THE QUALITY STREET GIRLS

A seasonal delight, inspired by the true story of the Quality Street factory.

Sixteen-year-old Irene 'Reenie' Calder lands a seasonal job at Mackintosh's Quality Street factory and feels like a kid let loose in a sweet shop, but trouble seems to follow her around. Beautiful and smart, Diana Moore runs the Toffee Penny line. The other girls in the factory are in awe of her, but Diana has a dark secret which if exposed, could cost her not only her job at the factory but her reputation as well. Then a terrible accident puts Quality Street at risk. Chocolate lovers have saved up all year for their Quality Street Christmas tin and Reenie and Diana know that everything rests on them...

THE QUALITY STREET GIRLS

THE QUALITY STREET GIRLS

by

Penny Thorpe

Magna Large Print Books
Anstey,
Leicestershire

British Library Cataloguing in Publication Data.

A catalogue record of this book is
available from the British Library

ISBN   978-0-7505-4743-7

First published in Great Britain by HarperCollins*Publishers* 2018

Copyright © Penny Thorpe 2018

Jacket design by Claire Ward © HarperCollins*Publishers* Ltd 2018
Jacket photographs © Ildiko Neer/Arcangel Images (figures),
© Robert Lambert/Arcangel Images (terraced houses),
Shutterstock.com (window frame) by arrangement with
HarperCollins*Publishers*

Penny Thorpe asserts the moral right to be identified as the author of
this work

Published in Large Print 2019 by arrangement with
HarperCollins Publishers Ltd.

Magna Large Print is an imprint of Library Magna Books Ltd.

Printed and bound in Great Britain by
T.J. (International) Ltd., Cornwall, PL28 8RW

The 'Quality Street' name and image is reproduced with the kind permission of Société des Produits Nestlé S.A.

In loving memory of Mary Lowes Walker, who made even more friends than Reenie.

Chapter One

It was late, and the Baxter's store on the corner at Stump Cross was closed, but the lights in the main window illuminated a sparkling display of Mackintosh's Quality Street; the latest success from the sprawling factory they called Toffee Town. As Reenie rode her nag closer she could see that someone had taken the coloured cellophane wrappers from the chocolates and taped them between black sugar paper to make little stained glass windows. Between the tins and tubs and cartons were homemade tree baubles; an ingenious mixture of ping-pong balls, cellophane wrappers, glue and thread.

While there were plenty of other confectionery assortments that Baxter's could have chosen to feature, Reenie couldn't imagine they'd have had much luck making a stained glass window out of O'Neil's wrappers. Besides, Quality Street was the best, everyone knew it; plenty of girls from Reenie's school had left to work in Sharpe's or O'Neil's factories, but it was the really lucky ones that went to work at Mackintosh's.

Reenie's enormous, ungainly old horse shuffled closer to try to nose the glass, the explosion of colour bursting forth from the opened tins on display had caught his eye and was drawing his curious nature to the window. Reenie didn't blame him; it was a beautiful sight and he deserved a treat when he was being so good about coming out after putting in a day's work in the top field. She had a great deal of affection for the old family horse, and she liked spoiling him when she got the chance, so she let him dawdle a while longer.

Reenie gazed at the window display, and dreamed of growing up to be the kind of fine lady that bought Quality Street, and had a gardener, and got driven around in an automobile. For the moment she would have to be content with being a farmer's daughter who had a vegetable patch and occasional use of her family's peculiarly ugly horse. Fortunately for Reenie, she found it easy to be content with her lot, she was an easily contented girl. As long as she didn't have to go into service she was happy.

'Come on, Ruffian. We've got a way to go yet.' Ruffian reluctantly allowed Reenie to steer him away from the bright lights, and continued up through the ever steeper streets of Halifax, over quiet cobbles she knew well. The night was cold for October, but she knew she had to ride out to get her father nonetheless.

Reenie didn't mind; Ruffian was technically her father's horse, and most fathers would not allow their daughter freedom of the valley with it, so she supposed she ought to feel pretty grateful. And it wasn't as though she had to come out to get her father very often, she thought to herself. He only got this blotto once a year when the Ale Tasters' Society hired out the old oak room and had their 'do', apart from that she thought he was pretty good really. He was very probably the best dad.

Reenie's thoughts kept drifting back to the

sandwich that was waiting in her pocket, wrapped in waxed paper and bound up with a piece of twine. The sandwich contained a slice of tinned tongue and some mustard-pickled-cauliflower that her mother made for Reenie to give to her father to eat on his way back. Reenie's stomach rumbled and she was tempted to take a bite out of it before she got to the pub, even though she'd had her tea. Her mother frequently told her that she was lucky to live on a farm where there was no shortage of food, but Reenie pointed out that there was no shortage of the same food: mutton, ewe's milk cheese, ewe's milk butter, ewe's milk curd tart, and ewe's milk. She rode in the dark past the Borough Market. There was a clamour outside The Old Cock and Oak. As she approached, Reenie didn't like the look of what she saw. Ahead of her, she could see brass buttons glinting in the old-fashioned gaslight from the pub, and the tell-tale contours of Salvation Army hats and cloaks. It was going to be another one of those nights.

Reenie knew before she'd even rounded the corner that this was not the regular Salvation Army, they would be off doing something useful somewhere involving soup and blankets. This was a Salvation Army splinter group, who the rest of the Salvation Army considered to be nothing but trouble. Reenie tried to feel friendly towards them as she wasn't in a hurry, but she did wonder privately why they didn't just go to the cinema when they got time off like everyone else.

'Think of your wives! Think of your children!' Reenie couldn't tell where in the throng of ardent

13

believers the call was coming from, but she knew that they wouldn't be popular with the pub regulars. There were several other pubs along Market Street, but the faithful had chosen to cram into the courtyard of The Old Cock and Oak to protest against the annual meeting of the Worshipful Company of Ale Tasters. Reenie couldn't see what they were so fussed about, but this wasn't anything new.

Reenie decided not to dismount this time and walked old Ruffian as close to the pub door as she could, keeping a loose, but expert grasp on the fraying rope that served as Ruffian's bridle. 'Comin' through, 'scuse me, if you'd let me pass, please.' As the ramshackle old horse nosed its way through the faithful, the crowd parted, some out of courtesy but others to avoid being stamped on by a mud-caked hoof, or bitten by an almost toothless mouth. Ruffian may not have had the aristocratic pedigree, but like his rider, he encouraged good etiquette in his own way. Reenie was close enough now to see a few faces she knew guarding the doorway; exasperated men waiting for the do-gooders to move on, their arms folded. 'Is me dad in there still?'

'Now then, Queenie Reenie, what's this you comin' in on a noble steed with your uniformed retinue.' Fred Rastrick gave her a wicked grin as they both ignored the small, rogue faction of the otherwise helpful Halifax branch of the Salvation Army.

'Don't be daft, Fred, you know full well they're nowt to do wi' me. Now fetch us me dad, would ya'? It's too cold for him to walk home, he'll end

14

up dead in a ditch. Go tell him I'm here and I'm not stopping out half the night so he has to be quick.'

'Young lady! Young lady, how old are you?' Reenie recognised the castigating voice of Gwendoline Vance, self-appointed leader of this band of Salvation Army members who'd taken it upon themselves to object to most things that went on in Halifax, including the Ale Tasters annual 'do'. Reenie could have mistaken the woman's face in the dark, even this close up, but there was no mistaking the way she was harping on.

'What's it to you?' Reenie was not in a mood to be cross-examined by strangers, especially those in thrall to teetotalism.

'Shouldn't you be at school?'

'Well, not just now as it's half past ten at night.'

'Well I meant in the morning, shouldn't you be at home in bed by now so that you can go to school in the morning?'

'No, and I'll tell you for why. Firstly, I'm fifteen and I finished school at Easter; secondly, some of us would rather be spending our time helping our families than wasting it on enterprises that won't get anyone anywhere; and thirdly (and forgive me if I think this is the most important), because today is a Friday, and when I were at school they taught me that the day that comes after Friday is Saturday, and that, madam, is when the school is closed. Now if you've quite finished, I want me' dad. Fred!' Reenie had to call out because Fred had disappeared further inside the pub. The Salvation Army devotee blanched and choked on her words. Reenie ignored her and turned her eyes to the doorway of The Old Cock and Oak.

'He's here, Reenie,' Fred reappeared, 'but he can't walk.'

'Well then tell him he doesn't have to. I'm waiting with the 'orse.'

'No, I mean he can't walk. He's blotto; out cold.'

'Oh, good grief. Well, can someone drag him to the door, I don't want to have to get off the horse or I'll be here 'til Monday.'

'I'll have a go.' Fred turned to go back inside. 'But he's not as light as he used to be.'

'*Reenee*,' the do-gooder emphasised the Halifax pronunciation, ree-knee, and tried to assume an expression that was both patronising and penitent for her earlier mistake, 'may I call you Reenie?'

'No, you may not. Unless you're gonna help with m' dad.'

'We'd be very, very glad to help with your father; it must be terribly hard on you and your family. Do you think you could bring him with you on Sunday to–'

'No. I meant help lift him on the 'orse. Good grief, woman, are you daft? Fred! How's he looking?'

'Nearly there,' Fred called out through gritted teeth as he attempted to pull the dead weight of Mr Calder out to his horse and daughter, then turned to a fellow drinker. 'Bert, can you give me an 'and throwin' him over Ruffian?'

Bert held up a hand and said, before darting back into the pub, 'You wait right there; I think I know just the lad for this.' Bert brought out a be-mused-looking young man who Reenie didn't recognise, slapping him on the shoulder with friendly camaraderie and pushing him in the direction of the horse. He didn't have the slicked hair with razored back and sides that the other lads round here had. His hair wasn't darkened by Brylcreem; instead, he had fine, golden toffee coloured hair that fell over his left eye and gave him away as a toff. Straight teeth, straight hair, straight nose, and a smarter suit of clothes than anyone else there; to Reenie, he looked hopelessly out of place among the factory workers and farm hands. It made her like him instantly for joining in with people who weren't like him. She might not have a lot in common with this posh-looking lad, but there was one thing; he looked like the type who would make friends with anyone.

'Reenie, Peter; Peter, Reenie.' Bert skimmed over the necessary introductions. 'We need to get Reenie's dad here over the 'orse.'

Peter smiled and nodded, and with what seemed like almost no effort at all, he gathered Reenie's father up and launched him in front of where Reenie sat, with his arms and legs dangling over the horse's withers on either side. The landing must have been a rough one for Mr Calder because, though unconscious, he still managed to vomit onto the military-style black boots of the nearest Moral League man.

The sudden eruption caused a shriek from the group's ringleader who turned to Reenie. 'Oh you poor child. You shouldn't have to see such things at your tender age.'

'Oh gerr'over yourself, woman. Everyone's dad drinks.' Reenie bent over to check on her father because although she was confident that he'd be

17

alright, she thought it was as well to make sure. Her shoulder-length red hair dangled down the horse's side as she dropped her head level with her father's, reassured by his loud snore; *silly old thing, what was he like? Her mother would laugh at him come the morning.* Reenie looked up to thank the young man, but to her disappointment, he'd already gone. She had wanted to tell him that her father wasn't usually like this, and not to mind the Sally Army crowd because they weren't bad as all that if you weren't in a hurry to get anywhere. She had wanted to say so many things to him, but she supposed it was better she get a move on and take her father home to his bed. It didn't occur to her that the young man had gone indoors to fetch his coat and hat so he could offer to walk her home like a gentleman.

Reenie pulled on Ruffian's makeshift bridle and steered the horse away, then thought better of it and stopped to call over her shoulder, 'and my friend Betsy Newman's in the Salvation Army and she says you six are pariahs! Go and help 'em with the cleaning rota like they've told ya', and stop botherin' folks who've had an 'arder week at work than you've ever known!'

Ruffian snorted, as if in agreement, and guided his mistress home.

Diana waited for Mary on the street outside; her father's thick old coat wrapped tightly around her, and the wide collar turned up against the autumnal night. 'She's definitely not with him this time,' Mary said, leaning one hand on the door frame of her mother's soot-blackened one-up-one-down terrace as she hurriedly pulled on a well-worn shoe with the other hand. 'She's promised she won't see him anymore.'

Diana didn't respond; it was a waste of effort, and she was bone tired. She had spent all day at work in the factory, then had come home to find her stepbrother hadn't paid the rent and had taken off with Mary's sister Bess. Not that this came as a surprise; nothing came as a surprise to Diana any more. Mary's sister was in thrall to her no good stepbrother, as only a silly sixteen-year-old can be. Diana had been a silly sixteen-year-old herself once, although it felt like a lifetime ago and not the mere ten years that separated her from that other person she had once been. Diana had been in thrall to someone equally unsuitable, and she knew that there was nothing to be done for Bess now.

'She realises now that he's no good for her.' Mary was following behind Diana and kicking at her shoe to move back the loose insole that had shifted when she'd pulled on her winter shoes over bare feet. 'I don't know where she's gone tonight, but I'm certain she's not with him.'

Diana didn't ask why Mary was following her if she believed all of her sister's promises; she didn't need to. Diana was the oldest girl on their production line, and younger ones like Mary fell into line with whatever she said.

'I mean,' Mary went on as they turned the corner of Mary's street and past the midnight blue billboard that announced that Rowntree's Cocoa would nourish them all, 'how do you know that it was definitely them?'

19

Diana stopped suddenly. She disliked walking while talking; she disliked talking at all, and she thought that if she didn't stop to say what she had to say then Mary would carry on kicking at her shoe rather than ask her to wait while she fixed it. Stopping killed two birds with one stone. 'I saw someone who told me that your sister and my stepbrother were in The Old Cock and Oak in town and that if I didn't hurry he'd have all my rent money spent.'

'But could they have been mistaken? I mean, what were their exact words?' Mary hopped on one foot as she tried to arrange her shoe without letting her bare foot touch the ice-cold cobbles of the dirty street.

Diana sighed. 'He said "You want to get down to The Old Cock and Oak, Diana, before that no-good stepbrother of yours spends all your money. 'The Blade' as he likes to call himself is in there with the Good Queen, and he's buying everyone a drink." There's no mistake; your sister is there with him.'

'What does he mean "Good Queen"? Who's "Good Queen" when she's at home?' Mary looked genuinely confused.

There was a long silence as Diana tried to decide whether or not to tell Mary what people called her; it might help her to do something about it, but then again it might not. Behind their backs Mary and Bess were known as the Tudor Queens; the porters on their production line had started calling Mary 'Bad Queen Mary' because she had a short fuse and no one had ever been able to get her to crack a smile. Her younger sister Bess was her polar opposite; she was cheerful to a fault. She had no concept of the consequences of her actions as she floated along in a happy bubble, and Diana had been forced to speak to her about it on the production line on a number of occasions, to no avail. Bess was all smiles and affection, and they called her 'Good Queen Bess'.

It seemed odd to Diana that two people could look so different while looking so alike. They had the same large, upturned eyes, but where Bess's looked pretty, Mary's glasses made hers appear bug-like. They had the same porcelain-white skin, but where Bess's looked delicate, Mary's looked ghostly. They both had a strawberry mark on their left cheek, but where Bess's looked like a cherubic kiss, Mary's looked like she was crying tears of blood. They were their own worst enemies, Diana had told them so often enough; Mary had a short fuse because she tied herself up in knots with worry, while Bess was as useless as a chocolate teapot in the factory because she was too happy-go-lucky. Diana wondered if Bess would ever realise her job was to make toffees, not gaze dreamily into the middle distance. Diana could see why they'd ended up the way they had; Mary had to do the worrying for both of them, and Bess didn't need to worry with a sister like Mary. If they could trade places for a day, it might do them the power of good.

'Have you fixed that shoe yet?' Diana didn't want to wait in the road much longer, her step-brother liked to flash money around when he had it, and he'd be on to another pub before closing time if she didn't catch up with him first.

21

'It keeps moving around.' Mary huffed with annoyance and crouched down to unlace her shoe and fix it properly, fumbling as though she were worried that she was taking up too much of Diana's valuable time.

Mary looked pitiful under the streetlamp. Her frizzy black hair was pulled tight back and twisted into a bun at the nape of her neck. All the other girls at the factory had their hair curled like the girls in the magazines, but not Mary; there were dark circles around her eyes and in the winter of 1936, Mary didn't even have a warm coat. *Poor kid,* Diana thought to herself, *she needs someone to look after her for a change.*

'Alright, I'm ready.' Mary stood up and shook her foot in her shoe one last time. 'I still don't think it's him.'

'My stepbrother could hardly be mistaken for anyone else. Apart from the fact that he's the only person in Halifax to dress like some American mobster from the pictures, he also looks like a cross between a rat and a frog, so his face is hardly going to blend into a crowd, is it?' Diana started walking again. The trouble with Mary Norcliffe, she thought to herself, was that she couldn't just walk in silence.

Mary followed Diana with her arms folded around herself and her shoulders hunched forward; her eyes were on the tram rails that stretched out down the road ahead of them, but then she looked up to Diana and said, 'Thank you for calling on me though.' There was an anxious pause as though Mary feared that every sentence was saying too much or too little. 'I know she's a nuisance, but she has promised she'll change. Honestly she has.'

Diana knew that Good Queen Bess would never be capable of seeing the consequences of her actions, and her sister Mary would always be looking after her. It was none of Diana's business, and so she said nothing. She helped them in her own way, but she wasn't going to try to change them. 'There's something I want to talk to you about.' Diana looked up see that Mary was already panicking. 'I've arranged for you and your sister to work beside me on the new line. We move floors tomorrow.'

'But, if we–'

Diana didn't let her finish, 'Everyone knows that you've been helping your sister to get her work done, but we can't let the other girls cover up for you anymore. You'll have to move up beside me where I'll be the only person covering for you, and then if you're caught helping Bess, the only people that will be in any trouble will be the three of us. No more risking the other girls' positions, do you understand?'

Mary swallowed and nodded.

'I know you'll still have to help your sister for a while yet, but you do it in my section and no one else's. If Mrs Roth catches you, it's best I deal with her.'

Diana was eventually rewarded with her longed-for silence, but she couldn't enjoy it because she knew that Mary was wrestling with all kinds of questions that she wanted to ask, but didn't dare voice.

They turned the corner onto Market Street

where the rainbow of shops had closed their shutters for the night, like spring blooms closing their petals each evening. The street was by no means sleeping, it was alive with factory workers who were out for a payday drink. It was hard to imagine what Diana had heard this morning about the men in Barnsley on their way down to Westminster on a hunger march. The people of Halifax had seen lean times, but on this Friday there was merriment.

As they passed The Boar, the girls were met with catcalls from the drinkers who had spilled out into the street outside the various pubs that filled the centre of town. Diana supposed the catcalls were not unfriendly, but they irked her none the less. There had been a time when Diana had painted the town red; when she'd been bright-eyed and infamous in Halifax. Back then she'd been the queen of all she surveyed; and then six years ago all that had changed. Her carefree day in the sun had ended, and she would never go back to being that Diana.

'Ignore them.' Diana was saying it as much to herself as Mary, and they walked on. Six years was a long time, but no one could forget Diana. She might be wrapped up in her late father's old black coat, her shoes might be down at heel, but she still looked like she'd stepped down from a Hollywood movie poster.

'Look at the state of that!' A buck-toothed drinker in the doorway of The Boar called out. Diana cast a glance in his direction and realised that he was pointing at Mary, who was taking the abuse quietly, as though she thought she deserved it.

'What did you say?' Diana mouthed the words at him almost inaudibly, barely a whisper. She didn't need to raise her voice; when she spoke the scattering of flat-capped drinkers who had spilled out of the pub fell silent. The old light was back in her eyes, and her iron-ringed irises were locked on the insolent young man.

He laughed awkwardly, looking around to his friends for them to join in. It was near closing time, and the lamp-lit street was busier with friends and acquaintances than it had been an hour ago. The young man had assumed that they would all make fun of the plain-faced girl that followed the beautiful one, but he was mistaken. His friends quietly shuffled backwards; some could sense what was coming, and others knew from experience that to cross Diana Moore was a mistake you only made once.

'What,' Diana remarked as she stalked toward the young man like a predator slowly closing in on its prey 'did you say?'

'Well...' he laughed nervously, throwing his arm up to indicate Mary but with less conviction now. 'Have you seen the state of her?'

'What about her?' Diana was close to him now, and without so much as a wrinkle of her celestial nose, she conveyed a menace more potent than this young man was ever likely to encounter again.

He faltered and then said, 'Well ... she doesn't have a coat, does she?' He'd have said more; he'd have said that she was plain or ugly, or skinny, or that her skin was sallow and her hair unattractive, but he felt a cold fear at the beautiful and unmoving face that was so close to his.

Diana leant forward slowly; with the elegance and poise of a dancer, her lips were so close to his that for a heart-stopping moment he thought that she was going to kiss him. He lifted his chin a little in hope, but her mouth moved past his without touching it, and then her mouth was at his ear, her breath warming his skin with a tingle, and in a whisper that was all at the same time tender as a lover, and unforgiving as death she said, 'Then give her yours.'

In the silence that had fallen over the drinkers, everyone heard her words.

Diana gently stepped back and the young man looked around helplessly at his friends, his mouth falling open in hesitation, confusion, and fear. He didn't know how to respond, so he laughed nervously again and waited for his friends to join in. All he wished was for the moment to pass so they could all continue with their Friday night drinking in peace. But his friends didn't come to his rescue; they didn't do any of the things that he expected them to do, they looked at him in silence and nodded in the direction of the girl he'd been mocking; they nodded as though to tell him to hand over his coat.

When they arrived at The Old Cock and Oak Diana appeared to be in a slightly better mood as she had shocked Mary into another brief silence.

'I can't keep this.' Mary was wearing the coat that Diana had thrown around her shoulders as she'd led her away from The Boar, and she looked worried; she always looked worried. 'I can't take

26

his coat off him.'

'So leave it at the pub tomorrow, and they can give it back to him.' Diana pushed open the door of The Old Cock and Oak, holding it open for Mary to follow her into the tap room. 'But I forbid you to give it back to him tonight. He doesn't deserve it.'

The crowded saloon, and higgledy-piggledy layout of the pub made it difficult to see all the drinkers. A thick fug of tobacco smoke caught Mary square in the chest as they entered and she began coughing uncontrollably; Diana was used to it and immediately began looking for her stepbrother. She briefly looked around the corner into the Savile room, but realised that her stepbrother wouldn't be there; that part of the pub was mostly occupied by older folks who still smoked their tobacco in clay pipes to save money on cigarette papers and Tommo wouldn't deign to be seen with the likes of them.

Diana ducked her head under the minstrel gallery that spanned one side of the pub. It was a strange old place, like something from a fairy story. It was all carved oak mermaids and crazy staircases; Tommo tended to frequent billiard halls, or places where he could be a big fish in a small pond, this was not his sort of place at all, which meant that he was up to something. The pub was full, but the clientele were divided evenly into two groups: the first were the Worshipful Company of Ale Tasters who had come in for their annual ale tasting evening in the private room on the next floor up. The second group of drinkers were the relatively sober regulars who had stopped by for a small glass of bitter after a day at work and were trying to suppress their amusement at the ale tasters who were all stumbling down the 16th-century staircase in an attempt to make their various ways home. Diana overheard the barman telling another drinker that they'd had an incorrectly labelled ale submitted for their tasting that year and it was rather stronger than they had anticipated. She suspected there would be a lot of sore heads in the morning and was glad that she wasn't one of them.

Over in the snug, she found Bess with a group of engineers that she recognised from the factory. Bess was under five feet tall, so when she saw her sister coming to get her she had no trouble darting behind one of the engineers to hide. Bess seemed to think it was all a game because she was giggling happily; the look of desperate exhaustion on her sister Mary's face didn't seem to register with her.

Diana approached the group. 'Bess, your sister's been worried sick.'

'Don't worry about her,' Bess whispered conspiratorially, evidently still thinking that if she stayed out of the way her elder sister might not find her to make her go home. 'Mary's always angry about summut', it won't be 'owt serious, let her go and cool off.'

It was too late, Mary had caught sight of her sister in their midst and had come round to forcefully grasp hold of her wrist and drag her out of the bar, calling out, 'Landlady! My sister is under-age to drink, don't serve her in future!'

Mrs Parish the landlady came out from behind the bar. 'And when the bloody hell did you sneak in, young lady?' She looked at Bess with a mixture of annoyance, amazement and confusion; Mrs Parish was a third generation licensee, and you had to get up very early in the morning to catch her out. If anyone got into her pub without her knowing it would have to be by some witchcraft.

Bess giggled, 'I was hiding inside my friend's coat when we all came in, and then I ran round into the snug. Didn't you see us? We looked like a pantomime horse. Everyone laughed!'

The landlady's shoulders sagged in exasperation. 'I'll remember your face, young lady. You're barred.' Mrs Parish narrowed her eyes at Mary. 'And how old are you?'

Mary appeared to be mildly affronted by the question. 'I only came in to get her. I'm going now. I wouldn't come into a pub unless I had a good reason.' Mary hustled her sister from the premises.

'Oh, Mary,' Bess's contented, innocent expression hadn't changed even though she was being hauled out of the pub, her bouncing, honey-blonde curls falling over her eyes prettily, 'I was only coming out for a bit o' fun with the engineers, there's no harm in it. You should come out sometimes too; now you're old enough.'

'You'll be fit for nothing at work tomorrow, and then where will we be?'

Diana followed the bickering sisters out into the courtyard. 'Bess, have you seen my stepbrother? I need to know where he's gone.'

'Have you tried at home?' Bess meant well, but it obviously didn't occur to her that Diana would already have looked there; common sense was not Bess's strong point.

'He's not at his mother's house. Where did he say he would be? Where did you last see him this evening?'

'I didn't see him tonight. But maybe you could see him at the factory tomorrow? He wants to come and look round the factory in the morning.' Bess said it as though she were imparting a nice piece of news that would please her sister and their colleague Diana.

'What does he want to do that for?' Diana was suspicious.

'Well,' Bess looked around and then leant forward conspiratorially, 'I think he wants to get a job at the factory. I think he wants to get settled somewhere nice.' She smiled; she genuinely believed the best of the young man who called himself Tommo 'The Blade' Cartwright.

'Trust me, Bess, my brother is not trying to get a job in the factory. If he asks you to get him inside the gates you tell me about it straight away, you understand?'

'Do you think we could get him an overlooker's job on our line?' Bess's voice squeaked with cheerful optimism.

Mary and Diana sighed with exasperation. This was the last thing they needed.

Reenie rode home through the heather, and by the light of the moon. When there was moon enough she'd allow herself this luxury of travelling back over Shibden Mill fields instead of the road. There was good solid ground underfoot for Ruffian, and if the night was clear enough she could see out across the rooftops of half of Halifax (if she didn't mind being unladylike and sitting backwards in her saddle and letting Ruffian take them both home).

Her father was no trouble as he slept, helpless as a babe, over the front of their horse. She realised, to her delight, that she could eat that tinned tongue sandwich in her pocket. Her father wouldn't remember in the morning if she'd had it; she took the waxed paper package from her pocket, pulled away the twine and took a bite of the soft, fluffy bread. It was heavenly, and Ruffian plodded on while she tucked in. Reenie was just near enough to the lane that bordered her part of the field that she could make out the silhouette of a lone policeman on a bicycle, effortlessly freewheeling down the hill.

Reenie was in such good spirits that she decided to ride nearer to the fence and wish him a good evening.

With a mouth full of tinned tongue sandwich she called out, 'Nah then! 'Ow's thi' doin'?'

The officer pulled on his brakes and skidded the bicycle into a sideways halt just yards away from Ruffian. He didn't speak immediately, but narrowed his eyes and assessed the teenaged girl who grinned at him naively in the moonlight; the almost-lifeless bundle of clothes that appeared to be a man; and the knock-kneed, run-down old horse that couldn't have more than a year or two of life left in him. Finally, he asked, 'Is this yours?'

'What, the horse or the old man? The sandwich is mine, but you can have some if you've not had any tea.'

'No, the land; is that your *land?*' Sergeant Metcalfe became frustrated when he saw that the girl who was trespassing still didn't understand. 'You're on private land, lass. Look at the signs and the fences. Can you not read the signs?'

'Can you not go on it if you're just using it to go home?'

'No, you cannot trespass if you're trespassing to go home. Trespassing's a crime; you could be up before the magistrate.'

Reenie smiled amiably. 'But I always go home this way.'

The policeman pinched the bridge of his nose and sighed. 'Do you know what it means when someone says that you're not doing yourself any favours?'

'I don't understand; am I in trouble? Is it because I haven't got him on a saddle? Because he's never had a saddle. We just use him for turning over the field and fetching dad and the like.'

The policeman sighed in frustration and thought about how late he'd have to stay at the station if he arrested a minor, and all the extra trouble of taking an unconscious man and an unsaddled horse into custody. Sergeant Metcalfe looked up into the happy, well-meaning face of Reenie Calder and decided that this was a battle he'd never win. 'You know what,' the policeman took a deep, exasperated breath, 'no one died so just go home and don't tell anyone I saw you or I'll get it in the neck for not doing owt about it. Don't kick up the grass, don't wander about, don't let anyone else catch you, and don't do it again.'

Reenie looked earnest, as though she was doing her best to help him. 'Don't do what again, exactly? Is it the horse, or is it me dad?'

Metcalfe threw up his hands. 'Right, that's it, I'm going home. You win. You will be the death of someone one day, but not me and not tonight. Get thi' to bed and don't let me see you here again.' He knocked the kickstand back up off his bicycle ready to wend his way to the station to sign off duty for the night as quickly as he possibly could, but he stopped, thought, and asked: 'You're not Reenie Calder, are you?'

Reenie Calder looked him innocently in the eye. 'No. Why?'

He held her gaze, debating once again whether or not to risk the ridicule of the station by taking in a girl, a drunk, and their horse into custody... No, it wasn't worth the risk; and quietly, he went on his way.

'Oh, well have a nice night, won't you.' Reenie shrugged to no one but herself. Reenie loved a bit of trespassing. She wasn't sure if it was because she liked the thrill of naughtiness from this minor infringement of the land laws, or whether she liked the idea that she was taking a stand against all them rich folks that would seek to prevent a Yorkshireman from being taken home the quickest route in his own county. 'Well Ruffian, it's just me and thee. It's a nice night for it. Now would you look at that sky?'

Reenie drank in the night air, the beauty of the stars, the joy of being on her way home with Ruffian, and the delight of having made a monkey of two adults in one night; and dismounted from her horse. She knew Ruffian only too well, and she knew that although he would put on a brave face, he was too old now to carry two people home. He was becoming more and more useless as a workhorse, and more and more precious as a friend. As she walked alongside him, wishing he could live for ever, her heart broke a little.

Chapter Two

Bess sauntered along behind her sister Mary who was moving at a quick pace, eager to get home to bed. Mary walked awkwardly in the stranger's grey wool coat; she was glad of the warmth, but not the circumstances in which she'd acquired it, and the almost inaudible rustling of the fabric lining felt deafeningly loud to her.

Bess didn't seem to notice the cold, she lost her balance every so often in her silver, t-strap Louis heels, but then with a click against the cobbles, she'd right herself again, scattering some of the ha'penny bag of chip shop scraps in her wake. Chip shop scraps were all they seemed to eat for their tea these days, and on this occasion, Bess was lucky that they'd been passing a chippy that was still open so that Mary could get her something hot on their way home.

Bess offered some to her sister as she trotted faster to try to keep with her. 'Don't you want any? They're lovely and tasty; I love the smell of hot vinegar when it gets into the paper and goes all tangy.'

'You eat them. Mother's not got us anything in for breakfast so that'll have to do you until dinner time at work.'

'I don't mind. I don't get hungry in the morning.'

Mary's wandering mind was interrupted by a call from the house opposite to their own:

'You found her then?'

'Yes, thank you Mrs Grimshaw.' Mary tried to shove her sister unceremoniously through the soot-blackened front door. Leaping at the chance to start a cheery conversation with the neighbour, Bess called over Mary's shoulder:

'Goodnight, Mrs Grimshaw! Thank you for the lovely bread you left–'

'Don't start that, just get inside,' Mary whispered to her sister. 'You'll wake the whole street.'

'You're alright.' The neighbour sucked casually on her old white clay pipe as she stood on her doorstep, placidly waiting for Mary knew-not-what.

She always did that, Mary thought to herself, she was always standing on her front step in her slippers and housecoat smoking on a pipe waiting for nothing in particular when they got back late. It was an unfortunate coincidence that Mrs Grimshaw always seemed to go out for a pipe when Bess was out late, and Mary had gone to fetch her. What must the woman think of the pair of us? Then Mary realised that if Mrs Grimshaw thought her younger sister was a dirty stop out, then she was, in fact, correct. However, Mary preferred to think that her sister was somehow a special case and that it wasn't as bad as it looked. Then she remembered what Bess had told her the preceding week and realised that it was worse.

'I don't know why you won't let me pass the time of day with Mrs Grimshaw.' Bess tottered into the front parlour that opened straight onto the street. She clattered over the bare boards on silver high heeled shoes as silly as herself while her sister lit a slim, farthing candle from the table beside the front door.

'Take your shoes off; you'll wake Mother.' Mary didn't need to look over to the corner of the parlour to know that their mother was asleep under grandad's old army coat in her chair beside the dying embers of the range. As far as Mary could remember their mother had never stayed awake to see that they came home safely because, like Bess, her mother took it for granted that they always would. The reason she slept in the parlour was no late-night vigil for her only children, but the practical solution to the problem of space; since their father died they had been forced to make do with a one-up-one-down. Mary and Bess shared a bed upstairs in the only bedroom. At a squeeze, Mrs Norcliffe might have been able to fit into it with her daughters, but she had moved down to the parlour years ago.

Bess unfastened the dainty t-straps of her shoes and carried them with her up the creaking stairs to their bedroom. She didn't lower her voice because her mother was deaf as a post and wouldn't hear them, but they were both careful to tread softly, and in stockinged feet, to avoid shaking the floor and waking her that way.

'I like her ever so much.' Bess dropped the shoes onto the floor beside the dresser and hung up her coat on the open door of their wardrobe. 'I think she wishes you'd talk to her more because I know that she's very fond of you.'

'Mrs Grimshaw does not like me.' Mary said it as though it were a fact that she had come to terms with long ago and only shared in passing as she folded the stranger's coat neatly and laid it in the corner furthest away from her as though it were a dangerous animal that might attack.

'Oh, but she does!' Bess's large, blue baby-doll eyes were wide with concern and love, and she reached out to rub her sister's shoulder reassuringly. 'You worry too much, and if you'd just talk to people and let them get to know you—'

'You're too trusting.' Unlike her sister, Mary didn't have to remove cheap costume jewellery and climbed into their lumpy, old, but nonetheless welcome bed. 'You're used to everyone liking you, so you don't see when you're getting yourself into trouble.'

Bess had pulled on her nightdress and thrown her silk stockings carelessly over the top of her messily heaped shoes. 'Your trouble,' she threw her arms around her sister's neck to give her a goodnight hug, 'is that you're too hard on yourself!' Bess giggled, kissed her sister on the cheek and then wriggled down beneath the coverlet to sleep.

Mary was sitting up in bed, about to lean over and blow out the candle beside her, but in her exhaustion her mind caught up with what she had seen. Her sister had just taken off a pair of fancy-

37

looking stockings, so Mary picked the candle up to cast the weak light a little higher. 'Bess?'

'Mmm.'

'Are those *silk* stockings?'

'Mmm.' Bess hummed the affirmative contentedly into her pillow. 'They're lovely.'

'Where did you get them from?'

'Tommo, he gave them to me as a present at lunchtime when I saw him at the factory gates.'

Mary turned to look down at her younger sister who had already closed her pretty, long-lashed eyes, and put her head on her faded-grey pillow. The candle wax melted down Mary's knuckles but she ignored it. 'I cannot believe you sometimes! I thought I told you that you weren't to see him anymore. If he thinks that he can just–'

Bess pulled herself up in bed for a moment, leant over, and blew out her sister's candle, plunging them both into darkness. Mary could feel Bess plonking her head back on her pillow and settling down to sleep. She sat up for a moment longer, debating whether or not to waste a match re-lighting it and trying to pursue the subject, but she knew better than to try. Her sister would never see reason, Mary would have to take matters into her own hands.

Diana could hear a church clock striking four o'clock in the morning somewhere down near Queen's Road. She was standing in the dark, galley kitchen waiting for Tommo to return; she had waited all night. To pass the time Diana had attempted to clean up some of the usual detritus that littered her stepmother's kitchen. An empty

38

Oxo tin was lying on the flagstones, the crumbs trodden into the floor along with innumerable other ills. Diana had cleaned what she could without waking little Gracie and her stepmother. She had swept up crumbling shards of plaster that had fallen from the damp, mould-blackened walls; she had reset the rusted mouse trap and returned it to its place under the stove that badly needed blacking, and she had folded up the dirty sheets of newspaper that her stepmother had laid out on the kitchen table. None of them ever read much of the pages from the papers these days; the sheets were there to eat their bread and dripping off instead of crockery, and they were always a few days out of date.

As she had folded up the dirty sheets of the *West Yorkshire Gazette,* she'd cast her eye over stories about Italy, Spain, and Germany and fascists. The stories all seemed to weave into one another; the Spanish were fighting their fascist leader, the Germans were bombing the Spanish to stop them fighting the fascists, the Italians were with the Germans, and Londoners in the East End rioted. They'd shouted, 'They shall not pass' in Spanish when the British Union of Fascists had tried to march through Whitechapel. Fascism was spreading across Europe like the plague, and carefully constructed treaties were toppling all over the world like a flimsy house of cards.

A photograph in one of the newspapers caught Diana's eye; it showed a razor-necked Oswald Mosley in his black, military-style uniform. He wore a black peaked cap like a police sergeant but his was emblazoned with the lightning bolt of the

BUF, and the shiny peak was tilted rakishly over his right eye to disguise a slight squint. His uniform had echoes of Great War army officers, and an official status that he clearly longed for, but did not possess. Diana spat on his face before screwing up the damp-softened news sheets and cramming them into the empty grate of the stove. She didn't like leaving anything about Mosley and his lot lying around if she could help it. Her stepbrother had a weakness for joining with the biggest bullies he could find, and she worried that it was only a matter of time before he realised there were even bigger fish than the criminals in Leeds that he so idolised.

Diana laid out fresh newspaper and saw a happier headline: Essie Ackland was singing at the Crystal Palace. Diana's father had loved Essie Ackland, and she still had his wind-up gramophone in the parlour with his collection of records. She was feeling melancholy, and decided to put on one of her father's favourites very quietly in the parlour so that the family upstairs wouldn't hear. She crept through to the room at the front of the house and the cheap and dirty pine shelves that were built into the alcoves either side of the fireplace. In the right-hand alcove, a row of yellowing paper record sleeves stood as a lone reminder of happier times in a better place. Diana gently ran her fingertips along the record jackets that were so familiar to her now that she could tell them by their worn corners without reading their labels. She picked out Essie's recording of 'Goodbye'. It was an old favourite, and as she lowered the needle to the shining black disc, she felt she even remembered the pattern of crackles that preceded that haunting opening bar.

Diana lowered herself into the horsehair armchair that had seen better days, and closed her eyes, imagining she was in the Crystal Palace with her late father.

Her moment was rudely interrupted as she heard Tommo fighting with the lock of their front door. She pulled herself up out of her chair, lovingly returned the record to its sleeve, and its sleeve to its shelf, and returned to the darkness of the kitchen before he'd even managed to get his latchkey into the door. She waited with arms folded.

The house they shared with Tommo's mother was only a two-up-two-down which meant that from where Diana leant against the kitchen sink she could see straight into the hallway. As Tommo entered the house, he could see her in the shadows.

'Wharra you lookin' at?' Tommo was even more disgusting to her than usual. A cigarette butt clung to the wet bottom lip of his wide and ugly mouth. As he sneered at her, he revealed dirty, crooked teeth. It was times like these that she pitied Bess; the girl could do immeasurably better than Tommo Cartwright.

'You didn't pay the rent.' Diana walked through to the parlour but didn't get very close before the fumes of beer and gin on her brother's stinking breath hit her.

'You pay it for a change. What do you think I am? Yer bleeding...' Tommo waved a skinny wrist around '...money machine.'

41

'I buy the food. Where's the rent money?'

'I spent it.'

Diana knew that he wouldn't be short of money. It might not be his, but he always had some. 'Are you telling me you've got nothing? Are you telling me you're no better than anyone else on this street?' She knew that would rile him and if he had any money it would soon show itself just to prove his superiority; Diana had been pressing her stepbrother's buttons for years and it was second nature now, undignified though it might be.

Tommo pulled himself up an inch or two taller and with drunken slur said, 'I'm never penniless.' He reached into his various pockets and pulled out a crumpled, damp pound note and a collection of coins and detritus, all of which he threw onto the floor disdainfully.

Their rent was ten shillings, and Diana had no intention of taking any more or less than that. She bent down and picked it up coin by coin in silence and with as much dignity as she could muster.

'What's this?' she said, unfurling a slip of paper.

Tommo sniffed and snatched it out of her outstretched hand. 'That's me being clever, that is.'

Diana had seen what it was; a betting slip from an illegal bookmakers that had been written out by hand. They'd been taking bets on whether or not the coronation of the new King was still going to happen in a few months' time, and Tommo had put on five shillings against. 'How is that you being clever?'

'I saw it in the paper, didn't I? Everyone's saying it won't happen. He'll off hisself before then. That's how them toffs get out of a jam; no brains.'

Diana didn't say anything. There was no point telling him that he was disgusting for laying bets that another human being would take his own life; king or not. Diana turned to walk up the stairs. 'Keep your voice down,' she told him, 'I don't want you waking the house.'

Diana returned upstairs to the room she shared with little Gracie. All the houses in their street were two-up-two-down, but being the middle house in Vickerman Street, they had one small extra attic room that jutted out of the row of rooftops; to Diana, it was a lifesaver. When her stepmother had offered it to Diana, she had been apologetic about the damp, the smallness, the drafts and the mice, but Diana had been too relieved to care. Diana was still glad not to have to share a room with her stepmother; her stepmother was a kind woman, but she snored like a drain.

Diana went to her single small window that looked out over the town; it wouldn't be light for hours. The street lamps picked out the undulations of the valley and the warren of tightly packed tiny rooftops. Silhouettes of enormous factory chimneys rose up like an industrial forest of brick-built trees giving life and death to the town simultaneously, with their jobs and their smoke.

Diana couldn't go back to bed now; she was too wide awake, and she didn't want to wake Gracie. Now that she had money to pay the rent, that was one battle over, but as soon as she won one battle there was always another. Life was a never-ending series of battlegrounds, and she had no one to fight by her side. She missed her father so much it hurt; he had been her sole champion, and he had never taken any of Tommo's nonsense. Diana remembered the first time Tommo had talked about getting himself involved with the Leeds gangs, and her father had locked him in the coal shed until he had agreed not to go looking for trouble. What would her father say if he could see her now? Living in Ethel's attic room, the house full of stolen goods that Tommo was fencing to his Leeds connections, and not a hope of ever escaping. Her father would have laughed Tommo to scorn for giving himself a ridiculous name like 'The Blade', and he'd have made sure that Diana didn't have to live in a house with stolen goods inside. Diana wished her dad was there; she wished he'd been there to help her save Gracie from the dirt, the damp and the life they were having to live.

It was the tenth of October, and when Reenie woke up she remembered that it was Saturday and today was her birthday. Her little brother's present to her was to muck out Ruffian's shed, so she didn't have to and her sister had promised to bake the bread. They had both got up early to do her jobs and had given her the bed to herself, and she was delighted.

As she lay, like a starfish, across the lumpy mattress that she had shared with Katherine since as long as they could remember, she planned her day. Reenie liked to plan her day so that she could get the absolute most out of it she possibly could.

Today she thought she'd bring forward wash day; nothing gave her a feeling of achievement quite like the sight of sheets being bleached by the sun on a dry day. All those girls she'd known at school who had gone off to get fancy jobs in shops, and tea houses, and the coveted piece-work places at the sweet factories, they couldn't possibly know the true satisfaction of a successfully completed wash day. At least, that's what she kept telling herself. She was better off at home; those stuck up girls could keep their stinking jobs, she had enough to do. And as for going into service; she didn't even want to think about that.

Reenie couldn't help dwelling on the words of the Salvation Army lady that she had met the night before; it was too late for Reenie to go back to school now that she was sixteen, but her mother was always nagging her about secretarial classes, or teaching herself shorthand. 'If you don't do something with your life you'll end up living from week to week in the pawnbrokers like your Uncle Mal,' her mum was always saying. Reenie had just never been any good at school work or anything like that; she would always prefer to be useful at home than useless in a classroom. She didn't necessarily like all of the jobs that she did at home (the ones she particularly disliked she had farmed out to her siblings that day), but working at home gave her a sense of purpose, and that was what she wanted. Reenie did have a dream, but she tried not to think about it; better to be useful.

'Reenie!' Her mother called from the kitchen, 'Reenie, are you up yet?'

'It's my birthday! I don't have to do 'owt!'
'You've got a present!'
'I know, and I'm making the most of it!'
'You've got to come down here and open it!'

Reenie sat up. Open her present? She never had presents that you opened; there'd sometimes be something for one of the younger ones, but she was sixteen now and past all that stuff. Reenie threw off the thick, warm layers of blankets that she'd been hiding in like a cocoon, and fumbled for her father's old slippers and her coat to put on over her nightshirt so that she didn't freeze on her way down to the kitchen. Even though it was only October, it was still Halifax in October. She ran a comb through her shoulder-length, bright auburn hair and tied it back hastily hoping that if she did it herself, her mother wouldn't pounce on her with a brush while she tried to eat her breakfast. She turned and neatened the bedclothes, disappointed that she was having to leave her warm cocoon so early, and then made her way down the stairs that she'd swept only the day before.

'There you are! I thought you'd never get up. Sit down and open this.'

Reenie looked down at the scrubbed kitchen table where an ominous-looking parcel was waiting for her, wrapped in newspaper and tied with string. Reenie sidled into the middle of the bench underneath it and looked up at her family, trying to conceal her confusion. She lifted the parcel gingerly, the crisply ironed newspaper still warm against her fingertips; she could tell immediately what it was. She wondered what precious object they had sold or pawned to raise the money to

46

buy her something so unnecessary, and how long it would take them to buy it back. She hoped they hadn't pawned the kettle because she wanted her tea.

Reenie turned over the parcel in her hands and made a show for her family of being excited and surprised, but out of the corner of her eye, she was scanning the kitchen to see what was missing. The ramshackle, low-ceilinged, worn-out old farmhouse kitchen looked unchanged: the freshly blackened range was hot enough to be boiling the kettle (which was a minute or two off singing); the pink china that her mother saved for best was drying on the wooden rack beside the sink that was big enough to bathe in. The old pine table and benches, discoloured with age and use and her daily scrubbing, were all where they should be. Out of the windows, she could see Ruffian chewing up the paddock, and wondered how much longer he could last with no money for the vet.

'Are you checking on Ruffian!' Her brother had caught her furtive glance out of the window and was outraged. 'I told you I'd see to him, and I will, I just–'

'All right, that's enough you two, don't start.' Reenie's mother went to see to the kettle. 'Reenie's got to hurry up this morning. Reenie, open your present, love.'

'Why have I got to hurry up?'

'Just open your present, love, there's a good lass.'

Reenie tentatively pulled at the string of the parcel. She was almost certain she knew what it was before she opened it, but as the inky paper fell away, she furrowed her brow in puzzlement. There, as she had expected, was a ½ lb tin of toffees that they couldn't afford, but what she hadn't expected was the envelope stuck to the top of the tin with her name typed on a typewriter; they didn't know anyone with a typewriter. These weren't cheap toffees either, these were Mackintosh's Celebrated Toffees. Even the tin, decorated with dancing carnival figures, and a lid edged in red and gold, was alive with magic.

'Go on, keep going, open that too.'

Reenie was stunned into silence, and she was about to open the lid of the tin when her younger sister said: 'No, silly, open the envelope.' Reenie could see that Katherine was even more excited than her, and that her mother must have let her in on the surprise.

John looked around in annoyance as he realised he'd been kept out of their circle, but his mother shushed him.

'Is this what I think it is?' Reenie, usually so loud and confident was quiet and nervous now. She turned the white, business-like envelope over in her work-worn fingers and took a deep breath.

'Only one way to find out, love. But best hurry, eh?' Her mother passed a clean table knife towards her daughter, and Reenie picked it up and slid it along the gummed seal.

There was a long silence as Reenie held her breath not daring to look at the page, and then she read aloud the first official letter addressed to her in her short life. 'Dear Miss Calder, We are pleased to offer you the position of Seasonal Production Line Assistant in our Halifax factory...'

Reenie gasped in surprise and delight. 'Oh, Mum! I've got a job! I've got a job! I'm going to Mackintosh's! I'm going to Toffee Town! They've given me a job!'

'I know, love; I wrote to them. They got a reference from Miss Dukes at your school, and a reference from the vicar, and we had such a time keeping it a secret in case it didn't come off, and then they wrote and said they wanted you to start right away.'

'Right away? Well, when right away?'

'Today! So go and wash your neck and get a wiggle on. Your birthday present from me is a job.'

'Don't I have to have an interview?'

'What sort of job do you think it is? Chief Accountant? You're not going into the offices; you're packing cartons, and every day's your interview. Be faster than everyone else, and they'll keep you until Christmas.'

'If I'm faster than anyone they've ever had do you think they might keep me longer than–'

'Now don't go getting attached; you know what you're like. Just be glad that you've got until Christmas and enjoy it. It's not everyone that gets into Mack's.'

'But if I were really, really fast and they'd had loads of girls leave at Christmas for Christmas weddings–'

'Christmas weddings? How many droves of girls are you expecting to leave for Christmas weddings?'

'Well, just say if there were a lot, do you think there's a chance that I might not have to go into service?'

49

Mrs Calder dried her hands on her apron and sat down at the edge of the table. 'Now listen, you three, I know you all talk like goin' into service is the worst thing in the world, and I know I used to tell you some terrible stories of what it was like in my day. Being in service now isn't like it used to be; you hardly ever have to live-in, and they all send their laundry out. Look, what I'm saying is: if any of you do have to go into service I think you'll have a wonderful time.' Reenie's mother tried to appeal to Reenie's imagination, 'Reenie, what if you went into service in a little place, and then a fine lady visited and spotted you, and you got to go to work in a big house and make friends with all the quality? Can you imagine?'

Reenie's tight-lipped smile gave her away; she was trying to agree with her mother, but in her heart of hearts Reenie desperately didn't want to. Reenie had hope now, and it was a letter from Mackintosh's.

The overlooker who was showing the new girls their place marched them through the corridor of the factory walking two-by-two in what she called a 'crocodile'. As far as Reenie could tell the overlookers were to the factories what the teachers were to her old school, and Reenie was immediately in awe of them. The overlookers decided where the girls went, which jobs they worked at, and how long for. Everyone wanted to stay in the overlookers' good books.

'No talkin' at the back! Listen wi' your ears, not wi' your mouths! You are going to walk through here every day for the next several years if you're lucky, but no one is going to show you where to go after today, so remember where you're goin'.'

Reenie followed dutifully, memorising the plan of the building in her head: up through the old Albion Mill, along a wide corridor where she could see the railway line running parallel, down three flights of stairs and up another two. By Reenie's reckoning this older girl, who'd collected them at the gates, seemed to be doubling back on herself to make them go a longer route. 'Excuse me!' Reenie was a third of the way down the crocodile of obedient new girls, but she was near enough to the front to shout naive, well-meant questions. 'Why did you take us down two flights of stairs and then up another two? Is there not some—'

'No questions, you're here to go where you're told.'

'Are you lost, though,' Reenie tried to sound kind because she couldn't imagine that this girl enjoyed being lost, 'because if you're lost, we could just stop someone and ask them for directions. Excuse me!' Reenie called out to two gentlemen who were passing them in the echoing, whitewashed corridor. 'Sorry to bother you,' she paused for a happy moment as she realised that she recognised one of them, 'but we're on our way to the—'

'We are not stopping! Follow me, please.' The older girl tried to hurry the girls along, but the older of the two gentlemen raised his hand politely to indicate that they should all stay.

'Good morning, ladies.' He made a slight bow of his head in a style that was almost Victorian.

He was an older man, perhaps getting close to retirement; thick silver hair, bold silver moustache, dark blue neatly cut suit. 'I am Major Fergusson, and this is my colleague Peter McKenzie. Is this your first day at Mack's?'

A chorus of 'Yes, sir' rang through the corridor and the crocodile line of girls all fixed their eyes on the young man beside Major Fergusson.

'Well, isn't that nice. And what is your name?'

'Reenie Calder, sir.' Reenie tried to look at him as she spoke, but her eyes darted to Peter to see if he would recognise her. She willed him to recognise her.

'And where are you going to, Reenie?'

'Don't answer him!' The girl in charge was determined to get them away, 'They're the Time and Motion men, and you don't talk to the Time and Motion men without your Union present.'

In the face of such obvious rudeness, Major Fergusson and Peter remained pleasant and calm; this was a sign, Reenie thought, of what her mother called 'Good Breeding'.

'We are here to help everyone find a way of doing their jobs more easily,' the Major said to Reenie, 'sometimes we conduct tests on the way the line works and in those circumstances, we have to work with the Unions to make sure that we are all helping each other. You can all talk to us any time, there's no need to be shy, or to ask permission of your Union.'

'I think that's quite enough–' their guide was silenced with another polite bow of the Major's hand. He clearly out-ranked her but didn't enjoy showing it. The Major smiled at Reenie and permitted her to speak:

'Can we ask you for directions?' Reenie didn't like to contradict her guide, but she suspected that the other girl needed some help. Reenie, in her naivety, believed she'd be doing the girl a kindness if she did the asking for her. 'It's just an overlooker is taking us to our new workstations, and we've been told to memorise the route that we're going along because we'll need to go this way every day, but I don't think it's right.'

'What makes you think that?' The Major was either ignorant of the girls gazing wistfully into Peter's smoke-grey eyes, or he was used to it.

Reenie didn't need time to think. 'Well, we came in by green painted double doors at the end of the old mill. We passed the timekeeping office where there were three commissionaires having their breakfast butties; then we went under a staircase where some fella in shiny shoes was smokin' and chattin' up a lass. Then we went out a single door – which was right small for all of us – into a yard where there was some men unloading sacks of sugar off a waggon. At the other end of the yard there was a sign that said *no waiting*, and we went past that into a new block where we went up three flights of stairs, then down a big corridor with a pine floor and big window frame that smelled of new paint. From there we walked down two flights of stairs just back there through that door which you can see from the window is loopin' us back to Albion Mills, so why can't we just stay in Albion Mills in the first place? Are we lost?'

The Major gave Peter another knowing, amused look; he supposed that this rigmarole the guide

53

was putting them through was more imaginative then sending them for 'a long stand'.

'You remembered all of that?' The Major seemed to admire Reenie for it, and the other girls were intensely jealous of the beautiful, wide-eyed smile that Peter gave her.

'Well, it has only just happened. I'm not a total doyle.'

'Young lady,' the Major was addressing Reenie again, but eyeing her guide with suspicion, 'you mentioned that you had already met your over-looker. Where did she go after you met her?'

'Well this is her, this is our overlooker.'

The guide gulped the air like a fish and stammered out defensively, 'I'm the overlooker of the new girls on their first day when they go through to their new places. It's very easy for them to wander about and get lost and someone needs to give them a firm–'

The Major ignored her and spoke directly to Reenie. 'Overlookers all have coloured collars on their white overalls. They are either red, blue, yellow, or green. If you see someone with a white overall, you know that they are the same rank and file as you.' He didn't point out that their guide's collar was white, or that she'd been deliberately taking them a longer route so that they would be lost for the whole of their first week at Mack's; he didn't need to. 'Now, let's see if we can't get you all on to your first day on the double. Peter, we've got time for a detour this morning, haven't we?'

Peter nodded brusquely.

'I think I can guess where you're all going to. Quality Street line, by any chance?' the Major asked Reenie.

'Yes, how did you know that?'

'It's all hands on deck at Quality Street, my dear. Christmas is coming!'

Reenie and the girls followed the Major to their new line, and although Reenie caught Peter's eye, he didn't speak to her. He smiled, and then he smiled again, but he didn't speak.

When Diana arrived at the toffee factory gates that Saturday morning, tired from very little sleep the night before, she was disgruntled to be stopped by the watchman. Diana tended to go in by one of the lesser-used entrances on the Bailey Hall road to avoid the undignified crush at the start and end of each shift. It added a few minutes to her journey, but Diana didn't care; dignity was more important to her than an inconvenience. The morning was crisp but not cold; the Indian summer of 1936, but she still wore her father's coat and her plain work shoes. A light wave of her ashes and caramel-coloured hair fell over tired eyes, and she slipped through the factory gate with her head down, her collar up, and her hands in her pockets like any other working day.

'Diana Moore?' The factory watchman had stepped out of his gatehouse cabin with a note in his hand.

'You know I am,' she said with an exasperated sigh.

'Message for you.' He handed over an internal memo envelope and went back to his business; answering queries from men who'd turned up on spec looking for work.

Diana moved out of the stream of other workers and found a quiet recess in a soot-blackened brick wall where she could stand apart and read the message. The note was evidently from someone who knew which gate she always used, or they'd left a note at every gate; either way she felt a slight discomfort about it. Diana was well known, but she didn't like to be *that* well known.

Mackintosh's Women's
Employment Department
October 10th, 1936
Dear Diana,
Please present yourself at the office of
Mrs Wilkes on your arrival today.
Yours sincerely,
Miss Watson
Secretary to the Women's
Employment Manager

Diana realised that Mrs Wilkes of the Women's Employment Department was waiting for her. This was unusual, but it didn't worry her; she knew that her job was not at risk. Diana knew that the factory couldn't run half the lines without her. This wasn't arrogance on her part; arrogance would mean that she enjoyed her position. In reality, Diana simply didn't care anymore. There had been a time, years ago when she had relished ruling the roost, but now the daily pettiness was exhausting, and keeping the younger girls in line was just one more battle for her.

Diana assumed that she was going to be asked to use her influence, unofficially, with some wayward girl or other; perhaps put down a group of troublemakers before they could put their own jobs at risk. It happened often enough. The senior management of the Mackintosh's business had realised long ago that it was more efficient to allow the girls to manage themselves, and Diana would occasionally be invited to the grand old directors' floor of the Art Deco office block to be unofficially asked to 'Have a word.' She never met the directors themselves; they were all down in Norwich at the newly acquired Caley factory. Rumour had it that they thought Norwich was more refined and they were moving there *en masse* to run the business remotely. It didn't make any difference to Diana, they sometimes came down to the factory floor to talk to one another while pointing out different machines, but they didn't speak to her or any of the other girls.

She folded the note and slipped it into the inside pocket of her old coat and began weaving her way in and out of the workers, wagons, and factory outhouses to the opulent main office building, and her interview with Mrs Wilkes.

Diana knew her way to Mrs Wilkes' office; she'd had to go there nearly six years previously when a different Women's Employment Manager had been in place. Diana had gone there to make her case for an extended leave of absence to care for a sick relative in the country, and whether the manager at that time had believed her or not, she'd argued persuasively and they'd let her go. Diana went in through the deco door decorated with M's, and up the six flights of winding white stairs with crisscrossed iron bannisters like giant strings of cat's cradle. The upper landing opened onto a hexagonal hallway, lined with the doors to the director's offices. She didn't want to linger long, her objective was to get in and out and back to work as quickly as possible.

In the centre of the hallway was a large antique hexagonal table, decorated with an intricate pattern of walnut veneer. High above, there was a sparkling, domed ceiling in every colour of glass, as though the hallway were a tin of cellophane-wrapped toffees bursting into the Halifax sky. Diana marvelled at the extravagance of it.

Following the narrow corridor at the other end of the hexagon, Diana found the door of Mrs Wilkes' office. It looked like it would be less out of place in a stately home, oak-panels were decorated alternately with an acorn, oak leaf or the letter 'M'. The Mackintosh family were proud of the acorn from which their great oak of a business had grown.

Diana knocked three sharp raps and then waited.

'Come!'

Diana realised that although she knew Mrs Wilkes' name well enough, she didn't think she had ever seen her and was surprised by what waited for her on the other side of the door. A straight-backed woman in a cream silk blouse looked up from paperwork on her grand desk, but she was not an ogre like her overlooker Frances Roth; she had the potential to be far less easy to manipulate. Diana made immediate assumptions about this Mrs Wilkes: grammar school girl, father a doctor, comfortable upbringing but not so comfortable that she didn't have to work hard at school, turned down an offer or two of marriage from an earnest young man because they didn't have enough money. Probably thinks all the factory girls are no more than beasts of burden, or wayward children.

Mrs Wilkes was undoubtedly a woman who had always possessed good looks; she was perhaps ten or fifteen years older than Diana. She still had a trim figure, and her neat, glossy hair framed her face in a way that enhanced its symmetry.

Diana thought that she could respect Mrs Wilkes, but she didn't know if she could really trust her. Mrs Wilkes didn't mix with the factory floor workforce; she was strictly an office manager and rarely ventured out of the smart Art Deco tower. Diana was more accustomed to life in the old mill buildings where her co-workers made the chocolate and toffee. Diana didn't know Mrs Wilkes' first name; she knew that the woman wasn't married because married women weren't permitted to keep their jobs at Mackintosh's Toffee Factory. But then again, married women weren't allowed to keep their jobs anywhere after they married, unless there was another war.

'Mrs' was a courtesy title afforded to women of an overlooker's grade or above, although Diana sometimes had girls on her own line try to call her 'Mrs' as a show of respect for her unofficial position of authority. Each time she refused the title and instead was known by the number of her position on the line: Number Four.

Mrs Wilkes unnerved Diana, as she politely

gestured to the seat in front of her desk. 'Miss Moore?'

Diana nodded, waiting for more as she lowered herself into the fancy wooden chair. To be called 'Miss' by a superior rather than by her Christian name unsettled her; it was unexpectedly respectful.

'I'll come straight to the point as I'm sure we both have plenty of other people's work to be getting on with: we would like to offer you the position of overlooker on the new Toffee Penny line.'

Diana gave a wry smile; so this was what they wanted her for. Although it was a surprise to be called all the way up to the Employment Manager's office, it wasn't a surprise to be offered the promotion. She asked, with seeming politeness, 'Is it that time of year again?'

'Excuse me?' Mrs Wilkes shifted the balance of her delicately rimmed glasses, as though the very slight bite of sarcasm she'd detected had been a trick of her eyesight and not her hearing.

Diana regretted being flippant; it lost her her dignity. She explained, with a slightly apologetic tone this time, 'I'm offered an overlooker's job about once a year. You'll have read my employment file, I'm sure.'

'Yes; that's why I asked to see you personally this time. I hoped that we could help you to overcome any obstacles that might be preventing you from taking the position.' She paused. Diana suddenly had a horrible feeling that this woman knew her secret and that this was a trap, but she gave nothing away. 'The line that you presently work on is making, wrapping, and packing the

60

new Quality Street sweets by hand, but you know as well as I do that hand-making is only ever intended to be temporary in a factory; by Christmas the Engineers and the Time and Motion Department will have the new, mechanised line ready and you'll be able to do your job with the help of a machine, but it will be a very different job. There will be other hand-making positions that we can move you to, but those will be temporary too. Wouldn't this be an ideal time to think about your future? Wouldn't you like to take a step up?'

'As you'll have seen from my records, I always turn down any offer of promotion.'

'I understand in the past you've had family circumstances that have made you unable to accept the position, but it has not gone unnoticed that you have been performing several of the duties of overlooker without formal recognition and if your family circumstances have now changed–'

'My family circumstances have not changed.' Diana took in a deep breath and tried to disguise her weariness as she repeated the same words she'd recited for the last six years, 'Although I'm grateful for the compliment you're paying me by offering me promotion I must on this occasion decline. I have a young halfsister who I care for in the evenings, and if I took an overlooker's job I'd have to spend my evenings in Union meetings, or employment department reviews, or typing up reports and shift patterns.'

Mrs Wilkes removed her fashionable, tortoiseshell-framed spectacles as though to indicate that she were now talking to Diana woman-to-woman, and not in a professional capacity. 'But Diana, you have to think of your own advancement and your own prospects. Think of the extra money you'd be earning if you became an overlooker. You'd more than be able to pay for someone to care for your halfsister in the evenings.'

'I prefer to care for her myself, thank you.'

'Then think of the things that you could buy for her with the extra money, wouldn't you like to earn more to help your family?'

Diana thought about the money that her step-brother had thrown onto the floor that morning as though it were nothing to him and that she had picked up so she could pay the landlord's man. Money was a problem, but it wasn't her biggest problem. 'I'm very fast, and when I'm working with girls who are as fast as me, I can make good piece rates, and that's enough for my family.'

'You said "when". Is there a problem?'

It was Diana's turn to be confused. 'I don't understand you.'

'You said that *when* you're working with girls who are fast, you can make good rates.' Mrs Wilkes was determined not to let Diana get on with her job; she was determined to dig in. 'Are you saying that the girls that you are with now are too slow? Can changes be made on the line–'

Diana suddenly wondered what she was getting at. *Perhaps she's seen something in me that she can use to build her own status?* 'No, they are very good, but we're on a temporary hand-making line which not everyone can do fast. When we move to our next line, we'll be faster.'

There was a silence, and Diana wanted to leave, but she could sense that Mrs Wilkes wasn't finished with her.

Mrs Wilkes tried a different tack. 'There are several very senior managers at the firm who think that you could become a manager yourself one day and that taking the position as over-looker would be the first step. Major Fergusson has watched your progress through all the years since you joined us and he feels that you are more than ready for advancement.'

'I have a great deal of respect for the Major; he's a kind man and he tries to make time for the Halifax factory floor workers. But you know as well as I do that everyone calls him Major Mis-fits, and if he takes anyone under his wing, it's because they're a strange bird. I don't like the idea that the managers here think I'm a misfit.'

'No one thinks you're a misfit, Miss Moore.' The Employment Manager said, 'You're an educated young woman, I can tell that–'

Diana snapped, 'No. No, I'm not.' She pulled up her chin imperiously; the Employment Man-ager had touched a nerve. 'I left school as fast as I could. And for the record, telling girls that they're clever and that they're not living up to their cleverness doesn't help them, it just tells them that there's one more thing they've got to feel rotten about. I'm exhausted, and the last thing I need is some woman in shiny brogues tell-ing me that on top of everything else I've got to do I've got to live up to my cleverness as well. All the girls on my line are clever; it's just that people with posh accents think talking Yorkshire means you're daft.' Diana got up to leave, and as she pushed the chair back into its original position,

Mrs Wilkes said quietly:

'I heard you discussing European politics with one of the other girls.'

This took Diana by surprise. She couldn't imagine this woman deigning to come down to the factory floor long enough to overhear anything, but Diana had an answer for her. 'My father was a Union man. You'll find a lot of the girls around here are very learned thanks to the Union. They have free public lectures and a library. Will that be all?'

Mrs Wilkes rose from her desk to calmly show Diana out of her office. 'And what would your father say if he knew that you were turning down the opportunity for advancement; to better yourself?'

'He would understand,' Diana said, biting her tongue. 'And he would tell me that the job doesn't better me; I better the job.' With that Diana left, stalking down the corridor in a foul mood and with her head held high, not stopping to think why one of the Mackintosh's brass nobs should be taking such an interest in her and her conversations with the other girls.

Reenie had taken her mother's words to heart, and while the other new girls were concentrating on what their supervisor was telling them, Reenie was watching the woman's hands and learning far more about how to work fast. It was a school day like no other; Reenie and her new factory classmates were in a room as vast as a cathedral, noisy as a day at the races, and as exciting as anywhere that Reenie had ever been. A conveyor belt ran down the centre of the room, flanked on either side by girls who were older than her and who, Reenie felt, were so much more sophisticated. They scooped up sweets with uncanny speed and somehow, beneath their hands they magically covered them in sparkling foil and then red and green cellophane and then dropped them into a box ready to move on. Hovering on nimble, rubber plimsolled feet by the wrapping girls' sides were white-aproned girls of Reenie's age who were waiting to take the filled boxes and place them onto the next part of the production line.

'Your job, girls,' their supervisor called over the din of the workroom, 'is to keep the wrapping girls supplied with everything they need to wrap the chocolates, and move the chocolates on when their tubs are full; and you have to be as fast as you can be.' As if to emphasise the point the supervisor stressed the next words one at a time. 'If you are too slow you will slow down the production line and people won't get their sweets when they go to the shops. Do you understand?'

A chorus of 'Yes, Miss' rose up into the chocolate and strawberry scented air, and Reenie scanned the room for the fastest workers. There, at the back of the room, was her new role model. A girl a year or two older than her and a foot taller was supplying two wrappers at the same time by picking up multiple boxes with her fingers. Reenie had seen the landlady at The Old Cock and Oak do the same thing with empty pint glasses, and Reenie made a mental note to practice with flowerpots as soon as she got home. If she could build up the strength in her fingers, she could do the same thing. But as Reenie was watching, the taller girl caught her eye and shook her head. A second girl, like a prettified miniature copy of the first, appeared from the door at the far corner of the workroom and scurried to her place beside her older sister; she picked up where the other had left off, but not half as quickly, and they both looked round furtively to check if their switchover had been seen. The taller girl was no longer carrying multiple boxes at once, but she was looking daggers at Reenie.

Reenie realised that she had seen something that she wasn't meant to see, and her eyes snapped back to the supervisor. 'You go to the cages and fetch a box of the foils and put them on her right. Then you go back to the cages and fetch a box of cellophanes and put that behind the foils, before you pick up the tub on her left that she has filled and add it to the pile on the pallet nearest you at the edge of the room.' The young supervisor was about to use that trick again of stressing every word with a pause in between, Reenie could tell. 'When you place that tub on the pallet you must pull up the flaps at the side of the tub,' the supervisor picked up a tub and demonstrated in a manner as exaggerated as her voice. 'You must fold them over, like so, and then you must make sure that they overlap, like so. Does anyone not understand?'

'No, Miss.' All the new girls sang together.

Reenie dared to raise her hand. 'Please, Miss?'

'What don't you understand?' The young supervisor was abrupt, but not unkind as she frowned on Reenie.

'Why don't the girls pick up two boxes at a time to go faster?' Reenie mimed the action that she had seen with her fingers.

The young supervisor couldn't suppress a laugh. 'Well you'll go far. What's your name, love?'

'Reenie Calder.' Reenie wasn't quite sure what she'd said to amuse, but she thought she regretted saying it.

'Well, Reenie Calder, if you can carry more than one box at a time, and keep it up for a whole shift, and do it every shift for two weeks, I'll double your wages. For every day that you can do the work of two girls, I'll give you the pay of two girls. But don't get your hopes up, love, you'll have your work enough cut out for you keeping up with one job, let alone two.'

One or two of Reenie's classmates had looked excited at the promise of double pay, but most of the girls had smirked at Reenie's mistake. These were girls whose brothers and sisters and fathers already worked in the factory and who knew how hard it was to keep up the speed of everyone else, let alone double it. Reenie was a little embarrassed, but she was also privately sceptical; if she could manage her father and a horse at the same time, and if she got in enough practice to strengthen her hands, she thought she stood a fair chance at making good speed. Little did Reenie realise then that her speed would get her into more trouble than she could handle on her own.

Chapter Three

'Mother!' Reenie threw down her old canvas shoulder bag as she banged open the back door and bounded into their farmhouse kitchen. 'It's wonderful! I love it! It's brilliant!'

Reenie's mother was slicing up a freshly baked loaf at their kitchen table, and the house was filled with the welcoming aromas of warm bread, spicy sausage stew, and herb dumplings. 'Alright, calm down, no need to worry the livestock.' Reenie's mother was amused by her daughter's enthusiasm. She put down the bread knife and dusted the flour from her hands. 'There are sheep in the far field that can hear you all the way from here, and they're taking fright.'

'Oh mother, you should have seen it.' Reenie was in raptures as she hung her coat up on the aged brass hook inside the door. 'It's like something from a film or a novel. The girls are so glamorous, and–'

'Glamorous? Factory girls?' Mrs Calder moved to close the kitchen door that Reenie had left open, but her daughter darted out again and started looking through the dead summer plants that were drooping, brown and dry under the kitchen window in their boxes. Reenie carried on talking happily and enthusiastically to her mother in the open doorway all the while as though there were nothing out of the ordinary in her search of

68

their little kitchen garden in the corner of the farmyard.

'No, they were, they were glamorous. They've all got lovely manners, and they tie their turbans up in this fancy way at the front, so it makes them look all haughty, like. And I'm going to be in the strawberry cream room at the end where they wrap the sweets by hand and you should see them, Mother, they move like lightning. I'm going to be the fastest, but I need to practice with flowerpots.' Reenie parted some out-of-season honeysuckle vines and called back to her mother. 'Can you spare any?'

'Spare any what?' Mrs Calder was used to her daughter's mildly eccentric schemes and took it all in her stride, leaning against the kitchen doorframe with her arms folded and her hair tied up in a knot on top of her head.

'Flowerpots! I need flowerpots! It's essential to my plan. I'm doing what Donna, the landlady does at The Old Cock and Oak.'

Reenie's mother started to understand why her daughter was poking about among last spring's bulbs beside the kitchen door. 'Is this what the other girls do? Have they told you something about flowerpots? Because it might be a wind-up, you know. I warned you about the overlookers sending you for a "long stand", you remember?'

'No, it's my idea.' Reenie had picked up a couple of larger terracotta pots and tested them for weight, covering her hands in soil and slimy green moss in the process, before discarding them and reaching for another. 'I've been watching everyone on the line, and I can see how I can get

69

to be the fastest, it was my idea.'

'Well I'm glad you want to be fast, but I don't think you need to be the fastest. At least, not while you're new. You might put a lot of people's noses out of joint.'

'But why?' Reenie was waving their small stone gnome around as though the answers might fall out of it if she shook it hard enough. 'They said that if I work fast, then the girl I work beside gets better piece rates, so I thought that if I was the fastest, then–'

'Come and sit in here,' Mrs Calder beckoned her into the warm kitchen. 'Come on. Leave those plant pots alone, they're hibernating. Sit at the table while I put the kettle on.' Without saying anything, Mrs Calder took a wet cloth to her daughter's hands while steering her in the direction of the rough old kitchen table.

Reenie didn't try to resist but did complain. 'Mother!'

Her mother ignored her objection and carried on settling her down into a chair, closing the kitchen door, putting the kettle on and taking out a teacup for each of them. 'Now, I think you're right; they will be glad you're quick, but if you try to do things differently, then you might get their backs up. Do you remember what I'm always telling you about the difference between speaking up and being outspoken?'

Reenie turned on the dining chair, making it creak. 'But this isn't even speaking, this is working without talking.'

'The day you work without talking is the day the King gives the crown to your dad. I know you,

you'll be a non-stop chatterer.' Mrs Calder put the teacups down on the table and reached up to the top shelf of the dresser to bring down Reenie's birthday tin of toffees. She thought that her daughter might like one with her cup of tea. 'Now listen, love, it's the same thing. When you're here on the farm with your father you're used to being praised for speaking up if you see a way of doing something quicker or better; that pulley you and him put up outside the barn has saved a deal of work, and that was a great idea of yours. But in the factory, there are bound to be a lot of people who want to keep things the same way that they've always been, even if there's a better way of doing things. You need to be just a tiny bit better than average to start with, and then, when you've got used to the place and when they've got used to you there'll be time enough to start improving things little by little so's no one notices.'

Reenie's eyes lit up when she saw the brightly coloured toffee tin sitting beside their blue and brown teapot. She was not in a bad mood, she thought to herself, she was just puzzled. 'But *why* wouldn't someone want things done better? If they're going to make more piece rates–'

Reenie's mother sat down beside her daughter and squeezed her hand affectionately. She didn't like the way places worked any more than Reenie did, but she thought her daughter would fare better if she went in with her eyes open to what they were like. 'It's because everyone has their own little area. It's the same in department stores, big houses, and in the Union. There are always folk who like to be a big fish in a small pond. You

71

might think to yourself that everyone's like you, and everyone wants to be helpful and kind and friendly and do their best, but you don't realise yet how rare you are. Some people just want to be in charge of their own little kingdom, even if it's only the linen cupboard of Shibden Hall!' Mrs Calder poured out a delicious, steaming hot cup of Indian tea for Reenie, black enough to tar a fence and handed it to her saying, conspiratorially, 'I knew a girl who was in service there, the Housekeeper was very territorial over her linen cupboard.'

'Why would she be territorial over a linen cupboard?'

'Because she was in charge of it, it was something that was hers to control. Sometimes when people feel like they haven't got much control over their lives, they'll try to exert it over their little territory at work. It might be the tool shed in the People's Park if you're the head gardener; or it might be the telegram machine in the Post Office if you're the Post Mistress, or on your production line there might be a shift manager who prefers to have all the ideas and doesn't like them coming from other people.'

'But what if they don't have any ideas?' Reenie's marmalade cat crouched by her side, indicating that it wanted to jump into her lap, so she pushed her chair backwards an inch to give it room. 'Or what if I have an idea that's really good, but it's not the same as the idea they've had?'

'Then you still have to try and keep it to yourself, love.' Reenie's mother was sad to say it, but she knew that her daughter's happiness depended on keeping herself wise to her workplace. 'If you want to stay you have to keep those ideas to yourself. There are a lot of people who won't like to see a girl being outspoken; it's just not how the world works.'

Reenie thought about the girl who had called herself their overlooker but had turned out to be leading them a merry dance. She realised that all the other girls who'd been walking alongside her must have thought that she was wrong to speak up. They would all have rather been made a fool of than challenge someone of equal standing, let alone a superior. It went against the grain for Reenie, and the golden toffee that her mother offered her in consolation didn't shut out the thought.

It was not the Monday morning that Diana had hoped for. Diana had wanted to slip into her high chair on the strawberry cream production line and to wrap her sweets in perfect, dignified silence while the fresh smell of strawberries got into her clothes and made her feel serene. She'd worked nearly all of the lines in her ten years at Mac's, and she could pick up any production line job in her sleep; whether it be hand-wrapping toffees, hand-piping chocolates, or decorating their tops with a dainty wire wand. Diana had a wealth of experience on the lines and it was one of the reasons why she had been chosen for the team of girls that would hand-wrap the sweets on temporary lines until the Engineers Office and the Time and Motion men could set up a permanent mechanised line and replace her with a machine.

73

Quality Street had only been launched in May, and no one had anticipated that it would be as popular as it had been. The Mackintosh's old rivals over in York had launched their 'affordable' chocolate boxes in the shape of Black Magic and All Gold, but they were only affordable for the likes of the managers and the office workers. Mackintosh's wanted to make a tin of chocolate toffees that was inexpensive for everyone; they wanted to make something to share, and to celebrate with, and to get excited about; something that exploded with colour and helped make treasured memories. They'd invented Quality Street in a hurry, and demand was now outstripping supply. Scratch lines were set up to hand make it in larger quantities while new machines were brought in and set up to start in the new year.

When Diana arrived at her post on the production line, her overlooker Frances Roth was waiting for her.

'I'm sorry that I'm a little late, Mrs Roth.' Diana said it without a hint of apology in her voice. 'The Head of Women's Employment wanted to offer me a job.'

'And did you take it? Am I to be left to find someone else to fill your position at a time when I can barely keep the line running with the girls I have?' Mrs Roth said it with bitterness, melodrama and accusation. Diana knew that Mrs Roth was exaggerating. Mrs Roth's particular talent was that she could run two lines simultaneously. It wasn't merely a case of watching two places at once, but also of managing the shift rota and paperwork that accompanied it. It wasn't because she was unmarried, but her private life was run with a military precision around the Salvation Army. She relished time spent on departmental paperwork and delighted in petty bitterness.

'I turned the position down, Mrs Roth. I didn't feel worthy of it.' The other factory girls watched in awe as Diana managed to tread the fine line between false sycophancy and out-and-out sarcastic rudeness with the overlooker that they all loved to despise.

Diana and Mrs Roth had an old antipathy to one another; everyone knew that. They were usually kept apart because Mrs Roth seemed to want to teach Diana a lesson and put her in her place, and Diana outsmarted her every time.

Mrs Roth seemed to have an unhealthy fixation with Diana and what time she wanted to leave the factory. If Diana left early to look after her sister there was always an insinuation that Diana was neglecting her work at the factory, and if she didn't leave early, Mrs Roth would insinuate that she was neglecting her younger sister. With Frances Roth, Diana could never win, and this was one of the many reasons why it was so frustrating to the factory management that she wouldn't accept her promotion.

'You're wanted in the overlookers' office, Number Four,' Mrs Roth snapped, calling Diana by her position number on the line to emphasise her inferiority.

'But I'm not an overlooker.' Diana did not sound surprised; she was simply riling Mrs Roth.

'Major Fergusson from Time and Motion wants to conduct a study on your line today,' but the

Union shop steward is unavailable to approve it. I said that you could represent the girls as you're in the Union.'

This smelt fishy to Diana and she followed Mrs Roth into the overlookers' room in suspicious silence.

Major Fergusson was waiting in the overlookers' room hoping that his new protégé wasn't about to see another classic display of Frances versus Diana. The Major had tried to mentor both young women over the years, but the experiment hadn't worked, and Mrs Roth was now worse than ever.

'Ah, Ladies, so pleased to see you both on the same line for a change.' The Major beamed and was very plausible; no one would have thought putting them together was a disaster. 'Diana, I hear that you will be acting as Union representative for the girls this morning?'

The Major had known Diana's father in passing. He had been a Union man and had often been the only thing to keep Diana on the straight and narrow back in those days. Her father had got Diana her first job at the factory when she was sixteen. Diana had been a bit of a bully and a troublemaker those first few years, and the Major kept a close eye on her. She ruled the roost, but she had been a different person then. When her father had left the factory, Diana had become more troublesome than ever, and for a moment it had looked as though she would have to be dismissed. But then her father had died suddenly, and just as suddenly she changed beyond recognition. Diana had gone away for nearly a year

76

claiming she needed to care for a sick relative in the country, but the Major suspected that she was caring for her halfsister who was born about that time. Her father hadn't married her stepmother, but there had been a baby, little Grace. Diana's father had died before he'd seen the child, but Diana and Ethel had stuck together all the same.

Diana had gone from living in a comfortable flat above a rented shop in a shabbily respectable part of town, to living in the attic room of a woman that she called her stepmother. The transformation had been as unexpected as it had been remarkable; Diana was still the 'it girl' of Mackintosh's factory and she still commanded a following among the girls, but these days she used her influence sparingly to secure herself a quiet life. Six years before she had a nasty habit of using her power to torment and tease. The old Diana liked power and adulation; the new Diana was a woman wise to injustice.

Now Frances sensed her chance for revenge and took every opportunity to use her power over Diana. The pair were usually kept apart, but Quality Street production was ramping up faster than planned and their unique skills were needed on the same line.

'I can't let you run a study on my line,' Diana said boldly. She was aware that Mary was doing the work of her sister and she had to make sure that they were not discovered at any cost. 'You need the Union's approval, and you can't have it this time.'

'But really,' the Major was affable as always,

'this is just a simple one, just something to show the new lad how we run a study. What if we agree not to record our findings? It will be a dummy run. Nothing will come of it.' It wasn't an unreasonable request; the Time and Motion men didn't expect the girls to do anything out of the ordinary, they just watched them at their work while recording their speed with a stopwatch and making notes of their movements on a clipboard. Their purpose was to see if they could find a way to make the work more efficient, perhaps by giving the girls a higher chair, or speeding up the conveyor if it was slowing them down and keeping them waiting. The problem came when the girls thought that the Time and Motion managers were expecting them to work faster than they thought was possible; that was why the Union insisted on approving any study on the line.

'Major,' Diana hesitated, as though about to broach a delicate matter, 'if I could perhaps speak to you about it alone?'

'No, she can't!' Frances burst out, 'She is being consulted as though she's an overlooker! I want to lodge a formal complaint.'

The Major forced a tolerant smile and said, 'Of course, Mrs Roth, of course. Although perhaps we might wait until all your other outstanding complaints against Diana have been dealt with? For the sake of an orderly office.'

Diana tried a different tack and turned on the charm for her arch nemesis. 'I only wanted to protect your reputation, Mrs Roth.' She simpered and spoke conspiratorially to the woman. 'I've met this new lad, and I'm afraid to say that some

78

of the girls on our line are very distracted by him. I'm concerned that if he conducts a study on one of your lines, the girls will perform worse than usual because he's there, and it will reflect badly on you, Mrs Roth. You don't deserve that; you work so hard to run an orderly line. Perhaps we could run the study without the new Time and Motion lad?'

'But I'm afraid the whole point of the study is to show Peter how they are run; without him, it would be futile.' The Major knew that Diana realised this and was deliberately trying to avoid a study. He doubted that it was out of dishonesty, but he still wanted to know why.

'What about the four new girls?' Diana asked. 'They haven't been trained yet so it wouldn't matter if you took them to work on one of the dummy lines, or even if you took them to one of the new mechanised lines that you're starting up so that they can learn the new machines?' Diana gave the Major a look that told him there was more to this situation, and so he acquiesced.

'An excellent idea.' He said, 'Oh, but Mrs Roth, can you spare them? I would be so very grateful to you if you could do me this personal favour.' The old military man, with his Savile Row suits and his Sandhurst manners, knew that the battle with Frances Roth was usually won with flattery.

'Well, I don't know Major Fergusson. I haven't had a chance to vet these girls myself—'

'And it's a credit to you that you take the time to do it. I know very few overlookers that take the time that you do over your girls.' The Major wondered if he'd taken it too far, but Diana – the expert in these matters – chipped in with:

'She's very good, Major. The other overlookers try to copy her where they can. I expect they'll all be wanting to send their new girls to you to work on dummy lines now; it will bring them up to speed faster. It's really a very good idea.'

Brought around to the notion that it had been her idea from the start, Frances Roth agreed and told Diana to take the four new girls and walk them to the dummy line with the Major, and to come straight back.

'What was all that about?' the Major whispered to Diana as they made their way down the corridor to the dummy line, well out of earshot of Frances Roth.

'There's a problem on my line.' Diana had dropped the simpering charm. 'Nothing I can't handle, but I'd be grateful if you'd hold off any studies.'

'For how long?'

'I'm not sure yet.'

'Anything I can do to help?'

'Possibly. I'll let you know.'

'I heard that you didn't take the overlookers position; you're clearly up to the mark, so I don't understand why you don't take it.'

'It's the hours. It's the time away from home.'

'I'm Reenie Calder.' Reenie caught up with the Time and Motion lad as they walked down the corridor behind Diana and the Major. Reenie put out her hand to shake his. 'You won't remember me, but we met the other night. I went to fetch m'father from the pub, and you were very kind and hoisted him onto m'horse.' Peter shook her hand with a friendly nod, but when he didn't say anything, Reenie carried on. 'He's not always like that, it was just the once.' Reenie found herself embarrassed; she'd plucked up the courage to talk to the lad that all the girls had been making eyes at, presuming on their earlier acquaintance, thinking that they had made a connection and that she would pick up where they left off, but there was silence. She didn't know whether she was more embarrassed or crestfallen. She'd really hoped that she could talk to him again.

'I, um...' Peter hesitated, looking for the right words. 'I've never seen a girl ride bareback up to a public-house before.' He seemed to think it was amusing. 'In fact, that was the first time I've seen a girl ride bareback at all. I hope you managed to get his saddle fixed.' Reenie was pleasantly surprised by his accent, he pronounced 'was' as 'wuz' and to her it sounded cultured and refined.

'Oh, he doesn't have a saddle. He's never had one.' Reenie seemed to be working something out and then asked, 'Have you lived in Halifax long?'

'No, I'm from Norwich.'

'Ah,' she said, as though that explained everything.

'It's my first week in Halifax.'

'Well, that explains why you've never seen a girl ride bareback. Nearly all the farmer's daughters round here ride bareback if they can get the loan of a horse.' Reenie thought about what it would be like to be from Peter's world. 'I expect girls in

81

Norwich have to stay at home and embroider the Coleman's mustard cow onto prayer cushions, while reciting all the kings and queens of England in Latin.'

Peter tried not to smirk and said coolly, 'Actually it's an ox, not a cow. But you're spot on about the kings and queens.' He seemed quietly pleased with himself for cracking a joke, even though he'd had to be helped into it. 'Have you been here long? At the factory, I mean?'

'It's my first week.' They shared a comradely smile. They would have to be friends now.

Peter realised it was his turn to speak, and with great effort came up with, 'Do you think you'll like it?'

'I love it. I love it so much. I want to be the quickest girl on the line.'

'Well, we've got something in common. I want to help you to be the quickest girl on the line.'

The dummy line was a foil wrapping machine. It wrapped squares of soft pastel green around triangles of hazelnut praline at a breathtaking speed. The machine didn't interest Diana – very little did – but what did catch her attention was a girl who had picked up two cartons in one hand and was about to demonstrate to the Time and Motion lad how she thought she could make the line faster. She'd obviously seen Mary Norcliffe use that same trick when she thought no one was looking and was picking up the slack for her sister. These young ones were exasperating.

Diana dived in before Reenie could utter a word to the new lad and steered her over to a quiet corner away from the others. 'Were you about to tell those gents that you'd had a bright idea?'

Reenie was startled, she hadn't expected the older girl to notice her and was glad of a chance to share her idea with this girl too. 'How did you know? It wasn't really my idea, I got the idea from something I saw, and I thought–'

'Well don't. Don't try any fancy footwork, don't try to share any bright ideas or do anything differently. Just work slowly and carefully. Don't talk about what you've seen or heard, just stick to a simple job.' Diana softened her tone when she saw that she'd been too short with Reenie. 'Look, I want you to do well and be happy, but round here you can get in trouble for thinking. Just don't rock the boat. And if you've got any ideas you tell me and not the overlookers. I'll tell you when you're allowed to have a bright idea and you'll do alright.' Diana received no response from the startled girl. 'Do you understand?'

'Yes, I think so. Although I think that the lad who I was going to show my idea to is different from the others because–'

'No.' Diana stopped Reenie short. 'Don't go getting ideas about the management lads. That one is no different from the others. I've heard all about him; he's from some fancy family in Norwich and he's a friend of one of Lord Mackintosh's sons, or nephews or summat. He'll be here five minutes and then they'll give him a job running one of the factories abroad. Mark my words, he's no different. If he asks you to walk out with him say a polite no, because his type is not for the likes of you; you can do better. He'll show you a good time and then he'll be gone. You deserve better; look to the engineers, or one of the factory fitters, but don't make eyes at the management lads even if they make eyes at you. In fact, especially if they make eyes at you.'

Reenie nodded and looked crestfallen; she seemed to take the advice on board.

'Just remember,' Diana told her as kindly as she could, 'all these management types are friends of the Mackintosh family; they might seem down-to-earth, but on Sunday afternoons they're eating cucumber sandwiches in Lady Mackintosh's drawing room, so don't go thinking you can make friends with them. It's them and us.'

Reenie nodded again. She'd had the wind knocked out of her sails, but it was what she needed. Some of these new girls were so green.

For a split second, Diana didn't recognise the two men walking towards her with their hands in their pockets. Perhaps it was seeing them in an unexpected environment, or the worn blue overalls that she'd never seen them in before, but for a moment she took them for normal factory craftsmen, on their way to a repair job. And when one of them looked her full in the face and gave her a nasty grin she felt a jolt of discomfort and walked past them for several paces before her mind caught up with itself. It was her stepbrother and his friend – her former beau, Stewart, though it pained her to remember it. They were clearly up to no good.

Diana froze for a second in confusion, then spun around and caught up with the trespassers.

'What are you two doing here,' she hissed to her stepbrother, 'and who gave you those overalls?'

'What's wrong with our overalls? I think they're very fetching.' Tommo mimed a pantomime twirl like Fred Astaire in a song and dance picture on the polished floor of the deserted factory corridor. He was smirking; he obviously wasn't worried in the slightest about being caught by his stepsister.

'You know bloody well.' Diana looked around to make sure they were alone. It wasn't unusual to see craftsmen like electricians, or fitters, or joiners, walking through the corridors on their way to or from a job mid-shift. There were so many thousands of employees at Mackintosh's that no one could be expected to know every employee. If anyone else had seen them, they'd have assumed they were on their way to a line needing a repair, but Diana knew better.

'Maybe we felt like getting jobs at Mac's.' Stewart ran his hand through his soft, floppy hair in a habit that had been honed over the years by his innate vanity. The same vanity that had prevented him from holding down any regular job for more than a week. He provided a stark contrast with his friend Tommo. Tommo was scrawny for a grown man; he had thinning black hair that was combed back with thick Brylcreem. His wide, frog-like mouth made Diana feel sick to look at it, and his beady, rat-like eyes always made her think that he was up to something. He usually was up to something. Stewart on the other hand was tall, muscular, sandy-haired, and with a complexion that was like rich Devon cream. His long, light brown eyelashes framed azure blue eyes that looked uncomplicated and innocent to anyone who didn't know him; and vacant to the few who did. Today Stewart's summer suntan was all but faded, along with any feelings Diana once had for him. She'd liked him when they were kids because he'd been the best-looking boy around and she enjoyed lording it over the other girls, but she was a different person now. The trouble was that Stewart was ignorant, and stupid enough to follow Tommo around. One day Tommo would get them both into trouble, and Diana thought it would serve them right.

Stewart huffed in a petulant pretence at being hurt by what Diana had said. 'You're always banging on about how important it is to get a job, and now that I've got one you're rude to me.'

Diana wasn't fooled by Stewart or his overalls. 'I know full well you haven't got a job here. These are craftsmen's overalls; you haven't passed an apprenticeship overnight, so these aren't yours. I'll ask you one last time before I call for the Watchman: what are you doing here?'

Tommo rolled on his heels with his hands in his pockets. His smug expression had not left his frog-like mouth. 'And what are you doing here, sis?' He lowered his voice and moved closer to her, even though they were completely alone in the echoey factory corridor. 'Haven't they found out your little secret yet?'

So, that's how it is, is it? Diana thought to herself. *If I shop you, you'll shop me.* She knew that Tommo didn't care if she lost her wage and her last taste of independence and self-determination; the only reason he hadn't exposed her until now was because he enjoyed tormenting her with the idea that he would. They stared at one another in silence, both as determined as the other not to give an inch. Tommo stood, smirking with mischief, Diana fuming with rage. And then Stewart yawned.

'Are we going, or what?' Stewart sounded bored. 'We've only got half an hour to put that bet on, and it'll take us best part of a quarter hour to walk to the bookies. If I miss this one, so help me–'

'Alright, alright.' Tommo had evidently been trumped by Stewart, who hadn't cared two hoots about the spat between his former girl and his best friend. Tommo rubbed his eyebrows with his bony, nicotine-stained fingers as though this demanding day had taxed his great intellect. 'This tip better be worth it, Stewie.'

'He's doping the horse hisself. It's a cert.' Stewart looked at his wristwatch. It narked at Diana that he could afford a wristwatch but worked less than she did.

Diana could tell that Tommo wanted to save face. He thought for a second or two and then allowed a smile to stretch over his horrible lips. 'Don't say I never do anything for you, sis. We're leaving you in peace.' And then he added theatrically, 'For now.'

Stewart and Tommo began strolling unconcernedly towards the concrete stairwell, but even though they were leaving the factory, Diana made sure that she stuck to them like glue. If she knew Tommo he had planned this so that he could steal something to order for his gangland cronies in Leeds; he wasn't an opportunist thief.

Tommo had taken the boldest route through the basin, right under the view of the office block windows, the Albion Mills factory windows, the railway station platforms above, and the main entrance gate cabin. Diana resolved to say nothing while he was within earshot and then to tell the commissionaires what he'd been up to as soon as he rounded the corner. Diana thought she could always get the commissionaires a photograph of Tommo from home if they didn't catch a good enough look at him, but when she got to the gatehouse cabin she saw, for the first time in all her years at Mac's, that it was empty. Tommo must have paid someone to create a diversion so that he could stroll in and out unimpeded. There was no one for Diana to tell. She stood there, helpless, angry. She watched their retreating silhouettes in their stolen blue overalls and hated them. What a change, she thought, from when she'd first walked through those gates; how her heart would have leapt to see Stewart walk around the corridor all those years ago. She'd have boasted to all the other girls that she had a young man and that he'd come to work to see her. Now, ten years later, she felt nothing but dread. Stewart had found his way into the place where she felt safe, and she didn't like it.

Diana looked around, hopeful that one of the commissionaires or the watchmen would come back, but the basin, as they called the deep space between the railway bank and the Albion Mills building, was deserted. As she turned to walk back to her line, out of the corner of her eye she caught movement. She looked up toward the windows of the office building. There on the third floor, lowering a dainty teacup into a dainty saucer, was Mrs Wilkes; she had been watching Diana.

Chapter Four

Reenie's grandmother had always told her that she had a good heart, but she liked the smell of trouble too much. As far as Nanna Martin was concerned, Reenie was a lost cause, and they would all just have to do their best to keep her on the straight and narrow and keep her in work until she could be safely wed.

Reenie didn't think her family were fair on her. It was true that she found herself in the stew quite a lot, but she didn't deliberately go out of her way to *find* trouble; it just found her. It was just this kind of situation that Reenie was walking into at the Mackintosh's factory known as Toffee Town.

'Do you know those two girls up at the far end? The ones that work behind the pillar?' Most of the girls sat in the same space that they had found themselves in on their first day at break time, and talked to the same handful of friends, never venturing out into the territory of other girls. Reenie, however, went round trying to make friends with everyone during her break. Impervious to any snubs she mostly won them over, but there were two exceptions: the two girls that she had watched on her first day, and who had given her a warning look. One of them was small, with a doll-like face; the other was plain with a red birthmark on her cheek like a blood-red tear. Today Reenie was passing the time of day with the boys who worked as porters on her floor and who filled the cages with the materials that the server girls needed to do their jobs. When the workforce wasn't segregated by order it seemed to naturally segregate itself; it was typical of Reenie that she would drift beyond the bounds of shop floor etiquette and mix with everyone.

'They call the younger one Good Queen Bess.'

'Why's that?'

'Because her older sister's called Mary, and she's a Bess, so it's like the queens who were sisters.'

'Oh, of course.' Reenie had no idea who the queens were that the boy porter referred to, but she thought it was wise to act as though she did.

'She's the lovely one so she's Good Queen Bess, but her sister's miserable so they call her Bad Queen Mary.'

'Not always,' one of the older porters put in matter-of-factly. 'Not to her face.'

'Aye, that's true. But mostly she's known as the Bad Queen.'

'Bess and Mary? Right-o. Thanks for that. I'll go and see if they want to make a new friend.'

'Good luck with that. Those two don't talk to anyone except Sarah who works in the dining hall.'

'That's a shame for them. You wait here while I

go and find out why.'

The boys laughed and shook their heads. They liked Reenie, but she didn't know what was good for her.

'Everyone at home calls me Queenie Reenie.' She put out her hand to shake the other girl's. 'I hear they call you Good Queen Bess.' Reenie turned to smile at Mary too and hesitated, the words, *'and they call you Bad Queen Mary'* hanging in the air unspoken, but cracking like an electric storm. Her voice faltered as she said, '...and you're ... her sister, aren't you?'

Mary said nothing, but Bess laughed to break the ice and said, 'Two Queens! Oh no, Queenie Reenie, which of us will be Queen of Quality Street?'

Reenie tried to shake the other girl's hand, but as she touched it she felt the thin skin, the delicate bones, and worried that she would break it. Up close Bess seemed like a little bird, lighter than air and just as fragile; her huge blue eyes seemed all the sharper for the dark circles round them.

'What do they call you Queenie for? I've never heard of a Queen called Reenie.' Mary wasn't taking Reenie's hand to shake it, although Reenie did offer it.

'Well it just sort o' rhymes wi' Reenie. My real name is Reenie, but you know: Reenie, Queenie, they just sound...' Reenie trailed off in the face of such obvious hostility.

'I think we need to get back to work. If we're going to work as fast as you we'll need to start early.' Mary said it bitterly, as though she resented Reenie's pace.

'Oh no, don't think of it like that, it's not a competition. Everyone works differently. I just like trying to be the fastest because then I can tell me' mam that I've done as she asked.'

'And does your mam know that the faster you go, the more likely the Time and Motion men are to see that it's possible to do our jobs faster, and then force us *all* to work faster so that we can never keep up with all the work that we have to do? And does your mam also know that that will mean we'll all earn less, *if* we manage to keep our jobs at all?' Bad Queen Mary was squaring up to Reenie now, hostile and cold.

'Mary, love, there's no need.' Her sister gently put a worryingly pale hand on her shoulder and tried to draw her back. 'Reenie doesn't mean any harm–'

'I don't care what she means and what she doesn't. This isn't how we do things here.'

Reenie hadn't realised when she came to work at the factory that everything would be so complicated. Instead of being paid a set amount of money for the time she spent working on the line, like she would if she'd worked in a shop, Reenie had been told they would all be paid for how many pieces of work they completed; depending on which department she worked in it might be how many cartons she filled with sweets, or how many tins she could make on the tin making machine. If she got though twenty boxes of sweets a minute she would earn the minimum rate for the day, if she got through ten percent more boxes she would earn ten percent more; twenty percent more boxes meant twenty percent more pay or 'piece rates'. However, there was a maximum; once you made your maximum piece rates you had to carry on working even though you knew that you weren't earning any extra money. Reenie didn't mind this at all, she just enjoyed working alongside so many other girls her age. 'Oh, but I can give you all some of my extra work if you like, you can keep the piece rates if you want to. I always reach my maximum and then after that I can't get paid for any more so I just do it for fun–'

'It's fun for you, but not fun for the rest of us who have to keep up with you. Did you ever think what you having fun does to everyone else?'

'But I'll give you my extra–'

'*That's* a piece rate racket. You *cannot* share your extra work with other girls or they'll sack all of us. Do you understand? If you try to do what you're suggesting then there will be no more work for any of us because we will *all* be tarred by the same brush and no one else will take us without a reference.'

'But *why?* I don't understand! I can't see why they wouldn't just want me to work as fast as I can so that they get more sweets at the end.'

'Because, you total doyle, if it is possible for a human being to work that fast, they will make us work even faster, and faster, and faster if we want to earn our basic rates for doing the minimum, and they will go on and on and on until we are all in our early graves. The Time and Motion men do not care about you or I, they care about the time it takes to do the work.'

'But I've seen you do your sister's work lots of times. Why don't they complain about that if they're so fussed?'

Bad Queen Mary's eyes widened with an icy rage and her words came out in a controlled hiss. 'You have never, ever seen us do anything of the sort. And don't even think about telling anyone else that poisonous lie.' Mary turned on her heel and left. There was a stunned silence from the other girls, and though Bess tried to offer Reenie a look of apology, she had to go after her sister, who was marching to her place on the production line.

Reenie was hurt and angry that anyone would treat her like that when she had clearly not meant any harm. She was particularly angry at being called a liar. If her grandmother had been there she'd have told Reenie to let it go, but in her absence Reenie began hatching a plan to make certain that Bad Queen Mary would never be cold with her again.

Chapter Five

Reenie worked a little more absentmindedly that afternoon, thinking about how she might get closer to Mary and Bess, the Quality Street factory's very own Tudor Queens. She watched them carefully from her side of the conveyor, and every time Mary caught Reenie's eye Mary would give her an icy, threatening look.

Reenie noticed several things, that Mary had to look at her work all of the time in order to follow what she was doing, and could only look over at Reenie occasionally. This was Mary's first mistake, the trick to speed was not to look, but to work by instinct.

Reenie also noticed that Bess was markedly slower than everyone else on the line, as though she just didn't have the strength. She took work from her older sister almost constantly. If the overlooker could see them then Bess would keep going, but she'd struggle to keep up even with surreptitious help from her sister. The wrapping girls were clearly unhappy about the situation, but tolerating it grudgingly. There was an understanding with them, Reenie thought, but they were not allowing it to happen out of friendship. Here was Reenie's opportunity: she would target the wrapping girls.

'Do you want to earn the highest piece rates of anyone on our floor?' Reenie had not bothered with introductions; she just presented herself at dinner time beside the wrapping girls' table and stated her proposition.

The dinner hour was just as segregated as the workroom; the older girls who wrapped the sweets chose to sit on tables apart from the younger girls. While the younger ones gossiped animatedly and leant over one another's dinners, snatching at leftovers and sharing comics, the older wrapping girls looked as still and bored as the portraits of Hollywood starlets in *Vogue* magazine.

The dining hall was not so different from Reenie's kitchen at home; there were scrubbed wooden benches below scrubbed wooden tables, but the difference here was that there were six hundred benches, and a sea of women all dressed the same. It was like finding a needle in a haystack, but she found them, sitting in the warmth of the corner near the kitchen hatches that were serving everything with a rich, mouth-wateringly fragrant beef gravy.

'And who are you when you're at home?' Heather Rogers, a wrapping girl with long, platinum blonde hair looked up from her dinner, and down her nose at Reenie. This was exactly the reception that Reenie had anticipated; which was why she had chosen to skip introductions and start with what was in it for them.

'She's Reenie, my server. She's the fast one.' Reenie's wrapper (known to the overlooker as Number Twenty-Eight, because that was the conveyor position she occupied, but to the vicar who'd christened her, she was Victoria Scowen) didn't sound enthusiastic about it, but Reenie felt that this still wasn't going too badly.

'I want to move to your end of the conveyor. I want to be up top behind that pillar. If you help me move you'll get higher piece rates because I'll be your server instead of Bad Queen Mary who's always slow because she's naffin' about wi' her sister.'

'Hang on,' Victoria Scowen didn't like the sound of this. 'What about *my* piece rates? You're *my* server; what's in it for me if I let you go up to the far end and leave me with God-knows who?'

'You'll get the same as you've been getting wi' me.'

'And how do you figure that one ou–?' Victoria was about to ask about the logistics of the problem when Diana – who was Reenie's intended target since she was the girl who had already warned her that if she had any bright ideas she had to take them to her first, and who appeared to have sway over all the girls on their line – cut in with a more important question.

'What do you want to move up to my manor for? Are you planning a piece time racket? 'Cause it sounds to me like that's the only way you can be offering all three of us better rates. No one can be in three places at once so you've got to be talking a racket.'

Heather Rogers tried to move Reenie on by saying in a haughty Harrogate drawl, 'We've got enough trouble up at our end with the Tudor Queens; we don't need the aggro of some new kid who thinks they know all running a piece time racket right under Rabid Roth's nose, thank you very mu–'

'No, Heather, I've a mind to hear what the young 'un has to say.' Diana ostentatiously moved herself into a more comfortable position and then indicated that she was ready to listen. Reenie could see that what she'd heard about Diana Moore was right; if Quality Street had three queens, then this was their true empress; she really did command all the other girls, and Reenie realised she was in luck.

'Come in Number Four!' Mrs Roth didn't have

an office of her own, but she marked her territory so firmly in the overlookers' break room that it felt as though they were being beckoned into her domain.

The room was not salubrious, but it was large enough for ten women to sit and glare at each other over a chipped mid-morning teapot. A row of three desks along the far wall with typewriters for processing sick notes, shift patterns and the like, seemed to be the only thing that marked the space out as a factory work room and not the windowless, dingy, cave-like lair of an old witch.

Diana slid through the doorway with the lithe confidence of a cat, followed behind by wrapping girls Victoria and Heather, who were reduced to cowering in the presence of Mrs Roth.

'Do you have something you wish to tell me?' Mrs Roth's words were sharp and threatening, and many a girl had turned and ran with their words left unspoken at that welcome, but Diana didn't so much as turn a hair:

'We've grown tired of covering up for Mary and Bess. We've come to tell you what's what so that we don't have to put up with them anymore.'

'Covering up?' Mrs Roth's snakelike eyes had met Diana's and were holding them unblinkingly.

'They do nothing but talk all day long, and it makes them slow. They're both perfectly capable of working faster, and I've seen Bess work like lightning when her sister's not with her, but they will talk.' Diana's casual, regal drawl seemed to imply that she considered Mrs Roth to be an intimate equal, rather than her supervisor. 'It's all sneaky whispers when you're not looking, Mrs

Roth. I can't imagine what they find to talk about, but you always have trouble when sisters sit together, don't you?' She held her gaze while she paused for effect. Reenie had been lucky indeed; Diana knew exactly how to play the woman she reported to. 'We'd like to help if we can.' She gestured casually to the two wrapping girls behind her. 'If you move Reenie Calder up to my place, and Mary down to the far end to Reenie's old place they'll be as far apart as they can be. We'll see how fast they work when they're not gassing. I didn't like to bother you with such a triviality, Mrs Roth, but when you've worked in production as long as you and I have, one knows that it's the small things that make a difference.'

Mrs Roth seemed to be looking for some trap or trick, and she snapped at Victoria, 'You! Why do you want to move Reenie Calder?'

This was what they had been afraid of; they didn't want her to notice the Reenie side of the plan, because the answers to those questions were awkward. Victoria panicked and looked at their ringleader for a hint but didn't get one, so just blurted out, 'She's doin' my head in Mrs Roth.'

And that was enough for the overlooker, the idea that Reenie would do anyone's head in was plausible. 'Alright, but I don't have time for this kind of thing. You'll have to work it out amongst yourselves. And if I think there's been *any* monkey business...'

'I assure you, Mrs Roth, that this is not monkey business. I would ask you as a special favour to me to keep an eye on Bess and Mary's piece rates once they've been separated and see what you see.'

'You *can't* move me.' A crowd of girls was gathering around the top of the conveyor as Mary refused to move to her new place at the start of their shift. The overlookers had not yet appeared and Mary was clinging desperately to the hope that the girls were just throwing their weight around because she'd threatened Reenie Calder. Perhaps if she stood her ground until the overlookers came out, they'd all be told to go back to their usual places.

'Yer movin' and it's final, love.'

Bess looked like a frightened animal, wide-eyed and timid. 'Do I move down to her left or her right?'

'They're not moving both of us.' Mary was speaking through clenched teeth. Rage, and fear, and injustice were bubbling up inside her and threatening to spill over. 'They're separating us.'

'But they can't! You can't! We're sisters! We have to be together; Mary, tell them that we have to be together.'

'You two have been talking too much.' Diana announced it loudly enough for all the workroom to hear, 'and Mrs Roth has decided that Reenie and Mary will exchange places so that you are as far away from your sister as possible and then we can see how fast you work.'

'I'm waiting to hear it from Mrs Roth.' Mary's voice was breaking with emotion, and her knuckles had turned white as she clenched her hands up into fists.

'You can hear it from whoever you like. But the message is the same. We aren't going to put up with this nonsense any longer. And you better work fast, because Mrs Roth will be watching your numbers, and anyone who can't make their minimum will be out.'

Mary caught an implied threat and stood her ground. 'We *always* make our minimum. I thought you were–'

Diana stopped her short. 'I don't care what you thought, it's time to do as I say. I've decided that it's better for everyone if you two are separated.'

'This is because of Reenie, isn't it? She put you up to it.'

'No one puts me up to anything, Mary Norcliffe; I make my own mind up, and don't you forget it.'

There was a clatter as the door swung to and the overlookers came in to take their high chairs, just out of view of that one spot at the top of the conveyor where Bess and Reenie would now work side-by-side. The shift was about to begin and Mrs Roth looked down from her crow's nest position at the crowd of girls, and at Mary who was shaking with emotion and fighting to hold back sobs and tears. Mrs Roth jerked her head once, slightly, almost imperceptibly, in the direction of Mary's new place, and Mary knew that it was all over. She reached for her sister's hand and squeezed it, but couldn't bear to look up at her face. Then she walked purposefully down the conveyor as all eyes, including the beady eyes of her overlooker, followed her in her humiliation.

Within seconds the other girls had scurried

back to their places and the machines were whirring into life. Reenie and Bess were left standing side-by-side, and Bess could just make out her sister at the far end of the conveyor wiping her eyes on a handkerchief and then pushing it firmly out of sight.

Reenie offered her new neighbour a tentative smile. 'I hope you don't mind. I can move back if it doesn't work.'

'If what doesn't work? What's happening?' Bess was pale with fear.

'I could see you were struggling. You're not very strong, are you?'

Bess shook her head.

'It's alright, love, we understand. I have a sister like you, she isn't strong either; it's not your fault. But it's alright because I've had this idea. I reckon I can work twice as fast as your sister, and cover your place without Mrs Roth seein' so you can take it a bit easier, and your sister can have a bit of a break an' all.'

Bess whispered, 'Are you going to let yourself get in trouble for us?'

'I won't get in trouble.' Reenie laughed softly at the idea and pretty crinkles formed around her bright green eyes. 'They'll never catch me. I know how to keep out of the way of the overlookers.'

'But what if one of the other girls notices and tells on us?'

'Did you just miss all of what just went on? A very public proclamation has been made by the only person in this room that no one would ever dare cross; it has been announced that the official reason for our change in places is to stop you gassin'. That's our story, and every girl here will stick to it if they know what's good for 'em after they've seen who said it. No one crosses Diana from what I've heard. We had to let your sister get upset so Mrs Roth would believe it too. She won't be watchin' you now; she'll be watchin' Mary; we'll be alright all the way up here on this end of the line.' Reenie shrugged, 'I just thought you looked like you could do with some help, and if your sister isn't spending all her time helping you she can work faster on her own and get her piece rates for once. This way your sister earns more, you earn more, these two earn more because I can go as fast as they like.' She pointed her thumb at her fellow conspirators, Diana and Heather, who gave Bess a nonchalant nod as though it was a mere trifle for them to help. 'And my old wrapping girl, Victoria Scowen, she earns just as much because your sister is the second-fastest server here. If she can do her job and yours she's bloody fast indeed and she'll make her maximum. Everyone earns more this way; everyone is happy.'

'But what about you, what do you get from it? You're not earning any more if you were already at your maximum and you're having to work so much harder, and you're risking your position if you're caught.'

Reenie thought about it. It was a fair point. 'Aye, but it's a laugh, isn't it?' And she grinned.

Diana wanted nothing more than to leave the factory for the day and get home. She had just overheard a conversation in the cloakrooms about a sweepstake that some of the girls were organising, despite the fact that it was strictly against factory rules; Diana wished she didn't know anything about it. She'd stuck her neck out enough for her young server girls, and she didn't want to know about their illegal betting because that was the limit. They were all sailing precariously close to a piece time racket as it was, and she could not, under any circumstances, risk losing her job.

Diana shook her soft ashes and caramel curls out of her elegantly pleated mob cap, and slipped it into the pocket of her white cotton overall before hanging it up on her hook. The cloakroom was a chaos of muddy shoes, hats and coats; girls from all over the floor were happily gossiping as they reclaimed their outdoor clothes and made ready to leave for the day.

One of the many benefits of being the most idolised girl on the floor was that Diana didn't have to stop and chatter away to her friends to keep them happy; she could leave with a nod to one or two, like an empress at court.

Not that she cultivated her position. It was generally known that she was the oldest of all the girls, but none of them seemed to know, or care, by quite how much. Little did the others realise that she was the same age as Frances Roth. The packing girls talked about Diana as though she was only nineteen, and they talked about Frances Roth as though she was nearing retirement, but they were both just twenty-six, and they'd hated each other since the day they met as five-year-olds at the Ackroyd Place Infant School.

'Miss Moore!' One of the younger girls had plucked up the courage to approach her with a copy of *The Picture Post*. Diana occasionally tolerated being called by her second name because it helped to reinforce her seniority, but she didn't like it as a general rule. The overlookers were allowed to be known by their surnames, but the floor girls had to go by first names; occasionally calling her 'Miss Moore' was another way that the other girls showed deference to their Empress Diana. The girl who stood before her was one she didn't know, a new girl all wide-eyed with enthusiasm. 'Please, Miss, we found this picture of Loretta Young and we think it looks just exactly like you.' She proffered her copy of the magazine like an offering to royalty.

Diana looked at the photograph but gave no visible indication of how she felt about it and handed it back. 'You don't call me Miss; I'm not an overlooker.'

The younger girl nodded and held her breath, trying not to be overwhelmed by direct communication from *the* Diana.

'Is that you done for the day? You walking out now?' Heather Rogers, one of Diana's few particular friends (if her association with anyone could be compared to friendship) always made a point of walking part way to the tram stop with the Empress of the floor to show all the other girls just how close she was to greatness.

'I suppose so, but I'm not going your way today. I'll walk down with you in the morning.' Diana could see that the other girl felt slighted, so she made the small concession of giving her a knowing look as though some secret had passed between them that the others were excluded

105

from. She didn't have the energy for lengthy explanations, but she thought that would help her friend to save face in front of the girls.

Diana made her way down the cast-iron west stairs that made a ringing noise as you landed your feet on them, and out towards the gate by Water Lane. It was always busy at this time, and Diana had perfected the art of weaving her way in and out of the throng of people without having to touch anyone; she hated the squash of bodies that built up by the Bailey Hall Road gate when the shift ended and so she always avoided it.

Today she had a mission: she had made a little extra money now that her piece time rates were up, and she was going to buy oranges for little Gracie, and a quarter pound of strawberry creams. It seemed a trifle unfair that the makers of these morsels had to go out and buy them like anyone else, but Diana supposed that if they all got to take a bag home for free there'd be none to send out to the shops.

For the first time in a long time, Diana loved her work. Diana was not like Reenie; she didn't have a passion for solving problems, or setting herself challenges. She didn't revel in her first taste of being good at something; instead Diana loved her job for the freedom it gave her to pay her way at her stepmother's house and to be near Gracie. She had let the other girls think that she was 'walking out' with Stewart, and they assumed there'd be a wedding soon enough, but didn't press Diana too much on the subject because she did not invite intimacy; Stewart was useful for avoiding questions if he was useful for nothing

106

else. She'd been lucky so far that all Stewart's recent girlfriends had been over in Leeds but eventually she supposed he'd settle down with some girl and she'd have to find a new excuse for why she wasn't painting the town red.

Diana's heart lifted a little as she thought about the chocolate and oranges, and Gracie, and the look she'd see on Gracie's little face when she produced them. She would make a mess of her frock, and then Ma would be annoyed, and Diana wouldn't care.

'You look happy! Penny for them?' The green-grocer woke Diana from her reverie. She smiled at him as she handed over her money in silence and left.

The walk up Gibbet Hill was steep, but Diana didn't want to waste a single farthing on trams or buses. Everything she had she needed to save for Gracie. The closer she got to home the more her aristocratic nonchalance fell away. By the time she reached the door the tough Diana was transformed into Didi; the caring sister and sometime idol of a six-year-old girl called Gracie Cartwright.

'Didi!' Diana was barely through the door when the little girl launched herself into her arms. The oranges fell to the floor and Diana didn't care. She caught Gracie in a bear hug and planted kisses all over her blonde, curly head. 'Didi, I've got a ribbon! I've got a ribbon to put on our Christmas tree! Look, it's red! And when I was at school Miss Waites said that I had the nicest hair and that she could tell I brushed it a lot, and I told her that you always brushed it for

107

me, and she said that she always brushes her hair a hundred times before bed, and I told her that I think you brush mine two hundred times, and she said she thinks I'm very lucky to have a sister who takes such care of me, and I said that you're my best friend, and–' Gracie prattled on happily, oblivious to the row that was going on in the kitchen at the back of the cramped terraced house.

Diana could hear her stepmother and Tommo shouting at each other. He was back, then. Ethel Cartwright was miserable when her son wasn't around, but Diana knew that she was much better off without him.

'But, Tommo, how am I meant to explain all this away if the police come looking? They were here again. They said you'd–'

'I don't care what you say, just come up with something. Use your brain if you've got one. If you love me, you'll do this.'

'But I don't know what to say to them–'

'I don't think you love me. In all honesty, I don't think you do. Mothers who love their sons will do anything to–'

'Of course I love you! Of course, I love you!'

'Excuse me!' Diana was standing in the kitchen doorway with Gracie by her side holding her hand. Gracie was so used to rows like this that she was less frightened by them now, but she still leant close to her Didi. 'I've come to get a knife and a plate. What have you come for?'

Tommo ignored the question. 'Oranges is it? Don't mind if I do.' He reached for the string bag that Diana had carried them home in, but she slapped his hand away angrily.

'They're not for you. They're for me' sister. The doctor says she needs oranges.'

'She's my sister as well, remember?' And Tommo winked at Diana. It was a challenge and a threat. He knew a secret about the little girl, and he knew exactly how much Diana and his mother didn't want anyone to know it.

'Then you'll care about her getting strong, won't you?' Diana was openly hostile, but she'd learnt that she had to stand her ground if she wanted to survive in the Cartwright household. Ethel would never throw her out, despite her tenuous claim on the older woman's parentage; Ethel's weakness was her love for her children, and all the children she had informally adopted over the years. It was this love that Diana didn't want to see exploited by Tommo yet again. 'What's in the boxes, Tommo? I hope it's not anything that will make Gracie poorly. You wouldn't want her to be poorly, would you?' She said it pointedly.

'It's nothing for you to worry your pretty little head abou–'

'But still, maybe I should ask Doctor Walker when he's here to check them, to make sure that there's nothing in them that would harm her lungs. The smell of pine from those crates is ever so strong, and it might make her cough. Maybe I should get him to check?'

'You're calling out *Doctor* Walker? The free clinic at St. Luke's not good enough for the likes of us?' Tommo scoffed. 'You haven't got the money to call out the doctor unless you get it from me, and I don't have the money to call out the doctor unless these boxes bide here for the night. So it looks like–'

'I have got the money. Where do you think the oranges came from–'

'Who gave it to yer? Some man? Finally using your looks for something worthwhile? Stewart won't like that when I tell him–'

'I earned it! I made my piece rates today if you must know, and I made my piece rates yesterday, and I'm having the doctor out tonight! She hasn't seen him for months, which means she hasn't had her medicine for months. She's got worse, and she's got thinner. *I've* got the money, so *I'm* sending for the doctor.'

'And what about the next time? Eh? Who pays for your fancy doctor with his fancy medicines the next time? You know you need me; you might not like it, but the only way any real money is coming into this house is if I bring it. So, if you want there to be money for a posh doctor next time, and the time after that, I suggest you keep your mouth shut and let me leave my belongings in my own home.'

'One night.' It was an order, not a question. 'You've got one night, Tommo.' Diana looked around the dirty galley kitchen that her step-mother never cleaned; the peeling plasterwork on the walls where the damp seeped in; the black marks on the door frame where her stepmother leant her enormous hands every time she shuffled through from the parlour; the tell-tale signs of mice along the skirting board. Diana wondered if she and Gracie would ever get away. No wonder Gracie still hadn't got her strength back after the whooping cough; how could they ever hope to escape this? How would she ever afford a real home, with a fire in the grate, and a Christmas tree?

Chapter Six

'She's not a real Captain.' Lieutenant Armitage was appealing to Sergeant Metcalfe in the Halifax police station. He wasn't dressed in his Salvation Army uniform because this was a private meeting between him, his son, and his son's old school friend who just so happened to be the local policeman.

'Are any of you real Captains? I thought that was the poin–'

'No! I mean she's not a real Salvation Army Captain. There must be some law that says she can't impersonate or summat'. Isn't there a crime of misrepresenting yourself?' Lieutenant Armitage didn't like having to take the matter to the police, but his son had persuaded him that talking quietly to Stan Metcalfe about their options was not the same thing at all.

Sergeant Metcalfe considered for a moment. 'You're thinking of the crime of masquerading as a policeman or a Chelsea Pensioner. There's nothing about giving a false rank in a religious organisation.'

'But she's doing *harm*; she's genuinely doing *harm!*'

111

'What kind of harm, exactly?'

'Well she's got this band of gatherers, you see, and they follow her–'

'Begging your pardon Mr Armitage, but isn't that what you've got? You do a lot of good in Halifax, and in my line of work I've got more cause to know about it than most; but don't *you* have a band of gatherers following *you?*'

'They don't follow me, they follo–'

'Dad, let me.' Lieutenant Armitage's son had come with him because although he loved his father, he suspected that the man wouldn't be able to explain himself in layman's terms to the policeman and would get overexcited and upset; it gave him no pleasure to see that this was exactly what was happening. 'Stan, it's like this, Gwendoline Vance she used to be proper Salvation Army, but ... well, she started gettin' over-zealous and me dad tried to tell her ... and if you ask me, she makes it more about following her than about real Salvation Army work. She thinks there's been enough soup and soap, and now it's time for Salvation; but she's got a funny way of showin' it, it looks like berating to me.'

'So what you tellin' me?'

'Gwendoline Vance brings her little group to meetings on a Sunday, but they're nothing but trouble. She's trying to take over the Halifax Salvation Army and run it herself. Me' dad wants to go quietly about his business and help people, but she turns up everywhere, shoutin' and nonsense. Christmas is coming and me' dad's been gettin' the band ready to play in town to raise money for toys for children what won't have none otherwise.

But Gwendoline Vance is sayin' she'll be there every step of the way, shoutin' out her preachin' over the top of them because the Lord's told her to. There's got to be summat' you can do to stop her, Stan. Look at me' Dad, have you ever seen him like this?'

'Well, there's breachin' the peace. I might be able to get her on that.'

'But then she'll have to breach it for you to do anything. We don't want her to even start. No one wants her doin' this; she spoils it for everyone. The Salvation Army has been playin' in Halifax at Christmas since before any of us were born. Let's not make this the first year they can't.'

'A police officer *can* make an arrest if they suspect that the peace is *going* to be breached, but I'd have to have grounds. I can't just go around nickin' women who shout at yer' Dad.'

'This isn't just any woman, Stan. You have to meet her. She's wicked.'

'Mr Armitage.' Sergeant Metcalfe could do without this, but in all his years of policing, he knew that no one had worked harder in Halifax to feed and clothe the poor than the Salvation Army, and the Armitages were the glue that held it together. He softened and changed tack. '*Lieutenant* Armitage; I can't go round and arrest the woman straight off the bat, but if you give me a time and a place when you think she will be breachin' the peace I will go round and take a look; I will take a very close look; I will watch her like a hawk. And if I see an offence being committed, whether the indictable or merely common law, if I see her so much as breach the peace, I will act in the public good.'

Young Armitage bristled. 'And what's that supposed to mean? We need you to–'

'Shush lad.' Lieutenant Armitage had brightened as he saw both hope and mischief. 'He means that Miss Vance has met her match!'

It was the Sunday of Advent, and the good people of Halifax were gathering in the enormous courtyard of the Piece Hall to watch their Christmas tree go up. The Piece Hall had no roof; it was designed in the 18th Century to look like a fine Italian Renaissance piazza, with galleries of tiny shops all around the sides. On a day like this one, when the winter sun was warm and strong, and the walls seemed to have a glow of pride, it had a draw for the inhabitants of Halifax that was hard to resist.

Gwendoline Vance had not wanted to miss this opportunity to preach to the masses, and so she and a group of her followers were congregating by the west door. Their logic being that at least half the people would have to pass them to leave when the lights were lit on the tree. Although the paving along the inside of the west door was flat, the entrance way that the rogue Salvation Army officers clustered in was at the bottom of a steep hill, and they themselves were standing in a hollow where the cobbles had been knocked out, and that had filled with dust that the wind blew in. Gwendoline liked the idea of this because she planned later to quote the bible to her followers telling them to 'kick the dust from their feet' as they left.

'Corporal Smith, how many people do you

think are here?'

The Salvation Army man stepped up onto a cream stone ledge by the doorway and surveyed the crowd of people: there were men and women of all ages, some happily squeezing together to fit into the courtyard, other luckier ones watching from the galleries above that formed part of the Piece Hall. He could see children in their best clothes standing proudly beside their parents in the glow of the winter sun, and he could see the lone cornet player in his Salvation Army uniform waiting beside the tree. 'I'd estimate about five-thousand souls, Captain.'

Frances Roth waited eagerly beside her mentor, Gwendoline Vance. She wore the dark, maroon-trimmed, Victorian-style bonnet of the Salvation Army Uniform, pulled tightly down over un-styled black hair. She was several years younger than Gwendoline Vance, but she could have been ten years older; pettiness had aged her. Her hooked nose and beady eyes gave her the look of a plotting crow, watching for a chance to do mischief. 'Shall we start now, Captain?'

'Not yet, sister.' Gwendoline Vance had a flair for timing. She was waiting for her moment. 'I have a prophetic gifting, and the Lord is telling me to wait on His call. It's a terrible, fearful privilege to know that you're doing the Lord's work, but know that today we truly are.'

Sergeant Metcalfe was watching from a gallery in the north west corner of the Piece Hall. He was in plain clothes a thin, grey wool scarf around his neck against the cold, and tucked inside his high-

115

necked waistcoat. These were the clothes he wore when he wanted to be ready to jump into action, if he needed to give chase. His waistcoat, jacket and trousers did not match, and the earthy-coloured fabric wasn't expensive, he was only a Sergeant after all, but they were practical, and they helped him blend in with all the factory workers who wore similar garb. His cloth cap was pulled down almost over his eyes, but his eyes were on Gwendoline Vance.

Sergeant Metcalfe had already guessed her plan; the official branch of the Halifax Salvation Army had sent a soloist to play 'Once In Royal David's City' for the crowd. As the last bar hung in the air, they would pull the switch to light up the tree with vibrantly coloured electrical lights, and everyone would cheer. It was always a moving moment, and people looked forward to it. Stan Metcalfe suspected that Gwendoline was waiting for the crowd to fall silent and then seize her chance to start shouting and preaching. He'd positioned himself so that he could vault over the balcony balustrade and land at her feet if she tried it, and then usher her and her followers away quietly, under threat of arrest if necessary, to prevent an extended breach of the King's peace. At the far end of the Piece Hall was his wife and children, and Sergeant Metcalfe wasn't going to let Captain Vance and her crowd spoil this for them, or any of the other children who had been looking forward to this as much as they looked forward to a Christmas toffee or a nativity play.

As he watched he could just see the legs of a half-way knackered old horse walk up a few yards behind Gwendoline Vance and her crew, and a girl slide off it onto the ground. He recognised the horse, and he recognised the girl.

Reenie Calder was on her day off, and she was desperate to see the lighting of the Piece Hall Christmas tree with her new friends. She had less time these days to help around the house and the farm, so she had had to get up early and work flat-out to finish in time to get over to Halifax. She had wanted to give Ruffian the day off too, but she could only meet Mary and Bess at the appointed hour if she took him and got him to pick up some speed on the way.

Horse and rider arrived by the west door just in the nick of time. The courtyard was already packed, and there was no time to find somewhere to tie up Ruffian and then squeeze in to the courtyard. Reenie would just have to make do with the view through the west doorway. She slid off her horse and stood by his side on the cobbled incline, looking down at the people whose faces were washed with sunshine as they waited for the show to begin.

Reenie heard it before she saw it; that unmistakeable sound of water hitting stone. There was no stopping it once it had started, so Reenie scurried quickly round to Ruffian's nose, hoping he'd miss her shoes. Ruffian was tired from a long ride and didn't care where he was relieving himself. The hot stream raced down through the cobbles and then collected behind a channel of twigs and leaves, which formed a momentary dam, allowing even more liquid to collect and build up, before breaking its banks and flowing like a great tidal wave towards the east door. Reenie knew that horses could hold a lot of water, but this, embarrassingly, was something of a record for Ruffian; and he was still going. Reenie didn't know what to do, she looked around for a bucket or something that might do as a bucket, but she saw nothing. She tried to call out and warn the uniformed people who were waiting in the doorway below, but they weren't listening. One of them, a tall, square-faced ring-leader in her early forties, who was dressed as a Salvation Army Captain, had taken in a deep breath and then bellowed out to the crowd, 'Repent!' She didn't get any further with her call to Salvation because at that moment more than a gallon of hot horse pee hit her shoes and ankles and settled in the light hollow that she was standing in.

Gwendoline Vance leapt up with a scream, and her followers, who were also hit, looked up to see where all this was coming from. It was at that moment that Frances Roth locked eyes with Reenie Calder, owner of the offending horse.

'I'm ever so sorry!' Reenie was genuinely sorry; she wasn't the type to ruin a person's shoes for any reason. 'I couldn't stop him. He's quite old.'

The rogue evangelists scrambled out of the puddle of pee and up away from the east door. The cornetist began his solo, and Sergeant Metcalfe enjoyed it all the more for seeing natural justice done without him needing to lift a finger. He had recognised the girl with the horse from that trespassing incident a few weeks back, and he suspected, based on what he'd heard about her, that this was Reenie Calder after all.

'Would you look at the state of that!' Tommo hooted with laughter as he pointed out the followers of Gwendoline Vance jumping out of the way, further down the plaza at the entrance to the Piece Hall. 'That's not...? Is it...? It is! It's a horse – they've just been caught in a steaming puddle of horse p–'

'Shush, would you please!' Diana put her hands over Gracie's ears where the child stood happily swirling her red ribbon around her tiny pink fingers and looking up over the heads of the crowd to catch a glimpse of the very top of the Christmas tree. 'I know what you were about to say, and I don't want Gracie hearing it. You're spoiling it for everyone.'

'Oh, la di dah, we don't want Gracie's tender ears tainted with such foulness.' Tommo nudged his friend Stewart in the ribs to encourage him to mock Diana too.

'What's the matter with you, Didi?' Stewart had adopted the nickname that little Gracie used for Diana 'You've got a right mare on for someone who was so desperate to give the kid a "nice day out".'

Diana didn't bother to defend herself, she was entitled to be in any kind of a mood she wanted after the things she'd had to do to get Stewart and her stepbrother to give Gracie one happy family Christmas memory. At first Tommo had scoffed when she told him that she wanted him to get Stewart to come out with Gracie to see the Christmas lights lit. But he'd seen a chance to

119

bargain with her; he had another four crates that he wanted to store in the house, and he wanted to store them for a week. She didn't know what was in them, and she didn't ask. It would be something stolen; either stolen by him and that he was selling on, or stolen by someone else and that he was charging money to hide until it could be moved on the quiet. He disgusted her, and she had no choice but to tolerate it. Without him and his income and his mother's help, her precarious life would collapse.

'Hey, Tommo, do you see who it is?' Stewart leaned over slightly to get a better look. 'It's Frances from school!' This seemed to make it all the more amusing for Stewart. 'Frances *Roth*, you've got to remember Frances Roth. I asked her to that dance, do you remember?' Stewart ran his thumb and forefinger along the brim of his cloth cap rakishly as though it had been quite a feat.

'Not Rabid Roth who wrote you a love letter and tried to get you to go to church with her?' Tommo's frog-like mouth formed a horrible grin. 'Nah then Diana,' he called back to his stepsister, 'do you remember Rabid Roth?'

'She's my new overlooker now, at Mac's.' Diana was not joining in the laughter.

'Is she indeed?' Tommo indulged in a little more theatricality. 'Well isn't that a turn up for the books?'

Stewart snorted with laughter, 'I remember, we were all just leaving school, and one of the Mission Halls had some dance on–'

'It was the Salvation Army.' Diana interrupted, flatly.

120

'How did you remember that?' Stewart clearly felt that ten years ago was somewhere in the dim mists of time and that choices made back then were all but forgotten. 'Well, like I said, I could tell that she were sweet on me; I mean all the girls were sweet on me. So, I said to Tommo, I said, "Do you fancy a laugh?" and Tommo said "Yeh, I fancy a laugh." So I went and asked Frances Roth to go to this dance with me, and I told her where I'd meet her, and then I just never turned up.' Stewart snorted with laughter again as though he had just delivered a brilliant punch line to a brilliant joke.

'Best thing about it was,' Tommo joined in, beady eye's creasing up with laughter, 'she genuinely thought you were madly in love with her and that you were saving up to buy her a ring and ask for her hand.'

'What?' Stewart was now wheezing with laughter. 'How do you know that? I never told her any of that.'

'A little bird might have put the idea into her head.' Tommo acted like he was pleased with himself all over again at the memory of what he'd done. 'Oh dear,' he rolled his eyes at his stepsister, 'I don't think Diana finds it funny.'

Diana said nothing, her face stony.

'You thought it was funny at the time.' Tommo was obviously touchy because he was pulling back the ridiculously padded shoulders in his new coat. With his scrawny frame, it looked like he'd forgotten to take the hanger out.

'I didn't. As I remember it, you just told me that I thought it was funny.' Diana had agreed to let Tommo keep his dodgy goods in their house for another week, but she hadn't agreed to be a sycophant.

Stewart rolled his eyes at her. 'What do you want me to do, go and apologise to her after however many years it's been?'

'Ten years. It's been ten years. And no, I don't think you ought to apologise. If you apologise, she'll realise that you were lying and that you never liked her. That's worse.' Diana decided that it was time to go home and she looked around for the quickest route through the crowds out of the Piece Hall.

'What, you think she still believes I liked her?' Stewart was incredulous. 'Honestly? Even though I stood her up?'

'She doesn't think you stood her up though, does she? She thinks I stole you away from her. She thinks I'm still stealing you away from her now. For all I know that's why she's never married because she thinks one day you'll see sense and stop courting me and go off with her.'

Stewart laughed and said, half-jokingly, 'Are we courting?'

Diana looked at him with complete disgust. 'Only if anyone asks.'

'Come on Diana,' Stewart put an arm around her and tried to push her up against one of the stone pillars of the plaza. 'You know you want me.'

'Oh, get off!' Diana was angry. 'Don't you even care that we're in public?'

'I thought that was what you wanted?' Stewart was enjoying himself. 'Don't you want everyone to think you're with me, so you don't have to answer awkward questions about why you're not courting anyone else? We should make a show of it, make sure everyone knows we're an item.'

'He makes a fair point, sis.' Diana hated it when Tommo called her 'sis', like an actor from an American talkie. 'You don't want people asking why such a paragon of virtue as yourself never married. They might start looking at you-know-who and doing their arithmetic...'

'Hush!' Diana was fuming now. She hissed, 'People can hear you.'

Tommo shrugged, too pleased with himself to care. 'And I think you'll find that the reason our Frances never married is not because she's been carrying a torch for my best friend all these years – who, by the way, was getting his own back on her for making snide remarks about you in the school yard – but because she's so ugly no one would ever have her.'

'Well, that makes two of you,' Diana snapped, and picking up Gracie, who at six was too old to be carried far, pushed her way through the crowds as quickly as she could.

Frances Roth was scuttling away from the Piece Hall with sodden shoes when she collided with Diana Moore. Frances hadn't been looking where she was going because she was concentrating too much on the discomfort of her damaged foot-wear, and the disgust and embarrassment at how the damage had been caused. Diana was not looking where she was going because she was trying to carry six-year-old Gracie while hurrying away in the direction of the tram home. As they collided Diana stumbled, and Gracie slipped from her arms, landing with a thud on her left knee. Gracie howled with pain.

'What are you doing to that child?' Frances Roth had pounced on Gracie in outrage at some perceived misbehaviour on Diana's part, and was trying to help her up while simultaneously keeping Diana at a distance.

'She's my sister, and I might well ask you the same question. What do you think you're doing, tearing round corners like that.' Diana scooped her arm around Gracie and pulled her close, away from Frances.

'I saw you throw her to the ground.' Frances was looking around her for witnesses, and then started saying loud enough for everyone in the street beside the Piece Hall to hear. 'I saw you throw her to the ground.'

'I most certainly did not. You ploughed into us!' Diana was affronted, but she was used to this. Frances was a terrible bully, and on the few occasions over the years when she'd passed her in the street with Gracie the woman had tried to accuse her of ridiculous acts of child cruelty. They were ridiculous because Diana would never harm Gracie, or let any harm come to her. Diana could only assume that Frances Roth was jealous of the little girl in her life.

Frances pointed to Gracie's wrappings. 'Why have you got her all wrapped up in woollens? Are you trying to hide bruises? Have you been mistreating this little girl?'

Gracie was evidently frightened by the vehement woman with the stinking wet shoes, and she clung to Diana's knees while rubbing her own and stifling little sobs.

'For the last time Frances; no one is mistreating our Gracie. Now would you for heaven's sake leave us alone.' Diana looked round and saw her tram pulling up at its stop; if she was quick she could just catch it and have them both home before it started to get dark. She didn't bother to take her leave of Frances, or even look her in the eye; it simply wasn't worth it.

'It's only a packing job; are you sure you want to go to all that trouble? You'll be done with it after Christmas. Why not get a bicycle, or walk in. I've heard a lot of the girls who live further out find a family in town to lodge with during the week; wouldn't that be simpler?' Donna was wiping down the bar and gathering up glasses as she spoke to Reenie.

'But I want to bring Ruffian with me, and you do have a stable you're not using, don't you?'

Mrs Parish, The Landlady of The Old Cock and Oak pursed her lips; Reenie Calder knew what she wanted, she'd say that for her. 'I do, but it's not just a case of clearing out the rubbish in it, there's all the mucking out you'd have to do in the week once you were using it. None of my lads can spare the time, you'd have to promise you'd be in to muck him out.'

'Is that a yes?' Reenie held her breath excitedly as she realised Mrs Parish had given ground. 'If I promise to keep it clean as a whistle is that a yes?'

'Very well. I suppose so. As it's you. But you've

got to clear all that lot out yourself to make space. It's no good bringing a horse into the yard, let alone a horse Ruffian's size, with all that junk still piled up.'

'If we take it away, do you mind what we do with it?'

'Are you asking if you can keep all the old rubbish?' Donna was confused but amused.

'Yes. Would you mind?'

'But it's all worthless; it's old crates and the like.'

'But can we still have it?'

'Very well. So long as it doesn't come back to haunt me.'

'Thanks, Mrs Parish!' Reenie called out excitedly to the landlady as she ran from the bar and out to the yard behind The Old Cock and Oak where Mary and Bess were waiting.

'Well, what did she say?' Mary was waiting to hear the worst.

'I can keep Ruffian here in the day while I'm on shift down the road, and we can have *all* the crates.'

'That's a lot of firewood!' Bess sat huddled in a plaid wool blanket on one of the upturned crates. The stable in question was as old as The Old Cock and Oak itself.

'We're going to sell it. I reckon if we can break up the crates we can sell them off for cheap kindling; then any metal we put to one side and sell to the scrap yard, and then the rest to the rag and bone man. The money should pay for a blanket for Ruffian, and enough hay and provisions to start him off.' Reenie's eyes sparkled with the excitement of a plan.

Mary was pragmatic. 'And how do you expect the two of us to sort through all this lot before Christmas, let alone before tonight.'

'The three of us! I'm here to help too!'

Reenie looked kindly at Good Queen Bess, who was shivering but willing. 'Well, you're needed to look after Ruffian while we work.' Reenie thought that if she brought Ruffian into the yard and stood him over where Bess was sitting, he would keep her friend warm in the cold, damp yard. Ruffian didn't move once you put him somewhere; he disdained unnecessary exertion now that he was reaching his old age. Although, to be honest, he had always seemed to disdain unnecessary exertion as a point of principle. 'Here, you stay where you are, and if he tries to wander off just tap his tummy.'

'But wouldn't I be more use breaking up crates?'

Mary didn't say anything. It was cold enough for snow and she would rather her sister waited in the pub where there was a fire, but if she was in the pub, then Mary couldn't keep an eye on her. There was someone who Bess would arrange to meet, given half the chance, and her sister wanted to prevent that at all costs, which meant keeping her out in the yard with them while they worked.

'No, silly.' Reenie pulled the blanket a little tighter around Bess's shoulders. 'You're much more useful to us there keeping Ruffian out of the way so that we can get to work. And you can keep us entertained by reading to us from your magazine. What's happening in the world now?'

'Oh, well!' Bess opened her magazine up to the page that contained the most thrilling news. 'It's a magazine that Victoria Scowen's sister's friend got from America in the summer. Apparently the King was seen holidaying with a married woman on a yacht, but they can't print it in the British magazines, and that's why everyone's laying bets on there being no coronation!'

Mary said blandly, 'On second thoughts, let's not strain your voice. You read in your head, and we'll work.'

Bess didn't hear the slight, as Mary had known she wouldn't, and Reenie simply rolled her eyes at the pair of them and pulled on her father's rough leather work gloves that she'd borrowed for the day.

Reenie and Mary divided the work up between them; Reenie pulled the rubbish out and set it in different piles depending on what it was made of, and Mary attacked it all with an axe they'd borrowed from the publican. The jobs suited them well; Reenie enjoyed the puzzle of bringing order to chaos and dividing things up into their rightful places, and Mary was surprised at how cathartic she found the opportunity to hit things until they were in pieces.

The girls worked through broken earthenware pots; dented copper kitchen pans; splintered wooden crates and beechwood chairs with missing legs. All of these were treasure to Reenie, who became more and more excited about how much money they would make when the rag and bone man came.

'And what if it all gets stolen in the night before the rag and bone cart comes? It's only Sunday; he'll not be here while Tuesday.' Mary was concerned that all this work would be for nothing.

'But he'll be here in less than half an hour.' Reenie was breathless but triumphant as she surveyed their carefully organised loot. 'I told them all to come at six o'clock.'

Bess lowered her softly tattered, out-of-date magazine to call across the yard. 'Told who? Who's coming at six o'clock?'

'The rag and bone man who buys from the gypsies; the scrap man for the metal; David Simmo' said he'll buy the old bottles for half the deposit and the lad from Martindale's Stores who's pickin' up all the kindlin' wood to sell for farthings. I arranged it all with 'em in the week.'

'But you can't have done; you only got permission from Mrs Parish to clear her yard this afternoon.' Mary was unimpressed by Reenie's initiative, and more affronted at her nerve.

'I know, but if she'd said we *couldn't* clear it all out this afternoon, then I'd have had the afternoon free to ride around them all and let them know the deal was off.' Reenie shrugged. 'Seemed like the best plan to me.'

Mary was put out, but she didn't know why, so she changed tack. 'And why have you got this sudden bee in your bonnet about keepin' the 'orse in town? I thought you were going to make friends with someone in the factory stables and keep him there?'

'I was ... I mean, I have. But I realised that I should probably have somewhere for him in town

129

in case of emergencies, as well as somewhere at work.'

Mary was suspicious. 'You're being vague, Reenie Calder. What have you got to be hiding? One minute you're keepin' Ruffian at work, the next minute you're keepin' him here. What's to do?' she asked with narrowed eyes.

'It's nothing, really. I just thought it might be an idea to have both options, and I started planning everything, and then something happened today before I met up with you both that made me glad to get a wiggle on with this place. But it was nothing special. I was going to get this place ready anyway.'

'Come on Queenie Reenie.' Good Queen Bess was excited at the prospect of some juicy gossip and folded her magazine into the pocket of her thick wool coat. 'Tell us; we're your friends.'

Mary looked more fierce than friendly, and that possibly had more to do with why Reenie blurted out:

'I met Mrs Roth ... I mean ... I saw her, I didn't meet her.'

'And?'

'Well, I think she were about to do something right important at the Christmas tree lighting with the Salvation Army because she was standing with them in the Piece Hall looking ever so smart in her uniform with the rest of her Sally Army chums, and I think I might have ruined it.'

'What, just by seein' her?' Mary was probing for more information; she knew there was more to this story than Reenie was letting on.

'Not just by seein' her no...'

'Come on, out with it, before me and Bess die of cold.'

'Ruffian weed on 'er.'

'He did what?' Bess gasped with laughter and was seized with a fit of uncontrollable giggles.

'And her captain.' Reenie pursed her lips, waiting for the telling off from Mary that she was sure that she was about to get.

For the first time in their fledgling friendship, Reenie saw Mary smile. Mary shook her head and tried not to show her amusement. 'Reenie Calder. You are the limit.'

'I'm in a lot of trouble with Mrs Roth.'

'I'll bet you are.' Mary strode over to her sister and gave Ruffian an admiring pat.

'Mrs Roth said I'd be staying late every night this week to clean the machines. I was going to clear this out anyway, but I thought I'd accelerate my plans in light of this recent hiccup.'

'Hiccup? This is more than a hiccup. You let Ruffian wee on Rabid Roth.' Mary was now sitting on the crate beside her sister, with her arms folded, but for once they weren't folded in hostility, she was hugging herself to keep a straight face. 'I think we ought to make sure we walk you home for the next week.'

Chapter Seven

Diana Moore was the chief topic of conversation in the manager's dining room of the Mackintosh's toffee factory at Monday dinner time, although the menu for the senior members of staff always referred to it as 'luncheon'.

The claustrophobically Edwardian dining room was deserted all but for Amy Wilkes, Major Fergusson, and Laurence Johns who said that he couldn't understand why such difficult employees were kept on if they couldn't work together. Mrs Wilkes agreed that Diana Moore and Frances Roth couldn't be kept on the same production line for long, but she wasn't convinced by the Major's solution.

The Major had come up with the idea that they could send Diana to one of their overseas factories for a six-month posting. That way she could work on a project that would give her more management experience and develop her unique talents. It wasn't an unusual stratagem, Mackintosh's had transformed itself in the preceding two decades into an international concern, and such a thing had only been possible by nurturing the talent of the local young people who came to work for them. Diana might like to behave as though it was her against the world, and that there was a great gulf between Lord Mackintosh and the factory floor staff, but Lord Mackintosh's mother had run a cook shop that she'd turned into a toffee factory, and he was only too aware of what a working class woman from Halifax could achieve in the world if she was given some help.

The hope behind the plan to send Diana abroad was that Diana would benefit from the short break from her relatives, who the Major believed, in his infinite wisdom, needed to learn to be less reliant on Diana. It did not occur to the Major that Diana could be spending so much time with them out of anything other than an overdeveloped sense of duty. Major Fergusson was convinced that Diana would get a taste for freedom; who knew, she might even get a taste for travel and want more postings abroad. Better still it would send a message to the other girls that there were great possibilities for them; that is, if they chose not to marry.

Mrs Wilkes poured cold water on the Major's ideas by saying, 'You can't send her to Germany, she doesn't speak any German. And what would you be sending her to Germany for?' Amy Wilkes slumped back in her mahogany dining chair and threw her napkin into her empty, gilt-edged plate. She considered the Major a friend and a man of unusually good sense, but this was not one of his better ideas.

'But she doesn't need to speak any German, that's the brilliant thing about it. Laurence here was telling me that he has a couple of excellent chaps there already who would be able to interpret for her. You explain Johns.'

Laurence Johns seemed rather embarrassed, but then he always seemed rather embarrassed when asked a direct question. He was about Amy Wilkes' own age and had spent the last few years travelling through a variety of equatorial regions as the firm's chief cocoa buyer. His promotion to Head of Overseas Interests had surprised Amy Wilkes as she hadn't thought that he would want to return to Britain to settle down, but then who knew what went on in other people's minds?

Laurence Johns cleared his throat. 'It's really not an obstacle if she doesn't speak German. We just need someone from the firm that we can trust. Our factory in Dusseldorf is in a terrible mess; the girls there are at each other's throats. They're mostly good girls, but there are one or two who make trouble. They see government informers everywhere they look, and we don't know if any of the girls really are enthusiastic for the new regime, or if they're just accusing one another out of fear.'

'Diana would be perfect.' The Major thought the opportunity was heaven sent. 'No one can manage unruly girls like Diana.'

'I'm still not sure about Diana Moore. I spoke to her myself about the overlooker position, and she was quite resentful. I was reading in her employment file that there was a full month when she wouldn't speak to anyone; not a word.'

'Yes,' said the Major with enthusiasm, 'and the other girls still kept in line for her sake! And we had no complaints about her work if I remember.'

Amy Wilkes did not share the Major's positive view of Diana's past behavior. 'But do we really want a girl who is so stubborn she can refuse to

134

speak for a month?'

'Ah, well,' said the Major, 'it was a long time ago – six years if memory serves – and her father had recently passed away. Given the circumstances, I don't think we can really be so hard on her. My point is, that even when she says nothing at all, she still keeps the girls in line.'

'She does sound like just the person we need.' Laurence Johns was tentative. 'But of course this posting is voluntary, given the political situation there.'

'Well, I'd send Frances Roth to Germany if I were you.' Amy Wilkes took off her tortoiseshell spectacles and rubbed the bridge of her nose between thumb and forefinger. 'She could kill Adolf Hitler with a look.'

Major Fergusson barked with laughter. 'Yes, yes, very good. I like that; kill him with a look.' And then he said more seriously, 'Frances probably could, too.'

'Alright Major, you've got my permission, but you'll need to persuade Diana. How do you want to do this? I can speak to her, but...' Mrs Wilkes shrugged.

'No, no, you leave it to me. I knew her father in passing. I think I know how to tackle Diana. I'll introduce her to Johns here, see what she makes of him, and we can come round to it by degrees.'

'You'll have to catch her first. She doesn't like being kept late, and she doesn't like being taken off the line mid-shift.'

'I have just the thing; a reporter from the *Halifax Courier* has asked to come in and take photographs of the Quality Street line. She's the

135

best person to run a line for a photographer, and I can introduce her to Laurence while she works.'

'On your own head be it.' Amy Wilkes had faith in the Major, but she wouldn't lay any bets on him in a tussle with Diana Moore. 'I tried to offer her a promotion and she gave me a lecture on the value of union lending libraries and the nature of education.'

'Hang on a minute.' Laurence Johns brightened up. 'You don't mean *the* Diana Moore, do you? Father was a Union man, left the factory to open a shop?'

'Yes,' Amy Wilkes sighed. 'Who did you think we were talking about?'

'Well I know her!' Laurence was delighted. 'She comes to all of my lectures, I've spoken to her many times. Yes, yes, I know who you mean. Very smart girl, asks very sharp questions. I was giving a lecture about cocoa growing in–'

'I'm sure the lecture was scintillating.' Amy Wilkes had heard all about Laurence's travels to cocoa plantations before. 'But do you think that she would listen to you?'

'Oh yes, definitely. We're great friends. I loaned her a book.'

'That settles it then. We'll send Diana to Dusseldorf and that should solve your problems and mine Laurence.' The Major seemed to be delighted at the simplicity of it, but Amy Wilkes thought that their problems would not be as easy to solve as they hoped.

Reenie's first workroom, she had eventually discovered, was a temporary one. Girls could be assigned to a line and work on the same one for years, a thought that horrified Reenie. She had been lucky, as Mackintosh's were launching a new line, and while production was ramping up some of the work had to be temporarily done by hand. For now, Reenie's room was the wrapping department for the chocolate sweets in the new Quality Street assortment, and Reenie's line was the Strawberry Cream chocolates.

The girls in Reenie's workroom went through agonies of desire as one after another glossy milk chocolates marched past them on the conveyor belt, like soldiers in a neat line. Not only could most of the girls never afford to buy the chocolates themselves, but they weren't allowed to eat them when they saw them in the factory. Day-in-day out they watched wide-eyed as the tasty little morsels disappeared out of sight, destined for homes other than their own.

Reenie made friends with everyone in her workroom and was ready to help anyone with anything – and to answer back tartly if she thought she saw any of the smaller girls being bullied – and so she usually ended up staying late even if she wasn't being punished for something her horse had done. It was that Monday afternoon after the line had shut down and the other girls had gone to the cloakroom that Reenie was reunited with her Time and Motion men.

Even though her workmates had talked about them as cruel, wicked Victorians intent on driving them all into an early grave Reenie thought that the Time and Motion men seemed ever so nice.

'Don't mind us, love,' one of the factory engineers in his blue overalls called across the workroom to Reenie. 'I'm just showing these two fellas a machine.'

'Yes, don't worry.' The Time and Motion man with a mop of golden blond hair flashed her a winning smile. 'We promise we're not here to make you work faster.'

Reenie lifted her head up from where she'd been working under a machine covering. 'Oh, it's you again. Hello, nice to see you. Thrown any more men over horses?'

Peter opened his mouth to explain to the Major and the engineer about Reenie's father and the incident outside The Old Cock and Oak, but then thought better of it and just smiled at Reenie, who was talking on happily.

Without pausing to give him a chance to answer she went on, 'You didn't tell me what happens if I want to work faster. I don't understand why everyone's so fussy about it.'

'You're Reenie, aren't you? Reenie Calder? I don't suppose you remember my colleague–' Peter flicked a stray lock of loose hair from his eyes.

Reenie raised an eyebrow. 'And what was it you thought I was good at last time we met?'

Peter hesitated when he realised his mistake. 'Having a good memory?'

'Yes, I remember you, Major Fergusson, thanks again for showing us the way over here, we'd still be lost now if you hadn't stepped in. Now I want you to tell me honestly, if I've seen a way to make everyone's work faster, will you use it against us?'

Peter answered, 'No, never, I wouldn't–'

'I didn't think so. Can I show you what I mean about the work?'

Peter nodded, surprised at the enthusiasm of this quick-witted girl.

'I want to move the finished tubs so that they can be put on the pallets by the shortest girls.' Her matter-of-fact manner surprised Peter, and even Peter's older colleague began to smile under his enormous whiskers.

'Do you want to demonstrate what you mean on the line?' Peter gestured gracefully with his hand toward the conveyor belt like a gentleman making way for a fine lady. Reenie stood up a little straighter and before long she was completely lost in the excitement of explaining to the men what she'd been trying to tell her supervisor all along.

'...Because,' Reenie told them, 'if you just made hooks that went on the bottom of the conveyor here and pulled the work back a bit, each girl could hook her finished tub onto the bottom of the conveyor, and it would carry it down to the end where the younger girls could be waiting to pick them up and put them on the pallets. We'd all work much faster, and the girls would have an easier job and make better piece rates, so they'd be happy, I know they would.'

Peter nodded and walked around to the conveyor, jumped up onto one of the wrapper's high stools and mimed the action of wrapping the sweets and then hooking the tubs onto the conveyor. 'Hmm...' he said, frowning. 'I'm not sure, Reenie. It's a very good idea, and I like your initiative, but the tubs would catch on the girls' knees and get knocked off.'

'Then the girls can sit sideways.' Reenie shrugged; it seemed so obvious to her. 'The wrapping girls can sit sideways looking up the conveyor instead of looking across it. They'll be even faster then because they'll have a better view of what's coming down the line.'

Peter frowned, but this time there was an excitement bubbling under the surface and a growing realisation that this slip of a girl might have hit on something. He moved back to the work station and tried out her idea. 'You know I think she's really got something. Reenie, you're a wonder! Bert, could you make this work, do you think?'

The overall-clad engineer crouched down and took a closer look at the conveyor, pulling at it here and there to test its strength. 'Yeah, easy. We could fit it on Monday.'

'Major Fergusson, what do you say?' Peter said, deferring to the older Time and Motion man whose moustache pouted forward as he became lost in thought.

'Yes, I don't see why not. If we don't ask them to work faster for the same piece rates they shouldn't mind. And we can afford it for as long as the line lasts on hand-wrapping; it's only until we can set up the twist wrapping machines, after all.'

Peter was delighted, but Reenie didn't kid herself that it was anything to do with her. The wink Peter gave her was for her idea on his production line and nothing more; she was pleased with it, though, all the same.

'Oh, but Tommo, you know we shouldn't.

140

Reenie's only in the next room, and what if someone walks in?' Bess Norcliffe was turning the tortoiseshell button of her thick, blue wool coat and whispering, even though it was only the two of them in the cloakroom, leaning into each other, their faces close. She wanted Tommo to persuade her that no one was going to come in and she would have been willing to believe him even if it wasn't true. The hour was late, the winter wind howled outside the factory windows, and the smell of work plimsolls warming on the radiator in the corner mingled with the smell of boiled sugar from the next room. Bess's pale face flushed with embarrassment, and her eyes darted about watching for anyone that might be coming back after hours. Reenie was working late on the packing floor, and Bess had agreed to wait for her, but apart from that, she didn't think anyone else was around.

'Come on, doll, be a sport–'

A door creaked on its hinges and footsteps clicked into the corridor before Bess and Tommo had even had a chance to look up.

'And what do you think you two are doing in here at this hour?' The half-shriek from Mrs Roth made Bess jump and let go of her button and hide her hands behind her back, as though the act of turning it round and round was a sin. 'Elizabeth Norcliffe! Who is this man!'

'Please, Mrs Roth, he was just passin–'

'And what's it to you, you dried up old cow?' Tommo 'The Blade' Cartwright looked nonchalantly over the padded shoulder of his ostentatious new jacket at Mrs Roth with one eyebrow raised and his mouth hanging half open as he spoke.

Frances Roth stood for a moment in shocked silence. 'It's you.' She clearly recognised him; it had been several years since their paths had crossed, but she couldn't have forgotten Diana Moore's stepbrother and Stewart Edward's best friend. 'What are you doing on these premises?'

Tommo shrugged and lied with confidence. 'I'm working here.'

'Then you should know that it's a sacking offence to speak to an overlooker like that! Who is your supervisor? I demand that you tell me the name of your supervisor!'

'No.' Tommo stretched and yawned casually, as though he were quite at home in the girls' cloak-room of the third floor wrapping section. To reinforce the point he reached into his breast pocket and took out a comb which he ran along his black, Brylcreemed hair, and winked at Bess. Tommo recognised Frances Roth, but he wasn't concerned that she'd report him for being on the premises. He'd been invited by an employee to wait for her late after her shift, and nothing had been stolen from the factory – yet.

'What do you mean, "no"? I asked you a question and–'

'And what? And you think I have to answer just because you asked?'

Bess stood dumbstruck but moved away from Tommo's side. She knew the drill, Tommo had told her time enough: *if anyone asks my name just say you don't know it, because if you love me, you'll do as I say.*

'If you don't tell me the name of your supervisor, you'll regret it.'

'What you gonna do? You can't sack her, she an't done nowt; I was just walking past when she were 'ere. So why don't you just go back to your tambourine, and your hymn book?' Tommo grinned, revealing his gapped teeth and his ignorance.

'You can't talk to Mrs Roth like that.' Bess had found her voice, but it was reedy and cracked with nerves. 'It's not nice, and she's an overlooker, you've got to call her ma'am.' Bess stepped away from Tommo, hugging herself for protection, as things had begun to turn nasty.

'Oh, "Mrs" Roth, are we? "Mrs"? You're no Mrs–'

'It is a courtesy title.' Frances Roth stood up straighter and stuck out her chin, as though maintaining her dignity would compel the relation of her old enemy to obedience. 'Overlookers have the courtesy title of Mrs, and courtesy is something that you would do well to learn.'

'Why? Why would I do well to learn courtesy? Where's it got you, eh? Look at you: dowdy hair that ain't seen no hairdresser and tough old boots you've had patched and polished, and we know you're not married because you can't work here if you're a married woman, so where has courtesy got you? And where has callin' a spade, a spade got me? I've got a nice suit on; latest style from America, all the independent men of business in Chicago wear 'em like this. I've got a lovely pair of shiny new shoes, and I've got a lot of money in my pocket for the weekend, so who needs to learn from who, eh?'

Mrs Roth wrinkled up her nose. 'I'm having you dismissed with immediate effect. I don't need to know the name of your supervisor in order to have you dismissed, I can inform the Employment Department, and they will look up your employment file. I know your name, Thomas Cartwright, and I'm fetching the night watchman to have you removed.'

'You do that, love. I'll be right here when you get back.'

Frances Roth turned on her darned heel and marched off towards the east door, throwing Bess a warning look as she left.

'What are we going to do now?' Bess sighed, but as the immediate danger of a confrontation with Mrs Roth had passed, so had most of her concern.

'Go out the other door, stupid.' Tommo reached for her hand, but Bess pulled it away. 'I don't want to go. I have to stay here to wait for Reenie.'

'You're coming with me, and you're coming with me now.' Tommo wrapped a nicotine-stained hand around Bess's arm and tried to lift her off her feet towards the door.

Bess struggled as best she could. 'Why can't you just leave me here?'

'Because I know you, and you'll blab which way I've gone, and I can't have no one on my tail tonight until I've spoken to a man at the Water Lane gate about some boxes.'

'But you said that you were only here to see me, you asked me to get you through the gates because you said you missed my pretty face and that there was no other reason!'

'Where do you think that coat of yours came from?' Tommo snapped back. 'How can you be so ungrateful? After everything I've given you! Do you want me to get caught? Is that it? Do you want me to get arrested? Because if you don't you're cutting it bloody fine if you want us to get away before your boss turns up with the night watchman.'

Bess had never thought about where Tommo's money came from, and she felt stupid now. She'd snuck him in claiming that he worked for the Buildings Department, thinking that there was no harm in her young man waiting with her in the cloakroom for a kiss and a cuddle. 'What's in the boxes you need to talk to the man in Water Lane about, Tommo?'

'Never you mind.'

Chapter Eight

Mary woke in a panic. She always woke at five o'clock in the morning, ready to start the fire in the parlour, and usually when she woke she could hear the sounds of the street waking: the rattle of the milkman's waggon; the birds; the neighbours; the knocker-upper; but this morning there was nothing.

Mary had never asked her mother how she had become deaf, but maybe Mary had woken up today to inherit her mother's deafness, and this was the start of it. She leapt out of bed and ran to the window, not noticing that she could hear the slap of her bare feet against the cold floorboards, and threw open the curtains. The window looked strange, as though there were nothing outside at all. Mary wondered if it was frost, but she was used to frost on the windows, this was different, this was sinister, and it had a strange kind of blue-white glow in the darkness.

'What are you doing?' Bess had woken up. 'Come back to bed, you're making me cold.'

'There's something wrong outside. Can't you hear it?'

'Hear what? I can't hear anything outside.'

'Precisely!' Mary picked up the candlestick that sat on the bare floor beside their bed and lit it.

She carried it gingerly over to the window and inspected it more closely. 'It can't be!'

'Can't be what?'

'Snow! There's snow all the way up past the window.'

'Mmm.' Bess purred with contentment in her warm cocoon of blankets. 'Does that mean we don't have to go to work today?' She didn't seem concerned by the thought that they were completely trapped.

'No, it does not. If we don't go to work, we don't get paid.' Mary shivered. 'We have to find a way out.'

A similar panic was unfolding in the other houses on the southern end of Mary's street. The storm had blown the heavy snow in eddies and whorls through the night until it had settled in a drift on the steep hill. Then, as silent as death, the snow

146

drift had slid down like a creeping avalanche to cover nineteen houses to the tops of their chimneys. As the street began to awake for a working day the morning revealed a clear sky, but the houses of Back Ripon Terrace had vanished beneath a blanket of white. Neighbours on the other side of the street were chasing back and forth to one another's front doors. They were busy waking friends and relatives to help with the rescue mission, rummaging in their coal holes for scuttles to use as shovels. Everyone was doing anything to help dig out the people on the other side of their street who were, for all they knew, dead or dying.

Mary was ignorant of the rescue attempts going on outside. The snow had formed a perfect insulation against the noises of the world, and she was seized by a fear that the whole town, maybe even the whole country, was under so much snow that they would never live normal lives again.

Bess pulled the covers up over her dainty ears and glossy ringlets, and sighed in contentment. 'You worry too much. Just enjoy stayin' in bed where it's nice and cosy until it thaws and it's time to go back to work. They can't tell us off for not going in if we're buried in the snow.'

Mary couldn't think logically when she was afraid; the sheer number of problems to be faced overwhelmed her, and she froze. Mary told herself to focus and to think of just one thing that she could do; she decided to wake her mother.

'Mam!' Mary rumbled down the stairs making as much noise as she could, hoping that some of it would penetrate her mother's muffled, almost

147

soundless world. 'Mam, wake up!'

Mrs Norcliffe was sleeping in the chair by the fire; she always slept in a chair by the fire because their house had only two rooms, the bedroom upstairs and the kitchen parlour below. She awoke as she felt the rumble of her daughter's footsteps on the stairs. Seeing Mary's panic, she was immediately alert; she followed Mary to the window where Mary, candle in hand, was waving her arms and talking about the end of the world. Mrs Norcliffe nodded, and with a sigh picked up the tin bath, a coal shovel, and heaved herself up the stairs to the landing in her ragged slippers and old robe.

'Go and get your sister,' she said to Mary. 'She can sit on my shoulders.'

Mary's fear had now turned to an angry frustration that no one else in the house could see the full horror of their situation. She was dancing about on the landing floorboards in her bare feet trying to get her mother's attention, but her mother was otherwise occupied. Mary let out a loud sigh of exasperation and went and did as she was told.

Mrs Norcliffe was positioning the tin bath tub directly below the landing skylight when Bess appeared reluctantly at the doorway, being shoved along by her elder sister. 'Not dressed like that!' her mother said. 'Go and put some clothes on or you'll freeze.' Bess was hurried into some warm wrappings and then returned. 'Alright, now climb up on my shoulders, that's it.' She leant forward and manhandled her daughter up into a sitting position for straightening up again. 'Can you reach the latch on the sky light?' Mrs Norcliffe

148

turned to Mary. 'Is she reachin' it? Is she reachin' the sky light?'

'Yes, mother!' Luckily, her mother could lip read.

'Well then tell her to open it.'

'You tell her to open it; she can hear you!' Mary was hopping from one foot to the other, fists balled up in a pent up frenzy of anxiety.

'Mary, tell her I'm not going to open it. There's snow coverin' it, and it'll fall on me 'ead.'

'Good!' Mary snapped at her sister.

'What are you two saying to each other?' Their mother tried to crane her neck to look up at the daughter on her shoulders. 'Are you arguin'? I don't want arguin' I just want you to open the bloody skylight, do you 'ear?'

Bess pursed her lips, reached up to the latch of the skylight and unfastened it. The window pane swung down, nearly knocking Bess off her mother's shoulders and the pair of them wobbled precariously as Bess ducked and caused her mother to stumble. The snow did not fall. It was as Mary had feared; the snow was so thick overhead that it had formed a compacted mass that would defy gravity, seemingly forever.

'Well, what are you waitin' for?' Mrs Norcliffe moved back into position. 'Poke it, Bess. Poke it!'

'How am I meant to poke it?'

Mary was now fuming, face red. 'Mother. She says she doesn't know what you mean.'

'I mean poke it! Give it a poke!'

'But Mary, my fingers can't reach.'

'Mother, she says her fingers can't reach.'

'I don't want her to use her fingers; I want her

149

to use the coal shovel, what does she think I gave it her for? Poke the snow with the coal shovel. I'm not standin' here all day!'

Bess timidly stroked at the snow in the skylight opening and a little wet dusting of snow fluttered down all around them.

'Don't stroke it! Poke it!' Mary was on the verge of hysteria.

Bess made a jab at the tightly compacted snow overhead, and a large clump came away and fell with a thud into the tin bath that their mother had carefully positioned below it. Mary could take it no longer; she stormed past them on the stairs, causing her mother to totter backwards and knock Bess's head lightly against the swinging skylight window. Mary returned a few seconds later with a broom handle that she was carrying like a bayonet-wielding soldier charging into battle. She got to the landing and began attacking the skylight opening with the broom handle in a frenzy of stabbing as though the snow were some animate monster that threatened her very life. The snow was no match for Mary, and it collapsed into the tin bath rather than suffer any more.

'I can see the sky!' Bess squeaked. 'I can see the sky!'

Mrs Norcliffe seemed unruffled by her eldest daughter's murderous outburst. 'Is the hole big enough to climb out through? No? Then keep diggin' at it, the bath's not full yet.'

Bess had now become interested in the enterprise and was ready to put the shovel to use on the remaining snow above them.

'That's right, keep at it. There we are.' Mrs Norcliffe shrugged off her youngest daughter, who flopped to the floor like a ragdoll and then pulled herself up in triumph, brandishing the coal shovel as a symbol of victory, despite the fact that Mary had done most of the work for her. 'You can put the tea chest on top of the blanket box and climb out that way to get to work. Don't forget to shut it behind you, and you can dig a path to the front door when you come home. Now don't wake me again before six o'clock in the morning, it's ungodly.'

'But Mother!' Mary was looking with renewed fear at the open window. 'That's the roof! How are we meant to get down?'

'Put the old tea tray in a sack and slide down. Did I not raise you to have any sense?' And with that Mrs Norcliffe padded her enormous bulk back down the stairs calling back, 'And hurry up, you're letting all the heat out!'

When Mary eventually put her head out through the skylight, wrapped up against a cold that she was certain would be apocalyptic, she saw that the drift of snow was not covering the whole of Halifax, nor even the whole of her street. She could see other heads appearing in the same way through other skylights, and as she scrambled up onto the snow drift that was now their roof she became visible to busy figures below in the road who let up a cheer. In fact, every time another neighbour escaped the snow, there was a cheer and comradely laughter. The inhabitants of the street slowly recovered from the initial fear that half their residents might have been frozen to death in their beds. Each time they released another captive friend from their natural igloo there was fresh hilarity, embracing, and shoulder slapping as though they hadn't seen one another in years.

Mary crept cautiously down the steep bank of snow, like an upside-down crab, falling on her bum every so often and struggling back up again. Bess, meanwhile, whizzed by on a sack and tea tray as her mother had suggested, gleefully calling out, 'Wheeeeeee!'. Bess landed, as luck would have it, in the arms of a handsome young coal haulier. She fluttered her eyelashes demurely, as some of the other men made cat calls and wolf whistles in appreciation of Bess's overtly coquettish display. This made Mary even more annoyed.

Waiting for Mary at the bottom of the snow slide that was now their home was Mrs Grimshaw. She helped the girl to stumble down the last few feet of the steep bank, and then offered her a thermos of hot coffee. 'There you are now lass, take a sup o'that, it'll warm you.'

'Thank you.' Mary was sheepish as she'd always thought that plump, red-faced Mrs Grimshaw from three doors down didn't like her much, but here she was, brushing the snow off Mary's coat and making sure she got warm before she set off for the factory.

'Here, take this for later, luv.' Mrs Grimshaw took something from her coat pocket and pressed it into Mary's palm; it was a neatly wrapped coconut eclair, as blue as the shadows on the snow slopes around them. 'Just don't tell your sister.' And she gave Mary a wink.

It was a rare treat, but it meant more than that,

it meant that Mrs Grimshaw cared about her. Mary thanked the woman with the rarest thing she had to offer in return: a smile. At that moment a friendship was born. 'You don't know how lucky you are, lass.' Mrs Grimshaw called after Mary, who was heading off in the direction of the factory. 'I'd give my eyeteeth to be going back to Mack's for a shift. Best years of my life.'

Mary waved back to her neighbour, a little pang of guilt in her heart that she often took her job for granted. 'Come along,' Mary said to her sister, catching hold of her arm as she caught up with her. 'We can't waste any more time, we've missed an hour of shift already.'

As they pushed through the heavy sprung double doors to their workroom, Mary could see that Mrs Roth had been waiting for her. The wiry, sour-faced woman sprang from her overlooker's seat above the busy line of girls and scampered over to the door to intercept the two sisters.

'What time do you call this?'

'We got snowed in, Mrs Roth. I'm very sorry.' Mary looked contrite.

'I'm not,' Bess said it quite happily, and inwardly Mary sighed with a bone-deep exasperation. There would be repercussions for saying something so foolish, but Mary knew that it would be no worse than a telling off; the worst had already happened: they were losing an hour's pay by not being on the line.

'You are coming with me!' Mrs Roth snapped at Bess and drew her roughly by the arm in the direction of the overlooker's office.

Mary didn't try to object because she assumed that this was nothing more sinister than a telling off for answering back. Mary was mistaken. She took her place on the line and began apologising to the girl that had been struggling to do without her all morning, oblivious to what her sister Bess was walking into.

In the overlooker's office, the Union shop steward and the Quality Street production manager were waiting impatiently.

'Her ladyship has deigned to join us at last.' Mrs Roth pushed Bess forward into the office.

'It was the snow; I couldn't help it. You can't blame me for the snow.'

'You are not here so that we can discuss the excuses for your lateness.' Mrs Roth assumed a position of authority behind the desk, although she had to stand because Mr Booth the production manager had taken her seat. 'You are here to tell us what you were up to with that young man that I saw you with last night in the cloakroom.'

Bess's wide eyes became even wider as she saw the difficulty of her situation. She was glad that her sister wasn't there to hear this; her sister always worried unnecessarily. This situation was certainly unfortunate, but she thought it would probably be alright. Bess decided to follow Tommo's instructions and lied. 'I don't know.'

'What do you mean you don't know?'

'He was just some lad who was passin' and asked directions. I don't know him.'

'You seemed to know him pretty well last night when–'

'That's quite enough, Mrs Roth.' The shop steward intervened. 'If Bess says she doesn't know him then that's all there is to it.'

Mr Booth, the production manager, wasn't in quite such a hurry to jump to either conclusion. 'Bess, can you tell me please, in your own words, what occurred between you and the man you saw last night?'

Bess shrugged, and the naturally innocent look of her face did the work for her. 'I was waiting for Reenie, and this lad comes in askin' where to go to find the employment office, so I gave him directions and then Mrs Roth came in, and they had a shoutin' match.'

'I did not have a shouting match with him. And you seemed to be very well acquainted with him. As I walked towards you down the corridor, I distinctly heard you say the name "Tommo".' Frances Roth was ready to defend her reputation.

Mr Booth stopped her short and asked, 'Is this true, Bess?'

'No.' Bess contradicted her employer with a well-meaning smile. 'You must have heard me say "tomorrow". I told him where the employment office was, but I told him he wouldn't find anyone there until tomorrow.'

Mrs Roth had opened her mouth to speak, but Mr Booth got in first. 'Where did he go after the argument with Mrs Roth?'

Bess shrugged.

'And where did you go? You weren't there when she got back, were you?'

Bess shook her pretty doll's face. 'I had to go home with Reenie, she came to collect me. I didn't know I was supposed to wait.'

Mrs Roth was clearly incensed that Bess's version of events was being believed, but she kept her anger bottled up behind tight, white lips.

'I think we've heard all we need to hear.' The shop steward stood up and looked at Mr Booth. 'Can we let her go now, sir?'

Mr Booth took a deep breath and then said, 'Yes, yes, you can go now, Bess. Thank you for your time. And remember that if you do see that young man in the factory again, you must alert Mrs Roth immediately.'

'Yes, sir.' Bess said it as though she meant it and then darted off out of the overlookers' office.

'You didn't believe all of that, did you?' Mrs Roth was outraged.

'I don't see why we shouldn't.' Mr Booth stood up and fastened the buttons on his jacket. 'She seemed perfectly innocent of the whole thing.'

'Reenie! Now you're here you can tell Mary your big news! I haven't breathed a word; I wanted to save it for you,' Bess said.

'Don't say you're leaving. Oh, Reenie, we've only just made friends with you.' Mary looked genuinely worried; she didn't wish to be selfish, but having Reenie around was all that was preventing Bess from losing her job. As long as Reenie was keeping up Bess's piece rates they were safe for a while longer. And if she was honest with herself, Reenie was the best friend she had.

Reenie looked pleasantly surprised and shook her head. 'No, I'm not going anywhere. Why, would you mind very much if I did?'

Bess slipped an arm through Reenie's and gave it an affectionate little squeeze. 'Of course we would, you're our great friend.'

Reenie was so taken aback by the warmth of the sentiment – and the fact that Bess's older sister seemed to agree – that she was momentarily lost for words. Tough, self-reliant Reenie felt herself weaken for a moment as her eyes stung with tears that she was determined not to show. Did these clever, kind and funny girls really want to be friends with her? She came back down to earth in time to hear Bess excitedly chattering.

'...And then she told him that he should turn all the packers around so that they face the other way. Our Reenie told the Time and Motion man what was what!

'Oh gosh, Reenie, what was he like?' Bess was less interested in the changes to the machines and more interested in the eligible junior manager. 'Is he very arrogant? I expect anyone that handsome would be very arrogant and quite aloof. Like Clark Gable or Fredric March.' Bess said it with a sigh, as though she hoped that he embodied both vices as thoroughly as possible.

'I don't think he likes me, to be honest. He never talks to me, or almost never, and when he sees me in the corridor, he just nods. I've hardly heard him utter a word. I think he must be proud; you know, too high and mighty to make friends with just anyone.' Reenie shrugged, not knowing how else to explain Peter's behaviour.

'Never mind that,' Mary was frowning and rolling up the sleeves on her white overalls as she spoke. 'Are we all going to find out this morning that our piece rates have changed?' She lowered her voice and moved closer to the other two. 'Because if they have, then we can't let anyone know that it was Reenie.' Mary, ever the old soul, tried to say it kindly to Reenie, but she was serious; the Union wouldn't like what Reenie had done.

'Oh you don't think the Union would make it serious, do you? She didn't mean anything by it.' Bess had lowered her voice to a whisper. 'Reenie wasn't to know. They can't make a fuss if she wasn't to know.'

'This isn't school anymore.' Mary looked around to make sure they were not overheard. 'It doesn't matter if she didn't mean anything by it, they can't know.'

'Don't worry Reenie,' Bess said reassuringly. 'We won't tell a soul. And if the Union tries anything, we'll tell them it was Mrs Roth and not you that suggested it.'

'Do you really think I'll get into trouble? The Time and Motion men said they wouldn't change our piece rates; I heard them talk about it. They said they could afford it until we're all moved to another line. Honestly, I don't think they'll do anything bad; I've shown them what to do to make everything easier for us; it will be better, I promise.'

Mary was still concerned, but Bess knew only too well that Mary was always concerned. 'I hope you're right, but even if things are better for us, I still think we shouldn't tell anyone about this, Reenie. I know I sound silly, but the Union wouldn't want any of us talking to the Time and

Motion men at all, it's just how it is.'

'But what if it makes things better for everyone? I can see loads of ways that we could—'

Mary interrupted to tell Reenie to keep her voice down. The factory girls were starting to glance their way. The Toffee Town girls were not surprised by shrieks and loud laughter; but they did notice secrecy, ears were pricking up now, waiting to catch a morsel of whatever gossip the three friends were so keen to keep to themselves.

Chapter Nine

Gracie had another chest infection. Since she'd contracted the whooping cough the winter before, she'd struggled to recover and the doctor had told Diana that it had weakened Gracie's lungs. Diana didn't think that she was in any immediate danger, but she was glad she had got away from the factory in good time to be with her. She'd seen that Reenie was being kept late on the line by Frances, but she didn't try to get her out of it. The girl had angered Frances Roth in some way, and although the punishment was dispro-portionate, it wouldn't do Reenie any real harm, so Diana left her to look after herself and went home.

'I gave her a little sweet tea, and I thought per-haps I could fry her something tasty that would help her to feel brighter.' Ethel sat up in the tatty balloon-backed chair beside the sick bed and stroked Gracie's hair with her sausage-fat fingers. A basket of mending waited by her feet, all of it unrecognisable to Diana because it came in from strangers who paid by the piece.

'Didi,' Gracie called up pitifully from her pillow. 'I want Didi.'

'I know, my love.' Diana crouched down beside the bed that she shared with Gracie and kissed her damp forehead. Ethel was her 'Ma', but it was her 'Didi' that Gracie always called for when she was unwell. 'You've done enough for today, don't worry about cooking for us.' Diana preferred not to feed Gracie fried food all the time, but she also didn't want to offend her stepmother because she meant well. 'I'll go out with a basin and get us something hot.'

'I don't want you to go.' Gracie rubbed her eyes, and Diana's heart ached at having to leave her, even if it was just for a moment, but she wanted to find her something wholesome to eat. Sending Ethel, with her arthritic knees and penchant for chips, wouldn't do at all.

'Don't you worry, my love; I'll not be long. If I can find a neighbour's kid to go for us, I'll come straight back up. You be good for Ma and keep warm under the covers.' Diana rested the back of her cool hand on her Gracie's clammy forehead for a moment and then went down to the kitchen. She rooted through the dirty clutter beside the stove until she found a red enamelware tureen and a lid to cover it; they needed a clean, but luckily the kettle on the stove hadn't long boiled, and there was hot water enough to scour the dishes.

Diana went out into the yard behind the house looking to see if any of the neighbours' kids were still out. Most had gone indoors for their tea, but there were still a few kicking around a wad of old leather scraps.

'Do you want to earn a penny?' she called out to a group who didn't look like they were terribly engrossed in the game. A boy darted forward, eager to earn some pocket money. 'Take this down to Cowie's cook shop on Queen's Road and get me four penny worth of a hot special, and tell them it's for Diana Moore; they know what I usually get. Come back fast, and I'll give you a toffee as well. But don't spill it. Wait, hang on!' Diana called him back and looked around her for something to keep the heat in. She found a clean rag knitted from lengths of soft cotton string and folded it to put inside the basin. 'You'll need to wrap that around it so's you don't burn your hand on the way back.'

The boy lifted a bushy black eyebrow at Diana. 'Alright, Miss. I have done this afore you know.' And then ran off with the professional efficiency of an expert in his chosen field.

Diana and Gracie lived off four penny basin meals most of the time. The biggest problem was that Diana or Ethel couldn't cook; and they didn't have pots or a proper, full-size range. Ethel often fried bits and pieces in the frying pan over the kitchen stove, but she didn't know how to make a dish from scratch. Ethel was a seamstress by trade, and learning general domestic skills had never been part of her education. Ethel had been

161

lucky to always live in a factory town, where working men got their main meal of the day in the factory canteen and wouldn't expect to come home to much more than fried bread and potatoes. Diana hadn't learnt how to cook either, but unlike her stepmother, she did know how to clean and tidy up after herself, and she knew that fried food wasn't good for Gracie's health. Cowie's cook shop valued Diana as a daily customer and always gave her a little extra for her loyalty. The cook shops were waning in popularity as so many people had been cleared out of the slums and moved into Corporation housing with proper cooking ranges, or even electric ovens. The cook shop was a Godsend if you had no range, no pots and pans, no utensils, and no inclination to gather ingredients and cook a meal from scratch; over-worked mothers could send their children up to a cook shop to fetch a meal in a basin, and all things considered it wouldn't cost them a great deal more than they would have spent making it themselves. The cook shop wasn't like the restaurant in an hotel, you couldn't order a dish from a lengthy menu, you had to take what they were cooking a big batch of that day, but it would be tasty and hot. Another good thing about making the daily trips to the cook shop was that if her stepbrother Tommo were home he would give her some money to get him something hot to eat at the same time. Perhaps 'give' wasn't the right word, but money certainly changed hands, and he would pay for hers at the same time, so they rarely had to go hungry.

The boy knocked at the back door, holding a hot basin meal and four slices of bread wrapped in brown paper that the cook shop owner had thrown in for nothing because he'd heard who it was being taken to. Diana walked down from Gracie's room to open the back door, and gave the lad his well-earned penny and a Mackintosh's golden-wrapped toffee from the pocket of her coat as she nodded her thanks. The food smelled wonderful, and as Diana kicked the door closed behind her, she carefully unfolded the cotton cloth and lifted the lid off the basin to see what they'd got. Inside was a big, heavy slab of steak and kidney pie wrapped all round in a thick golden blanket of shortcrust pastry and oozing with good Yorkshire gravy. Cowie's cook shop made the best steak and kidney pie, with sweet onions, juicy brown mushrooms, and a good firm ox's kidney that held its flavour. Diana could smell the stout and black pepper mingling with the meat juices, and it made her mouth water. She gathered up some mismatched cutlery, a couple of the least damaged plates and carried them all up to Ethel and Gracie.

'Now then, love, we've got something hot for our tea. Do you want to sit up for me so's I can make you up a plate.' Diana doled out a serving for her stepmother and passed her a chipped plate and yellowing bone-handled knife and fork, which were the best she could find.

'I don't want Maggie Ann,' Gracie complained from beneath the covers.

'Well, you must be feeling better if you're worried about what's spread on your bread.

163

There's no margarine on it this time, it's just plain, fresh bread to mop up your gravy with.' Diana tended to eke out their meals with bread and cheap margarine, which Gracie hated the fishy taste of and called 'Maggie Ann'.

Gracie sat up and seemed a lot better than when Diana had arrived home that afternoon, but she still only toyed with her food and ate no more than a mouthful. Ethel offered to clear away their supper dishes and took them down to the kitchen so that Diana and Gracie could start to get ready for bed.

Once Ethel was gone, Diana reached up for the medicine box from above her wardrobe. She placed it on the end of the bed with care and looked inside for the lamp and the Cresolene. Diana knew that Tommo hated it when she lit the Cresolene lamp as the medicated fumes of coal-tar crept all over the house, and he claimed his clothes ended up smelling of the stuff, but he would just have to lump it this time; Gracie was ill, and she needed something to help open up her lungs.

Diana kept the brown glass bottle tucked well out of reach not just because she knew that her stepbrother would like to throw it out, but because she worried that Gracie might try to open it. The label warned of the dangers of its poisonous contents and instructed anyone who had spilt it to pour vinegar on their skin, and anyone who had drunk it to immediately take large doses of Epsom salts, presumably to induce the poor sufferer to vomit it all up again. She took the bottle and lamp over to the wooden wash stand under the window

164

and carefully decanted a few drops into the gilt-metal dish that curled up decoratively above the flame of the patented Vapo-lamp. The strong anti-septic smell hit her and was immediately reassuring; the house might be damp, dirty and festering with mice, but the Cresolene would drive all the badness away. She felt like a witch brewing up a potion and a spell, and she took comfort in the knowledge that she was doing something.

Gracie's cough, with its terrifying whoop, started up again in the late evening. Diana knew that she wasn't supposed to let it worry her, but she couldn't help it, the sound made her heart ache for the poorly girl. 'Try not to cough, Gracie. Deep breaths, now, that's a good girl.' But Gracie couldn't breathe and the more she tried to take deep breaths, the more she struggled to breathe at all. It was damp in their room, Diana knew it; the whooping cough had cleared months ago, but the damp and the mildew from the walls was getting into her lungs. Eventually, the coughing subsided, and the vapours from the Cresolene lamp began to do their work. Gracie whimpered quietly in bed, wheezing but breathing steadily. Diana wanted to sing her a lullaby, but she couldn't sing, and wasn't creative enough for bedtime stories.

'You lie still, my love, I'll be back in just two ticks.' Diana smoothed the bedclothes over the little girl's tiny shoulder and went quickly down the stairs. She knew just what she wanted; up on the book shelves among the paper-sleeved records was her childhood favourite. It was a silly thing, a comic song of Vesta Tilly's: *I'm Following in Father's Footsteps,* but she thought it would be just the thing for her tonight; not too frantic, but uplifting and gently funny. She struggled up the stairs with the wind-up gramophone clasped in front of her, the record she wanted already on the turntable. She put it down on the floor in the middle of their attic bedroom, wound it up, settled the needle on the shining shellac disc and then climbed into the bed beside Gracie.

'Here's a nice treat for you, Gracie.' Diana sat up in bed with her back against the wooden headboard and gently stroked the little girl's golden hair. 'It's not often we have music up here, is it?'

Gracie lay still, and Diana tried to whisper along with Vesta Tilley and the chorus.

Diana didn't mean to fall asleep, but when she woke to the sound of clattering downstairs she found that she was fully clothed and sitting on the bed in the dark, the gramophone having come to a stop some time ago. She was thirsty, and she decided to go down to the kitchen to get some water before turning in properly for the night. It must be late because there were no sounds from the street, and when she looked out of her attic room window, she could see that the lights of the factories down in the valley were out. Diana closed the bedroom door gently behind her and crept down the stairs.

'What is that bloody stink?' Tommo was home, and he had caught a lungful of the Cresolene. Diana realised she must have been woken by his key in the door, and she regretted coming out of her room.

166

'Smells like coal tar. I bloody hate coal tar.' Stewart was with him, and Diana debated whether or not she should retreat to her room as quietly as she could to avoid having to listen to them, but then she heard Tommo say:

'Didi, don't think I don't know you're standing there on the stairs. What you waiting up there for? Still reckon you're too good to mix with the likes of us, do you?'

Diana sighed and made her way slowly down to the parlour. 'Keep your voices down; Gracie's ill.' It wasn't a plea; it was an order.

'Well unless there's something wrong with her ears, us making a noise isn't going to make any difference.' Tommo had lit a small oil lamp and turned off the brighter gas light in the parlour.

'What are you doing with the lights?' Diana knew he was up to something, but that wasn't a great surprise.

'You're going to help us move a couple of things into a van. We don't want the whole street watching so we're doing it with romantic light.'

'What things, what van?' Diana wasn't going to help them move anything.

'A nice man from Leeds is buying what's in your boxes in the kitchen,' Tommo sneered. 'And he's even sent a van to pick them up. Isn't that kind of him?'

'If they're my boxes does that mean I get paid for them?' She was being sarcastic. Diana hadn't even touched them, but she was certain that whatever was inside them was stolen goods, and she didn't want her fingerprints anywhere near them.

167

'I've told you, sis; if you want in on the family business, I've got plenty of work for you.'

Stewart guffawed. 'I've got plenty of business for you if you'll get off your high horse for once.' He tried to grab at her, but she darted out from under his hand and made a dash for the safety of the stairs. 'Come on, you used to like it.'

'I've told you,' Diana's voice was cold, quiet, and restrained. 'I don't want you to ever touch me again.'

'You used to like it.' It was an accusation; Stewart was offended now, no longer joking. 'I know you liked it because the proof of it is walking around.' He made an aggressive step toward Diana, but Tommo put a restraining hand on his friend's chest and said:

'We're not starting all this again. It's the middle of the night, and I've got a house full of knocked off machine parts and a getaway van waiting in the street. One beat bobby walks past here, and we've had it. Get a move on, and leave her. She's a moxie mare, and you're better off without her.'

Stewart was in an uncharacteristically bitter mood which Diana knew meant he'd been at the gin. They must have been over in Leeds all evening, drinking fancy gin cocktails with their fancy gangland friends, and the drink had set him off. He never seemed to care that she'd refused to get back together with him after her father had died and her circumstances had changed. As far as she'd been able to tell their whole relationship had always seemed to be a joke or a bore to him. She didn't think there'd ever been any real love in it for him, and he'd never shown the slightest indi-

168

cation that it had hurt him; except when he'd been at the gin.

'Yeah, but I'm not starting it again, am I? Because she's never actually said why she did it–'

'Stewie, fella'.' Tommo was trying to push his friend back away from the stairs. 'Forget her. She's not worth it. We're going back over to Leeds, and I've got any number of girls who'd give their eye-teeth to show you a good time. And they're young, too; not like Diana, she's past her best, just look at her.'

Stewart hadn't heard anything his friend had said; his sights had been locked on the steel-banded irises of Diana's cold eyes. 'Why did you suddenly go off me? Eh? Do you think you can do better, is that it? You think some handsome prince is gonna come along and sweep you off your feet?'

Diana stood at the top of the stairs saying nothing, wondering if she should risk helping them move the precious bloody crates to get them out of the house faster and keep the noise down.

'Was I not good enough?' Stewart's face contorted with bitterness. 'You're a fallen woman now, anyhow,' he shrugged drunkenly with a kind of angry self-pity. 'So what does it matter if you show me a good time every now and then? It's not like anyone's gonna marry you anyway. It's been six years; your handsome prince isn't coming. I'm your handsome bloody prince.'

'I'm going to see to Gracie. I want you to keep the noise down.'

'Tommo and me care about the kid too, you know.' Diana was certain that Stewart was saying it to score a point rather than out of any interest

169

in the little girl that he usually ignored.

As Diana disappeared almost noiselessly up the stairs, she could hear Tommo talking Stewie down and persuading him to keep a look out while he moved the boxes so that they could get to those good time girls in Leeds all the quicker.

Diana didn't know it, but Tommo hated the new, mature Diana who kept herself to herself and persisted in rejecting the advances of his best friend. He accepted that they had to live under the same roof, but it made him angry that she was never grateful.

The two of them co-existed in a kind of stalemate of disgust; Diana was disgusted by Tommo's apparent moral bankruptcy, and Tommo was disgusted by her change of character. He had liked the old Diana who had tormented and teased everyone, and who had made his best friend happy. Stewart and Diana were too much like each other, Tommo had always thought; that had always been their problem. Too cool by half.

Chapter Ten

'Ladies!' Peter was standing on two pallets to shyly address the girls across the packing room hall, though he didn't need to as he stood over six feet tall. 'I must apologise to you–'

'What for; breaking all our hearts?' Heather Rogers heckled, and she was encouraged with cat calls from the other girls.

'Er ... I...' Peter blushed, cleared his throat, regained his composure, and started again. 'I ... I must ap ... apologise to you because I have inadvertently made you all famous this morning.' He intended it as a witticism, but not all of the girls understood. Reenie was watching and listening, and she thought she noticed something that the other girls hadn't seen: this lad was painfully shy. She thought she detected a slight speech impediment, and she began to deduce that this was why he didn't often speak to her; if she was in a group with the other girls and he felt himself to be under scrutiny he'd hardly be likely to feel motivated to speak. Now he was in a position where he had no choice; all eyes were upon him and Reenie felt for him. 'A press reporter with the *Halifax Courier* asked my permission to use a photograph of you all. Quality Street is the sweet that everyone is talking about and the local rag particularly wanted photographs of you all making it, I'm afraid. I hope that this will prove a nice surprise for all of you...' His voice faltered. '...And the management has laid on free copies of the paper for you to take home and share with your families.' Peter waved a hand towards two large piles of newspapers beside the doors, tied up tightly with newspaper twine. 'You may help yourselves if you–' Peter said anxiously, waiting to see if they would be angry that he had taken a liberty with a photograph that had not been intended for public consumption.

He didn't have a chance to finish his sentence before a stampede of excited girls dashed towards the newsprint like a pack falling on prey.

'Bess, look, you're right at the front!' Reenie was waving her copy of the *Halifax Courier* as she emerged from the crowd of girls that had descended on the two piles of papers generously provided by the factory.

'Hang on; these aren't all the same.' Victoria Scowen was inspecting her paper and then looking around at everyone else's. 'This is the *Daily Chronicle;* this is a national paper. Those are the *Halifax Courier.* There are two papers here.'

'Yes, that's right.' Peter was staying away from the piles of papers that were being destroyed by the eager, nimble hands of so many girls. 'I gave the photograph to a local man on the local paper, but they syndicated the photograph.'

'What does syndicated mean?' Reenie had no qualms about asking when she didn't understand a word; if people wanted her to understand what they were saying they would be happy to explain. That was the whole purpose of talking, to give a message to another person, but Mrs Roth was shushing her as though she ought to be ashamed of her ignorance. Diana Moore saw this and, just to irritate Mrs Roth, asked:

'Yes, what does syndicated mean?'

'It means it's in all the papers. They've sold the photograph so that everyone can feature the Quality Street girls on the Quality Street line.'

'Are we the Quality Street girls?' Reenie felt her eyes sting and took a deep breath willing herself not to cry. She was just so proud at the thought that she wasn't just a filler-in until Christmas, she was one of the Quality Street girls, and everyone reading the *Courier* or the *Chronicle* would know it.

'When you say "it's in all the papers", what do you mean, precisely?'

Mary was inspecting her copy as though looking for a hidden trap. 'Is there a chance that this could appear in the *Manchester Guardian* and be seen by my aunts?'

'I mean that it's been sold all over the world.' Peter's fragile confidence began to give way as a startled silence fell on the packing hall. 'It has been wired to America via cables beneath the sea, and it will appear in the American papers in the morning. People as far away as the colonies will see this in their newspapers with a delay of only a day... Or a day and a half. It will be in just about every newspaper in the country from what I'm told. Is ... is that all right?' Peter said, taking in the rare sight and sound of the silent packing girls.

'Oh my *God!*' Reenie's exclamation rang out across the motionless production line. 'Good Queen Bess will have her photograph seen by Dukes! Bess, you might get one of them fall in love with you and want to marry you from seeing your photo!'

Suddenly the room was alive again with noisy excitement. Heather Rogers wanted to know if her photograph would get as far as Hollywood; a girl with large, milk-bottle-bottom glasses wondered about the exact number of people in total that would see them. A helpful porter pointed out that the King would almost certainly see it. At this last speculation, Bess promptly fainted, causing even more excitement. Mrs Roth cut through it all with an angry shout:

'That's it, I've had enough of this. Back to your stations, all of you! I will not have the running of this line delayed any longer. Mary, take your sister out to the nurse's station to recover herself and then come straight back.'

'But Mrs Roth, I can't lift her on my own—'

'I'll lift her.' Peter stepped forward and scooped up Bess as though she were as light as air. 'Reenie, you're coming with us.'

Mrs Roth opened her mouth to argue, but the young man outranked her, and she clamped her mouth shut, looking daggers at them as they left.

As they rounded the corner of the corridor outside their workroom, Bess began to recover from her fainting episode.

'Please don't take her to the sick bay, she seems alright now.' Mary, to Reenie's surprise, was insistent that her sister shouldn't have any medical attention whatsoever.

'But wouldn't it be better to take her to the sick bay where they'd have smelling salts or something?'

'No, she's alright really—'

'Wait!' Reenie had an idea. 'What about the Mint Cracknel room?'

'What about it?'

'We could take her there instead. The mint oil is so strong in there that all you have to do is walk past the door and it makes your eyes water. I bet that a lungful of that would do her the power of good; better even than sea air. What do you say, Bess?'

Bess fluttered her eyelashes prettily at Peter, and Reenie tried not to feel annoyed about it. 'If Peter doesn't mind taking me.'

They agreed that they would go to the minty corridor and find a quiet spot to sit in until Bess was feeling better. Once they had found a windowsill wide enough for Mary and Bess to sit in, Reenie pulled a rolled copy of the paper out of her overall pocket and looked at their photograph again.

'How does it feel to be part of the biggest hit of 1936, Reenie?' Peter was glad she'd come along, not just so that he wouldn't be left alone with flighty Bess, but also because he wanted her opinion more than anything.

Reenie didn't have to think about her answer. 'Magical.' She sighed.

'And what did Lieutenant Armitage want with you? I saw him having a word with you after the Sunday evening meeting,' said Gwendoline Vance, who was wearing her Salvation Army uniform even though she was in her house and it wasn't a Sunday; she always wanted to be battle-ready for the Lord. In her early 40s, she was a tall, square-faced, large-boned woman. One of the benefits of the uniform was that it gave her a look of symmetry and a distinction that she didn't have in a regular floral frock.

'He was telling me they wouldn't let me go on the social rounds. I'd given them your letter of recommendation this time, about me joining the Salvation Army Social Services work, but he's said that I'm temperamentally unsuited.' Frances

Roth was speaking with a breathless outrage to her mentor as she perched on the edge of a low armchair in Gwendoline's best parlour. The wrapping and packing girls wouldn't have recognised their overlooker. She was transformed, in the presence of her mentor, into a naively devoted acolyte. Gwendoline Vance had known for a long time that her friend had wanted to join the official department of Salvation Army Social Workers at their Social Work Mission in Halifax, and it irked her that members couldn't simply volunteer for the work if they felt called to do it. Surely an individual Salvation Army soldier knew better than anyone else whether the Lord was calling them to the work.

'And what would he know? It's not about temperament; it's about vocation. It's your vocation; anyone can see that. You've been called by the Lord to work for the Salvation Army, and if he can't see it, the Lord will make him see it.'

'There's a little girl I want to help; she lives with her mother and some people that her mother *claims* to be related to but isn't, and she's very poorly. She'd be much better out of there, and with people who can look after her properly. I don't believe she's ever once been to a Sunday School or so much as seen a hymn book. And I believe she's being mistreated; whenever I see her she's wrapped up in so many layers you can't see her at all. Between you and me I believe they're trying to cover up bruises.'

'Perhaps you ought to tell the Lieutenant that; maybe he'd see that you have a gift of discernment for this work.'

176

'I told him, but he just says that I'm being too hard on the family. He says he's been a Salvation Army Social Worker for twenty years and he knows when to step in and when to step back.'

'Well someone has to be hard on the family for the sake of the little child. Sometimes you have to have a cold heart to do the Lord's work. Who's the mother, would I know her?'

'Well, Ethel Cartwright claims to be her mother, but I've long had my suspicions.' Frances Roth prepared to reveal the secret that she'd been keeping for six years.

Sensing a revelation, Gwendoline egged her on. 'Do tell.'

'I've known the family, distantly, for many years, and I remember seeing the supposed mother just before the child was born, and not long after. She looked no different to me and I believe that the child is illegitimate and has been taken in by her.'

'But who would the mother be then, if not her?'

Frances Roth enjoyed the attention of her mentor and made the most of it. 'Well, either her no-good son has brought home a child he's fathered with some tarty piece, or Diana Moore is no better than she ought to be.' Frances revelled in the moment and dived into the string bag beside her to pull out the photograph that she had brought with her. 'I have ... um ... let me see...' Frances took the rolled newspaper from her shopping bag.

'Is that the *Morning Herald?*' Gwendoline was pointing at the offending article as though it were a rodent or disease that Mrs Roth had smuggled into her parlour to contaminate its cleanliness.

177

'No, Captain; well, it is, but it's not what it looks like. I wouldn't ever buy it; I wouldn't, they just gave us all copies at the factory and I couldn't get a copy of the *Courier*. I brought it because they've written about my girls; they've written about my production line.' Frances fumbled over the rolled newspaper, found the correct page and smoothed it out with shaking, eager hands, before handing it to her mentor.

'The Loveliest, Luckiest Lasses.' Gwendoline read aloud with all the disgust she could muster. 'Quality Street is the sweet everyone is talking about, and while the quality are quaffing champagne with their toffee—' she thrust the paper back to Frances. 'Oh, really. The newspapers are obsessed with the rich and the beautiful, and never give a column inch to the real business of converting the lost for the Lord.'

Gwendoline indicated that she didn't want to see any more of the elegy to the latest luxury confection, but Frances persevered. 'But Captain, look; there she is.'

'There who is?' Gwendoline reached up to the mantle for her reading glasses and inspected the photograph that went along with the story.

'That's her, that's Diana Moore.' Frances pointed her bony finger with its stubby nails at the photograph of the girl she'd despised since her school days. 'She's the one who went away, and they let her come back. And if that wasn't bad enough now they're letting her appear in the paper!'

'Oh, yes, yes, you've told me about her before, haven't you? Did you say she'd been in the county

178

asylum or something of that sort?'

'No, not the asylum; she said that she went away to care for a sick aunt, but I've known her for more than twenty years, and she doesn't have an aunt. When her mother died there was no family but her father, and then when her father died she went to live with some woman her father had been knocking about with, but who was no legal relation at all.'

'She has a tarty look about her.' Gwendoline Vance wrinkled her nose up at the photograph of Diana Moore, the most dignified girl in Halifax. 'I expect she deliberately pushed herself to the front of the photograph.'

'She was always like that at school. All the girls would fall into line behind her like she was their high queen. She started walking out with a boy from our school, Stewart Edwards, he was called. He was like her; all the looks and all the friends, but she used to do cruel things and make him join in. I knew she'd get what was coming to her, and I waited, and I waited, and nothing happened. We both joined Mack's, we both started work on the same line, it was just like school, and all the other girls followed her and ignored me. And then, when we were nineteen, and we'd been there three years, she went away. She was gone for months, and all of a sudden she was back again, and her old stepmother had a new baby, and I was certain that she was keeping a secret. She'd changed, and I could see it.'

'Well, you would know better than anyone having known her longer than most.'

'Precisely.' Frances smoothed out the pages of

the newspaper as though they were velvet. 'If anyone would know when that girl was keeping a secret it would be me.'

'And what did her employers think about all this?' Captain Vance didn't think that a girl could keep something like that a secret for long.

'Well they never seemed to want to see it. It was as plain as the nose on my face, and the over-lookers and the employment managers were determined to turn a blind eye. I knew that the child was Diana's baby, of course, and I was sure that she'd get found out eventually and the factory would see her for who she really was. I was convinced that justice would be done and she'd be in the trouble that she deserved, that she'd lose her position and have no way to keep the child, and that it would be taken by social and given to someone better, but to this day she has never been found out. It makes me so angry that justice has never been done; I've worked hard all these years and done nothing but good, and Diana is nothing but bad and she's never had her comeuppance.'

'Yes, but look at you now, you're an overlooker, and where is she? Hmm? She's still on the factory floor, and she's spoiled goods for ever.'

'But it's the injustice of seeing her there and knowing that nothing has been done.' Mrs Roth took a gulp of tea and coughed as it nearly choked her. 'He never loved her, you know. I think she trapped him by having a baby, but there was a time when he thought about leaving her.' She pulled up her chin in a melodramatic pantomime of personal tragedy and sniffed.

'Did he take you into his confidence?' Gwendoline Vance gobbled up a Garibaldi biscuit along with this new morsel of gossip.

'He did more than that; he wanted to leave her for me.' There was an awed silence from her friend, which Frances enjoyed for a pause before continuing. 'It was ten years ago, but I don't believe his feelings for me have changed. I saw him in the Piece Hall that day they put up the tree; our eyes met, and I could see the longing in them.'

'But he isn't Saved, is he?' Captain Vance had known many a girl stray from the path of the Lord by falling for the attractions of a young man who wasn't 'Saved' and regularly attending church.

'That's what everyone thinks, but I know that in his heart it's a different story. He asked me to go with him to the dance at the Mission Hall, and he wanted to come to church with me, but at the last minute she did something to keep him away.'

'What did she do?'

'I never found out, but I did discover that he'd been saving up for a ring; his friend told me in an unguarded moment. He had wanted to ask me to marry him, but she wouldn't let him get away. I waited for him, I waited three years, and then I think she must have trapped him by getting herself in the family way. That's the only explanation for why he's avoided seeing me all these years.'

'Some women are vicious.' Captain Vance shook her head. 'She sounds like Mrs Simpson if you ask me. I feel sorry for the poor Prince of Wales – or King Edward as I suppose we'll have to get used to calling him – she's bewitched him, and he's in her power. I think he'll do the right thing and cast her aside for the sake of his country, but it's awful to see him in her thrall. Your Stewart will come to his senses in the end too and leave this tarty piece.'

'But he won't, though. Not now that she's had his child. He's honourable is my Stewart, if nothing else. I don't think he can stand her if I'm perfectly honest; no one ever sees them walking out together anymore, but I sometimes see them together with the child. He loves that little girl, and she's the image of him, she really is. Gracie is the only hold she has left on him.'

'It must be heartbreaking for him to see his little daughter so badly cared for by that tart of a mother. Especially as she'll never be at home as long as she's working for you. If he's a working man, though, he'll have no choice but to leave the child with her; he can't very well give up work and care for her himself. If only he had someone else who could care for the child so that he didn't have to see Diana Moore ever again. It would be better for the child, certainly.' Gwendoline pursed her lips as though she was drawing up the moral strength to say something good. 'You would make a wonderful mother for the child, and imagine how grateful he'd be to you if you were willing to take her on.'

Frances's eyes widened. 'Whatever do you mean? Take the child on instead of her mother?'

'Well, why not? The Social take children away from bad mothers all the time, and she sounds like the worst sort. You ought to write to them and complain about how ill she's making her little daughter. Tell them about how they wrap her up to disguise her bruises.'

'Well, I have written a concerned letter or two in the past when I've thought it my Christian duty.' Frances knew that it was more than one or two, but she received so few replies to her complaints about Diana's fitness as a parent that she hardly thought they all counted.

'Well then, why don't you register your willingness to take her on; just as a foster mother at first, of course. Perhaps that's the reason the social haven't acted sooner – perhaps there's been no one willing to foster the child. Then, when this tarty girl has lost her hold over your Stewart, and he is free, he'll be able to declare his true feelings, and you'll become her stepmother through marriage.' Gwendoline smiled mischievously over her tea cup as she sipped victoriously from it. 'I wonder if he still has the ring he saved up to buy you?'

'Oh,' Frances made a pretence of never having thought about it before. 'Do you think he'd have kept it all this time?'

'Well, have you ever seen her wearing it?'

'Not once; and she'd have boasted about it if he'd proposed.'

'*Mrs Frances Edwards;* it has a lovely ring to it. If you rescue his child you'll be rescuing him – think how grateful they will both be to you. And think how wonderful it will be to have a ready-made family.'

They smiled at each other; it was as good as done.

Chapter Eleven

'Reenie, come over here where no one can over-hear us.' The look on Diana's face was impossible to read. She always looked aloof and a little dangerous to the other girls, and this time it was obvious she had a particular purpose in mind. It was break time, and Reenie followed Diana back to the doors of the cloakroom where Heather Rogers stood sentinel. 'Heather: don't let anyone in the cloakroom 'til I tell ya'.' Heather nodded and closed the door behind them.

'Am I in trouble, because I–'

'Shush your mouth for a minute; we haven't got time. I need to get off shift early today; there's something I've got to do after work. What can you do?'

'What can I do?' Reenie was confused.

'Yeah, what can you do to help get me off shift early. I'm helping you cover for Bess and Mary Norcliffe; now I need you to cover for me for once.'

'I think Mrs Roth will notice if you're not in your place...'

'Then think of a reason why she would need to send our section home. You're creative with ideas; I'm not. Get creative. Think right now, what would be the best way to get our section closed down at three this afternoon?'

Reenie took in Diana's tightly clenched jaw and

184

narrowed eyes. Diana was worried about something. Reenie realised it wasn't laziness or throwing her weight around, it was a necessity; Diana really needed to get away. 'Well, I've been telling the Time and Motion men for a while tha–'

'Don't talk to the Time and Motion men, I've told you, you'll get into trouble. In more ways than one if the young one is anything to go by. Take my advice and don't get into trouble. How can you do this without involving the Time and Motion men?'

'I can't, really. I think I need to get a message to Peter to tell him that he needs to get the engineer out to the conveyor today. I'll say that I know it's catching on the end section and it's been wearing out faster than the engineer said it would, and we need to fix it now. They'll stop the line to look at it; I know they will. They'll send everyone home, though, not just our section.'

Diana put her hands in her pockets and paced around the cloakroom. 'I don't want to shut down the whole line. I just want our section to go at three. I don't want to defraud the company or lose them 'owt.'

'But if the four of us on our section go early then we're losing them two hours of work,' Reenie pointed out.

'Yes, but we'll work twice as hard so that we've done more than anyone else would have done if they'd stayed. Is there anything on our section that needs fixing? You're always saying that a stitch in time saves nine, now what else needs fixing that would be as well to fix now rather than later?'

Reenie sat down on one of the benches below the coat-crowded pegs and furrowed her brow in thought. She thought about the overhead lighting, maybe she could tell them it was getting too hot, warming the chocolates and needed to be replaced; but no, that wouldn't work, all the lights were the same. The more she thought, the more she came to the conclusion that going to Peter was the only way to get them out early. 'Look, I'm sorry, but I have to go to Peter and get him to do a study on me; it's the only way if you want to get out on time.'

'Is he the young one?'

'Yes, but he's alright, he isn't like you think.'

'They're all like I think.' Diana turned the thought over in frustration and then said, 'Alright. If it's the only way.'

'I'll go and fetch him now.'

Reenie didn't waste any time darting down the corridor to the Time and Motion office; she knew exactly where Peter could be found, and she knew what to ask him because she'd been trying to pluck up the courage to ask him it for days.

Reenie burst through the door of the high-ceilinged office to find the desks abandoned, all except Peter's. He looked up in surprise as this slight-framed whirlwind broke his reverie.

'I've thought of a way of doing our boxes faster, could you time it on my section?' Reenie was out of breath from running, strictly against factory rules, down the empty corridor.

Peter rose from his seat to offer one to Reenie. 'Yes, but I need to get the Union to agree to let me time a worker. That would take about a week

186

and by then you'll have been moved to another line and yours will have been mechanised so it doesn't really matter how fast it can be done by hand, but I'm still impressed that you keep finding ways to improve the line.' He offered her a winning smile as consolation. 'Your next line will be a mechanised one, so I suppose if you find a way to work that one quicker it would definitely be worth timing you.'

Reenie didn't sit down in the chair that Peter had drawn out for her, she looked earnestly at him and said: 'No, it has to be this afternoon, please help.'

'What's wrong? Why are you out of breath?' he looked concerned and laid a gentle hand on her arm.

'Where's everyone else?' Reenie looked round to check they were alone. 'They're not going to come back in, are they?'

'No, they're in a meeting all afternoon. Reenie, what's wrong?'

'Can I trust you?' Their eyes met and she felt an understanding pass between them. 'You're not going to tell on me are you?'

Peter looked more concerned than surprised. 'You can trust me. Take a deep breath and sit down.'

'I don't want to lose my place here, I love my place here, but I think I'm in more trouble than I can find my way out of.' Reenie's eyes were pleading, and at that moment she suddenly felt very far out of her depth.

Reenie let the whole story come tumbling out, about how she'd been helping Mary and Bess,

187

and now had to help Diana too. She was at risk from the Union for speaking to him and trying to work so fast, and at risk from Mrs Roth for helping Bess, even though it meant the company benefitted from all her hard work.

'Alright,' said Peter, 'let's take it one step at a time.' Peter was not the type to become involved in his colleagues' personal difficulties, so this didn't come naturally to him, but Reenie was different. 'First you need a reason to get Diana out of work at three. I think I can help with that; the Major has a new line that he's setting up. He's told me not to work on it while he isn't here. Perhaps if we don't switch it on, and you just have a look at it you could all report back to me on where you think it will work and where you think it could be improved.'

'Will that get Diana out for three o'clock?'

Peter was resisting the temptation to become caught up in Reenie's sense of urgency and said slowly and calmly, 'If you, Bess and the other girl on her section can come and help me work the dummy line and tell me what works and what doesn't we can send Diana home as spare once we get to the line. But we'll be in trouble with the Union later because it's a Time and Motion study, although technically it's not against the rules because it's not a study on your area of work, it's just setting up somewhere new for a new job.' Peter mulled over the technical details of the thing.

'Am I going to learn a new job?'

'Yes, is that alright?'

Reenie's face lit up, and she was all smiles again. 'Yes! I want to learn all the jobs there are.

And all the machines.'

Peter let out a sigh of relief that was almost a laugh, but not quite. He smiled too. 'Well, this is your chance to learn one of them at least. We'll send Diana home after we've got to the line, then your overlooker can't put her on cleaning duty and keep her here.'

'But wait! What if I work this line too fast for the other girls to work on it later, but not fast enough for you? I don't want to–'

'You worry too much. How about this: you can work as fast as you like when I'm around, and I won't record exactly how fast you're working because you're my statistical anomaly.'

'Statistical anomaly? What does that mean?'

'It means that you're different.' He was about to say something else, about how he liked her because she was different and suggest they walk out on Sunday, but his courage failed him and instead he said, 'You can be different as long as I'm around. My job is to make the line safer and better for the girls, not to push them harder.'

'I like the sound of being a statistical anomaly.' She looked up into his smoke-grey eyes and wished for another smile.

The moment had passed, and Peter was businesslike again. 'Come on, let's get back to the line before you're missed. We have to get Diana out by three o'clock.'

Peter and Reenie arrived back at the Strawberry Cream line with moments to spare. The girls were taking their places after their break, and Mrs Roth was striding through the doors from the overlookers' room. Peter intercepted her before she could reach her post. 'Mrs Roth, I wonder if I might have a word?'

'Mr MacKenzie, I haven't been notified by the Union that you've been permitted to conduct a study on my line. I presume you're not so new that you hadn't realised you can't be here without Union permission.' Mrs Roth wrinkled her long nose as though the smell of dark chocolate and strawberries that hung in the air was unpleasant to her.

'I'm not conducting a study; I'm setting up a new line: Toffee Penny. I need a few girls to help me set up, and–'

'You need porters if you're setting up; my girls are not here to fetch and carry for the Time and Motion Department.'

'No, you misunderstand, Mrs Roth. I am setting up a new mechanised line which will need four operatives to run one section. I want to check that the setup works and that I don't need to do things differently. I just want four of your girls to pretend to work on this as a dummy line.'

Mrs Roth was weighing up whether she could refuse; this lad reported into Major Fergusson, and the last thing she wanted was for him to come on to her line all smiles and undermine her in front of her girls. 'Very well. Thirty-two, Sixteen, Seven, and Twenty-nine!' Mrs Roth called out without taking her eyes off Peter MacKenzie. The corresponding girls looked round them in surprise and began climbing down from their places when Peter interjected:

'Er, no, I want that section up there. Those

four. Reenie Calder and the three girls with her.'

'If you want four girls then the four I've chosen for you are just as good as any others.'

'No, I very particularly want Reenie Calder's section.' Peter tried to sound casual, but it wasn't easy when Mrs Roth was so determined not to let Reenie go.

Mrs Roth was silent. She cast her eyes over to Reenie's section where Diana looked, as usual, bored; and where Reenie was squirming with anxiety. 'Calder! Come down here!'

Reenie leapt down from her place and scurried round to Mrs Roth, past a sea of faces that were half confused, half envious. 'Yes, Mrs Roth.'

'Don't you "yes, Mrs Roth" me. You're up to something. I know you two are up to something. What are you up to?'

'I don't think–' Peter tried to intervene, but Mrs Roth shot him an accusing look.

'I know when someone's trying to run rings around me, and you, Reenie Calder, are making my teeth itch.'

'Madam.' Peter had drawn himself up to his full height and was trying to appear dignified and business-like, despite only being nineteen to what he thought was Mrs Roth's ninety. 'I requested that Miss Calder here come and work with me, so as I'm sure you must agree, she can't possibly have arranged to–'

'Oh, pull the other one! I saw her come in here with you when she came back from her break. You two have been colluding over something, and I want to know what. I bet it's a piece time racket. I can smell it is.'

191

Peter was angry. 'It would hardly be a piece time racket if I'm taking her *off* the line, now would it? She'd need to be here to make extra piece rates, and where we're going, she'll lose them and only make her minimum. Now if you've quite finished I think you need to get this line started as you're three minutes late resuming from break, and that's not only the overlooker's responsibility, it's also something that I don't need the Union's permission to report on.'

Mrs Roth was white with anger; she knew when a battle was lost. She called out to Bess, Diana, and the other girl on their section. 'You three! You're losing your piece rates for the rest of the afternoon. You're wanted on a dummy line.' She then turned to Reenie and hissed, 'I'm watching you. I know you're up to something and I'm going to catch you, and then I'm going to sack you.'

In the hallway outside the Strawberry Cream workroom, Heather looked visibly shaken.

'Don't worry,' Reenie reassured her, 'she can't get us into any trouble for helping Peter with a new line.'

Heather couldn't be persuaded; this was too much adventure for her, and she wanted to return to the safety of the line she was used to.

'Alright.' Reenie was embarrassed by her friend's cowardice in front of Peter. 'You go back and swap with Mary and tell her to come out here and help us.'

Peter, Reenie, Bess, and Diana waited around in the hallway for the disapproving reappearance of their friend. Mary, of course, did not know the details of their scheme because she was still exiled to the far end of the conveyor well away from them, but she had watched the proceedings with growing annoyance.

'And what,' Mary demanded as she burst through the double doors into the corridor to find them waiting, 'the bloody hell is all this about, Reenie?'

'Mary,' Reenie smiled, 'so nice to have you with us. Now it feels like a proper jolly.'

'Answer my question.' Her arms were folded against any attempt to make her cheer up.

'This,' Reenie said, 'Is Mr MacKenzie, he works for the Time and Motion department, and he'd like us to take a look at a dummy line he's set up for the Toffee Penny; give him our expert opinion on it.'

'We don't have any expert opinions. What are you up to Reenie Calder?' Peter wouldn't have believed it if he'd known, but Mary was holding back some of her anger and suspicion out of politeness to him.

'Really,' Peter interjected, 'no one is up to anything. Reenie has very kindly volunteered to take a look at a dummy line that I'm about to start work on. I hear that you four are the fastest workers on the line by far, so I do think you have expertise to share. If you would kindly step this way, ladies?' Peter politely led them on towards the hall where the dummy lines were set up, and then, as they reached the doorway suddenly seemed to realise something. He was not good at deception and his sudden realisation had the air of a pantomime performance. 'You know, now that I think about it, having three of you here would be more than enough. If one of you would like to go home early...' It was very obviously contrived, but as Mrs Roth wasn't around to see his heavy hint to Diana it didn't matter so much.

'Yes, I would,' Bess piped up happily.

Diana gave Bess a withering look, and without saying a word to any of them, she walked imperiously away.

'What's got into her, do you think?' Bess was still oblivious to the real purpose of the exercise.

'I shouldn't worry,' Reenie reassured her. 'We'll have much more fun without her.'

Mary stiffened up. 'Who said we were here to have fun? I thought you wanted us to look at a machine?'

'Yes, just look, though, I don't want you to run it at all because I haven't got the settings quite right.' Peter opened the green doors to the hall and pulled a dust sheet off their latest mechanical marvel: the Toffee Penny double twist wrapping machine. 'All I need you to do is look at it while I finish off my reports in the office down the hall–'

'Wait!' Mary's eyes were wide with anxious surprise. 'You mean you won't be here to supervise? Who will be the supervisor?'

Peter smiled affably. 'Oh, I'm sure you can look after yourselves, can't you?'

194

Chapter Twelve

'Reenie Calder, *do not touch that switch!'* Mary was white with panic at the thought that Reenie would start a machine running without supervision. She had been on the brink of begging Peter to stay and not to leave them alone with a machine, but he had retreated to the Time and Motion office while her back was turned.

'Don't be so wet. I know how it works ... I think.'

'How do you know how it works? I thought you said this was a new machine?'

'Well, I can just tell by looking at it. I've got a feeling for machines...' Reenie was crawling under the twist wrapping machine to take a better look at its mechanics. 'They speak to me.'

'Do they really speak to you?' Bess liked the idea of factory machinery speaking to Reenie in a kind of song that only Reenie could hear.

'No, they don't. Don't listen to Reenie; she's looking for trouble–'

'What, under the machine?'

'No, she's not looking for it under the machine. I just mean that she's thinkin' of doin' something that we've been expressly told not to do, and – DO NOT TOUCH THAT SWITCH!' Mary threw herself between Reenie and the large red disc on the wall that controlled the electric current to the Baker Perkins twist wrapping machine.

Mary wasn't clear in her own mind which worried her more: the electricity; the lack of supervision or the sheer forbidden-ness of it, which made her feel horribly sick.

'Look, it's not complicated.' Reenie took a step back from the offending button to break the tension. 'Bess, you come over here and have a look. We won't touch anything; I'll just talk you through how it works.'

Bess happily bobbed over to look at the machinery in her dreamy, contented way that took in nothing of what she was being told.

'These here are dummy sweets; they're not real. They're made of plaster of Paris which is why they're grey. They're the same size and shape as the real sweets because they're for testin' the machine. They go in here … up here … round here … and then the machine sort o' spits them out into the foil wrap. This arm whizzes over here and catches it and wraps it. Then it gets wrapped by the cellophane arm, and then it goes onto the next conveyor … except we don't have another conveyor so we'll just have to catch 'em and put 'em in a box while we work out the line.'

'We will not be catchin' 'em and puttin' 'em in a box, Reenie, because we will not be switching on the machine.'

Bess saw two dials on the side of the machine that looked like smiling faces with big noses, and she smiled back at them. 'What are these for?'

Reenie squinted at them. 'Well, that knob says *fast* and *slow*, so I suppose that's for if you're a man what's usin' it and you don't know what you're doin'. We can turn it up to fast because

Mary an' me are the fastest packers at Mack's so we definitely know what we're doin'.' Reenie reached forward and gave the 'nose' a twist up to maximum speed. 'And this is height. I reckon this changes where the arms go because if you look right now, they're too low to catch the sweets, the dummy sweets would just sail over 'em onto the floor, and we'd have to pick 'em up and put 'em back. Here, I'll show you.' And before Mary could stop her, Reenie gave the power supply button a nonchalant jab which set the machine roaring into life.

Reenie was right; the arms were too low to catch the hard dummy sweets. Turned all the way up to maximum speed the machine was firing out plaster of Paris replicas of the Toffee Penny like bullets from a machine gun, and they were hurtling across the empty fourth-floor hall and smashing though the window on the other side. The girls panicked; they knew where the on switch was for the machine, but they didn't know where to find the off switch. It didn't occur to them that it would be the same switch, and they didn't want to hit it again in case that just spurred it on to go faster, like a horse being started with a crop.

Mary ran to the window to see where their missiles were landing. 'They're hitting a man! Quick, stop them!' Mary dived past the machine to scoop up a carton and, under heavy fire from the glistening gold dummy-wrapped Toffee Pennies, started trying to stop the sweets before they could reach the window. 'Reenie! Catch them! Get a carton! Catch them!'

Reenie grabbed at a carton and like a juggling

circus performer caught at the rapid fire of dummy sweets and flicked them into the carton below her arm. Bess stood watching the proceedings with benign interest, her fingers tucked into the cuffs of her cardigan sleeves which stretched them at the shoulders. 'Gosh, Reenie, you are the quickest.'

The double doors to the almost deserted packing hall flew open, and two men burst in. One was Bert, the engineer, and the other was an older man that Reenie didn't know, but who looked angry and was holding a handkerchief to a cut on his forehead. Hot on their heels was Peter who took in the scene of devastation from the smashed window to the scattering of dummy sweets across the maple wood floor, but didn't fail to notice Reenie's superhuman speed before he reached for the red button on the wall that would make the machine sigh to a stop.

'Don't stop that machine!' Bert was on the warpath.

'But the machine's gone wrong; it's not meant to be doing this.' Peter was tempted to ignore the engineer.

'This is Reenie Calder's doin' if I'm not very much mistaken, and the best punishment for her is to make her keep up with her bloody machine.' Bert scowled at Reenie.

Reenie tried to assume a confused but innocent expression while simultaneously juggling a mixture of dummy sweets and cartons in a rapid-fire movement that Mary was only barely keeping up with. 'What did *I* do?'

'You *shot* at Mr Arkwright!'

Mary tried to improve the situation with a heartfelt apology. 'We're ever so sorry, Mr Arkwright. We didn't mean to do it; it were an accident.'

Bert was unrelenting. 'He was in the war, you know!'

Mr Arkwright blotted at his brow with a shaking hand. 'I didn't get hit this many times at the bloody Somme.'

There was a smell of burning tar coming from the machine, and smoke was emitting from one of the wrapping arms as it went at top speed. Almost as quickly as the machine had started firing out its volley of dummy sweets, it ran out of them, and Peter leant over and knocked the round red power switch, bringing the whole thing to an exhausted stop.

Peter was about to speak when Bert interrupted him. 'Right, which of you was running this line?'

Reenie raised her hand sheepishly. The old man looked her up and down and then shook his head. 'I don't think I trust you to run a bath.'

'Reenie,' Bert said, 'it is your responsibility to make sure that everything and everyone on your line is safe before you start work, do you understand?'

'Yes, Bert.'

'Alright, what went wrong this time?'

Reenie was taken aback, she was expecting to be shouted at and marched off the premises, but Bert was giving her a chance to speak. 'I could see that the angle was set too high and that the sweets would overshoot the wrappin' arms, so when I turned it on I knew the sweets would fly off, but I didn't realise how far they'd fly, or how fast.'

'And what would you do differently next time?' Bert was folding his arms.

'I wouldn't start a new machine when I'd been asked not to. I would turn the speed down to near nothin' until I understood what the machine were capable of. I'd look at all the things that could go wrong around me, like the sweets goin' out the window, and I'd plan how to stop all them things goin' wrong so there'd be no more accidents.' Reenie finished and then waited out the awkward silence as they all looked at one another.

'That'll do.' Bert didn't look happy, but he seemed satisfied with her answer. She had learned. 'Now clear up, and I'll get the glazier.' He sloped off out of the workroom, followed by the old soldier who shook his fist at the girls on his way out.

The moment that they were alone Mary turned on Reenie. 'How could you? How could you?' She rained down slaps on the arms that Reenie held over her head to protect herself.

Peter tried to break up the fight. 'Wait, wait, don't do that–'

'I'll do what I want!' Mary was shouting.

'But don't you realise what you've just done?'

Mary stopped still, thinking that Peter was about to tell her about some as-yet-unknown rule they had broken and was waiting to hear the worst, but Peter just smiled and said, 'You've broken the Mackintosh's packing speed record; you two are the fastest workers in Halifax.'

Reenie was dazzled by Peter's smile, and her own face lit up to match his; she was the fastest worker in Halifax, and he'd seen it.

Chapter Thirteen

The waiting room of Doctor Walker's surgery had been tastefully decorated for the season with one robustly healthy-looking Christmas tree. The doctor's wife had decorated it herself with strings of shining beads in a shade of deep plum, and droplet-shaped glass baubles that matched. There were tiny wooden carved cherubim dangling from a green thread that appeared invisible against the green of the tree. To little Gracie they appeared to be really hovering on cherubic wings above the thin, white candles that had yet to be lit.

'Didi, when will we get a Christmas tree?'

Diana took a deep breath and tried to speak to Gracie in a whisper so as not to disturb the hallowed hush of the waiting room. 'I don't think there'd be room for one in our house, it would get knocked over in no time,' she lied, hoping that the other patients waiting in silence wouldn't judge her for depriving the little girl of something she so desperately wanted to give her, but couldn't spare the money to buy in place of other necessities.

'Is that because of all the boxes that Tommo put in the–'

'Gracie!' Diana interrupted her before she could say anything that might bring the police to their door. 'What did you do at school today?'

'We learned about the different countries and what they do at Christmas time and can we have

201

a tree if it's very small? I know somewhere that we could get a tree that's very small and then I could put my red ribbon on it and maybe if I asked Tommo very nicely he would move all of the boxes, and–'

'I don't think a tree would be very good for your cough, Gracie. Trees bring all kinds of dust into the house, and they're very damp–'

'I wouldn't mind a bit, and my cough is very much better, I promise it is.'

'Well that's as may be, but I think you would be better to sit quietly and think about all those children in other countries that you learned about at school and think about what they're doing for Christmas.' Diana breathed an inward sigh of relief when Gracie didn't say anything else. There was a special kind of sadness, Diana thought, reserved for those who want to hear all the things a child has to say, but have to keep them quiet for the sake of other people. It weighed her down that Gracie's cough wasn't getting better and that Tommo was putting them all in danger by keeping goods she presumed were stolen in their house. As she waited under the dumb cherubs she felt that her life with Gracie was so precarious that at any moment one of a dozen things could happen to make the whole house of cards collapse.

Diana gazed into the faces of the floating cherubs on the Christmas tree; they weren't smiling. Neither would I be, she thought to herself, if I'd been painted gold and had to sit naked in a tree holding a mandolin.

The doctor appeared at the door of the waiting

room and called Diana and Gracie to follow him. Diana led Gracie into the consulting room with a gentle hand between her shoulder blades and relaxed a little at the familiarity of it all; Dr Walker had always been good with Gracie. The room was a bright, daffodil yellow, and the doctor in his pin-striped charcoal trousers and black morning coat was a reassuringly familiar sight.

'I'm sorry to bother you again, Dr Walker, but she's been running a temperature on and off since yesterday. I was up most of last night with her. The whoop is back, and I know she can't have whooping cough again, but the sound of it is just tearing out my heart. She sounds like she's gasping for her breath.'

Dr Walker listened to Diana and warmed the end of his stethoscope in his hand before asking to listen to Gracie's breathing. 'Well,' he sounded optimistic after a thorough examination. 'I'm pleased to say that she's not in any immediate danger; and you're quite correct when you say that she hasn't contracted another dose of whooping cough. The bout she contracted last winter will give her immunity for decades to come, but as I said at the time she will still have a whoop – a sort of echo of the illness – for the next couple of winters. I know that it can be very distressing to hear it, but it really is only a ghost of that old illness.'

'I read something in the paper about white lead in house paint. I know that several countries have outlawed it, and it can make children very poorly. Could that be making her worse, do you think? Our house is held together with the stuff.'

'Well, it hasn't been outlawed in the Empire yet, so it can't be as bad as all that, but keep her away from it if it gives you peace of mind. It doesn't hurt to be cautious.'

Diana wished she had the chance to keep Gracie away from it, but flakes of the stuff fell into their bed while they slept. Diana had read that it could poison children.

'I'm afraid, though, that the damp at home isn't doing her much good. The whooping cough weakened her lungs and she's only likely to fully recover her strength if she gets out to the country or the seaside and has a good long dose of clean air. We've talked before about sending her to a cottage hospital, haven't we?'

Diana covered her daughter's ears and whispered, 'I don't want to send her so far away, not at her age.'

'I can recommend some excellent places that would be full of other children just her age. No? Very well, then she needs building up. Give her plenty of sweetened condensed milk, oranges, and strong beef tea. Do you still have the vapour lamp?'

'Yes.' Diana was surprised he couldn't smell the medicated stuff on her; they burned it almost every night.

'Well, use that as often as she needs it to help bring down the irritation in her lungs. Encourage her if you can to breathe through the coughing fits as coughing will only cause further irritation to the lungs and risks permanently damaging them.' The doctor consulted a memo on his desk. 'And take her up to People's Park. The Corporation is laying new tarmac on the paths there this week, and there's nothing better for the lungs than breathing in the vapours from a freshly-laid tarmac road.'

Diana nodded. She'd known that the doctor couldn't do anything for Gracie, but she'd brought her anyway just as she would inevitably take her to the park to smell the tarmac knowing that it was all humbug. As long as there was something that someone told her she could do to help the child she would do it.

Reenie was sneaking out in her dinner hour to check on Ruffian. She was confident that he would be content without her in the factory stables, what concerned her was how the factory horses would feel about their new stable-mate. Reenie often thought that if her horse were given the ability to talk he would probably refuse to utter a syllable on a point of principle. He was Yorkshire through and through, and Reenie was confident that he would be glaring daggers at any horse what tried to get him to so much as move unnecessarily, let alone sniff at his dinner.

A lot of the workers went home in their dinner hour, so Reenie didn't have to worry so much about being seen going into the stables; the Mackintosh's stable workers had kindly told Reenie that she could keep Ruffian there whenever she liked, so long as she knew that she had to brush him down and tend to him herself, but it was important that none of the managers or the overlookers found out. Especially Mrs Roth.

As Reenie wound her way around the outer

corridors of the Quality Street building she thought she detected the sound of footsteps following at the same pace as her. Reenie decided to follow a route so convoluted that no one could ever keep up with her; she threaded through small back corridors and out over winding fire escapes, down rattling cast-iron spiral staircases and through offices empty for the dinner hour.

It wasn't until Reenie was crossing a goods yard that she heard an East Anglian voice that she knew well call out. 'Why on earth are you doubling back on yourself? Is it some kind of game?'

Reenie spun around, and there in the doorway she had just passed through was Peter, holding a rolled up plan from the Mackintosh's drawing office and looking puzzled.

'It's like some gigantic game of hopscotch. Where have you dropped your jacks; Carlisle?' Peter caught up with her and shook his head fondly.

'I thought I was being followed, so I was trying to lose whoever it was.'

'Well I was trying to catch you so that I could ask you about something, but if you'd rather I left...'

'No, no, don't go. Honestly, I don't mind if it's you that's following me, I just thought it might be Mrs Roth, and–'

'And you didn't think to turn around and check?'

'Not really.' Reenie felt a bit silly but was relieved that Rabid Roth wasn't on her tail.

'Look, I just wondered if you'd take a look at these plans with me.' Peter gestured to some crates by the far wall where the sun was lighting up the brickwork and the pine of the packing crates, the better for them to see by. Peter effortlessly lifted one of the crates onto the other to create a tabletop, then unrolled the plans. 'This is a line that I'm planning for a new Quality Street sweet that we're introducing especially for next year. All of the machinery is being specially made at great expense, so I can't afford to get this wrong. If this line isn't going to work, I need to go back to the drawing board before we send off our order to Baker Perkins for their machines. You've got an eye for how a production line works in practice, what do you think to this?'

Reenie blushed; she was rather flattered that Peter thought she had an eye for anything, let alone the thing she loved most in the world. Reenie tried not to look at Peter for too long and instead frowned at the plans trying to feign studiousness. As her eyes skimmed over the ink and paper a whole world came alive to her mind's eye; to Reenie, these weren't flat plans, they were a treasure map, a magic spell, and work of art all combined. Reenie could see the cream and chrome machines popping out sweets; she could see her friends on the line and the arguments that would ensue if Betty Armitage got the position next to the door. Most of all, she could see herself performing her own unique kind of magic as she juggled two of the jobs on the line at once.

'Penny for them?' Peter asked.

'I just want all the jobs on this line.' Reenie turned around the plans to get a better look at one position in particular. 'Except this one; the door's going to hit them in the backside every time someone comes in or out of it. It'll be worse for Betty Armitage because she has the biggest backside. Put Bess here if you can't move the door; Bess is a bag of bones.'

Peter looked again. 'Why didn't I see that?'

'I don't know; she spends enough time fluttering her eyelashes at you–'

'No, I didn't mean why didn't I see... I meant why didn't I see that the door was going to be a problem.' It was Peter's turn to blush, although he had no interest in the physical appearance of either of the colleagues that Reenie had mentioned. 'What about this area here,' he pointed out the place where neat little ingots of golden toffee would drop from the conveyor into the gentle, mechanical arms of another twist-wrapping machine. 'How fast do you think we could expect the average girl to refill this with a roll of foil when it runs out; would we need to shut down the whole line every time?'

Reenie wrinkled her nose. 'No. Think of it like threadin' up a sewin' machine; the first couple o' times you do it you have to go slow and remember what you're doin', but before you know it you can do it one-handed and blindfolded while you sing "God Save the King". Leave it to us; we'll work out how long a roll of foil lasts and then before you know it we'll have the changeover down to fifteen seconds. It's like dancing; it's easy once you've got the hang of it and you know the tune.'

'If you could do it in fifteen seconds how long do you think the average girl could be expected to do it?' Peter was rolling away the plans.

'I didn't say how fast I could do it! If you gave that job to Heather Kilinbeck she'd do it in fifteen by her second week on the line.'

'Honestly as little as fifteen?' Peter was excited as this seemed to have solved some great problem for him.

'Honestly fifteen.'

'Reenie Calder, you're a wonder!' He gathered up his papers and hurried back out of the court-yard, turning back to Reenie and waving the plans at her to call excitedly, 'I could marry you!'

Reenie rolled her eyes, folded her arms and smiled. She knew that he was only joking, but she enjoyed hearing it all the same.

Chapter Fourteen

'Is it true you're going to marry the Time and Motion manager?' Heather Rogers was walking back to her place on the line with Reenie and Bess, filled with excitement at this new piece of office gossip.

'No, don't be daft; he's only jokin'.' Reenie shrugged, but she seemed to be enjoying the envy of the other factory girls that this handsome, charming young manager should have such a rapport with her. He'd suggested marrying her four times now, and she never had so much fun as when they were working together.

'But I heard that he said he was going to marry

you and take you back to Norwich with him. Why would he say that he was going to take you to Norwich if he didn't mean it?'

'Oh, he's just messin'. He's from Norwich, and he's always sayin' he's gonna marry me and take me home because I do half his work for 'im and without me, he'd have twice as much to do. It's just his way; he don't mean 'owt by it.'

'Where do you go when he takes you to "look at other lines"?' Heather Rogers winked at Reenie.

'We just go and look at other lines, and he lets me learn some of the machines that they're getting on other floors. It's nowt funny.'

'Does he not try to kiss you?' Bess asked wistfully.

'No, he just takes notes while I'll tell him which bits of the line I think will break down first, and we work out how we could move the conveyor belts round, so no one gets bashed on the bum by an open door. It's just work, honest.'

'Don't the other girls on the other lines get annoyed with you comin' and takin' their work?'

'No, they get to collect my piece rates because I'm workin' faster than them, so they're better off. He's not timin' me or owt, it's just about workin' out how to do things better.' Reenie moved around the pillar that marked their end of the Strawberry Cream line. 'I can't work that fast when the overlookers are watchin' though, or they'd tell me off. It's just when he knows there's a quiet line he takes me to have a go at learnin' it.' Reenie was as pleased as if she were talking about a date at the pictures, but she told herself that there was nowt funny about it, she just liked her job and Peter liked his, and they were working well together.

'We're being moved to a new line. We're not working under Mrs Roth anymore.' Diana delivered the news as she sat down at her place on the Strawberry Cream conveyor belt.

'Who's we?' Reenie tried to whisper to Diana and look as nonchalant as she could. 'Do you mean you and Bess, or the whole line?'

'All of us. This whole workroom. They've got a mechanised line ready to take over Strawberry Cream, and girls who they'll train for it. We're all being moved to hand wrapping Harrogate Toffee on the fifth floor and we're out from under Mrs Roth's nose.' Diana kept an eye on Mrs Roth as she spoke, ready to fall silent if her eyes turned in their direction.

'I don't know that line; I haven't had a chance to see it.'

'I thought your young manager had let you work on all the lines?'

Reenie wished Peter *was* her young manager. 'I only try out the machinery for the new mechanised lines, this isn't one of his.'

'Well, you need to find out what you can about it, and find out fast. You three,' Diana nodded toward Mary on the other side of the conveyor, 'have been lucky thus far, but it might not be so easy to hide Bess and her shortcomings in another workroom.'

Bess had been listening, but had been content to let them both plan without her interference. 'Don't worry, though,' she smiled, 'I shan't be

211

here after Christmas.'

Diana and Reenie both did a double-take; this was news to them. Reenie was about to ask what was happening at Christmas, but then Mrs Roth began pacing the hall in their direction, and they fell silent as they worked.

Reenie waited until their break to speak to Mary. Mary had mellowed a little since the incident with the Toffee Penny machine, but she was still too uptight for her own good if you asked Reenie. Mary turned a work stool on its side to form a bench for herself and her sister and sat down with Reenie and Heather. Mary was weary, and the red birthmark that ran down her cheek looked like a vicious wound from some horrible factory accident.

'Bess was just tellin' us that she's not goin' to be here after Christmas.' Heather offered up this bombshell as though it was nothing but a light conversation starter.

Mary looked at Bess and narrowed her eyes. 'What did you tell them that for?'

'Well, you know I can only keep workin' here for a little bit longer.' Bess's optimistic attitude puzzled Reenie who asked:

'Are you not feelin' stronger, Bess?' Reenie asked. 'You seem a bit stronger.'

Mary shot out of her make-shift seat and picked Reenie up by the arm, marching her out into the corridor beyond the changing rooms. Reenie realised she'd said the wrong thing.

Reenie couldn't decide if Mary was angry or if she was about to cry. She was a rum one; Reenie thought of herself as idealistic but resilient, whereas Mary was fragile as an eggshell for all her stoic pragmatism. Her sister looked as though her bones might break if you touched her, and Mary looked as though her heart might break at any moment. This, thought Reenie, will be the day she has a breakdown; a person can only put on the tough-guy act for so long.

'I've told you; you mustn't ask about Bess's health.' Mary said it in an urgent whisper as she leaned in behind the doorway, holding Reenie's arm to keep her close. 'Well, not in front of other people; not in front of people who aren't family.'

'But I *care* about her; I'm *worried* about her.' Reenie didn't try to lower her voice or hide her feelings. 'I'm worried about you; have you seen yourself lately? You might think you're a mighty iron lady, tough as a toffee tin, but you'll kill yourself with worry one of these days, and then where will Bess be? You want to look after her, so let us look after you for a change. You can't keep going like this.'

Mary had expected unwanted questions, unwanted advice, or unwanted drama, but it had never even crossed her mind that someone would care about her, Bad Queen Mary, the stone heart of Halifax. All the fear and frustration of the last two months and all the years of anxiety before came tumbling out in sobs and tears and words she couldn't hold back. 'I'm so afraid, I'm so afraid; oh Reenie, I'm so afraid.' She let go of Reenie's arm and covered her face with her hands, tears running between her work-worn fingers.

'Hush.' Reenie pulled her into an affectionate

embrace and took out her own handkerchief. 'It'll be reet; you'll see. Now I think that if Bess just sees a doctor she'll–'

'No!' At this, Mary looked genuinely afraid. 'No doctors. She can't see a doctor.'

'But hear me out, I know a way that we can pay for it; if we talk to the Union then–'

'No, Reenie.' Bad Queen Mary was back in command of her emotions, and she made her sobs subside by sheer force of will. 'No one at work can know that there is anything wrong. Especially not work.'

'But they can't sack her for being ill. They might even send her to Scarborough or some-thing. She just needs to get strong. Imagine if a doctor could give her something to make her better, then all this would be over. You want it to be over, don't you?'

Mary's jaw clenched a little, and her fist tight-ened around the handkerchief that she was de-termined not to need again. 'We have to be very careful about work. She will have to leave eventually, but for the moment, while she can still stand, we need to save every penny the pair of us can earn.' Mary realised that she was frowning at the friend who had given them both so much, and she tried to soften her expression. 'I'm sorry Reenie, I don't want to trespass on your kindness any more than we already have. You've been so good to Bess, picking up her slack and covering up for both of us. We couldn't have got this far if it wasn't for you.'

Reenie froze. 'What do you mean "while she can still stand"?' her arm loosened around the girl's shoulders. 'You know what's wrong with her, don't you?'

Mary gritted her teeth and nodded. She had lowered her eyes to the ground because she couldn't bear to meet the look that Reenie was giving her. Mary pressed the handkerchief to her mouth as the enormity of it all hit her again, and with her back against the wall she slid down to the floor where she crouched in a ball and tried to fight the fresh wave tears that were on their way.

'And what if she could have an operation? What if you're condemning her to death by not letting her see a doctor soon enough?'

In an odd reversal of their usual roles, Reenie was now the adult and Mary the shame-faced, pleading child. 'You don't understand; we've got no choice! Money doesn't grow on trees, and if things are bad now, they'll be ten times worse when she can't work anymore. An operation isn't going to help.'

'How would you know? You're not a doctor, are you? My aunt was took by the cancer, and the doctor said that if she had seen them sooner for an operation–'

'She's not got a cancer! I would not be keeping her away from doctors if she had a cancer! I'm not stupid!' Mary pulled Reenie back closer to the wall, looked around to make certain they couldn't be overheard, and then hissed in a low breath, 'She's pregnant. And you can't tell a living soul.'

Chapter Fifteen

It was a bright, sunny Sunday morning and Diana wanted to take Gracie on an outing to the market to get her something special for breakfast. She knew that Gracie loved the Piece Hall because the poultry stalls often had live, caged bantam chickens and the stall holders let Gracie talk to them through their bars; Gracie loved birds. She also loved ribbons, and if they walked the long route, they could look through the window of the haberdasher on their way.

Now that Diana was bringing home a little more money in piece rates her stepmother Ethel had tried to persuade her to spend it on a better coat from one of the second-hand stalls in the Borough Market arcade. Diana's father had died six years earlier, and she was still wearing his guardsman-style overcoat. It was a coincidence that the shape of the coat, with its big shoulders and wide lapels, had just come back into fashion. Diana's stepmother had spent hours turning it for her to give it another year or two, which was a remarkable feat even for such a good seamstress, but she still insisted that Diana needed a newer one.

Diana, however, didn't care about new coats. In fact, she liked having her father's old coat; it was like a hug from her father every time she put it on, and that meant more to her than what it looked like. Diana wanted to spend her money on Gracie; on little treats for her and happy memories.

Diana had taken nearly twenty minutes that morning wrapping Gracie up in warm layers under her pretty lavender overcoat, because poorly lungs need wrapping up when they go outdoors. She had a soft muffler – that she promised would not scratch – lilac mittens with a little bell sewn onto each cuff – which she promised would summon invisible fairies to good girls like Gracie – and a tam o'shanter in ballet slipper pink – that she assured Gracie was just like one she'd seen Princess Elizabeth wear in a newsreel. When they'd finally reached the window of the haberdashers Diana lifted Gracie up to see the ribbons in the window and realised that she was lifting up more knitted wool than child.

'They have a red one like mine!' Gracie cried out in genuine surprise and enthusiasm. It seemed to make her prouder of her own little strip of red ribbon that she carried around as a precious treasure. She didn't want another one, she just wanted to compare hers with all the others. Diana wondered what her family had done to be blessed with such an easily contented child.

As they walked on from the haberdashers to head down the hill towards the Piece Hall Diana told Gracie to get ready to hold her breath. The only problem with taking the long route via the haberdasher's window was that they had to pass the stinking premises of the slink butcher. In Halifax they were lucky; there were few families so poor that they couldn't afford to put a scrap of

217

meat on the table, but even then they sometimes resorted to the slink butcher. He sold diseased carcasses, sheep's heads for threepence, and even the flesh of prematurely born calves called 'slink'. For most families the shame of turning to the slink butcher was almost as strong as the natural revulsion; he painted his prices on his windows in chalk paint and even the most uncouth butcher in Halifax would shudder to be as brazen as that. Diana feared the day when things got so bad she had to turn to him for meat; even the abattoir didn't smell as bad as his shop.

As soon as Diana caught a whiff of rotten meat on the air she turned to Gracie and said, 'Alright, are you ready? Deep breath now.' She mimed pinching her nose and made a game of it. Gracie knew what was coming next because she loved this game and she struggled to hold her breath because she was grinning so much. When Diana said the word she pinched her nose with her left hand and held out her right to hold onto Diana's. It was time to run headlong down the road, holding tightly to one another's hands until they reached the bottom where the air smelled of nothing more offensive than bad drains and burning coal.

When they reached the bottom of the road, they let out their breaths and gasped in more fresh air. Gracie began to cough, and Diana crouched down to hold her close and rub her back, full of concern again, but then she realised that Gracie was coughing because she was giggling and her giggles became infectious, and Diana realised she would be quite alright.

Diana stood up again, took Gracie's little, mittened hand in her own, and led them on toward the Piece Hall market. It was a relief to her that she could keep sad things like the slink butcher from Gracie by turning them into a game. Diana's plan was to buy a kipper from a fishmonger in the Piece Hall, which had been brought over from Whitby ready-smoked. She had a fancy that something which had been smoked beside the Yorkshire sea must be healthier for Gracie, and if it were smoked there would be no need to fry it, or attempt to cook at all on their ill-tempered kitchen range, save for poaching it with boiling water from the kettle.

'I'll not split a pair, it's unnatural. You buy a pair of kippers or none at all.' The fishmonger could easily have sold Diana a single kipper and have sold its other half to another customer, but he seemed determined on a point of principle not to let her make this little economy.

'But I don't need a pair.' She gestured to Gracie, whose cornflower blue eyes she hoped would melt the fishmonger's heart. 'It's for the child; she's been poorly, and I wanted to give her a kipper for her breakfast.'

'You're not begging, are you?' a voice behind Diana said in accusatory disgust, and Diana knew exactly who the voice belonged to.

'Frances,' she turned to address her overlooker, glad of the opportunity to call her by her first name as they were out of the factory, and not Mrs Roth, 'I'm surprised to see you here. I would have thought you'd be at chapel.' She tried to make it sound warm and friendly, moving away from the market stall to give the fishmonger the opportunity to serve his other customers. She had a fancy that morning to keep the peace and show little Gracie how she could take the moral high ground and not let Frances Roth rile her.

Frances Roth was sticking her chin out as though she had the right to be judge and jury over everyone else and looked down her nose at Diana. She had a string bag bulging with little parcels wrapped in ivory waxed paper, and a variety of vegetables. Diana could just imagine her going back to her prim little house and cooking herself prim little dinners that she would eat alone in her bitterness.

'Is that a child or a ball of wool? Are you trying to cover her up because there's something you don't want anyone to see? Bruises perhaps?' Frances looked at the round bundle of wool wrappings that stood beside Diana. Her comments were more than offensive, but this time Diana was determined not to be goaded.

'You recognise my little sister, Gracie. Say hello to the nice lady, Gracie. You know her, don't you? She was friends with me and your uncle Stewart when we were at school. We met when we were just your age.' She tried to keep her tone light. Frances might be a bitter, vengeful old cow, but Diana knew that she herself shared part of the blame for what Frances had grown up to be. She regretted all the bullying when they were younger, and Diana was genuinely sad for Frances that she had been led on by Stewart all those years ago. If Frances had ever asked, Diana would have told her that Frances could find a much nicer man than Stewart Edwards because most men were nicer than Stewart Edwards. It was a tragedy, Diana thought, that this woman was wasting her life clinging to something that never would have been, and wasn't worth wanting in the first place.

Gracie lifted a lilac-mittened hand to her muffler and pulled it down from her mouth so that she could call up in her politest voice. 'Hullo, nice lady.' And then whooped and coughed.

Diana crouched down to rub her back and encourage her to breathe steadily. 'She's been poorly with bad lungs, but the doctor says she's getting better now. It's nothing to worry about.'

'I'm not surprised that she's coughing given where she's living,' Frances said matter-of-factly, and Diana assumed that she was talking about Halifax itself.

'When the weather's better, and we get our holiday I'm going to take her to Blackpool for the sea air. Not long 'til Easter.' Diana tried to sound optimistic and forced a smile as other shoppers jostled past her.

'And what does her "Uncle" Stewart say? Wouldn't he rather she were somewhere more wholesome; away from anything poisonous?'

'Well,' Diana thought about the flakes of white lead that peeled off the walls of her stepmother's house along with shards of damp-riddled plaster; was that what Frances was talking about? And if she were, how could she know? 'I'm sure all the family would benefit from a day by the sea.' Something was off here, and Diana didn't like it. She wanted to stand her ground, but she wasn't sure what she was standing her ground against.

'But that must be why he still sees so much of

221

you. He must feel some obligation to the child. I can't help but feel that if the child weren't living with you, he'd be long gone.'

Diana didn't like the tone Frances was using or the way that she was talking about Stewart as though she had some claim on him. Gracie was six, and she was perfectly capable of picking up on these things and asking questions later.

Frances had always been blind to Stewart's callous disregard for anyone but himself and seemed to nurture a delusion that he had a heart of gold but was led astray by Diana and Tommo. No one led Stewart Edwards astray, he was vain and shallow and feckless and Diana decided that Frances was welcome to him. She could fight him off when he was drunk and wanted to manhandle her, Diana had tired of him long ago.

'Well, I must say I think it's terribly sad. Sometimes separation is better for everyone.' Frances gave a pointed look at Gracie and sniffed.

Diana bristled; this was a threat of some sort, she was sure, but she couldn't understand what so she decided to misunderstand wilfully and called out to the fishmonger. 'Now then! This lady thinks it would be better to separate them.'

The fishmonger shrugged and tore the pair of smoked kippers down the middle. Before Frances Roth could realise what she'd been tricked into, Diana had handed over her coins, snatched away the quickly wrapped kipper, and darted away into the crowd with her daughter, leaving Frances Roth with the bill for one kipper that she had not asked for.

That'll teach her, Diana thought to herself.

'Gracie, I want you to remember that lady, and if she ever tries to talk to you, I want you to say, "Not today, thank you." Do you understand?'

'But you said she was a nice lady.'

'I know, but sometimes I'm wrong.'

'Reenie knows.' Mary had waited until she and her sister were in bed that night, and there was no chance of them being overheard. The rattle of the railway line shook the frame of their old metal bed as another freight train went past their bedroom window. One of the downsides to having a deaf mother was that she hadn't thought about the noise when she'd secured the lease of a house so near the branch line.

'Knows what?'

'About the baby. I had to tell her.'

'Is she as angry with me as you are?'

'No one is as angry with you as I am.'

'Please, Mary, don't be hard on me. It was love, and love is something you just can't help when it finds you. I love him, and he loves me–'

'He doesn't love anyone but himself. If he has ever told you that he loves you, he's lying, and you're a greater fool if you believe him.'

'He doesn't need to tell me that he loves me with words; I can tell by–'

'So he's never told you that he loves you? He's never actually said the words?'

'I don't need him to say the words; we have something that goes beyond words. He knows that what passes between us–'

'If he loves you, why is he still making you work in your condition? Why are we having to move heaven and earth to cover for you at the factory so that you can keep working? Why have we got Reenie doing your work and her own?'

Bess was silent for a moment. The cold sheets that covered the musty bedclothes were beginning to warm and release the scent of the lavender soap their mother had washed into them. She would rather enjoy the scent and her dreamy mood than answer questions about something that wasn't worth worrying about. 'I know you're only asking because you care about me, but really, you mustn't let yourself get anxious about it. He needs me to keep working that bit longer so that we can put some money aside for when we're wed, but it's not for much longer.'

'How much longer. Exactly how much longer? When does he say you're going to be married? What date has he booked the church for? Why doesn't he announce it in the papers? Why don't you have a public engagement?'

'It's not that simple. He has a lot of business dealings that mean he can't be seen to be getting married because people will think they can't rely on him between now and Christmas; they'll think that he's goin' off on honeymoon and they won't think of him for jobs.'

'So he's said that he's going to marry you after Christmas? Is that what he's said?'

'Oh, wouldn't a Christmas wedding be lovely? Or Boxing Day? Now that would be perfect because then everyone would already have the day off and they'd be in a mood for celebrating. A Boxing Day wedding...' Bess sighed into the cold air of their cramped, dark bedroom, dreaming of her Christmas wedding.

'Tell me what he has actually said. Tell me what his actual words were at any point. I want to hear the words he's used.'

'He hasn't used any words, I told you, he hasn't said anything, and he doesn't have to. Everyone misunderstands him because they listen to what he says, but that doesn't tell you anything about what a person is like on the inside, and he is a good man deep at heart, and I'm lucky to have–'

'What?' Mary interrupted her sister's charitable reverie. 'You mean he didn't actually say any of this? This is all just a story you've told yourself to justify all his–'

'It is not a story, I know it's true.'

'All this time I've been helping you keep working because I honestly believed that you had a plan. It might not have been what I wanted for you, but it was better than nothing, it was better than the prospect of being an unmarried mother and having a baby by that good-for-nothing leech, Tommo Cartwright.'

'Mary!' Bess rarely raised her voice, but this time she was angry. 'How dare you say that about the father of my child. You don't know anything about it.'

Mary waited in the light, airy hallway of the Halifax Salvation Army social service office. There was a row of chairs against the wall for visitors, but Mary couldn't bear to sit; she preferred to pace angrily in the hope of venting some of the pent-up rage she felt bubbling up within her. Eventually, it was her turn to go into the lady captain's office, and she had to try to put on a more civil aspect.

'Do you help people to adopt babies? Have them adopted, I mean; do you help people with babies they can't care for?'

'Yes, sometimes.' Captain Honeywood looked at Mary with a compassion that invited her to tell any secret without judgement. 'Are you asking for yourself? Do you have, or are you expecting to have a baby that you won't be able to care for?'

'Not I, my sister.' And suddenly, in the presence of this discreet and trustworthy woman Mary found herself opening up and telling all the truths she wished she'd been able to tell sooner. 'There's no chance of us being able to feed it when we can only just feed ourselves. She'd have to give up work and her chances of marriage after that; well, I don't like to think what kind of a life it would be for her.'

'And you're certain the father of this baby doesn't intend to marry your sister?'

'I'm almost certain, but to be honest, that isn't the problem. The problem is that he's a bad sort, and she'd be worse off married to him than any-thing else. I don't mean that he's just feckless, or lazy, or a bit selfish or 'owt petty like that; I mean he's bad, really, truly bad. He'd be the death of her, and the baby too.'

'Alright, well it sounds like we have a few things to talk about, but let's start with your sister's wel-fare: how is her diet, does she get plenty of fresh food? Is she eating well?'

Mary felt a pang of guilt; her sister was not well, and she wasn't eating as well as she could because Mary was secretly keeping back some of their wages from her mother and putting them into a savings jar she'd hidden away for when Bess eventually had to give up work.

'I take it from that silence that she's not eating properly. Well, I'm glad to say that this is an area in which we can easily give help. I can arrange food parcels for the duration of her pregnanc–'

'No!' Mary jumped to refuse when she realised that food parcels would rouse suspicion with her mother and the neighbours. 'I'm sorry, I can't take food parcels, but if you could tell me how to arrange for the adoption of the baby, I'd be most grateful.'

'Putting a baby up for adoption is a momentous step, it's not something to be taken lightly; and it's certainly a step that would have to be made by your sister, you couldn't make it for her.'

'I know, but if you could talk me through it now at least I'd know what's coming, and I can explain it to her when I think she's ready to hear it.'

'What kind of thing do you want to know?'

'Just how it works really. What happens when you give up a baby?'

'Well, in this country adoption is regulated by the 1926 Adoption Act, and all that really means is that babies can't be given to just anyone, there are laws, and that's a good thing for everyone. When someone gives over their baby to be adopted the baby is first put into the care of the local authority; they are called the *guardian ad litem*, that means they are the guardian of the child until the adoption is finalised. They then find a new family for the baby, and they help the new family to fill out an application to the courts to adopt the baby. The court then has to assess them and decide if they are suitable parents. These are the same courts that hear criminal cases and all the things relating to the laws of England, because the life of the baby is a serious business. At this point, the court asks if the parents, or grandparents in the case of a single mother with no father to acknowledge the child, have given their consent to the adoption. The local authority then usually present a permission document signed by the mother at the time she handed the baby over to them. Without this, it is very difficult to proceed, this is one of the most important aspects of the act. There are circumstances in which the local authority can act without the consent of the parents, but they have to have a very compelling reason.' Captain Honeywood sighed. 'Does knowing this help?'

'Yes.' Mary was thoughtful. 'Yes, yes it does a bit. I think I just don't like the unknown, but knowing all the ins and outs of it gives me something to hang on to. Yes … I just don't like the unknown…'

'No one does, and it will be harder for you because you're taking the burden of worry for your whole family. When does the doctor say the baby will arrive?'

'April,' Mary lied.

'Doesn't the line look lovely?' Charlotte Pantry was looking at a copy of the *Halifax Courier* with a fellow overlooker in the overlookers room at the end of their shift. 'The girls look so graceful.'

Mrs Roth was not interested in the story, it had brought her nothing but trouble, and she had been glad that afternoon when the girls, Bess, Reenie, Diana and Mary included, had packed up for the last time ready to move on to their new line the following day under a different over-looker. 'Are you still looking at that old thing? I thought everyone had read that story twice by now.' She said it scornfully because she resented anyone having fun chatting over a paper while she was typing her report sheets for the factory manager.

'But this isn't old,' the overlooker held out the crisp new paper to her colleague. 'This is this afternoon's edition. They've published more of the pictures from the Quality Street line. They're talking about how the new line that we open tomorrow will be the fastest sweet wrapping line in the world.'

Mrs Roth glanced across at the paper with dis-gust, but then stopped as something in one of the photographs caught her eye; it was Reenie Calder, and she was cheating. Mrs Roth took her fingers off the typewriter keys, turned slowly in her chair, and took the paper from Charlotte Pantry. 'She's doing the work of two girls.'

Charlotte and their other colleague looked over at the photograph benignly and smiled. 'Yes, that Reenie, she's a one. No one could beat her in a wrapping race.'

'But she's taken over another girl's place, look. She's doing the work of Bess Norcliffe; she's working a piece rate racket.' Mrs Roth was speak-ing with the energy of building fury.

'Oh Frances, no one worries about stuff like that anymore. You should be proud that one of your girls can keep up that sort of thing. Besides, there isn't anything you can do about it now.'

Frances Roth's grip around the newspaper tightened as she realised that the girls were no longer within her jurisdiction, and they had been making a monkey of her for goodness knew how long. Mrs Roth did not intend to let this go.

Chapter Sixteen

'Have you had any luck persuading Diana Moore to go to Germany?' Amy Wilkes was working very late in her office, and she called out to Laurence Johns as she saw him walk past her open office door.

'Er...' Laurence had been taken by surprise and looked around inside the doorframe as though he expected to see an ambush waiting for him behind it. 'No ... not yet, but...'

'Well have another go, would you? I've got Frances Roth breathing down my neck because she thinks she's caught Diana at a piece time racket and she's forcing my hand. Unless Diana goes away on that posting of yours, I'm going to have to launch an investigation. She's got photographs this time, and they're pretty damning.'

'But if she's guilty of a–' Laurence Johns stumbled over the expression that was entirely new to him since his work up until now had not involved him in the intimacies of the factory floor.

'Piece time racket.' Amy helped him.

'Yes, if she's guilty of a racket then do you really want her–'

'Yes, we do. They can all run a racket for all I care, it's no skin off my nose. You talk to her about Germany again, and I'll talk to the Major about Frances Roth.' Amy Wilkes gave her colleague an efficient smile. 'Goodnight, Mr Johns.'

'Er, yes, yes,' he said, still a little surprised to have been caught sneaking biscuits back to his office quite so late, and yet, at the same time, not caught.

Diana had always known that with Stewart Edwards bad things always happened in threes: like stealing from a shop, or getting into a fight in the pub or hitting someone. He didn't plan it, and he didn't always realise it, but these things would just happen in threes.

Diana was nothing like Stewart, and she thought that perhaps the universe was trying to reward her for it because when life sent her good things, it just seemed to send them in threes. Three wasn't just Diana's lucky number, but she also sometimes felt like it was her secret language with fate. Stewart used to laugh at her for it, but if he had been capable of being honest with himself for even a moment, he'd have admitted that it frightened him sometimes.

That first year when they were courting, back when they were still at school and didn't know any better, they had had an almighty row in Diana's Dad's shop. It was before Diana's dad

231

had died, and she could remember it like it was yesterday.

Stewart had stormed out of the shop with Tommo Cartwright, and Diana had got her first glimpse of his true colours. Stewart had been in the wrong, he admitted as much later, but Diana never mentioned it because she said that she didn't need to; fate would show him what was what. Stewart had been sceptical, but sure enough within three hours of leaving he took a tumble on his own front steps and broke three ribs. He went back to Diana repentant and self-pitying. That was the first time he saw her do it: she listened to what he had to say, nodded as though she had expected something like that would happen, then went out to the shop and bought three bread cakes to give to a beggar. She said that it was an offering of thanks to fate for seeing her right. Stewart scoffed, but a little voice had told him to be careful with this one.

There was not a moment in their courtship where Diana kidded herself that Stewart was a clever lad or even a good lad, but he was devastatingly good-looking. They got along well enough for a couple of years, but it was no great love affair. He talked about weddings and future homes, but it was always part of a joke or a tease; never serious. Diana knew that he would run if he were faced with a vicar, and a register to sign.

Diana had never been a prude, and even if her relationship with Stewart hadn't been the greatest love story of the century she had still had a good time. She'd made the other girls jealous and she'd made some of them blush. She'd revelled in being so grown up and she had never thought that she would fall pregnant. She'd never thought that she'd be stuck with Stewart for life, or that she'd be forced to rely on the kindness of other people for necessities instead of working for her own wage. Diana knew that she could get her father to make Stewart marry her, but the problem was that the thought of being trapped with Stewart for ever was too horrifying to bear. There were other options, but like all the other girls her age Diana knew that a back-street abortion was very dangerous if you hadn't already had a baby, and even if you found someone to do it for you there was no way of telling if they knew what they were doing.

When she'd told her family that she was expecting a baby her father had seemed like her only champion. He ran his own business, a little grocers shop, and he said that she could work in the shop and keep the kiddie out the back. There was no need for her to worry about what she'd do when Mackintosh's found out that she was in the family way because she would just accept her dismissal and start work in the shop the following day. If the neighbours didn't like it they could go and buy their goods elsewhere, but her father knew they wouldn't dare. Ethel had moved into the flat above the shop by that time, and she was ready and willing to help Diana with the baby in any way she could.

Stewart and Diana's daughter Gracie had arrived on the third day of the third month of the 1930s. Nothing went according to plan. When Diana's father died of a heart attack, it came as a

233

shock that they would have to leave the shop and the flat above it. Ethel's son Tommo found his mother a house with an attic room for Diana. Diana would have shown her gratitude, but the death of her father devastated her so completely that she struggled to even speak.

Diana didn't have an awful lot of choice about giving up work when Gracie was born. Before Diana started to show she asked the employment manager for leave to go and help an elderly relative in the country, and when she came back to work, she told everyone that her stepmother had given birth to an afterthought baby while she was away and that she had another sibling. It was ridiculous really, she couldn't believe that anyone was taken in by it, but they must have been, or she'd be out on her ear. Gracie had her father's cowlick fringe and bright, azure blue eyes and it was a daily miracle that no one mentioned the likeness. She lived at home with her stepmother and the bairn, and at first, she'd thought that it would be temporary and that by the time Gracie was old enough to know who her real mam was Diana would have sorted herself out, and she wouldn't be masquerading as anyone's sister anymore. But the years had flown by, and now she was sitting on a chair at Gracie's sixth birthday party – which was months late because they even lied about her birthday – pretending not to care as much as she did.

'It's lovely that you two can be such close sisters even though you're not close in age,' Mrs Royd from next door cooed. She hadn't lived there long, so she had no suspicions yet about the child's parentage. It was as well, Diana thought to herself, because so far Mrs Royd hadn't been able to keep any of their other neighbours' secrets, and Diana had found out eye-opening things from this woman about the people living around her that she had never wished to know.

'Mmm.' Diana pulled her face back into a tight-lipped smile that didn't reach her eyes, and nursed her glass of fizzing orangeade.

'Isn't he good?' The neighbour pointed to the boy from two streets away who had been persuaded to come in and show off in exchange for some cake and ginger ale. 'He isn't a professional, you know. He learnt all those magic tricks from books in the library, just books! Would you credit it? He's a prodigy, that lad, that's what he is.'

A hammering at the front door interrupted the one-sided conversation. 'I should get that,' Diana got up a little apologetically. 'It might be Gracie's stepbrother and his friend. They're expected.' Diana kicked the rolled up blue rag away from the base of the door where it had been keeping out the biting late-autumn draft, and opened it. 'Where have you two been? Get in, quick; she's been askin' for you.'

Stewart and his bosom pal Tommo loitered on the pavement, not making a move to go in. Tommo took a moment to smooth back his hair with his comb while Stewart jammed his hands in his coat pockets and stood stock still. He looked so much like Gracie it made Diana's heart ache; there was the cowlick above his left temple, the soft colouring, the long eyelashes framing bright

235

blue eyes, and the dimple in his cheek that was waiting to appear when he smiled. Simple Stewart they'd all called him when they were kids; he was still a looker, Diana thought, but there had never been much between his ears.

Stewart asked, 'Who's been asking for us? Tommo's mam?'

'No, Gracie.' And under her breath, she hissed the words. 'Your daughter. It's her birthday party, and where the bloody hell have you been? I expected you an hour ago.'

Stewart scowled and kicked the floor. 'I don't see why I should have to be here.'

'Yeh,' Tommo chimed in. 'If no one's supposed to know that he's her dad then it doesn't make any difference if he's here or not, does it?'

'*You*,' Diana jabbed an angry finger into Tommo's chest, 'are meant to be her brother; and *you*,' she did the same to Stewart, 'are meant to be her sister's boyfriend, so yes, you do have to be here. I'm havin' to look after all these kids practically on my own.'

'We don't wanna be anywhere where there's no kids.' Stewart was sullen as he struggled to find someone to blame his present discomfort on.

'Look, Didi.' Tommo was already taking a few steps backwards with his hands in his jacket pockets, pulling the lining open in a shrugging gesture of helplessness. 'We can't stay, we just came round to see if you could come out, we had a bit of a treat lined up for you.'

'I'll believe that when I see it.' Diana scoffed.

'No, we did, Sis, honest we did.'

Stewart smirked and leaned a bit closer, as

though this revelation would change everything and Diana would leap into his arms. 'We've got a car for the night.'

Diana looked angrily at Tommo. 'Have you stolen a car?'

'Oi, keep your voice down! Do you want to come out for the night or don't you?'

'No, I do not! I want you to come and help me with Gracie's birthday and keep out of things that are gonna get you locked up!'

'No one's getting locked up.' Tommo was wary of the neighbours who might be listening. 'We've just been asked to deliver a car somewhere tomorrow, and we're having a night out in it before we pass it on, that's all. The roads'll be clearer tomorrow; let the snow melt and all that.'

'Now you're moving stolen cars. I can't believe you two sometimes.'

'Well don't say we didn't offer, alright?' Tommo was walking backwards away down the street and turned around to pick up his pace once he saw that Stewart was following him.

'I hope you both crash it! I hope you break your noses!' Diana was leaning out into the street to shout after their retreating backs, heedless of the neighbours. 'I hope you both rot in hell!'

Diana closed the front door behind them with exaggerated care as she tried to compose herself. She had to crouch down to wedge the faded roll of rags back under the gap in the door, then she gritted her teeth, took a deep breath, and returned to the party.

The parlour was full of children, and a noisy game had kept them from paying any heed to the argument on the doorstep. One or two were in party clothes; there was a very nice violet purple dress worn by a girl, and one boy was sporting an emerald green bow-tie, but apart from that the children were dressed in the same old threads as usual. The difference was their hair; clearly, their mothers had given them a scrub up and a brush down, because for all their poor clothes every child looked as though they'd been turned out for something special. It meant a lot to Diana that so much care had been taken over coming to her daughter's birthday, her little Gracie was obviously loved by a lot of people, even those who lived so far away they took omnibuses through the black slush of the dirtying snow. It was easy to see why she was so loved, but then Diana told herself that she was her mam and she would think that.

Diana leaned in the doorway and watched as Gracie turned to Ethel Cartwright and said, 'Mammy, can I do a dancing game?'

For Diana, it always stung to hear her daughter call the wrong woman Mammy and to know that her daughter was oblivious to who really gave her life. At that moment Diana suddenly realised how much she had given up over the years for Stewart. She had kidded herself at first that it was a courtship to cut her teeth on, or a trophy boyfriend, or something to tide her over until she found someone better. Later she'd told herself that there was no one better so she might as well take what was on offer. But now she saw what it had really cost her; it had cost her the word 'Mammy'. If she ever found a way to get a home of her own, Gracie would be too old to call her Mammy. And even then, to finally reveal the truth to Gracie would break the poor kid's heart and Diana would never do that for all the world. It was never meant to be for this long, but now Diana felt she was trapped, and Stewart had stolen the best years of her life, and he hadn't even stepped through the door to see his daughter's birthday party. Diana was suddenly angrier about it all than she had ever been; that one minor omission on Stewart's part had opened the floodgates, and she wanted him out of her life for ever. She wanted to see him hurt, to understand what he had done.

Diana's stepmother began to sing 'Minnie the Moocher' so that the children could play a game of musical statues, and the boy with the conjuring tricks took a well-earned break.

'I was just telling Gracie's sister here that you're a prodigy.' Mrs Royd from next door beamed a smile at the boy who was taking a gulp of ginger ale. 'Did you really learn all them from library books?'

The boy blushed. 'I'm still not very good. There are some tricks you need special equipment for, like cups with hidden compartments, but these tricks I can do with things I make.'

'You're still a very clever lad in my book.' The neighbour folded her arms as though taking a stand against anyone who would have suggested otherwise.

'And it's very kind of you to come and entertain at our Gracie's party. I hope my stepmother has given you lots of cake to take home.'

The young magician blushed an even deeper

239

shade of red. He was fourteen, and he hadn't expected Diana to speak to him directly. He stammered, wide-eyed. 'Do you want to see a card trick?'

'Go on then; where are your cards?'

'I haven't got any.'

Diana burst out laughing at this. Her anger at Stewart had subsided when she was showing gratitude to the boy, and it freed her to see the funny side. 'Then how do you expect to show me a card trick?'

The magician produced a stack of beer mats, apparently out of nowhere. There was a little flurry of applause and coos of appreciation from Diana and Mrs Royd. 'I couldn't buy a pack of playing cards, so I nicked beer mats from round all the pubs and wrote numbers on them, see?' He offered them to Diana for inspection and then began hastily clearing a space on the table beside them that had been moved to the edge of the parlour wall.

'You know what you are?' Diana thought for a moment. 'You're resourceful. You'll go far my lad if you keep going like this.'

The beer mats were arranged on the table in a fan shape, face down, and Diana was asked to pick one. 'Do you want me to pick it in my head, or pull it out and look at it?'

'Pull it out and take a look, then put it back just the same. I'll turn my back, so I can't see what you've picked.'

Diana picked a card at random and then looked at the number that had been inked onto its makeshift face; it was a three, it was her number. She

240

put it back carefully and said a little prayer in her head that the universe would send her another three to tell her that everything was going to be alright. 'Alright, I've put the card back, what now?'

The lad turned around, and with a deft gesture, swept up the cards and made them vanish. Mrs Royd gasped with delight. 'Now, I want you to point to your card.'

'I can't; you've made them disappear.'

'Ah, yes,' he said, 'that is a problem.' He paused for effect, as though he'd really got the trick wrong, as though he were really lost. 'Well, I think your problem will be solved in one ... two ... three...' and suddenly Diana's card leapt into his hand as if from nowhere, as if he had control of the elements and there was her card, bold as anything, a number three.

Diana took the card and smiled, knowing what the number really meant to her. It was like fate giving her a little nudge of reassurance. *Things will change for the better, don't give up hope,* she thought. She nodded graciously to the lad and acknowledged his prowess.

'However did you do that?' Mrs Royd was aghast.

'A conjurer never reveals his secrets.' The boy took a deep breath of contentment and drained his glass of ginger ale.

Diana slept fitfully that night; she had the same old dream again where Stewart had found his way into her factory, the place where she was safe, and ruined everything. In the dream, he appeared on the packing line all of a sudden, as though he had burst through the thin brick wall at her back to materialise beside her. In the dream he always wore his best going out clothes, the togs he brushed down when he was going out on a spree. But in the dream he didn't have the swagger and grace that had helped to win her over all those years ago. Instead he stumbled, hand outstretched for help, a trickle of blood running over his left eye.

Diana woke at twenty minutes past one o'clock in the morning with a racing heart and stumbled over to the washstand below her bedroom window. Diana's room was at the top of the tiny house, and her attic window looked out across the rooftops below Gibbet Hill. The library book beside her bed had fallen open on the bare floorboards, and Diana just avoided tripping on it; Gracie slept on in their wrought iron bed. The bright moonlight of the cloudless sky shone in to illuminate the chipped pitcher of water that waited for Diana to wash herself with before work in the morning. She drank straight from it, glad of the icy coldness. Diana was careful to rest the jug lightly in the china basin in case the noise woke her daughter, but the child was in a deep sleep and hadn't stirred.

She steadied herself on the edge of the washstand in the milky moonlight. *He'll never get in,* she told herself, *it's only a dream;* but Diana sometimes dreamt things that came true, and it worried her. She looked out of the soot-flecked, cracked attic window, across the dirt of Vickerman Street, across the rooftops of the houses down the valley, and out across to the toffee factory; her toffee factory. Mackintosh's was still there, still in one piece, and it would still be there in the morning, she reassured herself. But there was something different tonight, something different about the factory. Diana leant forward to rub the smudge off the window that was creating the illusion of a shadow across the side of the Albion Mills, but she realised that it wasn't a smudge on her window, something really was wrong at the factory, and at that moment a burst of light appeared in its place that terrified her.

Chapter Seventeen

Bess pretended that she had a headache that evening, and while her sister was at the chemists buying her aspirin, had slipped on her silvery, Louis-heeled, t-strap shoes and slipped out of the house to meet Tommo.

Tommo had promised her a spree that night and when he'd picked her up from their pre-arranged meeting place she had not been disappointed. Tommo had the use of a Hillman Minx Magnificent for the night, and his friend Stewart was driving. Automobiles were Bess's favourite thing, and she was all giggles and wide-eyes.

'This seat is bigger than my bed!' Bess squealed as she ran a delicate hand over the smooth leather interior and luxuriated in the expansive upholstery. 'I wish my sister could see me in this!'

'I tell you what,' Tommo said, leaning over the back of the passenger seat to squeeze her silk-stockinged thigh, 'we'll drive down your road and shout her name as we pass the door, how's that sound?'

Bess thought it sounded super, and they decided to make a night of it, drinking stolen champagne and gin alternately from bottles that they passed between each other, and driving past the doors of people they knew hooting their names through the car windows with less and less coherence the drunker they became.

'I want to go to Mack's! I want to go to Mack's!' Bess cried out with enthusiasm.

'What do you want to go there for?' Tommo had hoped that Bess would suggest some friend of hers that they could pick up for Stewart, he didn't want to take her to her workplace.

'I want to shout "Lady Mackintosh is a strumpet!" Haha.' Bess hiccupped and looked so pretty for a gin sozzled tart, Tommo decided that he wanted to climb into the back seat with her.

'You heard her Stewart, we're going to Mackintosh's to shout "Lady Mack is a strumpet!" And then we're going past my place to get Diana for you. Time she got down off her high horse.'

'Right you are!' Stewart pulled the car sharply round the bend to change direction and head for Mackintosh's factory. He'd been mixing drinks, and he was not only drunk but bitterly angry. He sped round corners at breakneck speed, and Bess bleated with excitement and called, 'Faster, faster!'

They were turning onto the steep hill of Horton Street when Tommo began attempting to climb out of the passenger seat beside Stewart, and into the back seat of the Minx with Bess. There was a tangle of limbs and lips, and Bess slid down onto her back lying long ways across the back seat, as Tommo tumbled awkwardly on top of her, running a hand up her thigh, but then sliding sideways into the foot well, and taking Bess with him. Stewart turned in the driver's seat to tell his friend jokingly to pack it in, but as he did so he lost control of the car, and it swerved dangerously.

Stewie laughed and cried 'Whoa!' as though the car were a horse and brought it back under control again, which sent Bess into uncontrollable fits of giggles and made it impossible for her to pull herself together and help Tommo to get them both upright again.

Tommo was still lying on top of Bess in the deep foot well of the spacious car, but he pushed himself up to see where they were; there, at the bottom of Horton Hill, was the white chimney of Mackintosh's. 'I can see your factory Bess, get ready to holler!' He tried to catch a quick kiss down behind the driver's seat, knowing that once they'd passed Mackintosh's they'd be going to get Diana and she'd be a spoilsport.

Stewart sped down the hill dangerously fast, planning to turn at the last moment to show off. The snow had melted in places, and re-frozen again in others. He didn't see the black ice at the bottom of the hill until the car's wheels hit it. What happened next seemed to Stewart to be happening in graceful slow-motion. The brakes of the Minx Magnificent locked and the car was carried forward at a speed that took his breath away. There was nothing that he could do to stop it from the moment the car hit the ice, and that was the last thing he ever knew.

It was nearly one o'clock in the morning, and Reenie and Peter were finally leaving the factory for the night. The late shift had finished at half-past midnight, and the pair of them had dawdled over the machines long after everyone had left the Toffee Penny line. Peter had endless questions for Reenie, except the one that he was trying to pluck up the courage to ask. He had been offering to walk Reenie home ever since he'd met her, but she always brushed the offer away as unnecessary because she could walk herself, not seeing the intention behind the offer. Tonight, Peter promised himself, he would make his intentions perfectly clear: he would ask her to the pictures.

Reenie was chatting away as they descended the narrow back stairs to the Time Office, and every moment Peter was hoping that Reenie would pause long enough to give him the chance he needed. But she was lost in her enthusiasm for a new sweet that she wanted them to make, and her cheery Yorkshire intonation echoed up the shining cream-coloured tiles of the stairwell walls.

'Reenie!' one of the old commissionaires poked his head out of the Time Office service hatch as he heard her passing. 'Are you comin' in for a sup?' The warm glow of a stove and the smell of milky cocoa brewing in a pot was inviting on a cold night, and Reenie couldn't resist.

The three old commissionaires treated Reenie as though the Time Office were her second home, and it was clear to Peter that Reenie stopped there for cocoa frequently. When they finally left the Time Office to head out into the night, it was after one o'clock in the morning.

Peter wondered if there was anywhere that Reenie hadn't made friends. Even though he thought it was funny, and a virtue, he knew that Mrs Roth didn't like it one bit. He wished Reenie would try to be a little bit more reserved at work for her own self-preservation.

'Are you sure you want to go all the way back home tonight? You'll catch your death walking back in this weather. I bet they'd let you sleep at The Old Cock and Oak until morning.'

'I won't be cold; I've got Ruffian. He bellows out heat, he does.'

Peter was confused. 'Have you brought your horse?'

'A' course I have. How else do you think I get to work? Not everyone can afford a fancy bicycle you know.'

'But where do you keep him? He's not in the bike sheds.'

'Don't be daft, what would he be in the bike sheds for? He's in the stables out by the coal houses.'

'Have we got stables here?'

'A' course we've got stables; where do you think we keep all the Mackintosh's horses you see pulling wagons round the factory? We've got everything here, my lad.'

'Am I your lad?' Peter was nervous, but he thought he'd finally plucked up the courage to ask her. He kept telling himself that the worst she could say was no and that it wouldn't be so bad really, but his heart beat in his chest so hard that he could feel it in his throat as he tried to form the words to ask Reenie Calder to walk out with him on Sunday. The moon was full and bright, and as they stood in the yard below the railway line, even the stars seemed to be urging Peter on.

It was at that moment that Reenie turned to look up at the railway line. She heard it first; a sort of whistle. There was no screech of brakes, no skid of tyres on the steep road that led down to the junction just opposite, just a whistle through the air and the distant rumble of a car's exhaust.

The main railway line was on the edge of a tall, brick bank. It was a strange, precarious place for a train; and any passengers who passed through could see into the windows of the toffee factory that sat in the old canal basin below the bank. The fifth floor of the Mackintosh's toffee factory was so close to the railway line, teetering on the bank, that the girls who worked on the line could easily blow kisses at the window to the Station Master, if they wanted to make him blush.

The railway line was sandwiched between the danger of the sheer drop down the side of the bank, and the danger of the road that it ran parallel to. The railway line ran along the road that formed a T-junction with Horton Hill and for a car that failed to stop at the junction the only place for it to go was into the railway line, side on.

From where they were standing, among the

bike sheds at the bottom of the old canal basin, Peter and Reenie could see the empty platform if they craned their necks upwards toward the top of the brick bank, but they couldn't see the road on steep Horton Hill that the car was hurtling down. Nor could they see the black ice that it skidded on but they heard the car smash through the flimsy wooden fence that separated the railway line from the road. Then they both ducked instinctively as the heavy Minx Magnificent flew over their heads, jumping the gap between the top of the bank and the side of the factory, dipping its nose as it fell through the air and smashed into the windows of the fourth floor of the Albion Mills building.

The car was swallowed by windows and brickwork, and only a gaping hole remained as the car went on further inside the building to come to a halt as it hit the wall on the building's opposite side. A look passed between Reenie and Peter, a look that mingled shock and horror and fear.

'We have to get them out.' Peter was quicker on the draw because he was already full of adrenaline from the worry of the question he had been about to ask.

'There won't be anyone on the fourth floor tonight. Their shift is—'

'No, Reenie, the driver!'

'Oh, God! Some poor person—' Reenie didn't finish her sentence. Instead they both began running at the same time, sprinting towards the nearest doors of the factory. Reenie had never run so fast in her life, but everything seemed to be happening around her in slow motion; they passed the uniformed commissionaires who had heard the car hit the building and were running outside to see where the sound was coming from. They were panic-stricken and in their haste had left their hats behind. 'Fourth floor! The fourth floor!' was all Reenie could shout, and they followed her at a run.

Peter was taking the stairs two at a time, easily outpacing the others. He was the first on the scene, and silently thanked God that their lighting in this hall was all electric and not gas. That car, he thought, had the look of one that was going to blow, and gas would kill them all for certain. The fourth floor was a storage floor, where finished goods were wrapped on pallets and then taken away on bogies. The floor was dark and deserted, but the brake lights of the Minx cast an eerie red gleam over the smashed pallets that had slowed its powerful trajectory. The car had finally come to a stop when it had hit the wall on the other side of the packing hall; its crumpled nose hung out into the night air, with one of its front wheels caught on the smashed window frame.

The engine was still running, and Peter covered his mouth with his handkerchief as he darted towards the passenger side to pull open the door. There were two people in the car, that he could see. The driver's seat had disappeared beneath the bonnet of the car, and it didn't occur to Peter to try to prise it apart. It wouldn't have been possible if he'd tried.

Crushed into the foot well of the car, behind the driver and passenger seats were two injured people, moving slowly, confused by what had taken place.

When Peter began pulling on the doors of the car they seemed to come to and try to get out. 'The frame is buckled!' Peter shouted, but the passengers didn't seem to be listening. 'The doors won't open! You have to climb out through the windows! Wind down your windows!'

Tommo Cartwright looked up, and his broken nose streamed with blood. Bess Norcliffe was in the back with him in a crumpled heap behind the front seats; she had been lying across the back in a drunken haze when the force of the impact had thrown her forward and lodged her in the foot wells with Tommo, saving her life but crushing her ribs.

Reenie arrived in time to see Tommo pulling his skinny legs out from under the buckled driver's seat, ignoring Bess entirely.

Tommo had pulled at the door handle, but when it wouldn't open he began kicking at it impotently from the inside with both feet.

'It's no good!' Peter was shouting to him. 'You have to use the window! Hurry! The petrol tank has punctured! You don't have time for this!'

The commissionaires took a look around and seemed to allocate jobs to each other without even speaking. One ran back down the stairs after nodding to the others, and Reenie felt she knew that he was going to get the fire brigade and the police. The remaining two ripped the flimsy plywood cover off a cabinet that held an emergency fire axe. The younger of the two strode forward to Peter and grabbed a fist full of sweat-dampened cloth at the back of his jacket and pulled him away from the car. The oldest of the commission-aires, the man who Reenie had always felt rather sorry for working so far past his retirement, swung the axe powerfully and expertly into the passenger side window, then stepped back a pace. He spun the axe in his right hand so that he was holding the handle closest to the blade, and then ran the handle around the inside of the car's window frame knocking away all the remaining shards of glass which fell as splinters on Tommo's face. The old man grabbed the lad by the throat and pulled him out through the window. 'It's time to get out!'

Peter and Reenie pulled Bess out through the window and supported her under either arm.

The older commissionaire had thrown the axe to his mate while he wrapped Tommo in a half-Nelson and pushed him towards the door. 'Get thi' down them stairs!'

Peter looked around at the car and then lifted Bess quickly over one shoulder and steered Reenie's elbow towards the commissionaire who hurried her away down two flights of concrete stairs before they were thrown down onto their knees. The explosion shook the whole building and knocked the wind out of all of them. As the commissionaires were thrown forwards, Tommo was able to pull himself free. It took him a few seconds to recover himself enough to turn, pull Bess up onto her feet, and half carrying her, make a run for it, stumbling on ahead of them all.

Peter turned to look back at the commission-aires a few yards away, the ringing in his ears making his head spin. The commissionaires were waving at him to go on and to get out. It didn't matter now if Tommo got away, their priority was to get out of the building. Reenie was on her feet and ready to run; she was pulling Peter's elbow this time, and the commissionaires had caught up with them and were practically pushing them down the stairs.

They all tumbled out through the doors, into the clear air of the night. There was a moment to look up and see the blaze lighting up the fourth-floor windows before the fire brigade arrived and were occupied with other things.

Peter staggered over to the water trough at the bottom of the bank and slumped down beside it. He expected Reenie to follow, but she was gone. He looked around in panic and saw her a few hundred yards off, running towards the stables.

Chapter Eighteen

In the dark and confusion, it was difficult for them to tell where they were bleeding from, but Tommo assumed that they were both bleeding. He was still standing, though, and Bess could still walk. He thought he might have a broken rib, but he'd been lucky, and he knew it. Tommo hadn't seen any sign of Stewart when he'd scrambled from the buckled car and he had assumed his friend had got out first and made his escape ahead of them. Tommo was wrong.

There was only one place for him to go now,

and that was to his mother's house. That, he thought, was where Stewart would be waiting for them. Shock and adrenaline kept them moving, and when Bess fell on a steep pavement he pulled her up again roughly. 'Keep up, can't you? We've got to get away before all hell breaks loose.'

'Oh, but Tommo, I can't walk; I need a doctor, Tommo.'

'Move yourself; we don't have time for this. The police could be round this corner any minute.'

'Let them take us,' Bess sighed melodramatically. 'I love you Tommo and I don't care what happens to me now so long as we're together.'

'Well I bloody care; I'm not lettin' you get me locked up just because you've had a knock on the 'ead. And who said anythin' about love? If you keep dawdlin', I swear I'll knock you sideways.'

'But you love me; I know you love me. That's why you rescued me and brought me with you when you escaped.' Bess clutched at her side with one arm and wiped a trickle of blood from her brow with the back of her other wrist.

'Let's get one thing straight: I am only takin' you wi' me because if I leave you behind you'll blab to the coppers. You're comin' wi' me so's I can make sure you keep your mouth shut, then after that, I don't care what happens to yer.'

'But Tommo, what about our baby and our weddin'?'

'Shut up and walk faster, I don't want to hear another peep out o' you.'

'I can't, I can't,' Bess bleated as she sat herself down on the damp grassy bank and looked at the blood that had spoiled her dress.

'Fine. You stop here. If the coppers find you, don't say a thing. If Stewart comes by this way tell him I've gone to me mother's. Tell him after that I'm going on to Leeds.'

Bess gave Tommo a strange look, but he didn't have time for her nonsense, so he left her by the side of the road and went on towards Gibbet Street and home.

Reenie ran breathlessly to the Mackintosh's stables. She knew exactly which direction Bess had gone, and if they were on foot then Reenie was confident that she could get there ahead of them with Ruffian. She was worried about Peter too, but he had got out safely, and there were plenty of people arriving at the scene who would take care of him. Bess, on the other hand, was possibly bleeding and was with a cad.

Bess rounded the corner near the bike sheds and ran headlong into the stables. They were dark, but for a storm lantern turned down low beside the door. The horses were usually peaceful at this time of night, but the noise of the explosion had spooked them all, and this scene raised a new wave of panic in Reenie.

Ruffian's eyes flared with fear, and he pulled on his bridle, kicking up the straw and whinnying. Reenie tried to soothe him, but the sight of her grazed, and smoke-stained face must have unsettled him even more. 'Steady, now; steady old thing.' She smoothed the greying hair around his muzzle and pressed her nose to his nose. 'I need you now old fella'. Bess needs you. We need you to be strong for us.' She pressed her nose and brow against the soft fur of that blaze of white that streaked up his face from his muzzle to his ears.

Ruffian stamped his hooves and flicked his head up for a moment, as though in defiance of the night. He was ready, and if anything stood in the way of his mistress it should be ready for him.

Reenie deftly untied the horse with her left hand, led him out into the yard and leapt onto his back.

'Reenie! Where are you going?' Peter was walking towards her, off-balance and dazed. Smoke and perspiration had darkened his straw-coloured hair, and a rivulet of blood ran beneath his right ear and stopped at his torn and soot-stained shirt collar. 'You need to stay and see a doctor. There's a doctor.' He was pointing behind him, towards the doors they'd escaped from, but shook his head and banged his right ear with the palm of his hand as though he could unblock his confusion.

Reenie slid down from her horse and, keeping a hold of the bridle, put her face to Peter's left ear and placed a hand gently on his shoulder. 'You've burst an eardrum. Now get your bike.'

Like Ruffian, Peter seemed to recover himself quickly at Reenie's words. Peter moved his head from side to side, as though to recalibrate his balance in light of this new information, and shouted deafly, 'I'm getting my bike!'

Reenie watched as Peter tried to straighten up and find his feet on his way over to the bike shed. He re-emerged with his dark blue Reyhand racer, and after putting both feet on the pedals and rising to a racing position, he nodded to her that he was ready. Ruffian snorted in response, as though to show his approval of Peter's stoicism; they'd make a Yorkshireman of this lad yet.

Reenie steered Ruffian towards the Water Lane gate, with Peter following. Reenie knew all about Tommo Cartwright. Those she spoke to told her things about Tommo Cartwright that made her feel sick. He'd have headed over to his mother's house where Diana lived, and Reenie hadn't formed any sort of plan beyond getting there and seeing her friend. They wound round a steep street of blackened stone terraces, and over the bridge that led them up in the direction of Gibbet Hill. Everywhere there were cobbles to slow them down, and Reenie had to knock Ruffian's side with the sole of her plimsoll to remind him that time was of the essence. They didn't have to travel far to find the grass verge where Tommo had left his girl.

Bess was lying on the cold damp grass without her shoes or coat. Blood stained her doll-like face and Reenie wrapped her coat around her while Peter went to fetch help.

To Sergeant Metcalf the house was unmistakable; the only two-up two-down in Vickerman Street with the front door standing wide open and the lights on. As he approached the doorway in the darkness, he could see and hear an angry exchange within.

'If they come here say that I was in bed all night and–'

'But they'll see the cuts on your face, and they'll–'

'I don't care what they say; if you love me, you'll

do as I tell you.' Tommo Cartwright was in the galley kitchen at the back of his mother's house, bleeding profusely from cuts all over his ugly face. His mother was dabbing at them with a wet rag, and sobbing with fear. Tommo himself was throwing off his jacket and trying to unbutton his shirt cuffs ready to burn the clothes that might give him away. 'Give me that sodding rag and do something useful for once in your life!' Tommo snatched the rag from his mother and pressed it to his eyes while thrusting his other wrist in her direction for her to undress him. 'Where's Diana? Why doesn't she come down here and make herself useful?'

'She had to go out.' Ethel told her son through her sobs. 'She had to go to the police station. She saw a fire at the factory from her bedroom window.'

'She's done what?' Tommo was enraged.

Sergeant Metcalf knocked at the wide-open door.

Chapter Nineteen

Diana sat up in bed beside her sleeping daughter; she was nursing a cup of tea to calm her nerves and trying to think through solutions to the myriad of problems that now presented themselves to her, but the situation seemed hopeless. Gracie was sleeping so peacefully it was as though nothing had changed, clutching her red ribbon that was now as creased as her sleep-stained cheek.

In the small hours of that morning, Diana had seen a bright light streak up from the windows of the Mackintosh's factory all the way down in the valley. She may have been a long way off in her attic bedroom, but even from a distance on Gibbet Hill, she had known immediately that what she could see were fire and an explosion. Diana feared that at that time of the morning there would be so few people around that the alarm wouldn't be raised fast enough. Not only that, that the whole place would be destroyed, or – even worse – someone might be trapped inside and come to harm. Diana had thrown on some warm clothes and left her sleeping daughter, knowing that her stepmother was still in the house to keep her safe. She had run heedlessly through the ice and frozen mud, skidding dangerously and often, until she reached the police sub-station at the Burnley road junction just minutes away.

The satellite station had been closed when she'd arrived, and above the door of the squat little Edwardian building was a warning carved in stone in a language she didn't speak: *ignorantia legis excusat neminem*, ignorance of the law excuses no-one.

Diana hammered on the door with her fists, too exhausted to run all the way into town to the main police station. It was with a sigh of relief that she felt the bolts being lifted on the inside of the door as the duty sergeant opened up to let her in. She hadn't realised then that her troubles were only just beginning.

From then it was only a matter of seconds before the fire engines were out on the road because Sergeant Metcalfe had access to a precious telephone and he could summon the brigade to the aid of the toffee factory. The sleeping police sub-station had sprung into life shortly afterwards, as word reached them that the fire had been started by a car. Diana had accepted a cup of tea as she had sat in the warm of the sub-station parlour waiting for the lift home that Sergeant Metcalfe had offered her.

It was only a few streets back to her own home, but her bare legs were spattered with black mud and she was shivering in the thin jacket and tired old headscarf that she'd pulled on as she had run out of the house.

However, Diana began to regret ever leaving her bed as revelation after revelation brought the fire closer to home. A woman police Sergeant came and told her that they had reason to believe that her stepbrother had been a passenger in a stolen car that had hit the side of the Mackintosh's, and did Diana know if he had returned home? For a moment Diana had hesitated; perhaps there was still a chance to keep this all at a distance. She briefly toyed with the idea of saying that she didn't know, but then she thought about all the suspicious crates that Tommo was hiding in the house and all the wrong things she'd seen, and she realised that she had no choice but to co-operate and to take the police back to the house herself before they went there of their own accord and tarred Diana with the same brush as they were bound to tar her stepbrother.

Diana nodded to the WPC and simply asked, 'Can I take my baby sister to the neighbours' before you go in? I don't want her to be frightened by police in the house.'

Diana had feared this day for so long; the day when all of Tommo's lies and threats and thieving would catch up with him. She had always assumed that the police would turn up at the door one day with a warrant and she would have to tell them that it was all Tommo's doing, and it would be her word against his. Despite all the threats she'd made to him over the years she had never imagined that when the time came, she would be the betrayer and he the betrayed. Not for one moment did she think that she would be the one willingly leading the police into their home and revealing their awful secrets.

They had driven her, for convenience sake, in the back of a police waggon where she rubbed shoulders with four other Sergeants in their dark blue wool tunics who had tried not to look her in the eye.

Sergeant Metcalfe had thought of his own young children and when the waggon arrived in Vickerman Street, he offered Diana a few minutes to carry the sleepy little girl into the house of a startled and slippered Mrs Royd before he and his men knocked politely at the open front door and went in.

It was all over now, and as Diana surveyed the damage to the furniture in her bedroom in the weak morning light, she wondered what the police had found in their search, and how much her stepmother had known that Tommo was hiding in their creaking, dirty house. Ethel Cartwright was still at the police station with her darling boy 'The Blade', so the police inspector must think that she knew something. It was with bitter amusement that she found that Gracie's Cresolene lamp was one of the few things not knocked over or damaged in their chaotic search.

She didn't know what she thought about what had happened to Stewart. She'd heard the police officers at the station discussing his death with one another in matter-of-fact terms, but none of them realised what he was to her. There was some talk about not revealing his identity to the press until they'd informed his family, but Diana thought that could take until next Christmas; his mother was dead, and his father was at sea.

She wondered if she was heartless to feel so little at the death of the father of her child, but she told herself that perhaps she'd feel something later when she'd had time to make that child safe.

Diana drained her tea-stained cup; in the short-term, she needed to find a neighbour who would look after Gracie so that she could go back to work while Ethel was being interviewed. Once her stepmother was back they would resume her usual childcare arrangement, but Diana was beginning to feel that her stepmother's house had just become too hot to handle, and in the longer-term, she needed a better plan.

It was the same old formless plan that Diana had always had: *get somewhere else where we can be together and I can be her mam.* But that wasn't so easy; Diana needed to work, and even when she was working flat-out at the factory as she had been this run-up to Christmas, it was barely enough. Besides, the moment she acknowledged Gracie as her daughter she'd lose her position; it was an impossible situation. And then she had Frances Roth breathing down her neck, and she didn't even know yet if the fire reached her floor? Would her job still exist?

Everything, Diana thought, had just become too much, and she felt like she had no back up in life. Everything had just become utterly terrifying and she missed her father so very much.

Diana pulled herself out of bed and went to wash up her teacup, telling herself that things were about to get better, but little did she know that they were about to get so much worse.

Gracie woke with a sniff and rubbed her face. 'Where's my ribbon gone?' Gracie looked into her open hand and saw that it was empty; the ribbon that she had been clutching when she went to sleep was missing, but it couldn't have gone far, Diana had seen it in her hand only a few moments ago.

'It will be somewhere in the bed; we'll find it later.' Diana tried not to let the sound of her fears into her voice, but it was hard.

'Uncle Stewie gave it me.' Gracie said this as a passing comment; a matter of no moment.

'When did he give it to you?' Diana couldn't think of a time when Stewart would have had the opportunity. The only times he saw Gracie were the infrequent occasions when Diana herself forced him to spend an hour or two with them, on an outing she had contrived. Gracie must have been wishful thinking, the ribbon was, Diana had assumed, a leftover from her stepmother's mending basket.

'He took me to the ribbon shop to choose it when he got me from school.'

'Your Uncle Stewart doesn't get collect you from school; Ethel – I mean Ma always collects you. And the haberdashers is miles out of the way.'

'She doesn't always collect me. Her knees are too bad to go all over town collecting kids and collecting mending and fetching basin meals.' Gracie's little impersonation of the woman that she had been told was her mother was uncannily accurate. 'Uncle Stewie sometimes gets me from school, but I'm not meant to tell you because Ma says you'll be angry with her for letting bad knees get the better of her. But I don't think you'd be angry with her for having bad knees. No one can help it if their knees turn bad.' Gracie clambered above over the top the bed clothes. 'He takes me to the ribbon hashers on the trolley bus if I've been a good girl for you.' Gracie smiled, proud that she had been good enough to be bought her own soft satin piece of ribbon. 'Uncle Stewie's going to buy me a ribbon shop when I'm grown up so that I can be a ribbon hasher like the lady at the counter.'

Diana looked at her daughter's long caramel coloured eyelashes that framed cornflower blue eyes so like her father's. Stewart had never mentioned that he'd done this for Gracie; there'd never been so much as a hint, and even if there had it wouldn't have changed how she felt about him as a father. He'd shown an inconsistent interest in his daughter at best, and at worst he'd helped to bring real trouble to their door, but he'd been a part of her life for so many years and it was natural to feel emotion at his loss. She had put thoughts of his death out of her mind until that moment, but at Gracie's words something broke in her; she covered her mouth tightly with her hand, and for the first time in many years, she burst into uncontrollable tears.

Chester 'Sleepless' Parvin, the most diligent reporter on the *Halifax Courier,* was wiping tears from his cheeks with the sleeve of his old brown raincoat while he tried to make notes on what he was seeing. Whenever people asked Sleepless how he managed to do his job and not become emotionally involved, he would tell them, proudly, 'because I've seen it all, and I've seen it all twice.' Parvin had been to America and seen the poverty of its cardboard city in Central Park. He'd seen the soldiers in London and Paris who had lost limbs for their country but had no work and no money to keep them warm; but this was the sight that finally reached his heart.

News had reached his office late the night before that a fire had broken out in London, and the Crystal Palace was burning. His colleagues listened anxiously to the wireless as news came through that 400 firemen were fighting the blaze while 100,000 spectators watched the end of an era; the end of an age. The glow of the blaze could be seen, according to reporters, across eight counties, and famous men said that the world would mourn its loss. It was only a building, but the news announcer said that to people all over the world it was the symbol of something very important and that it could never be replaced. The Empire was thrown into a kind of mourning for a building that Sleepless couldn't pretend to understand. That was until the call came in from the King Cross police sub-station: Mackintosh's was ablaze.

When the night porter woke him up at his desk to tell him that there was a telephone call for him he thought it was a prank. Perhaps his colleagues had been so put out that he had not understood their feelings of loss for a glass building in London that they'd arranged a phoney message about a fire in a Halifax institution to see if he would react the same way. It was not the case; Mackintosh's factory really had been ablaze.

It was now after six o'clock in the morning, and it was starting to get light. From beside the watchman's cabin at the Albion Mills gate, Sleepless could see the tear in the side of the toffee factory where a car had ripped through the fourth floor. On the ground, he could see the pile of rubble and tangled window frames that had poured down the side of the building to land on a waggon that was just visible beneath it, all but obliterated. He could see the tell-tale streaks of soot blackening, some above the hole where smoke and flames had billowed up in a cloud, and some below that ran in rivulets down the exterior wall where water from the sprinklers had carried it.

The toffee factory had an extensive sprinkler

system, and when the night watchman had triggered it from the control box, the water had worked immediately to control the blaze. Even so, there would be no lines running in the main toffee factory that day; the fire had burned long enough for the smoke to spread everywhere and damage everything in the Albion Mills wing. The building would need engineers and surveyors to check it before it would be safe for anyone to return; and then the builders would have to replace the walls, the windows; everything. This would be devastating for the business.

Sleepless was surrounded by workers who were arriving for the early shift and who didn't understand what was going on but had followed the smell of burnt brick dust to the factory gates. Grown men were looking up at the side of the building in shock, shedding tears as though an old friend had died. That was when it had hit Sleepless; it was the way that these people cared about the place they worked in. Mack's was more than just a care for their own livelihoods, it was an attachment that ran bone-deep.

'Are you the reporter from the *Courier?*' The night watchman at the gate had spotted Sleepless scribbling away at his ink-stained notepad as he took in the scene.

'Aye.'

'They want you, come on through.' The watchman lifted the gate for Sleepless but called back through to the workers who were jostling to follow. 'I'm sorry, I can't let anyone else through just yet. If you could just wait there.'

'And what are we supposed to do? We've got a

shift starting in ten minutes.'

The watchman pointed Sleepless in the direction of the doors to the main office block below the railway embankment and then turned back to the throng of people who had endless questions. As Sleepless walked away, he could hear men voicing worries about pay, late production rates, and a host of questions that the watchman couldn't be expected to answer.

Outside the doors to the main office, a group of suited men were standing and talking with the Chief Constable. The Fire Chief stood with a man whom Sleepless recognised as Sir Harold Mackintosh himself; his pointed, owl-like eyebrows drawn together in heartfelt concern as he listened intently to the other men.

The factory manager saw Sleepless approach and detached himself from the group to meet the reporter half-way and speak to him privately. 'Mr Parvin, it's a bad day.' He shook the reporter's hand and welcomed him like a comrade.

'It is that. What have you got for me?' Sleepless Parvin knew that he could best be of use to the factory if he got to work and reported on what had happened there without delay. He smoothed down his pencil line moustache with the thumb and forefinger of his right hand, flicking the cover of his reporter's notebook open with the thumb of his left.

'I can't give you the details of the crash itself, I'm afraid.' The factory manager had dark circles around his pale eyes, and rusty stubble was showing through along his jaw where he'd had no time to shave. 'I don't know how the car managed to get here–'

'Don't worry, sir. We've got all that. Borough Police said it was a freak accident. How the car managed to jump the rails and get this far, we'll never know, but we know pretty much everything else.'

'Freakish is about right.' The factory manager looked up at the gaping, blackened hole that had opened up in the brickwork in the side of his factory. 'Well, it's a tragedy for the family of the man whose life was lost, but I think it's also going to be a tragedy for a great many Halifax families whose livelihoods depend on production. The entire Quality Street production line will have to go into shut down; we'll be lucky to still be in business this time next month.'

'Is it that bad?' Sleepless didn't stop writing for a moment and didn't take his eyes off the factory manager.

'Well, there's a car in the middle of the fourth floor, and the walls on either side are open to the elements where the vehicle smashed through, and there's the smoke damage besides, so it won't be fixed in a day. Although, saying that, it could have been worse; we were lucky that the watchman triggered the sprinkler system, so the damage of the fire was contained to this building, but that isn't saying a great deal. There's still a hell of a lot of damage.'

'How much damage are we talking?'

'Significant. All the work that we've done to build the fastest line in the world has been de-stroyed in one night.' The factory manager looked up at the side of the Albion Mills building; it was a fresh, misty, Autumn morning, and it felt like funeral weather. 'And that, Mr Parvin, is where we will need your help.'

'Anything the paper can do, you know we're here to help our town.'

'Can you take this down verbatim?' The factory manager didn't need to ask; Sleepless nodded to show that he was ready. 'We have decided this morning that we will build a new Quality Street production line and we will have it up and running in seven days' time.'

'In the same building?'

'No. We're going to reopen the old Queen's Road factory.'

'But that's as good as a ruin.'

'Not quite a ruin. It's true that we decommissioned it as a production line fifteen years ago. But it hasn't been completely empty, it has been in use as a warehouse which has kept it dry, but now we will need to work like stink to get it stripped down, scrubbed up, and utterly spotless in time to move in. We're looking for any able-bodied men, especially those with building experience, to present themselves at the Queen's Road factory from noon today.'

'And once all the machinery has been moved from the line here, will you be able to get up to the same speeds in Queen's Road?'

'We won't be taking the machinery to Queen's Road. The smoke damage means the machines need to be sent away so that they can be specially blast cleaned.'

'Then how will you make Quality Street?'

'We're going back to hand making, hand wrapping and hand packing everything. We're calling on any women who have previously worked at Mack's to return to help us meet the national demand for Christmas. We will be paying double for any woman with packing or wrapping experience who can make the minimum speed, and we're lifting the cap on piece rate work. Any woman who can work fast is encouraged to, and we guarantee no one will be penalised for doing so. The future of the factory is in their hands, and the faster we all work, the better our chances.'

'Do you think there'll be that many women who aren't already working for you who can help? I'm not being funny, but aren't you employing most of them?'

'We're lifting the marriage ban.'

Sleepless stopped writing; his jaw dropped. 'How's that?'

'You heard me, Parvin. We're lifting the ban on the employment of married women on the production lines. It's just until the factory is back on its feet, but between now and Christmas we are asking the women of our town–' the factory manager seemed to think better of what he was saying. 'No, we're *begging* them – come and help us. We're offering extra rates to past employees who know the ropes because we are determined to get Quality Street out at the highest possible quality for its first Christmas. The only way we can do this is if we have the help of the whole town to do the impossible: build a new factory overnight. The fate of Mackintosh's is the fate of Halifax; there's more at stake now than just sweets.'

271

'Ruffian.' Reenie sighed as she looked out of the window of her hospital ward room. It was late afternoon, and Reenie had been in the care of the doctors and nurses at St Luke's Infirmary since the early hours of the morning when she'd been brought in with Bess and Peter. Reenie had been thrown down the stairs during the blast from the explosion of the car, but she hadn't sustained any serious injuries. Her doctor had suggested keeping her in for one more night under observation, but Reenie was adamant that her place was at home. She had asked them to send a telegram to her parents to let them know where she was and she had been watching for them from the window ever since.

As soon as she saw her parents on the horizon with her beloved horse, she leapt from her chair and made a dash for the entrance to the hospital. 'Ruffian!'

'You found him alright then?' Reenie ran over to hug her horse before her father, who didn't seem to mind.

'Yes; eventually.' Mr Calder jumped down from the trap that was being pulled by one horse and bringing up Ruffian in tow. 'One Sergeant Metcalf had taken him into custody after he'd packed you off to the hospital and he said he'd been nothing but trouble. We borrowed Black Wanderer from down Shibden Farm to pull the trap so if you want to ride Ruffian home you can. Although he'll be sluffed by now after the night the pair of you have had.'

'I'm sorry.' The ward sister had chased out after Reenie when she saw her making a dash for the front drive of the hospital. 'I really can't recommend that your daughter rides home, especially not bareback. She's had some nasty knocks, and I think she'd be better returning home in a motor in a day or two, or perhaps–'

'It sounds like you don't know our Reenie,' Kathleen piped up. 'Seein' the horse will do her more good than seein' a doctor, honest to God.'

'Kathleen, language!'

'What, it's true?'

Reenie hugged Ruffian around his grey neck, and he snorted in scorn at the public show of emotion.

Chapter Twenty

'But I don't know anything about factory work; I'm a cocoa buyer, I wouldn't know the first thing–'

Major Fergusson held up his hand to sweep Laurence Johns' words away like so many motes of dust. On the other side of the door waited sixty Halifax women of varying ages, some of whom had worked in the toffee factory when Queen Victoria was still on the throne. They had heard the call and were the first to find people to mind their children or their husbands and come back to the work that was forever in their blood and bones.

'You don't need to know anything about it,' the Major reassured him 'the women know their work

273

and each other, and you'll find that they organise themselves on a line much more quickly than you or I ever could. But above all you'll find that they make good decisions; trust them, and they will make life easy for you. You are just here to administrate and to get them the budget for anything they need. It will be a good learning experience for you,' he smiled and added, 'you'll enjoy it.'

Johns was sceptical, but they needed to pull together at a time like this, and if he could make a difference by throwing himself in at the deep end then that was what he would do, and he would just have to see if he sank or swam. 'Alright, let's not keep them waiting.' He smoothed down his blazer, and they pushed through the smoke-damaged double doors to the production hall. The eager chatter of sixty women died down, and all eyes were turned on the men.

'Ladies, we are sincerely thankful to you all for–'

'Hey, is 'e alright?' One of the women interrupted the Major and pointed at Laurence, who had turned pale when faced with the prospect of so many people who would be looking to him for leadership, and was now flushing red with embarrassment under his red whiskers at the shame of being seen to show fear.

The Major clapped him on the shoulder and loudly announced, 'This is Mr Johns; he will be your acting supervisor.'

'E's a bit young, 'int 'e?'

'Not a bit of it! Johns here is just the very man for you; he has been tasked with assisting you in turning this hall into a noisette paté line in record time. Any equipment you need, you need only ask him, and he will have it obtained for you. I have high hopes for this working party, I handpicked you all for this special task.'

'Did you really handpick them?' Johns whispered to the Major.

'No,' he whispered back. 'They were just the first to turn up. But don't let them know that. Good luck old chap, and don't start work until this hall is shipshape and Bristol fashion.' The Major made his quick goodbyes and then left Laurence alone with his new department.

There was an awkward silence; Laurence needed so much from these women, and he didn't know where to start. Before he could gather his thoughts, Mrs Grimshaw said, 'Listen, love, we know what we're doin'. Any chance you could just leave us to it?'

Shock and relief mingled in Laurence's response. 'Yes, yes.' He waved a hand. 'By all means. Do you need anything from me?'

Mrs Grimshaw took off her coat and began folding it. 'We'll want a cuppa and a bun at half past ten. You go put the kettle on, and we'll make a start.'

Laurence didn't know if she was serious, but he was happy to take her at her word. As he left to find provisions, Mrs Grimshaw was asking how many buckets they had, and two older women were volunteering to fetch and carry water. For Laurence, it was totally unexpected, and it gave him hope.

The factory manager's meeting was held in the

275

boardroom of the office building which looked across at the shattered Quality Street factory. This was a place that Frances Roth would never have considered important enough to enter under ordinary circumstances, but these were strange times, and she was bringing evidence of widespread fraud.

Frances took in the opulence of the manager's suite of offices as she walked through them, and she relished every moment of it. The ornamental skirting boards, picture rails and door frames made her feel like she was going up in the world. The narrow corridor opened out into a hexagonal hallway that was capped on top with a great domed skylight of rainbow glass that looked just like an exploding tin of Quality Street. Mrs Roth looked around her at the five doors that bordered the hallway, each lit with a frosted glass electric light crafted to look like a flaming torch; she didn't know which room she wanted, so she waited until she was summoned.

Eventually, the door to the boardroom opened. 'Mrs Roth?' A spectacled young woman who she did not recognise bid her enter. Naturally, she ignored her as she would have done any secretary.

'Ah, Mrs Roth.' The factory manager sighed, trying to muster the charitable feeling to be halfway polite to a woman who he supposed was only doing her job. This felt like it had been the longest week of his life, and the men who were seated at the table around him bore the careworn, dishevelled look of men under siege. 'I understand you have some information about, er...' He rummaged through the untidy piles of papers that

276

littered the board table looking for a note that would remind him why Mrs Roth was there at just a time when they had no time for her.

'It's a piece time racket, Sir.' She paused for effect and then blurted out with energy, 'A fraud.' Mrs Roth was clutching a copy of the latest newspaper to feature a photograph of the old Quality Street line, and she laid it out on the table and pointed to Reenie Calder's outline. 'There, that's my proof. You can see that Bess Norcliffe is standing back to let Reenie take over her work, and Reenie is working two jobs at the same time–'

'I'm sure we don't need to worry about–' Mr Booth, the Quality Street line manager tried to dismiss the triviality of it but Frances Roth was now brimming over with pent-up energy, and didn't hesitate to interrupt him.

'But it's connected to the crash, sir, and another theft. I wrote it all down, Sir.' Frances Roth reached into her pocket for a carefully typed report which she had folded away neatly. The factory manager tried to pull his exhausted frame up in his chair and nodded at Mrs Roth to go on. 'The girl in the photograph was the passenger in the car that crashed into the factory. She is also the same girl that was seen with the man who stole the car here, in this very factory, outside of working hours when I raised the alarm and called for the night watchman. He got away that time, but I understand from the papers that when he was arrested crates of stolen machine parts from this factory were found at his place of abode. I believe that this girl, Bess, helped him to get into the factory to steal those items and she is part of a plot to defraud the firm wherever possible. The girl in this photograph is Diana Moore, the so-called stepsister of the thief, and she lived in the house where those stolen goods were stored. I have observed them at work over several weeks, and I believe that those three girls, Bess, Diana and Reenie, have been part of a wider plot, and at a time like this they could easily do even more harm to the business.' Mrs Roth pulled herself up to her full height and waited as though she were expecting applause.

The factory manager rested his elbows on the table and put his head in his hands. This was the last thing he needed; if the situation were not complicated enough now, he had theories of conspiracies and complicated family networks. He sat up again, took a deep breath, and looked to Mrs Wilkes, the employment manager. 'Mrs Wilkes, what do you say to this?'

Amy Wilkes, the smart woman in tortoiseshell spectacles who Frances had mistaken for a secretary, raised an eyebrow in thought. 'I think we shouldn't be too hasty with this one. Let me speak to the police officer in charge and get his thoughts. Certainly, there appears to be evidence for one isolated case of cheating on piece rates,' she gestured to the photograph in the newspaper which had now taken on more significance than its subjects could have thought possible. 'But at a time like this, we need those faster girls more than ever. I would recommend that we keep an eye on them to make sure that they can't cause any trouble, and schedule a disciplinary hearing to investigate the piece time cheating. The other matter is one for the police to investigate for us and I'll talk to them about that myself.'

'With respect, Madam,' Frances Roth was now bubbling with pent-up frustration that her revelations hadn't met with the astonishment and praise that she had believed she would receive. 'No one's going to bother keeping an eye on them at a time like this, everyone's busy, and no one cares. I'm the only one that has cared enough to bring this to you.'

'Then they will be placed under your supervision, and you will keep an eye on them until further notice.' Mrs Wilkes smiled as she watched the electrifying effect her words had on Frances Roth. This, she thought, ought to keep the woman happy for the moment. And it did.

Chapter Twenty-One

The Major knew that Peter could only hear him through one ear, so he leant over to make sure that he was speaking to the side that didn't have a burst eardrum. 'Are you sure you want to do this, Peter? We can give you more time to rest.'

Peter didn't shake his head; it hurt too much. 'No. I want to be useful.'

'Very well. I want you to set up five lines in this hall. It's the first room we could get cleaned up and painted, and it's yours.'

Peter was too tired to be surprised. He had fought through that night at the factory on sheer adrenaline, but once Bess and Reenie were safely in the care of the doctors he had felt the exhaustion of his injuries. He was lucky that no bones were broken after the force with which the explosion had thrown him to the ground; his badly sprained wrist was held in sling. He was painfully aware that he had cuts and bruises, but couldn't remember how he had got them. Reenie was in a similar way, and she too had returned to work as quickly as possible, but Bess remained in hospital because her injuries were more serious.

Peter surveyed the empty hall of the old Queen's Road factory and wondered where to start. He'd planned the Toffee Penny line when they had got the new machinery, but that was with the guidance of Major Fergusson, and with the luxury of a lot more time. He thought, and then asked, 'What kind of equipment do we have?'

'Only the most basic, I'm afraid Peter. Copper boiling pans, but they won't be connected to a mains steam supply, you'll need a source of heat for each one; we've got the toffee making tables that haven't been used since the war and with a blast clean they should be ready in a day or so. Then there are trestle tables for wrapping and packing, but no conveyor belts so you'll need to plan for movement and supply.'

'What about enrobing machines to cover the fondant centres in chocolate? And depositing machines to set the strawberry fondant into the starch moulds?'

'You should be so lucky. They'll have to use hand depositors for the strawberry cream–'

280

'What's a hand depositor? I've never even seen one.'

'Well, I'll say one thing for this situation: it will be wonderful for your education. You can assume that there isn't a scrap of automated machinery and that everything we need to do will have to be done with Victorian methods. Let's hope some of the older married women volunteer to help because if we're very lucky, some of them will remember the shortcuts of how to use it.'

Peter and Major Fergusson surveyed the empty hall in silence for a moment before Peter said, 'I want Reenie Calder and Mary Norcliffe. Mary is fast, and Reenie has a good eye for how to organise a line; she's smart with process improvements.'

'You'll have them. Are you sure that they're both ready to work?'

'They're ready. They came back before I did. They're both working on the clean up in the next hall. Reenie's so ready she brought her horse and put him on a waggon.'

Major Fergusson lowered his voice and tried to look casual. 'Oh, no, don't look now, Rabid Roth is on the warpath.'

'That's the last thing we need.'

The Major called out to Mrs Roth. 'Madam, what brings you to the Queen's Road factory this fine morning? We haven't readied it for production quite yet.'

Mrs Roth crossed the bare hall towards the two men, her heels clicking on the scrubbed floor as she walked briskly, and with menacing purpose. She was within reaching distance of the Major, and she handed him a slip of pink paper. 'These are the staff members who have been assigned to my supervision–'

'Ah, no, I'm afraid I have already agreed that these young ladies will be seconded to Mac-Kenzie's section as part of the emergency plans.'

'Mr Peter MacKenzie has also been assigned to my supervision.' Mrs Roth was quiet, reserved, and slyly triumphant.

'I'm sorry, I don't understand.' Major Fergusson gave the overlooker his full, puzzled attention and passed the soft slip of pink paper to Peter.

'Peter MacKenzie is no longer attached to the Time and Motion Office; he has been implicated in a piece time racket and a wider fraud. There will be a disciplinary inquiry, but until that time, while investigations are pending, he has been transferred to my supervision, and demoted to the grade of porter.'

'But that's ridiculous!' Peter burst out, screwing up the flimsy paper without a thought, 'I haven't done anything of the sort! Who is my accuser, what evidence do you have? What fraud am I supposed to have committed?'

'Now, MacKenzie.' The Major placed a restraining hand on Peter's shoulder and said, 'I'll handle this. Mrs Roth, there has clearly been a misunderstanding. I will speak direct to the factory manager–'

'No need.' Mrs Roth smiled. 'If you pick up that memo and smooth it out you'll see that the factory manager has signed it. Good afternoon, Major Fergusson. Peter, follow me.'

Sleepless Parvin was visiting his old friend in the

old factory. The production hall, which had sparkled with rainbow-wrapped Quality Street sweets only a few days before, was now streaked black with smoke and water damage from the fire that had raged above it. Sleepless wasn't surprised to hear that his friend had been requisitioned to run a working party. Laurence was one of the brightest men he'd ever met, but he was sensitive, and he worried too much about what other people thought of him. Sleepless thought he'd probably appreciate a friendly visit and some moral support.

'Is this hive of activity all your doing?' Sleepless took a notepad and pen from his pocket out of sheer habit.

'Not mine, I just make the tea!' Laurence appeared genuinely happy and relaxed, and Sleepless was glad to see it. 'I tell you, Sleepless, I have the best working party in the whole factory. These good ladies know what needs to be done before I do. You should have seen the place this morning, it was black as sin, and the windows were all thick with smoke grime, and the place smelt like a camp fire, but then my team got straight to work with their mops and their brushes, and look at it now!'

Sleepless could see a neat tidemark on one remaining patch of wall that was being rapidly eroded by a young woman with a scrubbing brush in one hand and a rag in the other. It was somehow satisfying to see the substantial progress that the women were making over the destructive work of the fire as black marks gave way to clean, gleaming cream tiles beneath. The sharp smell of borax and soap flakes was a pleasing pick-me-up first thing in the morning.

'Can I talk to one of them?' Sleepless gestured with his notepad that he was looking for a quote.

'Yes, yes, by all means. Let me get Mrs Grimshaw.' Laurence called over the motherly woman who had put him to work keeping the team fed and watered. 'Mrs Grimshaw, this is my good friend Parvin, he's reporting on the fire for the *Halifax Courier.* Parvin, this is one of the kind former employees who responded to your call for workers.'

'Oh, aye?' Mrs Grimshaw used the pause in her work to re-tie her headscarf around her greying hair. 'Are you the fella that wrote we should come in?'

'Yes, yes, that's me. Do you mind telling me what it's been like coming back to the factory, Mrs Grimshaw?'

'Oh, I'm Mack's through and through, I am. I left, what were it? Seventeen year ago?' Mrs Grimshaw sighed with satisfaction, 'It's like I've never been away, really. I were just sayin' to our Maureen, it's like comin' home. I'm workin' wi' all the girls who I joined with after school. We see each other in the market and that normally, but gettin' together again to work like this is just somethin' else; it's better than Christmas. I mean I were sad when I heard about the fire, an' all, but I wouldn't have missed out on this for the world. See that lass over there,' Mrs Grimshaw pointed out a woman in men's overalls that looked as though she'd borrowed them for the occasion. 'She's third generation Mack's, she is. Her mam is here somewhere, and her grandpa is outside movin' rubble. It's a family here, that's what's nice about it. Even the Mackintoshes have pitched in; two halls down you'll see Lady Mackintosh and her daughters cleanin' a cloakroom for us because Lady Mackintosh said she couldn't have us all come in to help and not have anywhere to hang our coats. Isn't that right nice of her?'

This, thought Sleepless, would be the best story he wrote all year.

Chapter Twenty-Two

'No, Mrs Norcliffe. Your daughter has been very lucky.' The doctor was raising his voice as much as he could without crossing the line into an out-and-out shout-off with Mary's mother.

Mary was pulling on both ends of a grey knotted handkerchief with her balled up fists. Her mother had initially been unwilling to come out to the hospital to visit Bess, saying that Bess should come home or stop out, but not bother her. When Mary finally made her understand that wishful thinking wouldn't make Bess well enough to walk herself home, she finally agreed to get on the bus. St. Luke's Infirmary wasn't so very far away, but the medical staff might as well have been from another universe. They talked about feeding her sister oranges and giving her lots of red meat, as though the money for these things grew on trees.

The ward smelled of carbolic soap, and the nurses had lined up all the furniture perfectly parallel with the wall, as though untidiness might spread germs. Bess was smiling away quite happily, a plaster cast around her ribs, and bandages around her head. She was gazing dreamily at the dashing Scottish doctor who was trying to communicate with their mother.

'I'm sorry, er, Mary, is it?' Dr Tennara was becoming desperate, 'I don't think your mother quite understands. If I were to write it down for her, would that...?'

'No. She can't read. What do you want to say to her? I can explain it to her if you like.' Mary saw the relief on the doctor's deeply-lined face; he had hoped that at least one of them would be able to speak to the mother in signs.

'Well, I want her to know that your sister has been very lucky. If she had been sitting up in the car as it crashed into the factory building she would have been thrown through the windscreen, but because she was lying across the back seat she was thrown down into the foot wells of the car and lodged there behind the seats. This is what caused her internal crushing injuries, and her broken ribs, and the nasty gash on her head. However, these will all heal in time. She will need several weeks' rest, and we have had to put a cast over her rib cage, but we are very optimistic about her recovery. She really has been a very lucky girl.' Dr Tennara paused, smiling, as though waiting for Mary to relay all of this to her mother through a complex series of signs and mime.

Mary nodded wearily that she understood, and

then turned to her mother to bellow out, 'Mother! Bess is poorly! She's staying here! We have to give her oranges!'

Mrs Norcliffe looked disgusted. 'We haven't got any oranges. And we can't leave her here; you two have got work in the morning.'

Mary turned a blank face towards Dr Tennara, as though to say *you see what I'm up against?* And then sat in silence while Bess tried to ask her mother cheerily for colour magazines instead of oranges and her mother doggedly demanded to talk to the supervisor. Arguments went on around her, but Mary wasn't listening; she was pulling at the knotted handkerchief trying to decide whether she could pluck up the courage to ask about Bess's baby, and then to ask about how much all this would cost them in hospital bills. She couldn't face asking, because she couldn't face knowing; and then suddenly, without her realising what she'd been doing, she saw that she'd torn her handkerchief in half.

'Careful, now Doreen, or we'll put you on pot washing duty!' Mrs Grimshaw grinned at her old friend who had been waiting in the make-shift dining room for two minutes and hadn't dived into work yet. The other women, on seeing an opportunity to be useful, had rolled up their overall sleeves and found themselves a place immediately. That's what they had always loved about being factory lasses: when there was work to be done anywhere, you could rely on factory lasses to organise themselves into an efficient production line without even thinking about it. They moved and acted as one, like dancers in a ballet.

'But I like pot washing; I'd be quite happy to. Although I think I should find somewhere for this lot first.' Doreen jabbed a thumb over her shoulder at some boxes on a trolley behind her that Mrs Grimshaw hadn't noticed until then.

'What are they? You'll have a devil of a job finding room for them in here for a day or two, this is about to become our new dining hall. We've got Margaret and Joan on sandwich making duty.' Margaret and Joan called out a 'cooee'. 'Winifred and Pearl getting the water boiled for coffee,' Mrs Grimshaw pointed them out behind a couple of old urns which they were coaxing into life with the expertise of wartime engineers, 'these lasses from the Quality Street line are putting up trellis tables, but we're still short a pot washer.'

Doreen surveyed the old church hall that had been offered to the factory as an emergency break room while they converted the old Queen's Road factory next door; it was a sight for sore eyes. The factory might be down on its luck, but it had lucked out with the lasses that had come in to help. Over the next days and weeks, there would be a never-ending stream of men and women through this hall, looking for food, a cuppa and a break from the round the clock work that they loved. She was glad to be back, even if it was only until Christmas.

'I'll be your pot washer,' she told Mrs Grimshaw. 'But I need to set these down first and return the trolley.'

'Are they for in here?'

'Yeah. They're for you. I thought you might like them.'

'Don't be saucy. What are they?' Mrs Grimshaw took a closer look at the boxes which were unmarked.

'They're for you, and they're mis-shapes.'

Mrs Grimshaw's eyes lit up. 'Oh you never! Are you kidding me?'

'I am not. I thought you might like to give out one with each cuppa.' Doreen shrugged it off but smirked as though she knew what a glorious gift she was bringing.

'Doreen Fairclough, as I live and breathe! I could kiss you!'

'We've got a whole batch of those purple caramel sweets, but they've got Emily Everard running the line, and she decided to put a hazelnut in the middle of all of them instead of a brazil nut, and now they can't use them.'

'Trust Emily Everard to go off and do her own thing. Mind you, I think it sounds like it would taste much nicer with a hazelnut instead of a brazil nut.'

'That's what she said, apparently. Couldn't understand why they couldn't just change the labels on all the tins to accommodate her whim.'

'Well, the nation's loss is our gain on this occasion. Bring them over here, and we'll pack them away under the sandwich table.'

The ladies dragged their trolley over to the far end of the hall and were about to stash them away when they noticed that it was 11 o'clock and time they stopped for a tea break. Mrs Grimshaw cracked open the first box so that they could each

289

have a sweet with their cup of tea. 'Hang on a minute, these are coconut eclairs.'

'Oh, yes.' Doreen looked over at them and nodded in confirmation. 'Emily also wrapped a batch of coconut eclairs in purple wrappers because she says she thinks they should all be purple. You've got that batch an' all. Perhaps we should put her on pot washing?'

'Emily Everard? Are you having a laugh? She'd be far too high and mighty to deign to do anything except run a line or run a country. Now, if you'll excuse me, ladies, I've just remembered I've got an errand of mercy to run.'

Mrs Grimshaw picked up two of the mis-wrapped coconut eclairs and went out through the church hall door, down the steps, and in through the back door of the old Queen's Road factory, where she only had to look for a few minutes before she found the person that she was looking for.

Mary Norcliffe was sitting on a box trying to unravel a knotted mess of string that she'd been given to wrap paper bundles with, and she had a face like fourpence.

'Now then our Mary.' Mrs Grimshaw beamed down at Mary. 'Hold out your hand lass.'

Mary was too miserable to ask questions and simply obeyed. Mrs Grimshaw pressed into her open palm two mis-wrapped coconut eclairs, which crackled as she delivered them. Mary looked down at them for a moment, then dropped her string, stood up, and silently hugged her neighbour.

'There now lass. I know it's hard, but it'll be

reet, you'll see.'

'But my sister's in the hospital and–'

'I know she is. And from the sounds of things it's the best place for her. Come on, sit down here.' She pulled up another upturned crate so that they could sit next to each other. 'Which hospital is it?'

'St. Luke's Infirmary.'

'Aye, well they're good there. She's in the best hands.'

'That's what I'm worried about! How much will it all cost? I want her to be well, but we can't afford to pay the hospital bill when she comes out, especially if she can't work now.'

'But isn't St. Luke's a volunteer hospital?'

'I don't know; I don't know what that means.'

'St. Luke's is what used to be the Workhouse Infirmary, although folks don't like to think of it like that, of course. Those doctors and nurses are volunteers, so you won't have to pay hospital bills when she comes out. However, you will have to pay a few bills when she gets home if you need to go out and get her any medicines. But if you and I can take her to the free clinic, then you won't have to pay to call out the doctor for her.'

'Would you really do that for me? For us, I mean?'

'Of course I would, lass. You know I'm always looking out for you two to make sure that you're safe. Now you eat that sweet before it melts in your hand.'

Mary smiled at Mrs Grimshaw and was surprised to discover that the sweet in the purple wrapper was a coconut eclair. It reminded her of the time she'd slid down the snow outside her house, and Mrs Grimshaw had been waiting to look after her.

'My sister was in the same place you know, back when it was the Workhouse Infirmary. She had a tram accident and was hurt very badly.'

Mary looked worried. 'What happened to her?'

'What happened to her? She married her doctor, that's what happened to her. Right now she's back at your burned-out factory helping put doors back on their hinges. She's done well for herself, but she hasn't forgotten the people at the factory who helped her back then when she needed it.' Mrs Grimshaw thought a moment. 'I don't suppose you two have been paying into the sick club have you?' Mary shook her head. 'The Girls Friendly Society, or 'owt like that?'

'I didn't think we could afford the extra cost. I was trying to save money.'

Mrs Grimshaw tried to disguise her exasperation. She'd seen this too many times before; girls would economise by stopping their payments to the sick club, but then when sickness came they'd have nothing to fall back on. 'What about the Union? Is your Bess in the Union?'

'Yes, we both are. I always make sure she pays her Union dues.'

'Have you talked to the Union yet about claiming for sickness for her? No, I don't suppose you have. You eat that up, and I'll take you to see the shop steward. He'll know what's what. If you've paid your Union dues you'll be able to claim sick relief from the Welfare Officer. It won't be as much as the sick club, but it will keep you both going.'

'So you are Irene Calder.' Sergeant Metcalfe was sitting opposite Reenie at the Calder family's kitchen table.

Reenie opened her mouth to say something, but couldn't think how to get out of that one, so she shut it again. She remembered meeting this policeman the night that she was trespassing, and although she didn't regret the trespassing, she did start to think that lying to him about her name that night had, in hindsight, been ill-advised.

'Of course she's Irene Calder,' her mother called over her shoulder from her place beside the kitchen sink where she was violently pulling at the feathers on a limp goose, 'who else would she be?'

'Who else indeed?' Sergeant Metcalfe folded his arms. 'Did I see you lead a horse to the Piece Hall on Saturday the fifth of December and then allow it to urinate on the feet of a group of Salvation Army members?'

'Reenie!' Mrs Calder put down the goose and spun around the better to give her daughter a look that told there would be trouble later if this were true.

'I didn't mean to!' Reenie pleaded 'He's a very old horse... I did look for a bucket...'

'Well, fortunately, that's not what I'm here to ask you about today.' Sergeant Metcalfe produced a photograph from the back of his pocket notebook. 'Do you recognise this man?'

Reenie reached out gingerly as though asking if she could pick up the photo, and Sergeant Metcalfe nodded his permission. She looked at it carefully and considered. 'I don't think I've seen him before, but I think he looks like someone that Mary has said we have to keep away from.'

'Mary who?'

'Mary Norcliffe, she's my friend at work.'

'And why does she say you have to keep away from him?' Sergeant Metcalfe made a note of Reenie's answers in a way so casual that it appeared he was merely doodling to pass the time.

'He's after Bess. From the sounds of things he's after all the girls, but he's after Bess too, and she's none too bright, so Mary spends all day and night fendin' him off like he's some vampire in a story. It wouldn't surprise me if she'd got Bess to draw a crucifix on her drawers.'

'But you've never met him?'

'No. Well, I might have done and not known I had, but I don't know that I have, if I have, if you know what I mean?'

Sergeant Metcalfe followed her logic, but didn't encourage her to continue it any further. 'What about Diana Moore; do you know her?'

'Oh, aye, she's a friend from work too.' Reenie pointed at the photo. 'That fella there is her brother, or summut', if it's the same man. She says he looks like a cross between a rat and a frog and she hates him even more than Mary does; he's away all the time, but when he's home he brings trouble so she's always kickin' him out.'

'Did Diana tell you this?'

'No, she's not much of a talker. It's all her neighbours; some of the other girls live nearby, and they hear her shoutin' and carryin' on, and they've told me about it.'

'What kind of things do they say they hear?'

'Last I heard was he'd turned up at his sister's birthday party and she kicked 'im out and said she hoped he'd die, so there's no love lost there. They have to live under the same roof, though because he's the one who brings home the money for the rent.'

'Do you know how he gets his money?'

'Oh, some no-good way, probably. I heard he'd been stealin' and that after he crashed that car in the factory, there were a lot o' stolen things at their house what he'd kept there. He's a bad lot in general.' Reenie shrugged as though this were something abstract and wholly unconnected to her and her friends, something that could not touch them and that it cost her nothing to mention.

'Has Diana ever asked you to help her with anything at work? Like moving things, or hiding things, or perhaps leaving the factory at an odd time or via an odd route?'

Reenie froze. She had helped Diana to leave early when she'd asked to and lent Diana her locker when she'd needed it. Come to think about it, Diana always left the factory for home by a strange route, but she'd always said it was just to avoid the crush at the main gates. What had Diana got herself involved in? Reenie tried to disguise her fear and simply said, 'No.' This conversation was taking a turn that she didn't like, and that she hadn't seen coming. She had not been on her guard because she hadn't thought that she had anything much to hide; she was not, in her mind, the one in the wrong.

Sergeant Metcalfe made a casual note in his

pocket notebook. 'So I suppose Diana would have to help her stepbrother sometimes, whether she liked him or not.' He looked up from his notebook. 'You did say that she was reliant on his money for the rent?'

'Well ... I ... er...' Reenie could see that she was trapping herself in her own words and tried to be more conscious of what she was saying and not saying. 'Like I said, she's not really much of a talker, but she's very honest and I know she doesn't like what he does, so I don't think she'd ever involve herself in it.' Reenie swallowed and looked around the family kitchen for some excuse to get the Sergeant to leave, but there was none.

Sergeant Metcalfe nodded thoughtfully. 'What were you doing at the factory so late on the night when that car crashed into the side of it?'

Reenie was about to answer, but then worried that she might be dragging Peter further into trouble. 'I was just looking at a machine. I'd been asked to look at a machine.'

'Is that your job at the factory?' The Sergeant sounded interested, almost pleased for Reenie. 'Have you been moved into engineering?'

'No...' Reenie tried to sound casual. 'But sometimes they do ask me to take a look at the machines, just if I'm around and that.'

'But your shift had finished, hadn't it?'

'I quite often stay late after my shift has finished to look over the machines; it's nothing unusual. It was just a very normal night.'

'It wasn't night, though, really, was it?'

'I don't know what you mean.'

'It was morning. You were still lookin' at your

machines at one o'clock in the morning.'

Mrs Calder was now facing the pair at her kitchen table. As she leant back her hands gripped the edge of the sink, turning her knuckles white. Her mouth was a grim, tight line and she watched in fear, not daring to speak. When she had let the policeman in it had been to ask some innocent questions to her innocent daughter, perhaps even to hear someone else praise her heroism for all she'd done to save Bess from a burning car, but now the situation had changed, and even she could read between the lines to hear the trouble that her daughter was in.

'I did stay a bit later that night, but it was just because I got chattin' to the commissionaires and they wanted me to stay for a cuppa.'

'What do you know about the machine parts that have been stolen from the factory over the last two months since you started working there, Reenie?'

'Nothing!' Mrs Calder broke her silence. 'She doesn't know anything! My Reenie is a good girl, she might be a bit cheeky, but she is not and never will be a thief!'

'Mrs Calder, I would like to hear Reenie's answer, if you please.'

Reenie didn't have to think. 'Honestly, I promise you, I don't know anything about any of that. I would never–'

'Tell me again about this man.' Metcalfe pointed to the photograph.

'I've never met him; he's just someone that I'm meant to keep Bess away from.'

'Do you know his name?'

297

'He's Tommo. But that's all I know about him, I don't know anything else.'

'Do you know where he lives?'

Reenie was confident. 'No, I don't know anything else about him.'

'But you just told me that he lives with Diana Moore and that you know her neighbours.'

In her fear and her desperation Reenie appealed to the policeman. 'I haven't helped him, honest I haven't, we're just tryin' to help Bess on the line because she's in the family way and she's too weak to work fast. Please don't think we've done anything wrong, we really wouldn't, it was only silly stuff on the line, please don't think we'd do 'owt serious.'

Mrs Calder wept. 'Oh Reenie, what have you done?'

The policeman leant forward and said very carefully, 'After the crash you got on your horse, and your friend got on his bicycle, and you both went in the direction of the house of Diana Moore, Thomas Cartwright, and Ethel Cartwright. Why did you do that?'

'Because I knew that was where he'd have taken Bess.'

'Where who would have taken Bess?'

'The man who got out of the car, I saw him and I–' Reenie's voice stopped short as she looked again at the picture, a dawning realisation. 'His face...'

'Whose face?' Reenie's mother moved across the kitchen and crouched down next to Reenie in response to the shock and fear in her daughter's face.

'His face, it was covered in blood. I didn't realise it was the same one ... or I forgot... I didn't know. I didn't, I just wasn't thinkin'—'

'Alright, Reenie.' Sergeant Metcalfe held her eye with a look that reassured the innocent and panicked the guilty. 'Do you want to go back to the beginning and tell me whose face was covered in blood?'

'That man, that man there. I thought I hadn't met him ... well, I hadn't met him, he didn't see me because he were being pulled out of the car. It were after the crash; I saw him pulled out o' the car... I'd forgotten what I knew! I'm so sorry; I didn't mean to lie this time, I didn't, I'd just forgotten what I knew and what I didn't know, I'm so sorry!' Reenie began to hyperventilate with strangled sobs as the enormity of her situation hit her; she was being investigated at work for running a piece rate racket, which was basically true although it had only been a small one. It had only been to help Bess and Mary but it looked so much worse because she'd been messing about with all the other machines at odd times to try to see more of Peter. She had lied to her overlooker to get the sister of a known felon out of work early for God-knows-what purpose and she had got Peter mixed up in all of it. Now the police were questioning her about her connection to criminal acts at the factory that everyone would believe she had masterminded with Bess's young man, even though she had claimed she'd never seen Tommo but after the crash she took herself straight off in the direction of his house without a second thought.

Now she had lied to the police, however inadvertently. This was more serious than trespassing on the way home from the pub. It was the kind of thing that got you put in prison; this was terrifying.

Chapter Twenty-Three

'You got yourself into this, Reenie, I never asked to get mixed up in bunkin' off work to get Diana out early, or chasin' after known criminals in the middle o' the night, that was all you!' Mary was holding up her gloved hands in a defensive gesture.

'But I did it for you and your sister, no one else!'

Mary looked around the deserted, snow-capped bike sheds to make sure they were not being overheard. 'You made your choices, I didn't make them for you. That first day when you got me moved down the line and took over my place, that was your choice, I didn't ask for it, I distinctly remember tellin' you to stay out o' it, and you wouldn't.'

'I'm not askin' you to do 'owt else that's wrong, I'm just askin' you to come to the hearin' and tell the director the facts: just explain that Bess was poorly, you don't even have to say why she's poorly, just that she's not very strong and so we rallied round to help her, and only her, and there was no piece rate racket, just a couple o' girls helpin' one poorly girl on the line, so the job still got done. That's all you have to say.'

'I can't.' Mary looked down at the pattern of dirty boot prints in the heavily compacted snow.

'Why can't you?' Reenie was becoming impatient. She didn't like it when other people couldn't see logic.

'I've made a promise to Mrs Roth.'

Mary's words hung in the sharp, cold air for a moment, and then Reenie took in a breath to shout almost loudly enough to shake the snow from the cycle shed roofs. 'You've done what?'

'You don't understand, I can't lose my job now, I've got Bess's doctor's bills to pay, on top of lookin' after her when the baby comes. If I lose this job—'

Reenie wasn't going to get dragged into the spiral of Mary's worries. 'But what have you promised Mrs Roth? Tell me what you've promised Mrs Roth.'

'I promised her that I won't come to the hearin'. I won't say anythin'. She says she can keep me out of it because I was down the other end o' the line from you so I couldn't have known...'

'Mary bloody Coldheart! Can you hear yourself? Can you even hear the words that are comin' out o' your mouth?'

'You don't need me! I've spoken to the Union, and they've said that they'll stick up for all of us, they'll be at the hearin', you don't have to worry.' Mary was defiant, but she wasn't meeting Reenie's eyes.

'Don't have to worry? *Don't have to worry!* Do you know what the Union shop steward said to

301

me? He said that they will stick up for all of us, and they will make sure that I get a good reference *if* I resign after this crisis is over, and we've moved back to the proper factory again. They said that I work too fast and they think it would be wise for me to consider goin' for work in a shop or goin' into service; *into service!* I pick up the factory work so fast that if I keep going at this rate the management will expect all the girls to work as fast as I do, and that isn't fair on the other girls. I'm very useful now while they're tryin' to pull together a scratch production line for Christmas, but after that, they'd rather I got out of factory work, thank you very much.'

'Well...' Mary floundered, looking for something conservative to say. 'Maybe it's for the best. I'm sure the Union know what they're talkin' about–'

'Does that mean you're handin' in your notice an' all?' Reenie folded her arms.

'Well, no, why would I?'

'Because you're just as fast as I am.'

'Yes, but I don't go causin' trouble with it! I don't go switchin' on machines I'm not meant to, or flirtin' with the Time and Motion managers and askin' to look through their plans for new lines, and stayin' late at the factory with 'em–'

'If I hadn't been late at the factory that night your sister would ha' been dead! We pulled her out that car, an' then Peter carried her all the way to the hospital. Do you have any idea how lucky she was that we were there when she crashed and that we went to find her after?'

There was stony silence for a moment, anger

302

and resentment hung in the air. The factory whistle sounded, breaking the quiet, and men and women, poured out of the doors, heading for home. Mary turned and ran away through the dirty snow, taking all of Reenie's hopes with her.

Reenie was devastated. She had truly believed that Mary was her friend, and it had never occurred to her that Mary wouldn't be as loyal to her as she would have been to Mary. Reenie made her way slowly up Cripplegate towards town. She needed to collect Ruffian from where she'd left him in the stables at The Old Cock and Oak.

As she trudged up the hill, Reenie's eyes began to sting with tears. She had been so brave until now, but her situation had become too much for her. She hadn't just lost Mary, but she seemed to have lost her friendship with Peter, too. Reenie had thought that they had shared something, a connection when he had taken her hand that night of the crash when they were in Diana's house. She felt that there was something special between them, but whatever it had been was gone. She had tried to see him, to talk to him, but he was obviously avoiding her, and there was nothing she could do about it. In a way it felt to Reenie like a bereavement, she was frightened of the trouble that she was in at work, and with the police, but the worst thing of all was mourning the loss of her friendships with Mary and Peter.

Reenie slipped into the courtyard behind the pub with her head down. A few early patrons hovered around the doorway, but none of them were paying any attention to a girl in a hurry.

Reenie could smell Ruffian before she could see him; it was the comforting, sweet smell of hay, and horse and warm oats. 'Now then old fella'. Reenie buried her nose in Ruffian's mane and wept. 'They've all gone, they've all gone. You're my only friend now, Ruffian, everyone else has gone.'

A commotion out in the yard made Ruffian fidget, and Reenie heard raised voices coming from outside the pub.

A woman's voice shouted. 'I can't let you in afore half past six. You know the law. I'm not risking my license!'

There was a gruff answer. 'We have to hear the wireless!' and another man called out, 'You have to let us in as citizens!'

Reenie came out of the stables and round to the side of the pub. Mrs Parish, the landlady, was leaning out of the open downstairs window into the courtyard where more and more patrons were arriving; but this wasn't the usual six-thirty clamour, this was something else.

'You've got eight minutes; you can wait while eight minutes.' Donna was pleading with the patrons who were obviously restless.

'We need to hear the wireless! We need to hear the King!'

'There's nothing to hear about the King just now, they've moved on to some silly thing about books. There won't be another news broadcast on the National Program 'til nine o'clock tonight. I promise you I'll be open and the wireless will be on for all to hear and I will call silence so's we can all hear it.'

A man stepped forward and asked suspiciously, as though Mrs Parish was trying to keep something from them, 'If they're just talking about books on the wireless what book are they talking about?'

The landlady sighed, pursed her lips and ducked her head back inside the pub for a moment to check. They could hear voices inside as she asked her son what was being discussed and then put her head out again to tell them, reluctantly, 'Some fool thing called *Follow My Leader*.'

There were a few snorts of derision, and someone said, 'Well how are we to do that if he's buggered off with some American?'

A young woman appeared round the corner, running at full pelt into the courtyard, light blonde hair and high cheekbones marking her out as the landlady's daughter. 'Mother,' she asked, out of breath, 'is it true?'

Her mother nodded. 'Your brother had the wireless on in the taproom and it was on the six o'clock news just now. Late-breaking news they said.' Mrs Parish shook her head in disappointment and then said to the assembled crowd, 'alright, it's half-past six, we're opening up.'

Reenie watched as Donna opened up the pub and some patrons wandered absently inside, while others stood in the yard, shocked into silence and motionless. One or two seemed to think it was futile to wait for the next broadcast on the pub wireless and went instead in search of family or friends to tell the news to, or perhaps to neighbours who had their own radio sets.

'What's happening?' Reenie asked as she followed the landlady into the public bar, 'Why's everyone acting so funny?' Reenie was beginning to panic; the thought that they might be at war never far from anyone's minds these days.

'It's the King,' Mrs Parish said, struggling to hold back tears.

'He's not...' Reenie stumbled over the words. 'He's not dead?'

'No. He's handed in his papers. It's all over, he's going. He's leaving us.'

'But he wouldn't, would he?' Reenie was incredulous. 'Only yesterday they were saying in the papers that Mrs Simpson was finishing with him and going away; she said she would. All the worrying's over. They'll find him a nice princess to marry. He doesn't want to marry the American lady, she's old and not a bit pretty.'

'The Prime Minister announced it in parliament this afternoon, lass, and they're saying it will be official from tomorrow because they're rushing it through. They're discussing it now in the Houses of Parliament, but the BBC are broadcasting some bloody talk about nothing.' Mrs Parish took her handkerchief from the pocket of her slacks and wiped briskly at her eyes.

A clatter at the door made the pair look up. Lieutenant Armitage in his full Salvation Army uniform came rushing into the tap room. 'Is it true?' he demanded, and when Mrs Parish was too shocked to respond, he asked again with even more urgency, 'Well, is it?'

'Yes.' She said it almost in a whisper. If Lieutenant Armitage was stepping through the doors of a licensed premises, then this news really was as earth-shattering as they all seemed to fear. 'King Edward VIII has written to the Prime Minister. He's abdicated the throne. The papers are signed. We have a new king.'

Lieutenant Armitage staggered to a seat beside the door and sank into it. 'A year of three kings. I never wanted to live to see a year of three kings.'

'Would you like a glass of soda water, Lieutenant Armitage?' Mrs Parish worried about the old man, he was white as a sheet, but she didn't want to offend his sensibilities by offering him a strong drink; the Salvation Army prohibited it.

'You're very kind. I'll take a glass of soda water.' He said it absently, gazing around him as though the world had a different look about it now. 'There'll be a revolution.'

Reenie moved toward the old man and sat down on a stool beside him. 'You don't mean it, do you?' she asked him, tentatively.

Lieutenant Armitage seemed to wake up and realise what he had said. 'Europe is a powder keg. Revolution may be only the start of it, lass.'

'But not in England, surely.'

'We've got families starving so badly in Jarrow that they marched on Westminster to demand food, and nothing was done for them.' The Lieutenant took off his uniform cap and rubbed his brow. 'Of course there'll be a revolution; there's no other way. This king we've lost today was the only one who defied the government to say that something must be done for the poor miners who work but starve. If he goes, there'll be an uprising in the North.'

307

'Won't the new king help?'

'He might do, but the Duke of Gloucester is not a man of the people.'

Donna returned with the soda water. 'It's not the Duke of Gloucester.'

'You what?' Armitage was confused.

'It's not Gloucester. We've got the Duke of York. He's king from today. They said he's King Designate. He's the next eldest in line, they can't skip over him just because he has a stammer and he's a bit shy.'

'Oh, well that's all we need.'

'But isn't he nice?' Reenie asked. 'His daughters are lovely.'

'He wouldn't stand up to his own reflection, that one.' He reached up to take the glass of soda water that Donna had brought him. 'Thank you, you're very kind.' He drained it quickly and then asked, 'Is there any more news? Did they say anything else at all?'

'Nothing. They said that the Prime Minister had announced it in the commons a bit after four o'clock, then they postponed discussion until six. There'll be nothing more until the nine o'clock news program.'

'What a world we live in where we can hear the latest news before the newspaper office has even had a chance to print an extra.' Lieutenant Armitage said it with a sigh and shook his head, perhaps thinking back to a time when tabloids seemed just as remarkable. 'We lose King George, the Crystal Palace, the Mackintosh's factory, and now this. We live in troubling times.' Lieutenant Armitage thanked Donna but said that he wouldn't linger.

He thought that the best place to go to would be the office of the *Halifax Courier,* at least then he could pick up the latest extra edition as soon as it came hot off the presses.

The landlady watched him go. 'I don't have much time for some of those Salvation Army lot,' Mrs Parish confided in Reenie after the Lieutenant was out of earshot. 'But old Armitage is the salt of the earth, he really is.'

'Mrs Parish, I'm worried.' Reenie felt frightened; the world was becoming so hostile, and she didn't know what to do.

'Don't worry, lass. There won't be a revolution, not here, not in England. The new king will surprise us all, you'll see.'

'But it's not just that; it's everything.' Reenie didn't know where to start. There were so many problems, and everything was in such a mess. Bess was in the hospital; she'd lost her friends; she was going to lose her job; she was going to lose Diana her job; she was probably going to be in trouble with the law; she was never going to be able to work in a factory again, and everything was all her fault. She couldn't see a way out, and she felt that she'd already burdened her family with too much worry. 'I think I'm going to lose my job.'

Donna gave her a sympathetic look. 'You were always too good for that lot down at the factory anyway. They don't deserve you as far as I'm concerned. If they can't see how good you are, then good riddance.' Mrs Parish picked up the Lieutenant's empty glass and said, 'Why don't you come and work for me? I need someone to work in the Oak Room; a kind of part-waitress, part-barmaid. It wouldn't be behind the bar it would be up in the private room, so it doesn't matter about you being on the young side so long as you stay out of the licensed premises. I get a lot of old fellas wanting to hire out the Oak Room: the Antiquarian Society, the Buffs, the Rotarians, your Dad's lot. I need someone to run up and downstairs with food, and to put out the tables and the tablecloths, and gather them up again for the laundry hamper once they've gone. It's the kind of work that keeps you on your toes, but if it helps you to worry a bit less to know that you can walk away from the factory now and have a wage here..?' The landlady paused, perhaps waiting for an answer. 'You think it over. You wouldn't get piece rates, but I bet it would be more fun than the factory, you'd have all the old gents to chat to. We've got a ghost here somewhere I'm told, and you could probably talk the hind legs off him if I know you.' The landlady waited again and then said, 'Come on Reenie, say something love. You're never usually this quiet.'

'I'm very, very grateful,' Reenie said earnestly, more tears welling up in her eyes. 'But I just don't want to ever leave the factory.'

'Why not? Surely you don't want to be a factory lass for ever?'

'But I do, I honestly do. I've always had a dream one day to be a manager and buy a house, and now it's never going to happen.' Reenie covered her face with her hands and sobbed. She realised now that it had been a silly dream; even if she hadn't ruined everything at the factory she would never have been a manager, and never in her wildest dreams was she ever going to have a house. If the king had to hand in his notice, why should she expect not to have to hand in hers?

Mrs Roth was feeling smug after her small victory at the factory. As far as she was concerned, the disciplinary hearing was exactly what these girls deserved, and the thought that it was going ahead thanks to her initiative gave her spirits a remarkable lift. She was feeling invincible, and it led her to make a bolder suggestion to her mentor Gwendoline Vance when she next visited for tea.

'On the night of that fire at the factory, the police went back to the house of the young man who had stolen the car and found all manner of stolen goods there in crates.' Mrs Roth's eyes shone with excitement. 'And do you know what else they found?'

Gwendoline Vance stirred an extra lump of sugar into her tea and eagerly asked: 'What did they find, dear?'

'Diana Moore's child had been living practically on top of stolen machine parts from my factory.'

'No!' It was a kind of pantomime of incredulity, as though Captain Vance enjoyed the scandal too much to be surprised.

'I told you she was being raised among bad people. The house belongs to Diana's stepmother, and Diana shares it with the stepmother and stepbrother. In fact, the stepbrother is the young man who stole the car. You know I've never approved of the way that Diana Moore goes about things; she shouldn't be allowed to work at Mack's at all, but she's been on my line, so I keep a close eye on her.'

'You do right.'

'Well, they call the young man who stole the car Tommo "The Blade", and would you credit it, I saw him in my section of the factory not two weeks before that crash. He threatened me; it was a terrifying ordeal. Would you believe he was with one of my girls and she swore blind she didn't know him.'

'I remember you telling me about the young man; it did sound terrifying.'

'Well, of course, I wasn't frightened at the time because I remembered him from my school days; he was plain Tommo Cartwright then. I was more annoyed than anything, but that's because I didn't know that he'd grown up to become Tommo "The Blade".'

'It sounds like you had a lucky escape. The Lord protects his followers.'

'Indeed! Well, can you guess who the other passengers were in the car with this young man when he crashed his *stolen* car into the side of my factory?'

'Oh, I can't think,' Gwendoline Vance said as though this gossip were tastier to her than all the mince pies she'd put out on the lacquered occasional table between them.

'It was Bess Norcliffe, the very girl that had sworn blind she didn't know him, and some anonymous mobster from gangland Leeds whose family cannot be traced.'

'You don't mean that the little girl is mixed up with mobsters?'

'I certainly do.'

Gwendoline shook her head. 'And what does the child's father think about all this? Surely he must want her taken away from a place where *mobsters* are hiding stolen goods.'

'He doesn't know a thing about it.' Frances sipped her tea, oblivious to the fate of the young man she'd pined for all these years. 'I haven't seen him since the end of November, no one has. Personally, I suspect he's gone to sea like his father. There's nothing for him here; going away to sea would be the only way for him to be free of Diana, which is what I know he really wants. There's a rumour going around the factory that he was in the stolen car when it hit the factory, but I don't believe it. My Stewart would never be involved in anything like that, and if he had been there the police would have confirmed it; it would have appeared in the papers. No, I'll never believe that he would willingly get mixed up in anything illegal.'

'And you'd know that better than anyone else, I'm sure.' Gwendoline meant what she said, and Frances was foolish enough to take it to heart.

'Anyway, the police went round to the house and found that they'd been keepin' all kinds of stolen goods there, so they arrested the step-mother, Ethel Cartwright, for hiding them. So, that little girl has been living with not one, but two criminals; her father has vanished; and her mother is unmarried. And...' Mrs Roth smirked at this new piece of information. 'Her mother is about to lose her position because she has been part of an illegal piece time racket at the factory.'

Gwendoline Vance clutched her hands to her heart and rocked backwards in her plump armchair, cackling; this was quite the most salacious gossip she had heard, and she was relishing all of it.

'Well, the more I thought about it, the more I realised that it was my duty to inform the authorities that this innocent child was being raised among dangerous criminals. Never mind the impoverished surroundings that had become, one might say, *precarious.*' Mrs Roth took a theatrical sip of her Darjeeling tea to pause in her narrative for dramatic effect. 'I decided that Captain Armitage might think me "temperamentally unsuited" to the Salvation Army's Social Services work, but that wouldn't stop me from going to see the Local Authority Social Services at the town hall. So off I went in my uniform, which I just happened to be wearing–'

'Of course, what a coincidence.' Gwendoline Vance winked.

'I never said that I was there in an official capacity with the Salvation Army social work section, I suppose they just assumed it. Anyway, I told them about the poor child, and they said that they were going to investigate.'

'Well, didn't I tell you that you ought to report that mother for the way she was bringing up her child? If you were to petition them to foster the child, you would be doing her a kindness. And just think, when your Stewart comes back you'd be able to tell him that you'd rescued his daughter and solved all his problems in one fell swoop; you'd have a ready-made home waiting for him.' Gwendoline Vance offered her friend another homemade mince pie. It was made with a rich, buttery shortcrust pastry, which covered the mincemeat with a cut-out of icing-sugar dusted star.

Frances Roth allowed herself another one as a special treat because she was feeling so pleased with herself. As she bit into it the sticky, juicy mixture of preserved citrus fruit, apples and spices oozed out and dribbled onto her chin from the broken pastry casing, and she quickly pulled out a dainty handkerchief to blot it away. She and her friend chuckled at the little mishap, feeling safe and warm in their self-righteous nastiness.

Chapter Twenty-Four

Diana sat in silence as she felt the strings that held her precarious life together unravelling around her. She hadn't just worked harder than anyone else at Mack's, but she had also been the most conscientious worker, accepting the fact that she would have to lose piece rate bonuses to reluctantly cover up for Mary and Bess when they were in trouble. Over the years she had kept the peace when more boisterous girls had tried to disrupt the harmony of their workplace. She had discouraged troublemakers; rearranged lines to give bright girls a chance to improve; and she'd even tolerated Mrs Roth's bullying without so much as thinking of reporting her. All this Diana knew, and she couldn't say any of it in her own defence. Instead, she had to listen to Mrs Roth's poisonous lies and hope to God that whatever the punishment was, it wasn't more than she could bear.

The disciplinary hearing was presided over by one of the directors and bore a chilling resemblance to the courtroom scenes she had watched at the pictures. They were assembled in the wood panelled boardroom, where large oil paintings of John, Violet and Harold Mackintosh gazed down on them with looks of mild curiosity, mingled with slight menace. The director in charge, the factory manager, and the women's employment manager formed a panel of judges at one side of the board table. On the other side were Mrs Roth and a few overlookers that Diana didn't know well, and then she, Reenie and their Union shop steward. Each party was huddled around either end of the table; a panel for the prosecution, and a panel for the defence.

The cast iron radiators around the edge of the boardroom were belting out heat and the room was fearsomely, unseasonably hot but Diana's palms were clammy with cold perspiration. Why couldn't they get this over with? If they were going to sack her, she wanted them to hurry up and do it so that she could get out of being in the same room as Frances bloody Roth.

'Mr Hitchens, sir,' the Union shop steward addressed the director personally, 'this is highly unusual, I would expect an investigation of this nature to be conducted immediately after the accusation has been made, but in this case these girls have been expected to wait for two weeks, with an accusation hanging over them, and not just to continue working, but to continue working in demoted positions and under the close supervision of their accuser.'

'This has been noted, Mr Parks.' Mrs Wilkes, the women's employment manager was unruffled by the observation. 'It was not expected that it would take so long. The girls' cooperation has been taken into account, and it is to their credit at this difficult time.' Mrs Wilkes glanced down at a printed agenda on the polished walnut table in front of her. 'Mrs Roth, would you like to begin?'

Diana suppressed an urge to roll her eyes and groan, and instead settled for cracking the bones in her neck.

'Yes, thank you, Mrs Wilkes.' Frances Roth organised her notes in front of her and, quite unnecessarily, chose to stand to deliver them. 'I have reason to believe that both Diana Moore and Irene Calder have been using their work here at Mackintosh's to run an elaborate fraud against the firm. I have submitted evidence to the factory management, in the form of a newspaper photograph that shows that Reenie Calder was doing not only her own work, but also the work of another girl on the line, and that Diana Moore knew this.'

Reenie was watching wide-eyed as the director nodded appreciatively at Mrs Roth, as though he not only believed the old tartar but was ready to give her a bonus for her diligence. Reenie felt sick.

'I have witnessed,' Mrs Roth continued, 'un-professional behaviour from them both when they are in the presence of a certain employee from the Time and Motion department–'

Mrs Wilkes interrupted to clarify for the director. 'This is Peter MacKenzie.' The director nodded.

'Yes, Peter MacKenzie,' Mrs Roth stumbled a little over her words as the interruption had caused her to lose her place, but she refocused her attention quickly. 'I have witnessed strange behaviour around this man, and it is my belief that they have offered him some bribe to facilitate a scheme associated with their piece rate racket.'

'What kind of strange behaviour?' Mrs Wilkes unscrewed the cap on her fountain pen and poised it over clean lined paper ready to take notes.

'Switching places with other girls; switching to other lines; disappearing to look at factory machinery late at night after their shift has finished; looking through drawings and plans of machines; taking machines apart; making notes on machinery that has not yet been commis-sioned for production, and *practising* on that same machinery.' Mrs Roth added the last sentence with an emphasis that implied she was revealing a thing most shocking.

'And is that unusual for girls of their rank and position in the firm?' Mrs Wilkes must have known that it was but asked as a matter of form.

'It's not just unusual; it's unheard of. No one that I have ever had on one of my lines has ever done anything of the sort. Reenie Calder has been memorising the inner workings of all of the machines, and it's unnatural.'

The director turned to the factory manager and muttered a question to him, and a conversation was conducted beyond the hearing of the rest of the room, but Reenie could see the look on their faces, and it looked bad. She was certain that she was going to lose the job that made her feel, for the first time in her short life, like she was good at something.

The director turned to Mrs Wilkes and muttered something, and Mrs Wilkes replied, 'Yes, I'll bring him in.' She rose, went out the door, and called to someone who had apparently been waiting in the hall for just such a summons. It was Peter, and for the first time since she had met him Reenie didn't feel glad at the sight of him; he walked in very deliberately ignoring her, refusing to so much as cast a look in her direction. Mrs Wilkes offered him a seat on the other side of Mrs Roth, and Reenie knew that he had come to testify against her. The thought that he could do such a thing broke her heart, but she could see why he was doing it, he was doing it for the same reason as Mary; his only way to keep his job and his fledgling career was to testify against her. Peter had years of working life ahead of him; one day he'd have to provide for a wife and children and put a roof over their heads, and for the sake of that future family Reenie could see him selling her out.

'Mr MacKenzie,' the women's employment manager flashed him a welcoming smile, 'we've been hearing a lot about the unusual working methods of some of the girls on the Quality

Street production line, but particularly Irene Calder. Can you tell me if you have noted anything unusual about her work?'

Peter took a deep breath as though he had so many incriminating anecdotes he could share, but that it bored him to have to decide which to share first. 'Well, where to start? She is faster than any of the other girls on her line, or on any line at the factory that I have observed. She often takes over the stations of other girls to work at three times the normal speed just to test whether or not it is possible, or to gain a better understanding of the machinery, or to see if there is a better method of carrying out a particular task in the factory.'

'And has she indicated why she does this?'

'She wants to know everything about our machinery and working methods. She is compiling a sort of mental encyclopaedia of every machine and process so that she can understand exactly how Quality Street is made.'

This woke up Mr Hitchens, the director, and for the first time, he raised his bluff, cracked voice to speak. 'Is she capable of remembering these things in any detail?'

'In perfect detail, sir. She is like a music hall memory artiste; she can retain everything. Although she has dabbled in reproducing some of the machines as drawings, it is only ever to tell me where a machine is going wrong and to suggest a remedy. She simply watches, or takes them apart, or asks the engineers questions, and then she understands.'

'Extra-ordinary.' The director pronounced the word as if it were two separate ones, and he sat

320

back in his chair looking warily at Reenie as though she were a witch and he feared her magic. 'I think we need to see some of these drawings and notes. I want the girl's locker emptied and any papers that she has submitted to me when we reconvene.'

The rest of the hearing was a blur. Reenie was dimly aware of an argument with her shop steward on one side and the director on the other, but she had stopped listening; she couldn't hear anymore. The disciplinary was not over; it was only postponed until every scrap she had ever written had been found and brought to the director. Nothing good could come of it, they would think she had been plotting to steal machines with Tommo, and it was all her fault for not doing as her overlooker had said. And then she remembered all the notes that Peter had written to her, and that she had kept and treasured, and that they would find, and the embarrassment and heartache were too much.

'Diana, don't go,' Laurence called out to her as she hurried away down the busy factory corridor; keen to get away from Frances Roth as fast as she could.

'Diana now is it? Not Miss Moore anymore?' Diana stopped to allow Laurence to catch up with her, but she wasn't looking back at him. She was waiting, with her head turned down to look at her feet.

'I'm sorry.' Laurence was obviously disappointed. 'I had thought we were friends. I know that we haven't known each other long, or–'

Diana interrupted him. 'I don't have much time Mr Johns. What did you want to speak to me about?'

Laurence Johns was patient; he knew as well as anyone some of what Diana was going through. 'This disciplinary procedure is ridiculous, and you shouldn't have to sit through it; no one wants you to sit through it.'

'Then why is it happening at all?'

'You know why; because Frances Roth has backed the employment manager into a corner. She has photographic evidence for God's sake.'

'Do you think I did it?'

'Of course not. It's ridiculous.' Laurence paused. 'But it does look damning. They have to investigate.'

'Is that why you stopped me, Mr Johns?' Diana fixed him with her iron-banded irises. 'To tell me that no one wants this to happen, but to be a good lass and bear up while it happens all the same?'

'No,' Laurence stood his ground, 'I stopped you to tell you that the offer is still open. If you want to take the posting to the Dusseldorf factory, I'll send you tomorrow. You could leave all this behind, and I would arrange it for you.'

Diana seemed to be thinking about it. 'You'd arrange it for me?'

'Yes.' Laurence was emphatic; this was not an offer made lightly, there really was valuable work that Diana could be doing in Germany.

'Tell me, Mr Johns.' Diana seemed to soften. 'Do you know Lady Mackintosh?'

He hesitated. 'Not well, not very well. I've dined

with her on a number of occasions. She's very hospitable to the factory managers, especially us waifs and strays with no families. I'd say I see her four, or maybe five times a year. Why do you ask?'

'Is she a kind woman?'

'Yes, very. Although she has nothing at all to do with the business if that's what you're thinking.'

'No, that's not what I'm thinking.' Diana seemed to weigh up two options before asking. 'She is a mother, isn't she?'

'You know she is.' Laurence couldn't see where Diana was going with this, but he trusted that she had her reasons for asking.

'I'm sorry Laurence, I can't go to Germany.' Diana said after a lengthy pause. Her tone was softer, and took his hand for a moment. 'But I am sensible of the compliment that you've made in your kind offer.' With that she turned and walked away, leaving Laurence none the wiser.

Chapter Twenty-Five

The lady from social services arrived at the house of Ethel Cartwright and Diana Moore to find no one at home. Out in the street two children were walking home from the corner shop singing their own version of the old carol at the top of their lungs:

'Hark the herald angels sing;
Mrs Simpson's pinched our King.
She's been married twice before,

Now she's knocking on Edward's door.'

The front door of Diana's neighbour's house opened and Mrs Royd shouted out of it, 'Oi! Don't be so bloody unpatriotic!' It was a fortuitous moment because it gave Mrs Royd the chance to see the lady from social services and to invite her in for a cup of tea.

Mrs Royd had been shut up in the house all day. Since establishing herself in the street as someone to whom nothing could be told without it being repeated and embellished, no matter how private, she had found herself short of people to talk to. The lady from social services had seemed like a godsend to Mrs Royd, and she ushered her into the parlour where, on the edge of a horse hair settee, little Gracie had cried herself to sleep.

'So sad about Ethel,' Mrs Royd said, as she poured the social worker out a cup of bitter tea.

'Ethel?'

'My neighbour next door, the house you were going to. Mrs Cartwright, you'll know her as, but we were on first name terms. She had such a lot of trouble with her son, and no one can say she didn't do everything to push him back on the straight and narrow, but some people can't be saved. He was one of those. Well, I read in the paper that it's prison for both of them! She helped him burn his clothes, and that's destroyin' evidence, and she lied for him too, and a whole host of other things. I can't see that she did anything wrong herself, she just tried to cover up her son's wrongdoings to give herself time to try to redeem him, but it was spending good time after bad if you ask me. Biscuit? Here you are, take two, you look like you need feeding up. Anyway, where was I? Oh yes, well, her poor daughters, I don't know what they'll do now. Diana, that's the eldest, very pretty girl, very; she works day and night, she does; day and night. She's never here, and that's why I've had to offer to keep an eye on this little one, she's her sister.' Mrs Royd nodded to the little girl with tear-streaked cheeks on the settee. 'Well, I say her sister, they aren't blood relations, halfsisters, you know. Well, anyway, Gracie will have no one to mind her now that her mother is–' Mrs Royd mimed *going to prison* so that the little girl wouldn't hear the offending words in her sleep.

Mrs Royd thought for a moment and wondered if she wouldn't be doing Diana a favour, in the long run, if she freed her from the burden of caring for her younger half-sibling. She was, after all, in the presence of a social worker, and it would be so easy to suggest that a better home could be found for the child. Perhaps Diana, in her relief might even thank Mrs Royd, and the whole episode might cement some life-long friendship of the sort that Mrs Royd had always dreamed of. Yes, she told herself, Diana would be relieved when she heard that she didn't have to worry about her half-sister any more. She began to tell the social worker a dramatic tale of stolen goods, drunken fights, rodent infestations, and a child left alone for hours on end. She enjoyed having an audience so much that she lost sight of where the truth ended and the embellishments began. She listed all the reasons why Gracie couldn't stay at home another minute, as the social worker took notes.

Reenie slumped in the beech wood captain's chair at the head of the kitchen table where her younger sister was painting Christmas cards, and her mother was carefully weighing out ingredients for their Christmas pudding.

'Well, it can't have been that bad if they haven't sacked you.' Katherine swished her brush in a jam jar of water to clean off the red paint before dipping it in the green.

'They just didn't get around to it this time, but it were obvious that they were goin' to. They had to stop the hearin' early because Mrs Roth got called away, but before that, all kinds of people turned up to tell them how troublesome I am.'

'Like who?' Mrs Calder asked.

'Like Bert the engineer who came in to say that I operated a machine that no one had operated yet, and it shot a man in the bum–'

'It what!' Reenie's mother dropped her wooden spoon with a ringing clatter in the earthenware mixing bowl.

'It wasn't as bad as it sounds, it were just Toffee Pennies, and it was because the machine wasn't set up right, but I knew it wasn't set up right. I were just demonstratin' what would happen if you used it wrong.' Reenie folded her arms and slumped further down into her father's usual chair. 'So then the man that we shot came in and said that he wouldn't trust me to run a bath, let alone a production line. Then they brung in a lad from the drawin' office who said I learned off him how to draw machines, which I did, but it were just for fun, I wasn't doin' 'owt bad, and then they brought out all my notes and drawin's, and now I think Peter is tryin' to make out that I'm a spy for Rowntree's or summut, and that all this was a big plot to steal the secret o' Quality Street.'

Reenie's mother sighed. 'And did they say you're to go back?'

'Oh, yes, it's not over yet. The whole ruddy thing will go on for ever at this rate. After every man and his dog had traipsed through to make it sound like I was a great industrial spy, then the police turned up for Diana because they had more questions for her. This made Mrs Roth very animated, and she made them adjourn until Monday and ran off without her cardigan.' Reenie blew her soft auburn fringe out of her eye. 'I hope she catches her death of cold.'

'Well, that's not very nice.' Katherine blotted at a smudge of indigo paint on her sleeve cuff.

'She's not very nice.' Reenie said. 'And nor is that Peter neither. You know I really thought he...' but her voice trailed off as she realised that she didn't know what she had thought, or what grounds she had ever had for thinking it.

'I tell you what,' her mother suggested, 'why don't you come here and stir the pudding and see if you can make it better with a wish?' Mrs Calder knew that the situation could not be improved by anyone in the Calder household, not even Reenie herself, but her first instinct was to comfort her daughter. Sometimes a mother's love could sooth if not help.

Reenie brightened a little and pulled herself out of her father's seat. 'I don't even know what to wish for.'

'Well don't tell us.' Katherine didn't look up from the painstaking work of painting a beak on her robin. 'It won't come true if you go blabbin' it.'

Reenie sighed and took hold of the spoon; the mixture smelled of warm cinnamon and cloves. There was a pleasing zing of citrus peel, and a bottle of her uncle's homemade cherry brandy was already open at her elbow casting a merry fug over the table. It was calming, and as she took the spoon, she thought to herself, *I wish I could do something nice for my family.* As she opened her eyes, she remembered the booty in her coat pocket: three fresh Toffee Pennies. She darted around the kitchen table, being careful not to overturn the cherry brandy bottle, and went to her coat hook by the door. After some rummaging, she announced triumphantly, 'I've got them!'

'Got what?' Mrs Calder draped a peach linen tea towel over the Christmas pudding mixture in her old earthenware bowl and looked curiously at Reenie.

'One each,' Reenie said happily. 'Peter gave me these to look at to give me ideas for the production line, but I can't take them back in now, we'll have to eat them.'

'But isn't that–' Mrs Calder was about to say *theft,* but stopped herself in time.

'These were given to me quite legitimately by a manager, and we are now perfectly at liberty to enjoy them because we don't allow sweets to go out to the shops once they've been in people's

328

hands or pockets. Sorry, they've been in my pocket for a fortnight, I keep forgetting that they're there.'

Kathleen abandoned her Christmas cards and gleefully took a toffee. 'Now *this* is more like what I expected when you got a job at Mackintosh's.' She pulled the creamy toffee disc from the squeaking cellophane wrapper with her front teeth. 'Ooh, it's lovely.'

The sisters were silent for a moment as they contemplated their shared toffee and enjoyed it. This moment, Mrs Calder thought to herself, was all she could have wished for.

Chapter Twenty-Six

'Where is she? Where is she!' Diana had burst into the King Cross police station and was screaming at the Custody Sergeant. 'They took her! They can't take her!'

Sergeant Metcalfe had been expecting this. They had released Diana only two hours earlier, after an evening of exhaustive questioning which had convinced both him and the duty inspector that she was innocent of any involvement in her stepbrother's criminal activities, numerous and long-ranging though they were; it would not have been in the public interest to pursue a prosecution against Diana. Interrupting her during a workplace tribunal hearing, and taking her away for questioning in front of so many of her work colleagues had been unfortunate, but necessary in Sergeant Metcalfe's eyes.

Only once Diana was well on her way back to her stepmother's house (which was now minus her stepmother because Ethel Cartwright was, in fact, in custody) did Sergeant Metcalfe have the chance to read the urgent memorandum that had come in by wire from the clerk at the Social Service Office: '*Grace Cartwright taken into care of the local authority pending further investigations by local authority. Request Sergeant Metcalfe inform sister of child, Diana Moore.*'

Unbeknownst to Diana, the paperwork on her daughter Gracie had been piling up on the desk of a social worker in the Calderdale office. Mrs Roth had formally lodged her concerns about the criminal influences in Gracie's home and also filed a correct and proper application to foster the child until she could apply to the courts for formal, permanent adoption. Gwendoline Vance of the Salvation Army had written to file her concerns about the safety and upbringing of little Gracie, but also to supply a personal recommendation that the child be placed into the care of Frances Roth, who she called a pillar of the local community, and who she claimed had long held a personal interest in the welfare of this particular child. Mrs Vance's acolytes followed suit and sent letters of recommendation for Frances.

The weight of the incoming paperwork became too much for social services to ignore. When word reached them that the stepmother of Diana had been taken into police custody that was the final straw; a representative was sent to check on the child. When the child was found with a neighbour who insisted in her old-fashioned way that Gracie would be better off 'with the parish' and that the sister wasn't a relation by blood anyway and would be 'glad if the social would take her', the child was taken to the Calderdale Social Service department. Here she would await collection and processing, like a parcel returned to the sorting office owned by no one.

Diana returned home to find that her secret child had been stolen from her, and all the demons in hell would have quaked at the ferocity of her rage. Diana left Mrs Royd weeping in her shabby little kitchen and then ran at speed all the way to the Social Service office, adrenaline coursing through her veins like she had never known. The office was closed, and the lights were out, and after she had hammered at their door until her fists bled, she turned and ran to the King Cross police station.

'It's alright, Miss Moore.' Metcalfe tried to calm the hysterical woman that he'd already spent so much of the day with as he led her back into the warm of the station. 'She's quite safe–'

'But she isn't with me!' Diana burst out, looking around her for something to do, or something to throw. 'Where is she? Tell me where she is?'

'We don't know,' Sergeant Metcalfe said, honestly. 'We just know that she was taken by the social while you were here, but we didn't get word until after you'd left or we would have told you and tried to make them wait. I know it's a shock, but–'

'But what? There's no buts; you just have to

find out where she is so that I can get her back and get her back now.'

Metcalfe sympathised with the girl, but his hands were tied. 'We don't have the authority to do that.'

'Why not?'

'Well, she's not a blood relation, is she?' He said it slowly and tactfully, with no hint that he suspected the truth.

Diana was silent for a moment, a feeling like cold water running through her veins and starting at the back of her neck. She wanted to scream to the world that Gracie was her daughter and always had been, but six years of secrecy had made her wary of giving away the truth without first calculating the risks. If she did what she longed to do now, and blurt out all the truth, she would certainly lose her job, and Gracie might be taken away from her anyway because without Tommo and her stepmother there would be no one to pay the rent and no one to care for Gracie while Diana worked. This was the terrifying situation that Diana had always feared and it had finally come to pass. Now she knew that her best chance was to keep her mouth shut until she could come up with a plan. The thought made bile rise in her throat.

'That shouldn't matter,' Diana whispered, her voice strangled with emotion.

Sleepless Parvin, the pencil-moustached newspaper man, leant against the painted brick archway in the outer corner of the room, quietly taking notes. He was so casual in his attitude that he was almost invisible; it was a skill that he had mastered over many years. He had called into the police station late that Friday night looking for a story, but he sensed that there was an injustice too. If there was anything that kept Parvin going in his lonely life it was the belief that investigative journalism could sometimes right wrongs. He listened without appearing to do so, and he remembered everything. To Sleepless this girl had the passion of a mother, not a concerned sibling, and he decided that he would discreetly see what he could find out.

'No, give it to me, we'll buy you a nice doll instead. Or a bear, would you like a bear?' Mrs Roth was trying to wrestle a red ribbon from Gracie's hand, but Gracie had a tight grip and wasn't letting it go. 'Mrs Vance bought you a tambourine, why don't you play with that instead?'

Gracie was resisting and repeating over and over again, 'Not today, thank you, nice lady.'

'Leave her dear,' Gwendoline Vance advised. 'She'll drop it soon enough. Children are always losing things. Now, shall we go on to buy the goose?'

They stood looking around them at the multitude of market stalls selling Christmas goods, and they didn't seem to mind that they were getting in everyone's way by standing three-abreast across the thoroughfare.

'I thought I'd leave the goose a little later–' Mrs Roth said.

'Well, you don't want to leave it too late, dear. They'll all be sold. You want to get one now and hang it up.'

The stall nearest them was a riot of colour in luscious fruits and vegetables that were just begging to be taken home to grace a Christmas table. Beyond that were poultry dealers with fat, feathery birds; a stall with fir trees bound up in tight gauze like green teardrops ready to burst out of their stays. Off in the distance were stalls selling lovingly-made toys, potted preserves, fizzing drinks and all manner of delights. It was among these stalls that Diana had chosen to wander, with her head down and her collar up, passing the long and unhappy hours until the social service office opened on Monday and she could beg to know what had happened to Gracie.

It was two o'clock on Saturday afternoon, and the sun was low and red in the sky, like strawberry cream filling. Perhaps that was why they didn't see her, but Diana saw them.

Frances Roth and Gwendoline Vance had been so excited at the arrival of little Gracie that Gwendoline had gathered some of her friends to her house to sew through the night so that Gracie would have a completely new outfit to wear in the morning. There Gracie stood, to Diana's horror, holding the hand of Frances Roth, and dressed from head to toe in a miniature Salvation Army Uniform, exactly like that of her new foster mother. To see her in the custody of that woman was frightening enough, but the uniform in miniature caused her a special kind of chill, a promise of a life to come.

Diana did not wait for them to see her; she began running immediately. She was not far off, but there were several rows of stalls between her and her daughter, and weaving in and out of them was like running through a maze, but run Diana did. Trying to keep her eyes on her daughter she dodged past cheesemongers and florists, knocked over displays of produce and bumped into people carrying bags of oranges. As she stumbled forward to the place where she had seen Gracie, the girl was gone. She looked around frantically for a glimpse of the direction they had taken and chased up and down nearby lengths of stalls, but they had vanished. Mrs Roth had her daughter, and she was out of sight.

Diana returned to the spot where she had seen Gracie, and there on the ground beside fallen orange crates and tissue paper, was a tattered piece of red ribbon that Diana would have recognised anywhere, but she knew its little owner was long gone.

Chapter Twenty-Seven

'He's in 'ere an awful lot, isn't 'e?' The overalled woman nudged Mrs Grimshaw and pointed in the direction of the supervisor's office, where once again the newspaper reporter was visiting Laurence Johns. The wall of the office that divided it from their factory workroom was nothing but panelled glass, and they could all see him looking with urgent concern at a file of papers that the newspaper man handed him.

'It's none of our business, although I'll admit it looks worrying.' Mrs Grimshaw had fit back into her old working routines so happily that she had to remind herself she wasn't staying much past Christmas, and whatever this was it was none of her business. She was just there to clean up, set up, and wrap up. But still, they did look caught up in something that shocked Mr Johns and animated the journalist. Laurence Johns handed the file back to his friend and waved his hand as though to say that he had read enough, and then they both agreed on something. The journalist shrugged and then Johns waved him out. Mrs Grimshaw looked around and saw that all eyes in the hall were now furtively on the glass-paned office and the two men. It was just like the old days, she thought; none of them could resist wondering at the stories that went on behind closed doors, and like Reenie and so many other women before her, Mrs Grimshaw hoped she'd get to stay on longer than Christmas. This was all too good to miss.

Laurence Johns thought in his office for a few minutes and then decided that he had to send for Diana Moore.

'This isn't about the piece rate investigation; you're not in any further trouble.' Laurence closed his office door behind her and gestured to the chair in front of his desk.

'Well, I didn't think I was. I wouldn't be talking to the Cocoa Manager if I was in trouble, would I? I'd be talking to Personnel or my overlooker.' Diana had a point, Laurence hadn't thought of that, but he had wanted to put her at her ease all the same.

They sat in silence for a moment; Laurence hesitating over where to start, Diana patiently biding her time as always.

'You know, er ... Diana ... may I call you Diana?'

'If it helps. Is there something you're having trouble saying?'

'Well, no ... I...'

'Alright, Mr Johns, let me help you out a bit.' Diana thought she knew where this was going and she wanted to get it over with so that she could go back to work. Work was the only thing that helped her to forget what was happening to her. 'I'm guessing you didn't invite a packing girl here to talk about the cocoa growing people of the African colonies, and I *know* you didn't invite me here to ask me to step out with you in the park come Sunday.' She held his eye as she made that last statement to make sure that they were both clear that she was not a helpless damsel in distress, and that she would not be treated like one. 'I suspect Lady Mackintosh has heard about my stepmother and our situation, as she hears about all the great tragedies among her husband's workforce, and she wants to suggest some charity that might give us blankets or soup, and you have been nominated, as her particular friend, to suggest it to me. Is that about the size of it?'

What Laurence said next, he said gently and quietly, but it took the wind out of Diana, and she was left speechless. 'I know that the little girl that you call your sister is your daughter and that

Frances Roth knows it too, and she's trying to take her from you. I'm sure it's not because she cares about the little girl, but because she cares about winning out over you. I don't know why, and I don't need to know why, but I don't like it.' Laurence waited to see if Diana would try to deny it.

Diana began to wipe away tears that had taken her completely by surprise. She had been ready to say a sarcastic thank you to an offer of inadequate help, and then to get back to work. She felt like this softly spoken young man had seen the real her, and for the first time, she had no defence.

'I haven't told Lady Mackintosh. I haven't told anyone; but yes, Lady Mackintosh is a personal friend, and I do have some influence with the family.' Laurence moved around from behind the desk and drew a chair nearer to sit beside the troubled girl. Laurence reached for her hand, and Diana, shocked at what was happening, let him take it. 'I want you to know that no one here would ever come between a mother and her child. If you were married it would be a different matter because then you would have a husband to provide for you and duty would keep you away from the factory. For the moment you need a wage and we will not prevent you from earning one here merely because you have a child. If it comes to it, I will personally involve Sir Harold, and he will make certain that you can keep your place.'

Diana was grateful, but she was beginning to see that this man was naive and that he offered false hope. 'But I'm a fallen woman, Mr Johns.' She said it as though it was her armour against the world; she knew what she was and it didn't hold any shame for her anymore. 'You've seen the world outside of Halifax, but you forget what people are like here at home. Every overlooker is going to complain that I'll lead the other girls astray and put ideas in their heads, and you'll try your best, but soon enough you'll have to stand aside as they let me go with a reference and a week's pay. It's how things are. You're a kind man, but you can't stop it happening if they know what I've done.'

'I can and I will. You'll need a place to stay where both of you can–'

'You are very, very kind, but I have to do what is best for my daughter. I have to protect her the way that no one ever tried to protect me. I've never told her that I'm her mammy because I couldn't risk it; she'd have told someone at school and then word would have got out. Then I'd have lost my wage and she'd have gone hungry and barefoot, and that was when we had Tommo payin' the rent. If I tell her now that she's my baby what will happen later when we have to be separated? When I can't earn enough to pay someone to mind her, feed and clothe her and keep a roof over our heads? It will break her heart. I'll not do that to her Mr Johns; if it kills me I'll not let her get hurt anymore. I've made my decision,' Diana's voice began to break again with emotion, but she gritted her teeth and composed herself. 'I've decided that Gracie will have the best possible life if she's adopted by a good family. A family where she'll have siblings and toys and a doctor whenever she needs one; and lots and lots of love. I do need your help Mr Johns, and I do want you to speak to Lady Mackintosh for me, but I want you to ask her if she knows of a family who would adopt my daughter and keep her safe.'

Laurence was speechless. He'd never seen such ferocity and vulnerability and love; it was over-whelming. 'You can't... I mean that you shouldn't have to–'

'My mind is made up, Mr Johns. Gracie is a poorly little girl, and she'll never be well as long as she has to live in the places that I'd be able to afford, if I'm lucky enough to afford anywhere at all. If you know a kindly, rich old man who wants a wife to cook for him and doesn't mind her bringing an illegitimate daughter in tow then by all means I'll take him; but I think that only hap-pens in moving pictures, don't you? I need to be realistic, and I need to act fast to get her away from Frances Roth. The Social won't leave her with Frances if Lady Mackintosh recommends a family. They don't have to be rich, they just have to be able to keep her well and happy.'

There was silence again. Laurence noticed that silence with Diana was easy. They could pause and take stock in each other's company and neither one of them was racing to fill the gap with chatter. She was a rarity, and she was right.

'I think you're starting to understand Mr Johns. Sometimes you can't have what you want, and you have to give up the one you love to keep them safe.' Diana stood up to leave, smoothing out the skirt of her white overall to indicate that she was leaving the real her behind and returning to the battleground of work with her mask of apathy. 'I want Lady Mackintosh to think that Gracie's my halfsister. I've given it a lot of thought, and I believe that if her new family think I'm her sister, they'll let me visit and write, but if they know I'm her mother they'll want a clean break. When will you speak to her?'

'Are you sure about this?'

'As sure as I've ever been about anything, Mr Johns.'

'I think you should call me Laurence.'

The nurses were turning on the lights over each patient's bed as the sun over Halifax disappeared behind dark clouds. Heavy snow was on its way.

'You'll need to say your goodbyes to your sister quite soon, it's time for her to get some rest.' The kindly nurse touched Mary on her shoulder to gently encourage her to think about heading home for the night. Privately the nurse didn't like the idea of the girl leaving it any longer or she'd be caught out in a blizzard, but that was none of her business.

Mary nodded to the nurse and then began tidying up the piles of brightly coloured magazines, get well cards, toffee wrappers, and general clutter that had piled up around Bess.

'You can leave all that,' Bess said contentedly. 'I don't mind where it is.'

'I don't want the nurses thinking we're more trouble than anyone else, I'll tidy up if you won't.'

'Oh, but leave me *Harper's Bazaar* where I can reach it, I like looking at the lovely actresses.'

Mary scowled; her sister had no concept of the difficulty of their situation and hadn't once asked after anyone else. If only Reenie were here, she thought to herself; she would know what to do with her. But Reenie was no longer on hand because Mary had chosen to betray her to Mrs Roth for the sake of a job at Mack's. Mary's only consolation was that it would at least give her the chance to take overtime to pay towards the doctor's bills and the cost of the new baby. The consolation was very slight.

At the thought of the baby, Mary decided it was finally time to pluck up the courage to ask the question that had been hanging over her for months. She clutched her tattered little purse to her chest for reassurance and crept like a frightened mouse over to the nurses' station. The nurses were all busy with other things, but now that she had come this far Mary was determined to persevere and quietly ask the question that she had hardly dared to think of until now, let alone ask. 'Excuse me, I'm sorry to bother you, but I wanted to ask about my sister and the baby. Is the baby going to be alright? It wasn't hurt too, was it?'

The nurses looked up from their teacups, patient files, and textbooks. They were puzzled for a moment, but then one of them asked, 'What baby?'

'My sister,' Mary tried to whisper across the counter. 'She's going to have a baby.'

The nurse gestured to her colleagues that she would handle this one, and led Mary off to a quiet corner to explain. The nurses felt sorry for the girl and her sister; they were just kids, really, and it was rotten that they had to manage all this on their own. Where was the mother? They'd seen her once, and then that was only for five minutes to shout over the top of everyone.

'Is it bad news?' Mary felt the cold of anxiety as the nurse paused at the dark, far end of the corridor where they wouldn't be overheard.

'I'm sorry, my love, there wasn't any baby. Your sister Bess wasn't expecting. She was anaemic, is all; it's very common for girls her age.' At the silent look of shock on Mary's face, the nurse continued in a reassuring, confiding tone. 'It quite often takes ladies that way. A change in her diet will do her the power of good, you'll see. We're giving her plenty of oranges, and lots of good food, and she'll be brighter in no time. She's had some nasty knocks, so you'll have to expect her to get better quite slowly, but she will get better.' She paused. 'Your sister isn't married, is she?'

Mary shook her head.

'No, I didn't think so. Bit young for that. Well, there's plenty of time for babies when she's older. For the moment she just needs to get her rest and get well, and I think you need to get your rest too. Now, go on home love, there's a blizzard brewin' outside if I'm not very much mistaken and you don't want to get caught out in that, do you?'

Mary shook her head again. She felt so many things at that moment that all she could really manage was a quiet, but earnest, 'Thank you.' And then she made her way out towards the street without stopping to wish her sister goodnight.

Out in the cold, buffeting air of the street below

343

Mary was suddenly very, very angry. All of this worry about the future had been for nothing, and her sister had been too caught up in her dreamy fantasy world to check the reality of the situation. She'd spent so much time talking about the baby and her plans for it, but she'd never been to see a doctor to check whether or not it really existed. Mary was angry with herself too; she didn't make Bess see a doctor to have the pregnancy confirmed which she could easily have done. Then she had insisted on keeping back some of their wages for savings so that their diet became even worse. She'd convinced all their friends at work to cover for Bess's tiredness, taking all kinds of risks themselves; and worst of all she had hurt Reenie by throwing her to the wolves when she needed a friend the most.

Mary realised that she needed to go and make amends with Reenie because Reenie was one of the best friends she'd ever had. It was Christmas Eve, and if she knew Reenie, she would be stopping late with her beloved machines. If she hurried she might be able to catch her at the factory before she left.

Chapter Twenty-Eight

It was the final day of the disciplinary hearing for Reenie and Diana, and although Reenie was expecting the worst, for Diana the worst had already happened; her eyes were red and puffy with a night of crying, but as she took her place silently in the beautiful boardroom, her face was a mask of indifference.

Reenie was already seated when Peter entered, and for the first time, she caught his eye long enough to poke out her tongue at him. Peter looked mildly surprised, but when he realised that no one else had seen he took his seat and continued to ignore her.

There was some shuffling of papers and moving of seats, but the room finally came to order when Peter was asked to comment on the evidence that he had given thus far.

'I hope that I've demonstrated just what a unique talent Reenie has, and what a valuable asset she is to the firm. She isn't just a remarkably quick worker, she has a prodigious eye for process improvements on the line, and she knows the machines so well that she can predict their breakdowns, and knows exactly the required repairs. The fitters and engineers can plan their working time on shift much more productively in the areas where Reenie is working.'

Reenie was looking at Peter with a face of suspicious confusion. This wasn't headed in the direction that she had thought it would go.

'And do you think you could use her at Norwich?' the director asked.

'I would say that she'd be essential. If the fire at the factory has taught us anything, it's that we need two factories making Quality Street so that we can double our production capacity immediately to meet public demand for the sweets, but also so that if one factory goes down, the other can ramp up production to compensate. Reenie could set up duplicate Quality Street lines in Norwich blindfolded.'

'And should we be concerned about competitor interest?'

'Most definitely. If Reenie were poached by a competitor, she would be an invaluable source of information to them, and it would be devastating to us. Reenie is fiercely loyal to the firm, but she's on a temporary contract. It would be in the best interests of the business to make that permanent and to offer a salary that would encourage her to remain with Mackintosh's.'

'Agreed. Mrs Wilkes I'll let you take care of that.' The director said it so casually that Reenie didn't notice that in those ten words her life had been changed.

The oak-panelled door creaked open behind Peter, and a pale face with a streak of red upon the cheek slipped in. All eyes were on the interloper who looked as though she had been crying, and whose strawberry mark made her look as though she had been crying tears of blood. 'Am I too late?' it came out in a hoarse whisper. 'Am I too late to tell all I know?'

Reenie held her breath. She saw a look pass between Mary and Mrs Roth and she couldn't see what it meant. Had Mary come to give evidence against her?

Mrs Wilkes looked at Mary over her tortoise-shell spectacles and asked, 'Do you have something to add that would make a difference to this case?'

'I do.' Mary clung to the edge of the exquisitely

decorated door as though it were some shield that she could duck behind if the going got tough.

'Then would you take a seat, please?' Mrs Wilkes gestured towards the table before them and fixed her with narrowed eyes.

Mary slid into the chair that the Union shop steward pulled out for her and then launched into what she had to say. 'There was no piece rate racket, we were all just helping my sister because we thought she was a bit poorly. Reenie was very kind, and so was Diana Moore–' Mary corrected herself as she realised that the office managers in their suits wouldn't understand shop floor etiquette, 'I mean Diana. They helped my sister keep up when she couldn't work fast enough, but we all worked well over our maximum rates. Diana said that we should so that the firm got what was owing to them. Their pound of flesh she called it.'

Mrs Wilkes lowered her spectacles to look over them at Mary. 'You said that your sister was unwell. What was the nature of her illness?'

'Oh, don't worry, it wasn't 'owt contagious. We wouldn't let any girl on the line if we thought she had something catching.' There was a pregnant pause, and then Mary mouthed to Mrs Wilkes. 'She was just a bit anaemic.'

Reenie looked happy, but Diana pressed her face slowly into the palms of her hands and took a deep breath; happiness was not Diana's principle emotion.

The director consulted his notes. 'Mrs Wilkes, you had something to add on the false accusations of criminal activity?'

'Yes,' Mrs Wilkes pushed her spectacles back up

347

her nose as though to conclude her business with Mary Norcliffe and turned to speak directly to the director. 'As to the matter of a piece rate racket, or any criminal activity, I think we can dismiss those out of hand. I understand that the police released Miss Moore on Friday evening without a stain on her character and that their investigations have now concluded. These girls have been the victims of a bad sort of young man, and not in any way accomplices of him. In fact, I hear that they have gone to lengths at times to keep him away from them as best they could. I myself saw Diana Moore marching him off the premises at the end of October when he'd managed to gain entry to the factory site. I suggest that they are reinstated with a clean record.'

The director was pleased that the whole affair could be wrapped up quickly; they had far more urgent worries at the time. 'We should, of course, commend Mrs Roth for her diligence in bringing this matter to our attention.' He didn't sound convincing, but waved a hand in the air as though that would help to emphasise his unenthusiastic point. 'Very important to know what's going on among the rank and file; one's not connected enough to the factory floor where it really matters. Good to know that we can rely on our overlookers to be our eyes and ears. Mrs Wilkes, I'm sure you can take over from here.'

'Yes, sir.'

With a general scraping of chairs across thick carpet the disciplinary panel began to disband, leaving Mrs Roth fidgeting and fuming at what she saw to be a monstrous injustice. She gathered up her papers angrily and flounced out with a look that told Diana that their confrontation was not over; there was more to come. 'You're coming with me,' she said to Mary Norcliffe, and Mary followed her.

Reenie looked around her, unsure what had just taken place. 'Are we sacked, or what?' She asked Diana as only she, Diana and Peter were left.

'No, they've promoted you. You get to play with all your machines and no one can tell you how fast or slow to go.' Peter was smiling from ear to ear as he enjoyed the look of confused suspicion on Reenie's freckled face.

Diana sighed. 'He stuck up for you. He told them you were good. You get to stay past Christmas.'

When Reenie realised what this meant she immediately began hitting Peter with her factory mob cap. 'I thought you were gettin' me sacked! You could ha' told me that you hadn't gone bad!'

Peter laughed under the rain of impotent blows and Diana said, 'Would you two just hurry up and get wed.'

Chapter Twenty-Nine

'We were so sorry to hear about what happened to your stepmother and stepbrother. I can't imagine the worry you must have had over it all.' Mrs Hunter sat beside Diana in the courtroom, and was all care and compassion.

Diana felt that she had exchanged one trial for another. She had left her tribunal at Mackintosh's the day before, knowing that she would be in the County Court the following morning, watching as the fate of her daughter was decided. Reenie had been celebrating her success, but Diana was too heartbroken to contemplate anything but the loss of her daughter. She couldn't go home to the empty house straight away, so she had walked around the market again, passing the time among the happy, busy Christmas shoppers who were too concerned with their own lists of things to buy to notice an unhappy girl who felt that she had lost everything in the world.

Diana had found her way to the courtroom expecting to be relegated to a corner on her own; she was always left to fend for herself, so the prospect held no fear for her. She was surprised, then, when she arrived to see Laurence Johns sitting near the front of the court and beckoning her to join him with a friendly wave of his arm and pointed to a seat beside him that he had clearly reserved for Diana. Frances Roth had taken over a corner of the courtroom on the opposite side with her friend and her solicitor. She cast Diana a look of smug triumph and Diana turned away from her with as little show of emotion as she could muster.

'What are you doing here?' Diana asked it politely enough as she slid into a chair at the end of a row. She was not annoyed, but merely puzzled; what would he have to do here of all places?

'I couldn't abandon a friend in need.' Laurence

took her hand and linked her arm through his so that he could squeeze it in a small, reassuring hug. 'You'll need all the moral support you can get today. Now, let me introduce you to the Hunters. I've already told them all about you and they've been asking to meet you.'

To Laurence's left sat a well-dressed couple in their early forties, Diana supposed, who were leaning around to greet her with expectant, kindly smiles. There was another man with them, who from his dress, armful of paperwork, and general lack of interest in her, Diana assumed to be their solicitor. She realised that the room had settled itself into such a way that Frances and her posse were where the prosecution would usually sit, and she and the Hunters were in the position of the defence. It was like her tribunal all over again, but this time the outcome could only ever mean pain for her, there would be no miraculous last-minute reprieve where she would get to keep her child. The best she could hope was that Frances Roth would leave dissatisfied.

'Mr and Mrs Hunter share a mutual friend with Lady Mackintosh.' Laurence had explained all of this to Diana before, but he thought it might be reassuring to remind her. 'They have children of their own, but they wanted to adopt a little girl. Here, you swap places with me and then you can sit next to Mrs Hunter and get to know her properly.' Laurence stood up and guided Diana gently round into his place.

Diana felt like she was sleepwalking. The Hunters were shaking her hand and showing her photos of their other children, and the garden

351

Gracie would be able to play in. Mrs Hunter was smartly dressed in an expensive-looking orchid pink suit with an unashamedly mis-matching reticule that appeared to have been made for her with love by an enthusiastic but inexpert child. She opened it to produce reams of drawings and carefully scrawled letters addressed to Gracie from her children in which they told her how glad they would be to have her as their new baby sister and listed all of the toys they had, all of which they said Gracie could share to her heart's content.

Diana was beginning to feel faint. Her eyes were hollow with lack of sleep and crying, she longed to both postpone this and to get it over with. The Hunters were kind and thoughtful and perfect, but she couldn't take in another word they said. Diana looked dazed and then turned to Laurence and asked, 'Will there be a judge? Can I speak to the judge? Can I speak to him in private now?'

Laurence looked concerned but nodded. He got up and spoke to the clerk of the court who understood and summoned Diana to follow him to a doorway at the front of the court, beneath a large royal coat of arms inscribed with more words that Diana couldn't read.

'She shouldn't have a say in it if she's not a blood relative.' Mrs Roth was arguing with the solicitor sitting next to her who had been hired by Mrs Vance to help them proceed with the application to adopt Gracie. The overworked, hen-pecked legal man was only too aware that this comment wasn't really intended for him, but had been spoken loudly enough for all the court to hear.

Diana didn't respond or even look around; her mask of indifference was back in place; she steeled herself to keep going without feeling it all, just for a few moments more. She walked through the centre of the court, past the bench, and into the Judge's room as though it were a tiresome affair. The Judge and the clerk of the court alone waited to speak with her in their imposing black robes ready to enter the court and begin the work that could never be undone. The room was a surprise to Diana; it was like a private office for the Judge. She had never imagined that he might need a space away from the court where some private work would be conducted like any mortal man. The room had the same sienna brown wood panels around the walls that the courtroom did, but where the courtroom intimidated Diana this little space had a feeling of mundane office duties that made her feel as though she had a right to speak.

'My clerk tells me that you have some information relevant to this case, Miss Moore.' The judge was a small, owl-like man, whose face Diana found difficult to read. 'I must warn you that although I understand that you have lived with the child, you do not have any of the privileges of–'

'I'm her mother.' She produced the folded birth certificate from the inside pocket of her jacket and laid it neatly on the desk between them.

'Ah.' The judge sat back in his chair and connected the tips of his forefingers like the steeple of a church. 'That puts a different light on the matter. And what brings you here today, Madam?'

The clerk of the court pulled out a chair on the

other side of the judge's desk, and Diana lowered herself gracefully into it. She paused to decide where to begin and then said, 'I never really expected to be able to keep my daughter as long as I have. I was lucky because my stepmother has always been a woman of strong maternal instincts, and although those instincts have led her to help a son who has got them both sent to prison, those instincts also compelled her to help me when I most needed help. She agreed to pretend that my daughter was hers, even though our relationship was slight. My stepmother lived with my late father, but they were never married, and in truth, she had no duty to me, but she's a kind woman, and she did more than I can ever repay.

'As soon as Gracie was weaned I went back to work, and she cared for the child, pretending she were hers and that she'd had her out o' wedlock; she said at her age she had no reputation to lose. The money I earned was only just enough to feed us, and we were reliant on her son for rent and other monies. Now that they're both facing long prison sentences I know that I will not have the resources to be able to keep my daughter any more. It is simply not going to be possible.'

'You have not touched on the topic of paternity.' Again the owl-like look of the judge made Diana unsure whether this was a question or a criticism, but she told herself that she did not and could not care, and went on:

'Gracie's father was a young man I knew at school. Sadly he was killed in the accident which led my stepmother and stepbrother to be arrested. He did not acknowledge our daughter on paper for reasons that don't matter now. His name was Stewart Edwards and his family will never be of any material help.'

The clerk of the court felt compassion for Diana and he wanted to reach out and squeeze her hand in reassurance. Instead he settled for offering her a glass of water from the walnut table behind where the judge sat.

'Frances Roth,' Diana continued, 'was in my class at school. I know her very well indeed.'

'And you would like to recommend her to the court as an adoptive parent?' The judge said it casually, almost disinterestedly, as he leafed through the papers on his desk.

'No. I would rather die than see my daughter in the hands of that woman for a moment longer.'

The judge looked up and raised a thick eyebrow. 'You wish to lodge an objection to the placement of the child with Frances Roth?'

'I do. She knows that Grace is my child and she hasn't tried to take her for Gracie's own good; she's tried to take her as an act of revenge on me. I'll admit that I was cruel to her when we were children, and I regret it. But she has repaid all that cruelty sevenfold. She is now my overlooker at my place of work, and I can't begin to describe how wicked she is.'

The judge had in front of him the years and years of paperwork generated by Frances Roth's complaints to the local authority about the care of the child in the Cartwright home, but it might be either the work of a genuinely interested party or a mischievous harridan. He made no comment on Diana's assessment of Frances Roth's character. 'Are you handing your child over to the local authority for adoption?'

'Yes.'

'You understand that once you have given her over to the local authority as *guardian ad litem* you will have no further power to influence her ultimate destiny? It will be for the court to decide whom is best placed to become her adoptive parent or parents.'

Diana had feared this. She had done her best to secure an alternative family for Gracie, but there was still a chance that the court would decide to place her with Frances Roth. After all, Frances had submitted her application first, and she was already Gracie's foster parent. This felt like a gamble, but if she chose to withdraw her consent for the adoption, she risked having Gracie forcibly taken from her at another time. By then this nice family, who were ready to take her daughter, might no longer be in a position to give her a home. It was now or never, and she didn't like the odds, but she had to hope for the best.

'I know.' Diana looked down at her work-worn hands. 'I know that I can't tell you who would be best for her. I've thought about this, and I know what I must do, and I just hope and pray that it works out for the best. I asked to speak to you to explain that my daughter doesn't know. I don't want her to know that I'm her mother because I don't want her to have the distress of losing a second mother after she's lost a first. Besides, if everyone thinks I'm her sister she might be allowed to write to me sometimes, and I might be allowed to send her cards, and that would keep me going, I think.' Diana reached into the pocket of her thin jacket, pulled out a clean, pressed white handkerchief, and opened it to produce a tattered, but carefully washed, red ribbon. 'This is Gracie's, and it's very precious to her. Can you make sure that she gets it back? If she is handed over to Frances Roth, I shan't get the opportunity to give it her, but I thought you could.'

The judge gestured to the court clerk to take the ribbon but made no reference to it. 'If that is all, madam, we will return to the courtroom.' He rose, and so did Diana.

Diana went back to her place and looked up at the judge with a pain in her heart unlike any she had ever known.

'Miss Roth, can you confirm your date of birth please.' The judge looked over his half-moon glasses at her with his beady eyes, and then glanced back to a sheet of foolscap that he had taken from the file in front of him.

Frances Roth beamed a smile of triumph which stabbed at Diana's heart; this was the beginning of the formalities that would make Gracie her daughter; it was all over. 'January 1st, 1910.'

'Yes, as I thought.' The judge was impassive. 'I'm sorry to inform you, Miss Roth, that under the terms of the Adoption Act 1927 you cannot ever be awarded adoptive custody of the child known as Grace Cartwright. The law requires all adoptive parents be at least twenty-one years older than the adoptive child; you are too young; in this case, by one year and three months.'

Diana sank back into her chair as though she'd had the wind knocked out of her; Gracie was safe

357

from Frances. Gracie was safe for ever; there would never be a time when Frances Roth could adopt her because the age gap would always be too small. It was a crumb of comfort in a situation where she knew that she would be losing any chance of keeping her child.

'Mr and Mrs Hunter,' the judge addressed the couple who Lady Mackintosh had helped to find. 'Your application to adopt the child known as Gracè Cartwright has been approved by this court.'

The contrast between the happiness of the Hunters and the anger of Frances Roth could not have been greater. Gwendoline Vance was quick to turn on the solicitor to demand that he object, but he was busy gathering up his papers ready to scurry away. The last thing he wanted was for anyone to ask why he hadn't noticed the discrepancy in their ages before they'd filed the application.

'Miss Roth,' the judge called out across the clamour of the court. 'Approach the bench if you please.'

Frances Roth looked around her with sharp eyes, as though to assess whether there might be some merit in pressing her case, and scurried suspiciously forward to hear what the judge had to say.

He had perfected the art of speaking in a tone that could not be overheard by the rest of the court, but was clear as crystal to the ear in front of him. 'I believe you have some information about the true parentage of the child.'

Mrs Roth's eyes lit up as, for a moment, she thought that she might be able to change the outcome of the day by revealing Diana's secret. She did not have the opportunity to respond, however, because the judge went on:

'Under the terms of the 1927 act, this child's past is now sealed. All documents relating to her parentage are the property of the local authority and will be kept secret by the local authority. Anyone who shares information relating to the child's parentage will be committing an offence under the law and will have to come here to answer to me. Is this clear?'

She took in a startled breath as she processed the information, and then pursed her lips in silence.

The judge did not feel the need to say any more, he left Frances Roth clutching the polished wooden rail around his bench, and he walked away towards the happy new parents, carefully unfolding a neatly pressed handkerchief that he had collected from the clerk of the court.

The Hunters were shaking Diana's hand over and over again. 'Oh I'm so glad she has a big sister,' Mrs Hunter kept saying. 'I'm so glad. You must come and see her. You must come to us every Sunday that you can, will you promise?' Diana nodded, her face pale with shock.

The judge approached and shook Mr Hunter's hand. 'This young lady wanted you to pass this ribbon on to her sister and gave it to my clerk in case she didn't have the opportunity of presenting it to the child's new parents herself. It seems the child is most attached to it.'

'Of course,' Mr Hunter said, 'of course. We'll make sure she has it right away. We were just saying how glad we were that the little girl has an older sister.'

'Ah yes,' the judge said sagely, looking at Diana with shrewd eyes over half-moon spectacles. 'I have been very impressed with her. I think she will be a fine influence on the child.'

It was the twenty-third of December and Diana had no Christmas chores to complete. Wherever she went, people seemed to be bustling about trying to tick one last item off their list of things to do before they could settle down to their well-earned Christmas break. There was only one thing Diana had left to do, and that was visit her stepbrother in custody. Her stepmother had been transferred to a women's facility too far away for Diana to reach in the snow, but Diana had written her a long letter and hoped to God that the woman wasn't suffering as much as she believed she would be.

Tommo had been kept on remand in Halifax, and his trial would be early in the new year. They both knew that he was looking at a long sentence and neither of them felt the need to waste the short time they had in the stark prison visit cell by speculating over it.

Diana was blunt. 'Have they told you that Stewart is dead?'

Tommo looked as though his stepsister had crossed a line before they'd even begun but then he rubbed the bridge of his eyes with cuffed hands and said, 'Yeh. Yeh, they told me. I hadn't realised; not at the time. I just thought...' His voice trailed away; he obviously didn't know what he'd thought.

'They can't find his dad to tell him, so not everyone knows. The police have to tell his family before the papers can print his name. Frances Roth still thinks he's alive.'

'She can't do.' Tommo was subdued and it was strange to see. 'Everyone must know by now. It'll be all over town.'

'She's heard the rumours, but until she sees it in print she doesn't have to believe it.'

'Poor old girl. She's never been right since he stood her up.'

'Poor old girl nothing. She tried to have Gracie taken off me by the social so that she could be a happy family with Stewart when he got back from wherever she thinks he's swanned off to.'

'Where's the kid?' Tommo sat up at the suggestion that anyone would try to lay a finger on Gracie. 'Why didn't you bring her to see me?'

Diana snorted. 'Why do you want to see her all of a sudden?' Tommo gave Diana a look of reproach but bit his tongue. 'You won't be seeing any more of Gracie. I arranged for her to be adopted by a family who–'

Tommo was incensed. 'You did what?' He nearly rose in his chair, but then looking over his shoulder at the prison officer seated in the doorway behind him, reluctantly settled down.

'It's for her own good. Ethel can't look after her anymore, and–'

'It wasn't Ethel that was looking after her! Stewart used to get her from school, and him and me were both risking our necks to make enough money to make sure that you two were never

361

hungry. It was the boys who were looking after her.'

Diana was taken aback momentarily; Stewart and her stepbrother had been worse than useless, she knew that, but every new revelation made her question her own judgement and wonder if she'd been wrong all along to think that it was her against the world, against her stepbrother, against everyone. She had to keep reminding herself of the wrong that Stewart and Tommo had done over the years, the drunken fights in the house, the emotional blackmail, the missed birthdays, the stolen goods piled up in the kitchen risking all their necks. If her father were there he'd have wanted her to fight her corner.

'Oh, don't give me that. You could both have earned an honest living if you'd wanted to. You liked being the grand mobster of gangland. If my father had lived–'

'You think I don't miss my stepdad?' Tommo wasn't teasing now, he was raw, and he was honest. 'He was your dad, but he was my stepdad; you always seem to forget that one, don't you when you're wallowing in self-pity.'

Tommo's words took her by surprise; her father had lived with Ethel, but he'd never married her. She'd never thought about how Tommo felt towards her father, it had never occurred to her all these years that Tommo had thought of him as a father figure. His claim on her own dad made her angry and she snapped at him. 'He hated you; he thought you were ridiculous.' Diana regretted the words as soon as she'd spat them out.

Tommo raised an eyebrow as though to acknowledge a glancing blow. 'No, sis, he just didn't like the stuff I did sometimes, but we respected each other, and I'd have made him proud if he'd lived–'

Diana could feel hysteria rising in her chest. She had been prepared for Tommo's scorn, and for his melodramatic recriminations, but not for him to be human, and not for him to bring her dad into it. 'You think what you've done would have made him proud?'

'No, of course I bloody don't, my best friend is dead, my mother's gonna serve two years hard labour and when I get out, I'm gonna have to work twice as hard to pay back the men in Leeds whose car I wrecked. But then I'm only having to do all this because he didn't live. If he'd lived, I'd have done something like drive a fruit and veg van, and I'd have done everything I could to make him proud. You don't get it, do you? Once he was gone, you just disappeared. You were still walking around, but you'd gone somewhere else in your head. We had to find another house, work out what to do with the baby, keep you both alive. God, Diana, you didn't speak for a whole month! We did all this so you could keep my niece and keep your precious job. You didn't want anything to do with Stewart anymore. I told him to keep his distance for a bit, see if you came round, and if you didn't, he'd just have to let you go your own way.'

There was silence; the old stalemate. Diana shuffled uncomfortably in her chair; her eyes turned away from her stepbrother. 'I had to give her up.' Diana's tone had changed. She was almost pleading; pleading with the only kind of brother she'd ever had to reassure her that she'd done the right thing. 'She needed to be with people who could look after her. She's been poorly too long.'

Tommo seemed to think about it for a moment and then shrugged. 'When I get out I'm taking her back off them because she's my niece.'

Diana could see that he meant it and was almost sorry for him; like Frances Roth he too was in a kind of denial. As she got up to leave she said to him very calmly, 'It's done, and not you or anyone else can undo it. You're no blood relation and you're no good for her. Just because you paid for things doesn't mean you did the right thing. You helped put a roof over our heads, but you're also the reason we lost everything. I'm not telling you where she is. No one is ever going to tell you where she is.'

Chapter Thirty

Mary had accepted a sound telling-off from Mrs Roth after she had come to her friend's aid at the disciplinary hearing, and several more tellings-off since; but to Mary's profound relief she had not lost her job. It was Christmas Eve and try as she might Mary still hadn't been able to find Reenie at work to apologise to her. She had been to visit her sister again in St. Luke's, and now she wanted to go back down to Mack's one last time before the Christmas break to see if she could find her friend.

When Mary arrived at the factory, she knew that the best way to check if Reenie had already left for Christmas was to head straight to the stables. Ruffian would be waiting for her if she was still here, but which stables? Would he be at the factory or the pub? Mary decided to run to the factory first; knowing Reenie, she'd probably put Ruffian to work while she was on the production line. As Mary rounded the corner, she caught Peter's eye just as he caught hers. He was walking alongside Reenie who was talking away, and Mary could have sworn he had been reaching out about to take Reenie's hand, but his dropped when they were face-to-face with Mary.

The wind whistled around the almost deserted goods yard, blowing dustings of snow from the rooftop of the factory stables and carrying it in eddies and whorls around the former friends who stood frozen in anxious silence looking at each other. Mary was waiting for Reenie to speak first, a show of penitence on her part for all that she had put Reenie through, but Reenie was holding her breath and Mary couldn't read her expression.

Mary Coldheart decided that she couldn't be cold-hearted any longer. Risking the rejection that she knew she deserved she ran to Reenie, threw her arms around her and hugged her. 'I'm sorry, Reenie, I'm so, so sorry.'

Reenie hugged her back and rubbed her shoulder. 'You're a silly one sometimes, Mary Norcliffe, but you're my silly one and I've missed you.' Reenie pulled away to look Mary directly in the eye. 'I've been worried about you too, though. How are you?' It was an earnest question; Reenie knew her too well.

'There's–' she was about to speak but then looked at Peter, wondering if he already knew.

Peter took the hint and said, 'I'll go and get your horse,' before trudging off into the stables, hands balled in his pockets against the cold.

'What is it, Mary?' Reenie asked, 'Are you alright?'

'How can you still care about me so much after everything that I put you through?'

Reenie shrugged. 'Sheer bloody-mindedness? I don't know; I just knew you were bein' a fool because you care about your sister. It wasn't because you wanted to be mean, it was because you were stuck between the devil and the deep blue sea. You had your sister's baby to think about, and that baby should always come first.'

'There is no baby.' Mary felt a wave of relief and remorse all at the same time; she had been so worried about it that she had done things she would never forgive herself for.

'Oh, Mary, I'm so sorry. Was it the crash, did she–?'

'No.' Mary's eyes stung with tears, and she reached into her pocket for a handkerchief. 'There was never any baby. I've just come from the hospital; the nurse said that Bess made a mistake. We both did. We should have taken her to see a doctor, but we were so sure because she was so weak.'

Reenie looked frightened. 'Was something else the matter? Something worse? She was so weak...' her words trailed off as she thought of the other possible more sinister reasons for Bess's inability to keep up.

'Anaemia. Just anaemia. They're giving her oranges.'

Reenie put a hand to her chest and breathed a sigh of relief. 'Well, that's one load off our minds. Bloody hell, though. You've been through it, haven't you? I can't believe how long you carried all that worry on your own.'

'But I should never have taken it all out on you; I should never have–'

'Hey,' Reenie squeezed her friend's arm affectionately and softened her voice to soothe her. 'All that's forgotten, it can't hurt us now.' She broached the question that she had been worrying about. 'How is she now? I went to see her yesterday, and she was ever so happy. But I was worried for her. Will she be alright?'

'They said she has to stay while her bones heal, but she'll be reet.'

'Well then!' Reenie squeaked in delight. 'We can both have a happy Christmas, can't we?' She tried to encourage her friend, but something was still weighing Mary down. 'Can't we? Mary, there's something else wrong, isn't there?'

'What do I do with her, Reenie? She'll never get a job back here at the factory, and I need to keep an eye on her to make sure she doesn't go off getting herself into trouble. I just don't know what to do.'

'Well, funny you should mention that because I've been talking to Mrs Parish the Landlady at The Old Cock and Oak and we've had a bit of an idea.'

'We can't get her doing bar work; she's not old enough.'

'Hear me out.' Reenie was enjoying this, it was like the big reveal of a conjurer producing a rabbit from a hat. 'She wouldn't be doing bar work, she'd be waiting on the old Oak Room upstairs where all the private parties are. Donna would keep an eye on her, and the private parties are all old married fellas, like the Rotarians and the Worshipful Ale Tasters so they'd all keep an eye on her too. It's alright money, and Donna says she can hang on until April, and if Bess is better, she can start then. What do you think?'

Mary didn't answer, she just hugged her friend and choked back a sob. She didn't feel like she deserved such a good Christmas, but she felt Reenie did.

A familiar neigh caught their attention; Peter was returning with Ruffian in tow, although Ruffian didn't appear to like being led by someone who wasn't Reenie and would stop still every so often in a protest.

'I should go and help him,' Reenie said. 'He knows a lot of things, but he's daft with horses.'

'Thank you, Reenie.' Mary dabbed at her eyes with her scrunched-up handkerchief and sniffed.

'Don't you worry, love. I promise you everything will work out fine. Have a happy Christmas, and don't forget to enjoy yourself.'

Peter and Reenie bade their farewells to Mary who plodded up the hill in the direction of her mother's little one-up-one-down which would feel empty this year without Bess.

'Are you staying in Halifax?' Peter asked her.

'Eck as like. I'm away home.' Reenie gave Ruffian a rub on his nose out of habit.

'But the snow.' Peter was frowning at the dark clouds that were gathering overhead.

'I wouldn't worry, I'm headed out east, and those will blow over west. I don't want to stay in Halifax on Christmas Eve, I'm going back to the farm. Ruffian'll see me right.'

Peter took a deep breath and lowered his voice before saying clearly and calmly, 'Can I walk you home?'

Reenie was speechless for a moment. 'But won't you miss the last train to Norwich? Don't you need to get home to your family for Christmas?'

'No trains. The snow.' Peter shrugged it off as though he didn't mind missing Christmas with the McKenzie clan.

'Alright then. If you're sure you don't mind. I mean, it's a fair few miles.'

'Finally!'

Reenie laughed at Peter's unexpected vehemence. 'What do you mean *"Finally"?*'

'I have been asking to walk you home for three months now!'

Reenie giggled because she couldn't understand why her friend was so animated about it. 'But I never needed you to walk me home.'

'That,' said Peter, with uncharacteristic emphasis, 'is not why I have been asking.'

The truth dawned on Reenie, and her eyes brightened with surprise, and she grinned.

Chapter Thirty-One

'What if she's got lost and she needs our help?' Reenie's sister Kathleen was determined to believe that Reenie would still try to come home on Christmas Eve, despite the snow.

'I've told you, she won't have tried to come back at night in this weather, she'll be hiding out at the The Old Cock and Oak with Ruffian until it's light; there's no use watching at that window, you won't see her.' Reenie's mother was trying not to show the worry she too was feeling; if anyone was mule-fool enough to try and come out in knee-deep snow drifts, it was her Reenie. But she told herself that she had the horse with her, and if she had set off, he'd see her home safely, or dig his hooves in and make her turn around and go back to the pub.

Kathleen scowled at her mother and then went back to looking out through their faded crimson curtains at falling snowflakes so large they looked like goose feathers. It was dark, and the heavy, gentle snowfall made it darker, but they'd left a storm lantern alight over the porch, and by its glow, she watched with her heart in her mouth for her absent sister.

'Maybe I should go out, love; just to check.' Mr Calder hovered in the doorway. He knew his wife's bravado, and he knew Reenie; he really should go out to be certain she wasn't on the road and having trouble with the horse.

'Don't you dare! I've got enough to worry about without you playing silly buggers in the snow. She's got the horse; what have you got? The last thing we need is you getting lost in a blizzard–'

'It's not a blizzard, woman, it's fallin' straight down, and there's not a gust of wind.'

'I don't care if it's falling upwards; you're not going out in it without the 'orse, and that's final. Reenie will be tucked up at the pub or bunkin' in with one of the girls from work. She won't have tried to get home in this weather. I'll say this for my Reenie: she's no fool.'

Mr Calder looked at his wife, and his look said, *are we talking about the same Reenie?*

'If I'd known she wasn't gonna bring us a tree in time for Christmas I'd have got one m'self.' Young John was looking gloomily into the grate of the parlour range which glowed with wood that his older sister had scavenged from the stable yard of The Old Cock and Oak, and had held back from the scrap men.

Kathleen opened her mouth to argue. 'How can you be so bloody selfish–'

'Don't start!' Their mother quelled them with a look. There was an uneasy silence in the cosy parlour. John looked longingly at the box of Christmas tree decorations that waited on the table for a tree to hang upon, while their marmalade cat tugged at a string of paper chains on the wall with a white paw. A pot of tea steamed on the sideboard where a tealight kept it warm and stewed the leaves until it was strong enough to stain a fence. Kathleen wriggled on the soft, tatty cushions of the battered window seat, and released a leg that had gone numb with pins and needles.

'Come away from there; there's no use watching, you'll only put us all on edge. Come and sit at the table, I've got a spot of tea for you. John, move those decorations now, you can put them up on a branch tomorrow when it's light enough to go out and get one.' Reenie's mother sighed; both children were in a sulk, and she herself felt like crying and going to bed. 'Kathleen? Did you hear me?'

'I'm not movin'.'

'If you leave those curtains open you're just lettin' more cold in. We'll be nithered–'

'She's here!' Kathleen leapt up from her place and ran to the door; the rest of her family froze in surprise. 'She's here!' Kathleen flung the door open, heedless of the fat snowflakes falling on the stone-paved parlour floor. 'Reenie! Reenie!' she shouted into the night. 'It's Christmas! It's Christmas!'

'I know!' shouted back a heavily wrapped figure in tough boots that had been lashed to tennis rackets, leading a nearly toothless horse, and accompanied by a lad who carried a tree. 'What d'you think I'm here for?'

'Reenie Calder! What do you think you're playing at coming out on a night like this!' At the sight of her daughter the tears that Mrs Calder had been holding back all evening suddenly began to fall.

Reenie reached the front porch. 'I do apologise. I'll turn round and go back again, shall I? Peter,

372

welcome to the Calder household. Mother, this is Peter MacKenzie; he's been trying to walk me home safely every time he's seen me for God-knows how long, and I decided tonight to let him because he hasn't got anywhere to go for Christmas, do you mind if he stays?'

'Well, I...' Mrs Calder faltered as she worried about the quantity and quality of the hospitality they could offer a lad who clearly deserved the best. She was so grateful that he'd kept their daughter safe and brought her home to them on Christmas Eve in a blizzard.

'If that tree's for us Peter can have my bed!' John piped up from behind them.

'No one would want your bed, it's sunk in the middle,' Kathleen was quick to remind her brother. 'And he'll not be sharing with Reenie and me.' She turned and spoke confidingly to the young man who was lowering the tree. 'Reenie kicks in her sleep.'

'I'll kick you in a minute if you keep telling all about me to our visitor.' Reenie was fiddling with something on the horse's back. 'Give us a hand with this so we can get inside.'

Mr Calder stepped into action. 'Why didn't you put the tree on the 'orse?'

'Because the 'orse is carrying the 'amper.'

'What 'amper?' Mrs Calder was trying to herd her family, the newcomer, and a tree into her parlour kitchen.

'It's a Christmas hamper, Mrs Calder.' Peter kicked his boots, which were also lashed to tennis rackets, against the doorframe to shake off the snow before he crossed the threshold. 'All the employees got one from Mackintosh's; it's a hamper of Christmas food to thank Reenie for all her work on the Quality Street line.'

'Why have you got tennis rackets on your shoes?' Young Kathleen was less interested in the food they'd brought with them than the strange footgear they were both wearing.

'Because, nosy, it makes it easier to walk on snow. It was Peter's idea; we picked them up from Sandow's gymnasium on the way here. Peter is a member, so he's allowed to take them.'

'They're very old.' Peter seemed apologetic. 'No one will miss them.'

'Alright, that's enough chat.' Mrs Calder was wiping her eyes with her apron. 'In you come, all of you. Reenie, what are you doing with that 'orse; is he coming in, or staying out?'

Mr Calder was feeling charitable to the old nag for bringing his daughter safely home. 'Oh, let him in; it's Christmas and he's family too. He can lie by the fire like he did when he was a foal, the parlour's big enough.'

'I'm not sure that's such a good idea, dad. Continence is no longer one of his virtues.'

Mr Calder looked as though he was mulling over potential solutions to that problem, but Reenie shook her head with a knowing look. 'Alright,' Mr Calder took the rope that served as Ruffian's bridle, 'You lot go in and get warm, I'll settle the horse into the barn for the night. He's earned his hot mash and his rub down.'

'Don't you go out like that, you'll ruin those slippers, and you'll catch your death of cold–'

Mr Calder nodded through his wife's nagging.

374

'Yes, dear. I'll put my boots on, don't you worry … yes, yes, and a coat and hat…'

While John and Kathleen wrestled the tree into the parlour, Reenie and Peter followed with the over-stuffed hamper which contained both Reenie's and Peter's Christmas gifts from the firm. Reenie plonked the hamper down on the kitchen table, sending the marmalade cat scarpering.

'What's in it?' John's eyes were bigger than his stomach at that moment, and he was eager to see everything that his sister had brought in.

'Aren't you going to say thank you to your sister for bringing you that Christmas tree all this way in the snow?' Mrs Calder tutted at young John who apologised, and thanked both Reenie and Peter profusely. 'Now then, Peter, can I get you a nice hot cup of tea?'

'Yes, thank you, just a very weak one for me.'

Reenie smirked to herself, knowing that her mother's tea would be strong enough to dissolve a teaspoon. 'Mother, perhaps you'd like to brew some of this.' She held up a package with elegant gold lettering and a satisfying crackle to the paper. 'In our hampers, they gave us *coffee*.'

Mrs Calder cooed with delight. 'Ooh, now aren't we posh? Coffee! Well, I never. Let me smell it.' Mrs Calder took the packet and took in a deep breath. 'Oh now that's wonderful, it really is. John, Kathleen, come here and smell this; this is what posh people's houses smell of.'

'And that's not all.' Reenie began producing one treasure after another with the flourish of a conjurer. 'We have a whole cured ham–'

'A *whole* ham?' John was giddy with delight.

'Yes, a whole ham. And...' Reenie paused for effect. 'Another whole cured ham!'

There was a ripple of applause and cheers from her younger siblings, and her father came back in to join them.

'Dad, you'll like this, we have a Dundee cake ... and another Dundee cake.'

'My goodness, and I thought Ruffian was lucky with his oats!'

'That's not all; we've got water biscuits, and ginger beer, and lime cordial, and two kinds of preserves, and stilton cheese, and drinking cocoa, and all kinds of things!'

'What kinds of things?' Young John asked earnestly. 'I want to know all the things.'

'There's Caley's Christmas crackers...'

'Real Christmas crackers? The kind with hats and a bang?'

'Yes, *real* Christmas crackers, *with* hats, *and* a bang. But best of all, better than two cured hams, two preserves; boxes of Christmas crackers, *with* hats and a bang, better than all of that, I have for you ... wait for it,' Reenie reached into the hamper and lifted out the prize tin, 'Mackintosh's ... celebrated ... *Quality Street!*' and she pulled off the lid with a flourish to reveal a sparkling jewel-chest of delights, all ringed round with paper bunting.

'Oh, it's Christmas, Reenie, it's Christmas!' Her sister jumped up and down on the spot, unable to contain her glee.

'It's a fact I'm well aware of. Now, shall we get the tree up? I want to have a cup of coffee, get the tree up, and then go to sleep for three days.'

Reenie had hung up her coat and Peter's and was now sitting on the floor pulling off her boots.

'Mr MacKenzie?' Reenie's mother almost curtsied to the young visitor, but to Reenie's relief, she appeared to stop herself just in time.

'Please, call me Peter.' Peter was warming himself by the parlour range until he was given permission to take off his boots in company.

'Oh,' Mrs Calder sounded both pleased and surprised. 'That's very nice; Peter it is. Peter, you shall have our room and my husband and I will spend the night down here in the armchairs–'

'Oh no! No, I wouldn't hear of it, I couldn't possibly turn you both out of your bed. I'll be quite happy down here in a chair, honestly.'

'Wouldn't he be warmer down here, though Mam?' Young John cut through the niceties with bald pragmatism. 'This here's the only fire in the house.'

After some polite awkwardness, it was agreed that Peter, having travelled so far in the snow, would be better off in an armchair by the parlour fire to ward off pneumonia and other cold-related ailments. Reenie's mother went off to find blankets and a spare pair of her husband's pyjamas, privately wishing to herself he had some that were not frayed at the collar. Reenie drank and relished her hot cup of coffee while her siblings dressed the tree in Christmas decorations that were so old and wonderful they were practically family heirlooms. John showed off the holly decorations and paper chains that he had made to dress the room with – in the absence of the lately arrived tree, which was a sore point, and a joy to him, in equal measure. Kathleen asked if Peter was Reenie's sweetheart, and at that moment her mother loudly decided that it was time to send everyone to bed because it was late, and Father Christmas wouldn't bring them anything if they were awake when he arrived.

Reluctantly the whole family made their way up the wooden hill to bed, leaving only Reenie behind to finish her coffee by the fire.

'There's only two stockings on the mantle.' Peter sat on the kitchen bench beside Reenie, steam rising from the wet clothes he was still wearing. He would change into Mr Calder's kindly loaned pyjamas once Reenie had gone.

'That's a good point.' Reenie started pulling one of her wet socks off, and then the other, before hanging them on the mantle with the help of a brass ornament. 'I must put mine up if I want Santa to leave me an orange.'

Peter guffawed with laughter. 'Do you not care who sees your feet?'

'We're not Victorians, Peter, I can't go dying of pneumonia just to keep you from seeing my ankles. Is that why you're still wearing your wet boots? Are you trying to be polite, or summat?'

'Well your mother didn't invite me to take them off, so I kept them on.'

'Oh, give over. You'll catch your death with wet feet. Pass one here.' Reenie didn't wait for Peter to move but leant across him and pulled at his laces while he tried to fight her off. He then pulled at the boot, which came away only with a tug of war by both of them. Once she'd got both boots she set them on the range top to dry out.

'And peel your socks off and give them here.'

'I can't take my socks off as well; there's a limit, you know.'

Reenie rolled her eyes. 'Do you want Santa to leave you a satsuma and a drum? If you don't leave him your socks, you won't even get coal.'

Peter relented and handed over his snow-sodden socks to be hung over the mantle to dry.

'Now, if we pull this bench right forward we can put our feet on the rail and get them really warm.' Reenie shuffled their seat forward and then settled herself down to thaw out. They sat in companionable silence, watching the wood crackling in the grate, and admiring the light as it reflected off the baubles on the Christmas tree every time the cat moved beneath it. 'Thank you for walking me home safely.'

'Thank you for finally letting me.'

'I'm sorry I got so angry about what you'd said at work. I just thought you were agreeing with Mrs Roth to let me get in trouble; I didn't realise you were paying me a compliment.'

'It wasn't a compliment; it was just a statement of fact. You really do know all the lines, and I really will need you in Norwich. Besides, how could I betray you to Rabid Roth? You know I solemnly agreed that you were my statistical anomaly.'

Reenie burst out laughing. 'Did you just call her Rabid Roth?'

'Yes. That's what everyone else calls her, isn't it?'

'Well it is, but it's everyone except the managers! The managers don't call her that; you're a junior manager!'

'I promise you; it's what the managers call her as well.'

'Do you honestly want me to come to Norwich with you?'

'Haven't I been saying so since we first met? I can't live without you.'

'Here we go; making fun of me again.' Reenie rolled her eyes and tried to give him a shove to push him off the bench.

'I've told you, I'm not joking. I've thought it all out: I've found a boarding house where you could live with several other young ladies who are secretaries at the Norwich factory. The landlady is very strict and takes the welfare of her young ladies very seriously; she doesn't allow gentleman callers, so your mother would have nothing to fear and you'd be well looked after. You would be on a secondment so the firm would pay your board and lodging, and give you the rail fare to go home one weekend a month like I do. After six months, when the new Quality Street lines were up and running, you'd be coming back to an even better job in Halifax, we both would.'

Peter was so earnest that Reenie was speechless for a few moments. Once she's had time to think she asked: 'Are you saying I'd be an overlooker at Norwich?'

'No, no, not at all.'

Reenie tried to disguise her disappointment. 'No, I didn't think so, that would be silly. I've only been at the factory five minutes; it takes years to be an overlooker, I expect.' Mentally she was scolding herself for getting ideas above her station and getting carried away.

'No, you'll be above the overlookers; you'll be a junior manager like me.'

Reenie gasped and then remembered her parents and siblings upstairs and covered her mouth so they wouldn't hear her squeal of excitement. 'But wait, is this a plan where you'd have to persuade a lot of people—'

'No, everyone is persuaded. You heard the director at the hearing; he agrees that we need you in Norwich. The Women's Employment Department have already drawn up the contract and the offer letter, and they are waiting to get you to sign it when you get back.'

Reenie was smiling so much it made her face ache, and she laughed out loud. 'Does this mean I won't have to go into service after the Christmas rush has died down?'

'Was that what you've been afraid of? That you'd be laid off after the Christmas rush and have to become a kitchen maid?'

Reenie nodded, thinking now about how silly her fears had been.

'I think I can safely say that you, Irene Calder, will never have to go into service. Do I take this as a yes? Will you come with me to Norwich?'

Reenie nodded. It would be a big step because she had never left Yorkshire before, but it would be an adventure.

'I can take you to meet my parents and my grandmother. She'll like you, I've already told her all about you. I've said I'm going to marry you one day and she thinks that's very wise.'

Reenie giggled. 'Are you winding me up?'

'No,' Peter was emphatic. 'I've been trying to ask you to walk out with me since I met you, why won't you believe me?'

'Yes, but you never said "walk out", did you? You just jumped straight to weddin's which couldn't ha' been serious. If you'd h'a been serious you'd have asked me to the pictures or summat; you wouldn't have jumped straight into this business about weddins'.' If this was going to be their first argument, Reenie was thoroughly enjoying it.

'I was showing you how serious I was.'

'No, serious would have been a specific invitation, like "do-you-want-to-go-to-the-pictures-on-Thursday".'

'Since when is an offer to share a lifetime together vague? I wasn't going to set a date now because we're too young, but I let my intentions be known.'

Reenie refilled their coffee cups, sidled closer to Peter, lifted his arm and put it round her shoulder, and then arranged herself to get comfortable curled up on the bench beside him. As she nestled in, she decided she was prepared to go on answering him back until morning. 'Call those intentions? I'll give you intentions, Peter MacKenzie!'

It was time for the ghost stories. This was apparently a Christmas tradition at the Hunter household, and Diana had arrived just in time to hear the start. Mrs Hunter had been worried that Diana wouldn't be able to join them because of the heavy snow. It broke her heart that Diana might spend Christmas day alone, as she now considered Diana an extended family member.

'Heaven knows how thick it will have fallen by morning!' she had said to her husband, who had agreed to send their driver out in the motor car to fetch Diana that very night. That way she would be safely tucked up in one of their guest bedrooms, and would save Mrs Hunter at least one Christmas Eve worry.

Diana sat in the large, cosy sofa beside Mrs Hunter and watched her daughter's new family. The other children, who seemed very taken with little Gracie, were all sitting cross-legged on the hearthrug waiting for Mr Hunter to find the correct page in the ponderous leather-bound volume that evidently contained some ancient story of a haunting. The fire glowed; the tree baubles sparkled; the children giggled, and everything seemed so comfortable and happy.

'Do you have very many servants?' Diana asked Mrs Hunter in a hushed tone so as not to disturb the story time atmosphere.

'Well not tonight we don't, we sent all the servants home to their families.' Mrs Hunter was laughing quietly as though it were some private joke. 'It's yet another one of our Christmas traditions, I'm afraid; we send the servants home to spend Christmas with their loved ones, and the cook leaves us instructions in the kitchen. It's merry hell; I can tell you,' Mrs Hunter seemed very amused about it all the same. 'The whole family descend on the kitchen, even the little ones, and we all try to fathom how to cook ourselves dinner. We make an awful mess and luncheon is a wonderful disaster. The children love it. I do hope you don't mind?'

Diana grinned from ear to ear. 'Not a bit.'

'Come along, Charles, haven't you found it yet?' Mrs Hunter knew that her husband fully intended to make the ghost story up as he went along and was pretending to have lost his place in the Yorkshire history book as part of the game.

'Hang on, I know it's here somewhere.' Mr Hunter flicked through yellowed, crumbling pages muttering the names of supposed stories that they contained. 'Hmm... *The Curious History of the Witches' House,* no, that's not it... *An Incantation for Making Naughty Children Behave,* no, no we don't want that one, no use for that one at all round here.' He winked at his assembled brood. 'Ah ha! I've got it! *The Mysterious and Sinister Tale of the Rattling Christmas Ghost!'*

There was a cheer from the happy children, and Gracie cuddled closer to another little girl of about the same age who had become her particular playmate.

'Now, once upon a Christmas Eve, many, many, many, many years ago, there was an old, dark house...'

Diana looked around at the room; the furnishings were comfortable, but a little worn in places. *Good,* she thought to herself, *they obviously aren't the type of people who care more for the look of things than the substance.* She noticed that some of the tree baubles had the names of the children written on them, and hoped that Gracie hadn't been too disappointed to have arrived too late to have a decoration of her own. She took in the lush green boughs heavy with sticky candy canes, the strings of brightly coloured beads, the chocolate decorations shaped like plump fruits and wrapped in foil, and then, as her eyes took in the final stem, she saw something that made them sting with tears: there at the very top, occupying the most prominent place on the tree for all the world to see, was a china-faced angel all dressed in white, except for the tattered, ugly piece of red ribbon that someone had tied around its waist as a silken sash. This was the kind of place where they would let her daughter put an ugly ribbon on their tree and take pride of place, just to make her happy; it was bittersweet for Diana, she knew now that she would never be able to tell her daughter who her mother really was, but she would be able to see her grow up happy, safe, and loved. Even though a monstrous injustice was being enacted on Diana, as she was being wrongfully separated from her child, at that moment, all she could think was, *she'll be safe.*

Diana quickly pulled a handkerchief from her sleeve and dabbed at her eyes as discreetly as she could.

'You must be missing your stepmother terribly.' Mrs Hunter said it with warm sincerity and placed a reassuring hand on Diana's arm.

In a move uncharacteristic for Diana, she nodded in agreement and let a little of her guard down while trying to look brave.

'We are so very glad to have you here with us for Christmas. You can't imagine how pleased I was when I heard that our little Gracie had a big sister. We will be very glad to have you any and every Sunday you can spare; you are part of the family now. And you must call me Lydia, for I am sure that we are going to be great friends.' Lydia Hunter tactfully didn't wait for a response and instead turned to heckle her husband's ghost story. 'Do you call this scary?'

'The ghost,' Mr Hunter said, 'approached me, rattling as he walked. It was a terribly frightening rattling noise – hang on, I'm going to demonstrate – close your eyes all of you. You too Monty, don't think I didn't see you peeking.' The children shut their eyes, and heard a strange muffled rattling noise. 'The ghost took the form of a floating sheet, and I was sure when I heard the rattling noise that there must be a *skeleton* beneath it, so imagine my surprise when he threw off his sheet, and it was the butler with a tin of Quality Street!'

The children opened their eyes and squealed with delight to see that the rattling had been a 2lb tin of Mackintosh's Celebrated Quality Street which their father had been teasing them with. He popped off the lid and pushed his nose in to inhale deeply and then said, 'Ah, now that's what Christmas smells like!' He offered the tin to the children. 'Here, you have a smell – but no eating them 'til after supper, mind.' He grinned at Diana and asked wistfully, 'What's it like to work somewhere day after day that smells just like this?'

All eyes were upon her and, in a bittersweet moment, Diana simply answered: 'I love it.'

Acknowledgements

There are so many people without whom this book could not have been written, but chief among them was my grandmother Mary Walker. When she heard that I was writing a novel set during the time of her own childhood she was full of excitement and memories for me to include. The day the manuscript was ready to be seen I had it printed, bound and posted to her. She died the following morning; too early for the postman and too early for me. I wish she could have seen her name here.

I have been lucky to work with some wonderfully kind, talented, and generous people during the writing of this book. Oliver Malcom at HarperCollins Publishers took a risk on me and I will be eternally grateful. Kate Bradley, the best of editors, guided me through a steep learning curve with skill and patience. Jemima Forrester gave me confidence in my work (and much more) when she took me on and added me to the books at the literary agency, David Higham Associates. Pav Gahunia and Jon Smith at Nestlé made this project possible by championing it – and suggesting storylines – at the moment when it mattered. Matthew Evans offered the kind of support that only a 'green' manager could, and kept me going more times than he knew. Fiona McIntosh, who had already given so much time over the last few years to mentor me, took time out of writing her own book to fly from Australia to give exactly the advice I needed at the very moment I needed it. My family were patient to the point of sainthood when I had to disappear to get writing done, and I hope that all of them: the Hutchinsons, Joyces, Baums, Walkers and Forrests, know how grateful I am to them.

I count myself rich in friends, and particular thanks are due to Beckie Senior, John Thompson, Kate Hawley, Sarah Richards, Kate Maunsell (I'm still sorry about missing the wedding), Alison Murray, Helen Main, the Dejagers, the Stows, the Bissmires, the Edmondsons, the Longs, the Pallants, the Molyneuxs, and the Sprays.

Toffee Town

The sweet heart of Halifax

In the twenty-first century it's easy to forget that the town of Halifax in West Yorkshire used to be known as the Devil's Cauldron. Back in the Industrial Revolution the cauldron-like scoop of the valley, the forest of smoking chimneys, and the soot-darkened buildings gave the place an evil look. When Ted Hughes wrote about 'Black Halifax, boiled in phosphorous', he knew what he was talking about, but there was another Halifax that he failed to mention. Hidden beneath that shroud of smoke was a hive of toffee factories and confectionery workshops that gave the town its other, sweeter name.

One of the wonderful things about the Mackintosh's Toffee story, is that it begins with young love. John and Violet were devoted members of their local Methodist church, and after having saved up to open their own pastry cook shop in the King Cross area of Halifax, they spent their honeymoon fitting it out. Their busiest trade day was on a Saturday when the town's factory workers had the afternoon off. John suggested that they create one special line to sell just on Saturdays as a treat to attract more customers.

John may have had a good head for business, but he didn't have the culinary experience to know what they should make as their special line on Saturdays, or how they should make it. Fortunately for toffee lovers everywhere, this story has a hero behind the scenes who saves the day: Violet Mackintosh had worked as a confectioner's assistant before she was married and she had an idea for a new kind of confection that would be just right for the factory workers' weekend treat.

Violet created a new kind of chewy toffee; at that time the only toffees were either the brittle kind like a boiled sweet, or runny American-style caramels. Violet combined the two confections to make a chewy, creamy sweet that quickly became known as Mackintosh's Celebrated Toffee. Her husband believed in her work so much that he organised a promotion of it through the local paper. Next, he opened up a market stall to sell it in another part of town, and finally he applied all his years of factory experience to opening up their first factory building and beginning mass production. Mackintosh's Celebrated Toffee quickly conquered the world.

One of the things that helped to make Mackintosh's Toffee successful was its affordability. In the latter part of the nineteenth century, and the early part of the twentieth, chocolates were expensive luxuries that were beyond the budget of most working people. Cocoa was an exotic, foreign ingredient that had to be shipped in from a long way away, and the process of turning cocoa beans into chocolate bars was labour intensive, which also pushed up the price. Toffee, on the other hand, could be made with much more affordable local ingredients, like sugar from British sugar beet, and butter from British cows. Mackintosh's Toffee was the ultimate affordable treat, and John and Violet helped to bring confectionery to the masses.

John's hard work took its toll on him, and he died prematurely in his 50s. It was a terrible blow to the family and the factory, but his sons did an admirable job of taking over the business. By the 1930s John and Violet's eldest son, Harold, was making his own mark on the history of the firm.

Harold had been watching his competitors; over in York two of his rivals (Rowntree's and Terry's) had launched more affordable chocolate box assortments in the shape of Black Magic and All Gold. Although these were significantly cheaper than the Fancy Boxes they'd been selling for decades, Harold still didn't believe they were affordable enough for a working family to enjoy together. Harold came up with a plan to launch an assortment that was a mix of chocolates, toffees, and chocolate coated toffees. The toffee element of the product would be much less expensive to produce and would help to keep the overall cost down for his consumers when they came to buy it in the shops. Mackintosh's had tried to make chocolate toffee assortments before, but they simply didn't have the expertise or experience in their business to make anything really complex. All of this changed one day in 1932 when Harold Mackintosh was eating his lunch in the Savoy in London. The Chairman of Lever

Brothers happened to see him and asked, 'You don't want to buy a chocolate factory do you?'

The chocolate factory in question was Caley's of Norwich, an old family firm which Lever Brothers had bought up, but no longer wanted. Caley's had started out making table waters and Christmas crackers, but were now solidly a chocolate business. Harold thought it over, and then decided to snap up the bargain.

When Quality Street came along it wasn't so much an idea as a challenge. In early 1936 Harold Mackintosh asked his senior staff to create a new assortment that mixed chocolates from their newly acquired Norwich factory with toffees from their Halifax factory; he wanted something really special, with a mix of twist wraps, foils, paper bands, and even a double row of coloured tissue paper bunting around the lip of the tin. This new product needed a name that proclaimed its quality, but also something that could become a brand, and cater to the 1930s trend of nostalgia for a bygone era of courtly love. Harold was a fan of the works of writer J. M. Barrie (famed for his Peter Pan story) and the name of his lesser-known Regency-era play *Quality Street* seemed perfect for the assortment. The name gave the Mackintosh team an excuse to cover the packaging in the characters and scenes from the story which gave it a pleasingly old-fashioned look.

Mackintosh's confectionery business went from strength to strength, adding new lines (like Tooty Frooties, Toffee Crisp, Caramac, Week End) and acquiring new businesses (like Anglo-Bellamy bubble gum and a liquorice factory in Castleford).

By 1969 the family firm was ready to enter into a new era, in the form of a merger with that old York rival Rowntree's, which finally brought Black Magic and Quality Street into the same family. John and Violet's sons and grandsons were still on the board, but now they were part of a much bigger business, and were equipped to take on even bigger challenges.

During the 1970s and 80s Rowntree Mackintosh, as the new business was named, bought up all kinds of businesses that made products that might have baffled John and Violet. The confectionery family grew to welcome Sun-Pat peanut butters, Pan-Yan Pickles, Tom's snacks and crisps, and even a business that sold freshly baked cookies from a cart. Wackier products appeared, like cheese spread in a jar and powdered fizzy drinks. Despite their departure from their sugary roots, Rowntree Mackintosh was hugely successful, which meant that they became a tempting prospect for larger companies.

In May 1988 a dawn raid was launched on their shares by the Jacob Suchard company (now part of Kraft). Suchard wanted to buy up the Yorkshire-based firm, and in the end they put in an offer of £1.7 billion. Then along came Nestlé who had been saving up to make an acquisition just like this.

Since Nestlé took over the business in July 1988, they have invested over £500 million in the confectionery businesses they acquired from the Rowntree Mackintosh take over. They have even chosen to base their international sweet inventing centre in Yorkshire so that their brightest sweet makers from all over the world can benefit from the knowledge that has been handed down through generation after generation of Yorkshire workers since those first days in the back-room kitchen of a young bride, Violet Mackintosh.

We do hope that you have enjoyed reading this large print book.

Did you know that all of our titles are available for purchase?

We publish a wide range of high quality large print books including:
Romances, Mysteries, Classics
General Fiction
Non Fiction and Westerns

Special interest titles available in large print are:
The Little Oxford Dictionary
Music Book
Song Book
Hymn Book
Service Book

Also available from us courtesy of Oxford University Press:
Young Readers' Dictionary
(large print edition)
Young Readers' Thesaurus
(large print edition)

For further information or a free brochure, please contact us at:
Ulverscroft Large Print Books Ltd.,
The Green, Bradgate Road, Anstey,
Leicester, LE7 7FU, England.
Tel: (00 44) **0116 236 4325**
Fax: (00 44) **0116 234 0205**